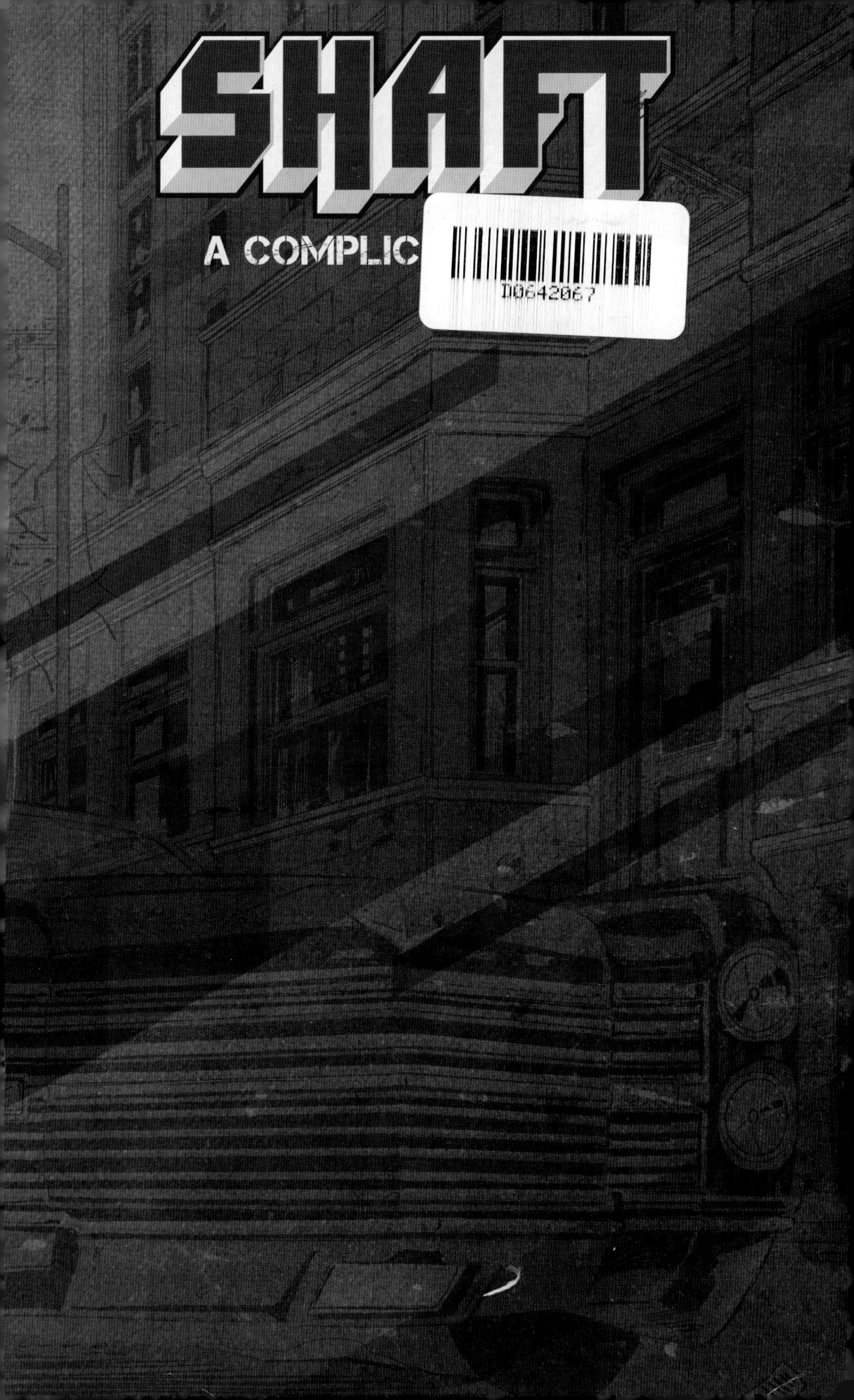
SHAFT
A COMPLIC

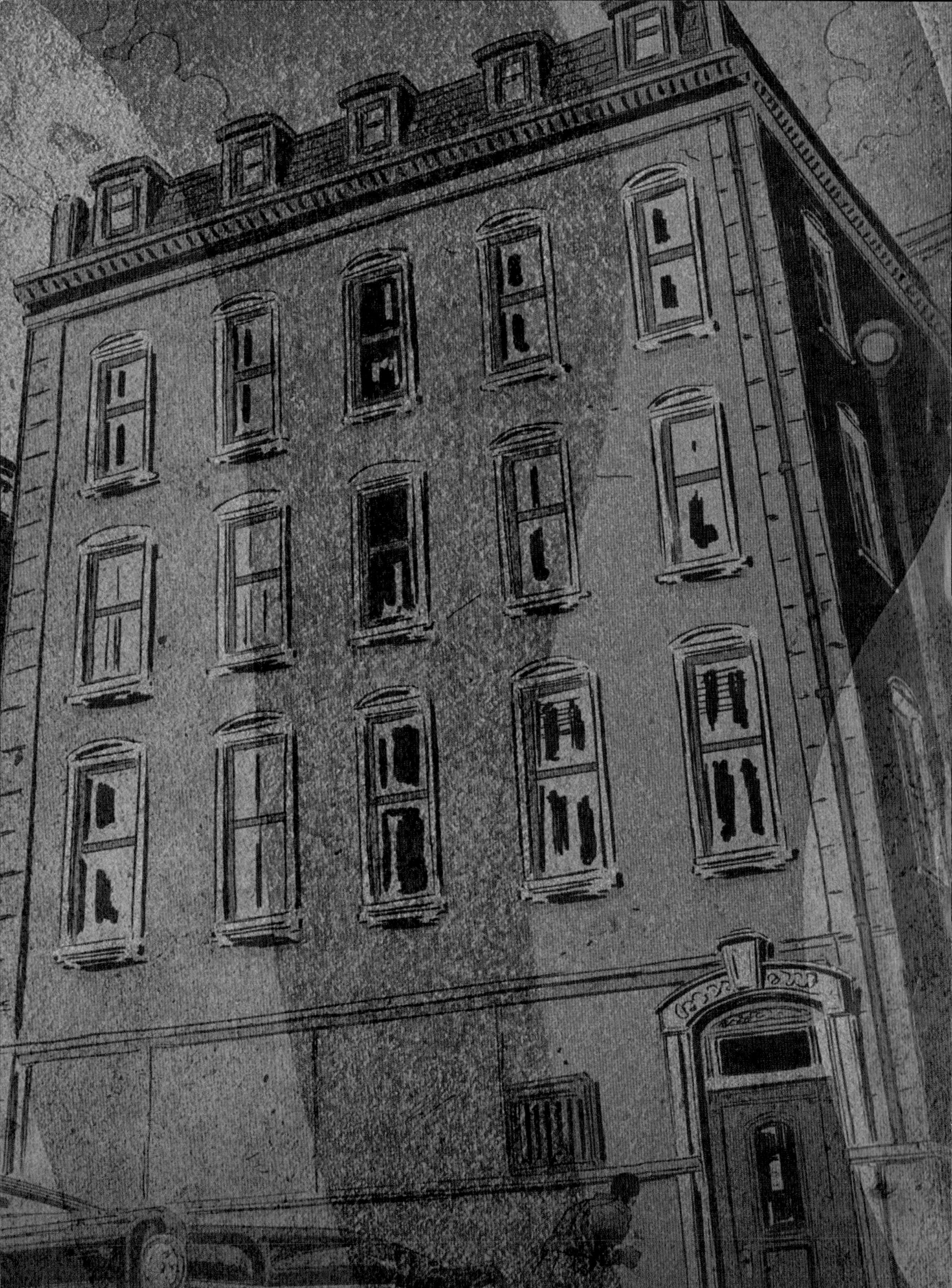

DYNAMITE®

Nick Barrucci, CEO / Publisher
Juan Collado, President / COO
Joe Rybandt, Senior Editor

Jason Ullmeyer, Design Director
Katie Hidalgo, Graphic Designer
Geoff Harkins, Graphic Designer
Chris Caniano, Digital Associate
Rachel Kilbury, Digital Assistant

Rich Young, Director Business Development
Keith Davidsen, Marketing Manager
Kevin Pearl, Sales Associate

Online at **www.DYNAMITE.com**
On Twitter **@dynamitecomics**
On Facebook **/Dynamitecomics**
On YouTube **/Dynamitecomics**
On Tumblr **dynamitecomics.tumblr.com**

ISBN-1-60690-757-3
ISBN-978-1-60690-757-3

First Printing
10 9 8 7 6 5 4 3 2 1

For information regarding press, media rights, foreign rights, licensing, promotions, and advertising e-mail: marketing@dynamite.com

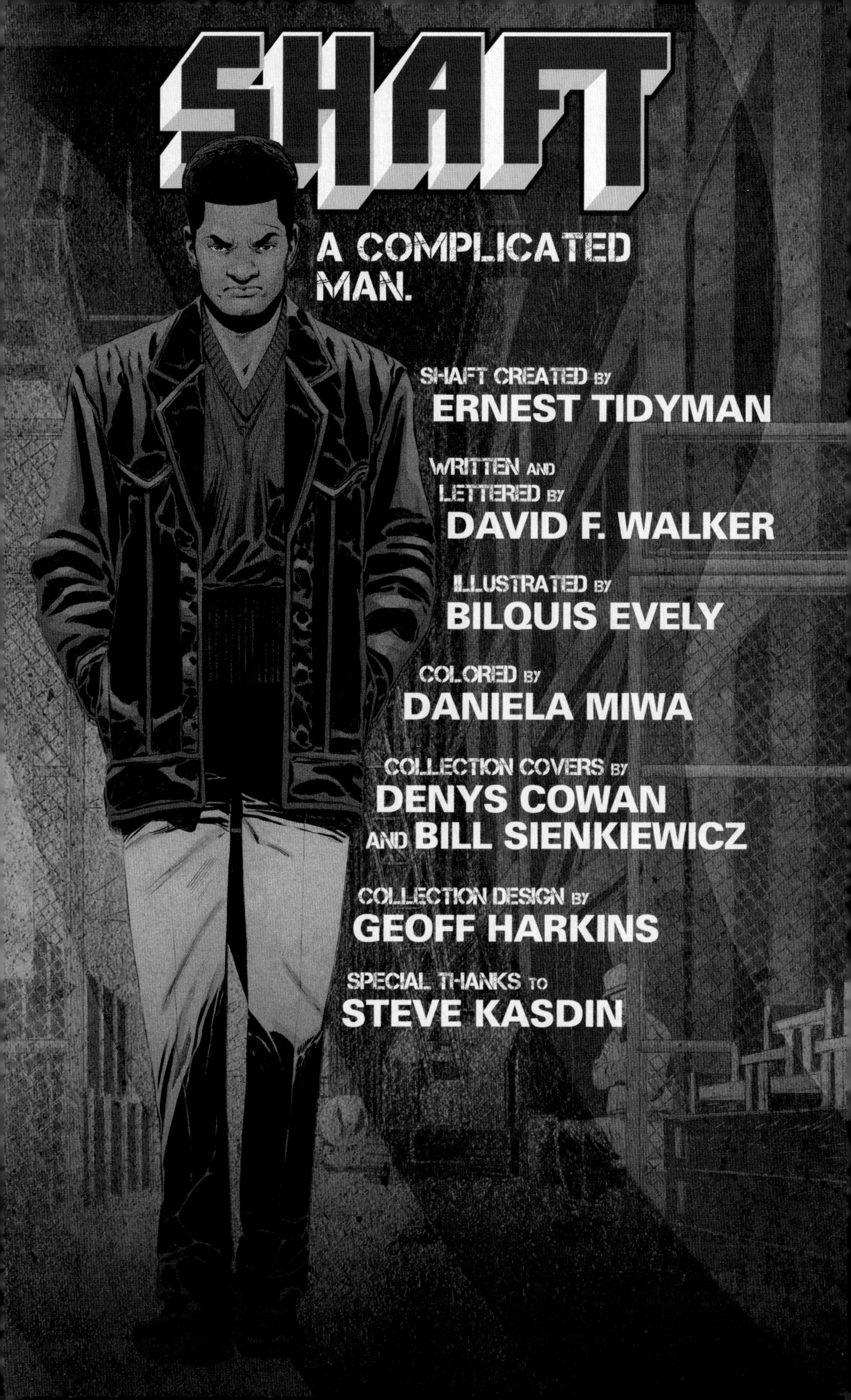

SHAFT

A COMPLICATED MAN.

SHAFT CREATED BY
ERNEST TIDYMAN

WRITTEN AND LETTERED BY
DAVID F. WALKER

ILLUSTRATED BY
BILQUIS EVELY

COLORED BY
DANIELA MIWA

COLLECTION COVERS BY
DENYS COWAN AND BILL SIENKIEWICZ

COLLECTION DESIGN BY
GEOFF HARKINS

SPECIAL THANKS TO
STEVE KASDIN

When I first heard that Detective John Shaft was going to have his own comic, I was incredulous. In this current racial climate, especially in comic/geek culture, I figured that there was no way any publisher would be so daring. Then I heard that David F. Walker was going to write it. The BadAzz MoFo himself was going to write Shaft for Dynamite Entertainment. I thought, 'Do they know that David isn't going to pull any punches? Do they have any idea that Walker is one of the rawest dudes to walk the planet? 'Will they back him up when he accurately reflects the language and the violence of both the genre and the world of John Shaft?' David F. Walker is pretty much the leading authority on any and everything Blaxploitation, from films, to music, to literature. If anyone alive was going to do Shaft justice, it would be him.

When David asked me to write this, I wanted to say no. How would I ever be able to do justice to the collected edition of one of my favorite comics from the last several years? For many Black people, John Shaft is as folkloric as Robin Hood. Despite being created in the early 1970s by Ernest Tidyman as a James Bond analog, Shaft feels like he has been around for as long as African-Americans needed justice. Shaft is the direct descendant of mythical strong men Stagolee and High John De Conquer. While it would be ridiculously easy to pepper this forward with Shaft-isms referencing the nascent detective's sexual prowess and his general bad-assery, he deserves much more than overused pop culture sound bites. He deserves to be respected for the cultural icon that he is.

Seven novels (eight, if we include Walker's Shaft's Revenge), three original films, a short-lived television series, and one remake starring Samuel L Jackson in 2000 comprised the entire mythology of John Shaft. But we still did not know him. We knew of him, the adventures he had, and the villains he faced. Shaft's backstory was not so much shrouded in mystery, as it was never elucidated. That is until issue number one of Shaft exploded into comic shops.

As a die-hard comic book fan, I am a sucker for well-done origin stories. Few have been done better than what is collected here. We finally are made privy to what demons are driving John Shaft. We see the situations that were instrumental in forging the unstoppable urban avenger he will become.

As a die-hard Black comic fan, this book is one of the most important in my lifetime. It is so rare to see Black characters in comics, particularly those who are three-dimensional, virile, and non-stereotypical—John Shaft is no one's sidekick or emasculated token. When he appears, it is almost as if the entire panel expands. He owns his space and is the total focus of his world. John Shaft is the hero I (and so many other comic fans who rarely see themselves represented) need right now.

Now sit back, relax, and brace yourself for the adventures of the Harlem Knight.

Shawn Taylor, June 2015.

Shawn Taylor is the author of Big Black Penis: Misadventures in Race and Masculinity. He blogs for www.thenerdsofcolor.org, is a lecturer on popular culture and interdisciplinary humanities at San Francisco State University, and is the author of a forthcoming speculative fiction novel—his first foray into fiction.

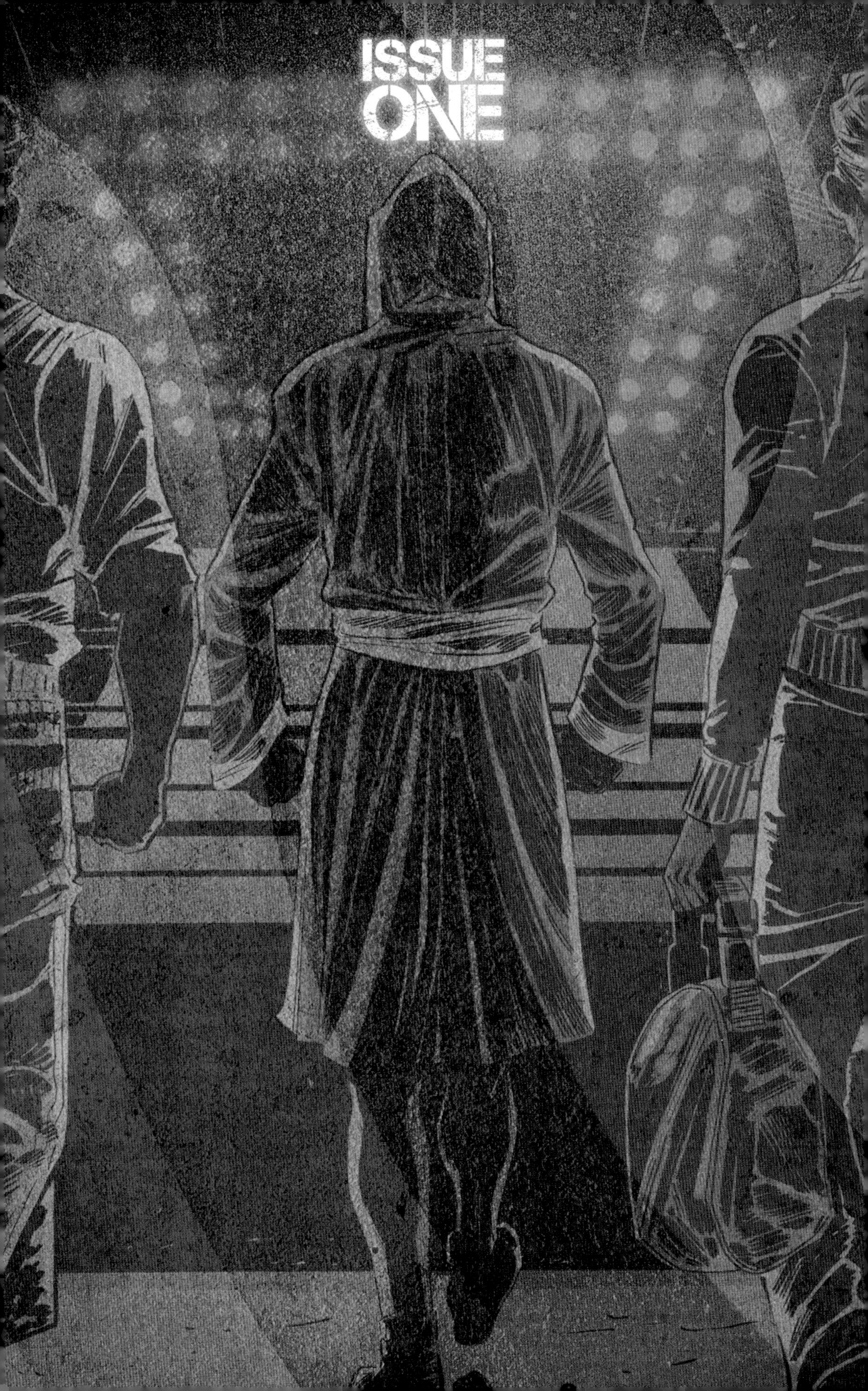
ISSUE
ONE

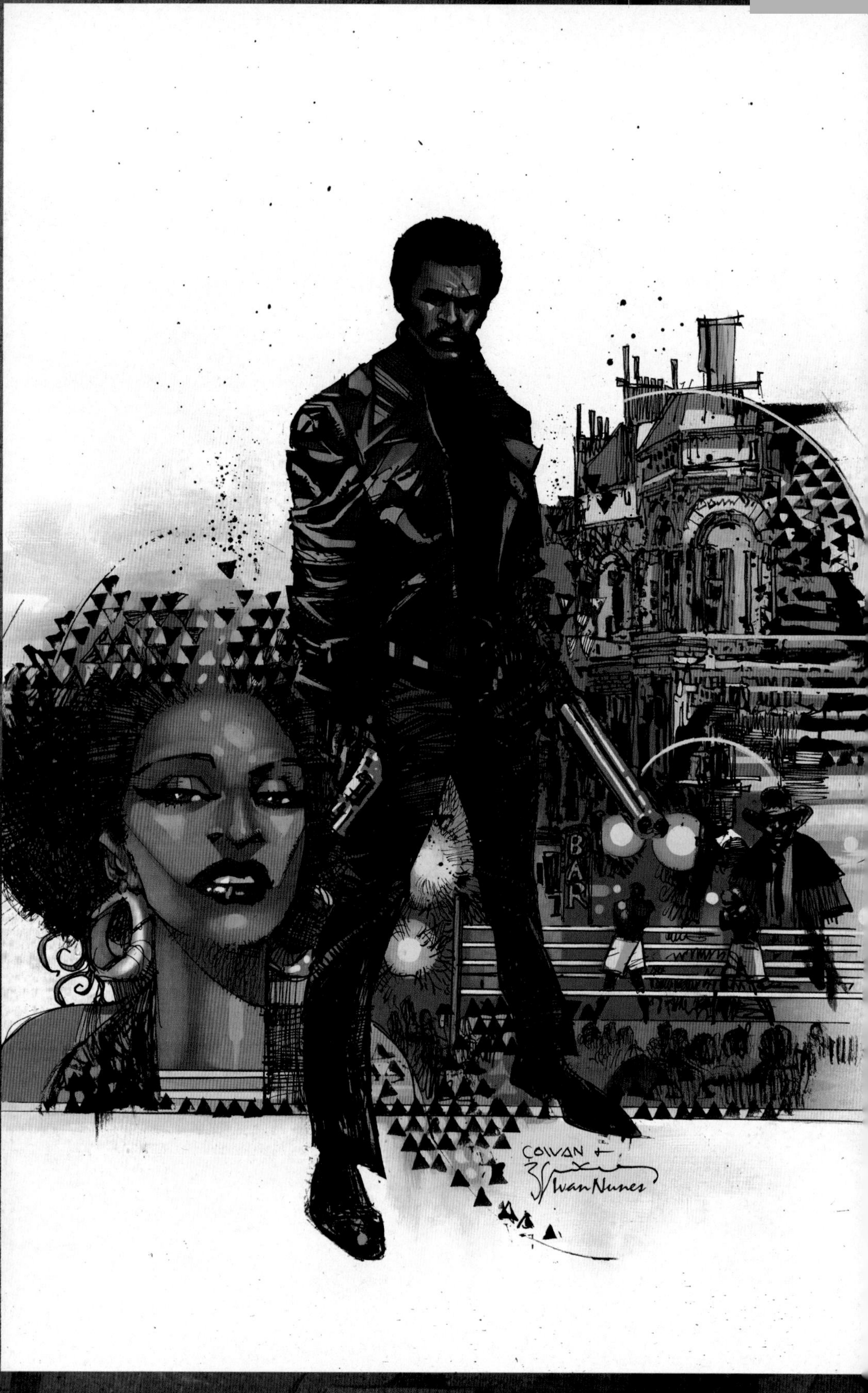
BAR
COWAN &
Ivan Nunes

ISSUE ONE MAIN COVER BY
DENYS COWAN AND BILL SIENKIEWICZ
COLORS BY IVAN NUNES

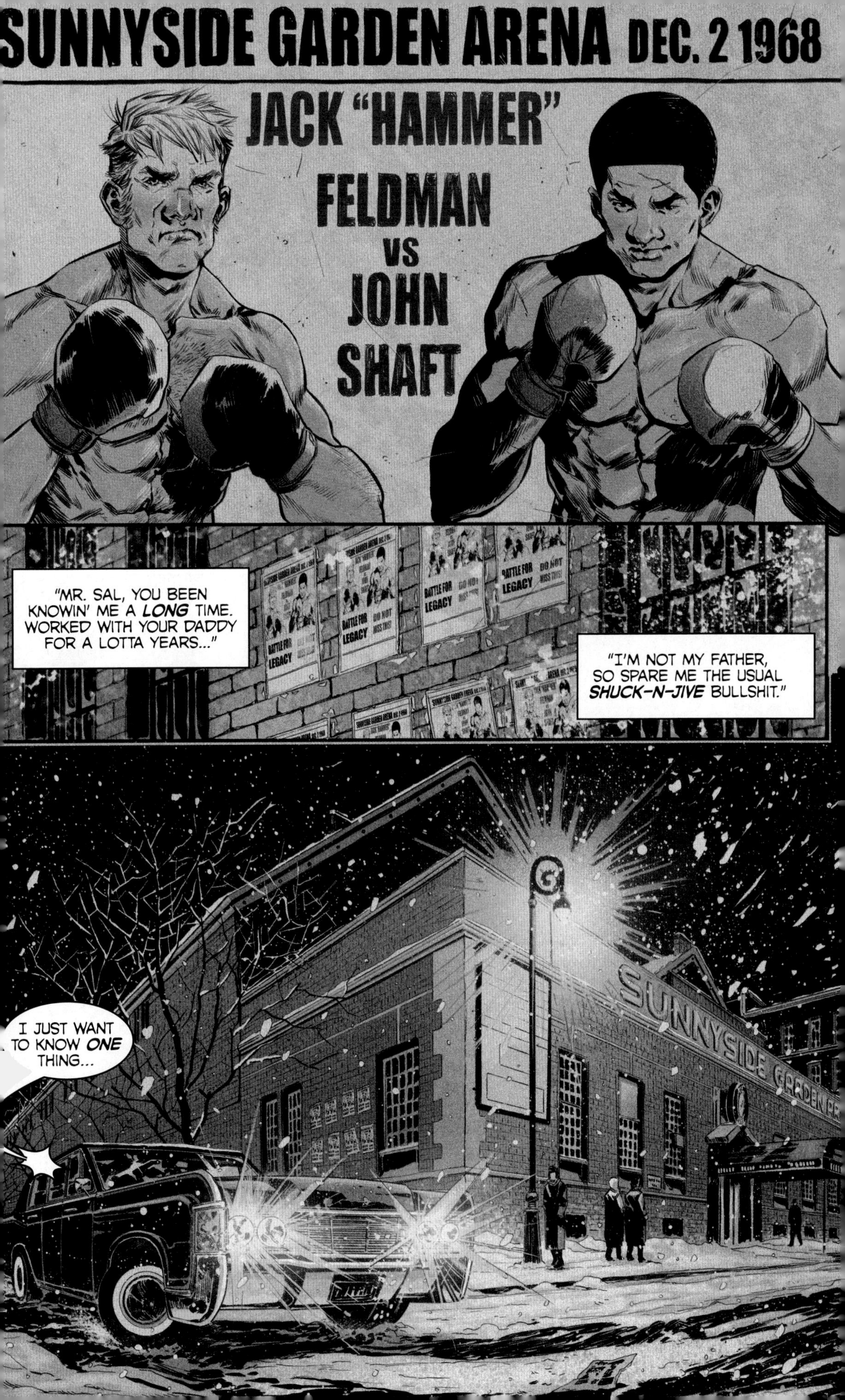
SUNNYSIDE GARDEN ARENA DEC. 2 1968
JACK "HAMMER" FELDMAN VS JOHN SHAFT
BATTLE FOR LEGACY
DO NOT MISS THIS!
"MR. SAL, YOU BEEN KNOWIN' ME A LONG TIME. WORKED WITH YOUR DADDY FOR A LOTTA YEARS..."
"I'M NOT MY FATHER, SO SPARE ME THE USUAL SHUCK-N-JIVE BULLSHIT."
SUNNYSIDE GARDEN
I JUST WANT TO KNOW ONE THING...

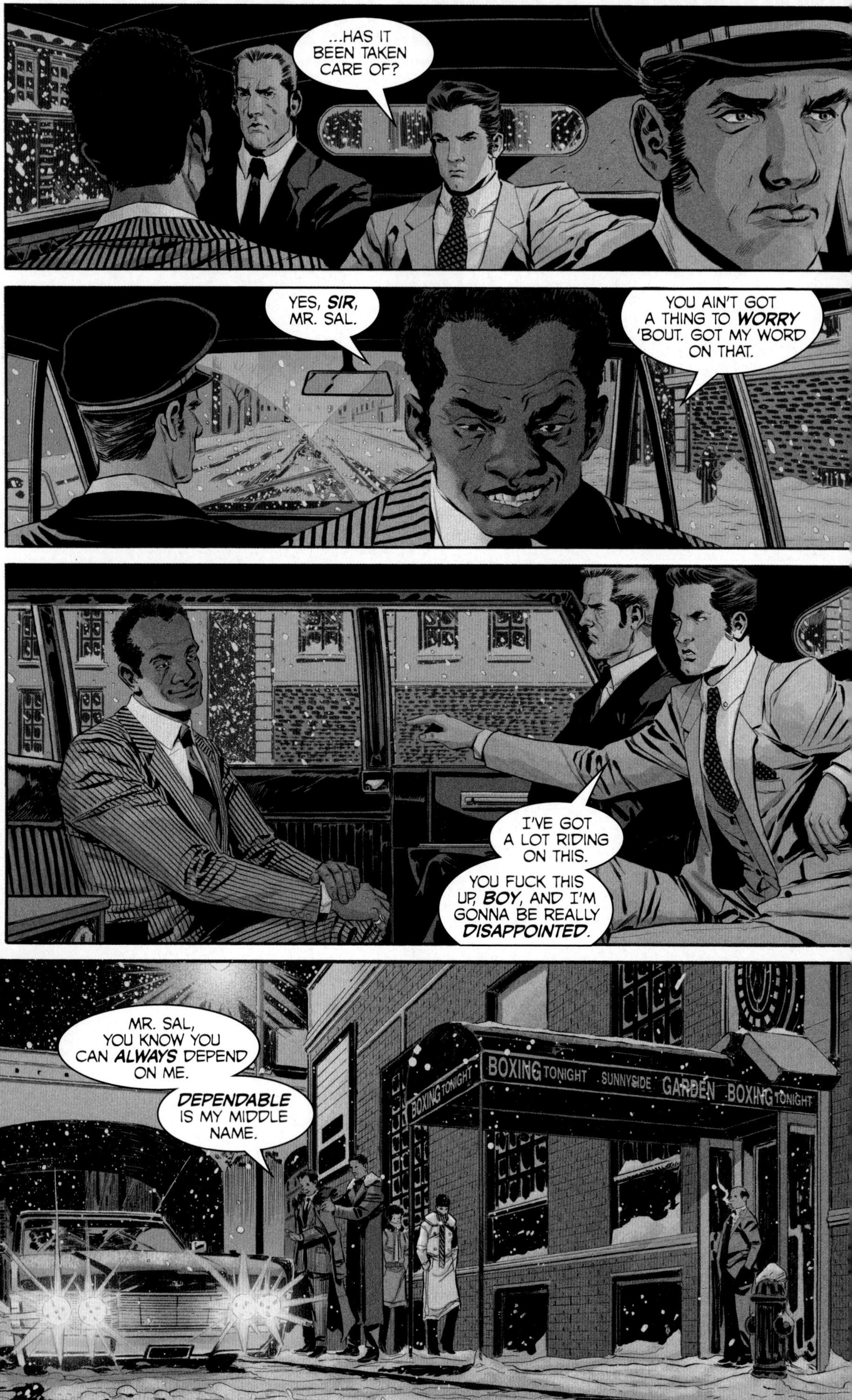
...HAS IT BEEN TAKEN CARE OF?
YES, SIR, MR. SAL.
YOU AIN'T GOT A THING TO WORRY 'BOUT. GOT MY WORD ON THAT.
I'VE GOT A LOT RIDING ON THIS.
YOU FUCK THIS UP, BOY, AND I'M GONNA BE REALLY DISAPPOINTED.
MR. SAL, YOU KNOW YOU CAN ALWAYS DEPEND ON ME.
DEPENDABLE IS MY MIDDLE NAME.
BOXING TONIGHT
BOXING TONIGHT SUNNYSIDE GARDEN BOXING TONIGHT

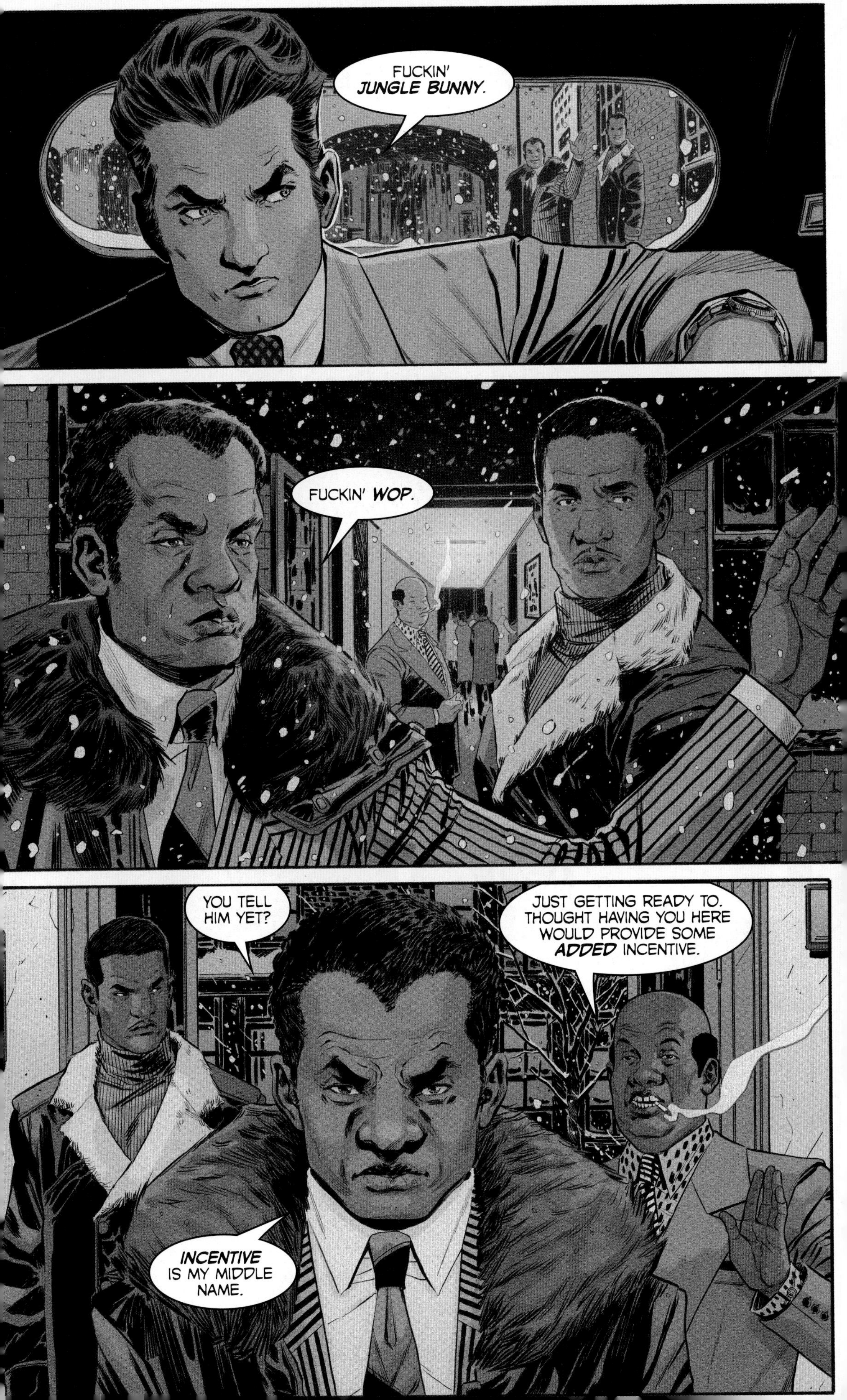
FUCKIN' *JUNGLE BUNNY*.
FUCKIN' *WOP*.
YOU TELL HIM YET?
JUST GETTING READY TO. THOUGHT HAVING YOU HERE WOULD PROVIDE SOME *ADDED* INCENTIVE.
INCENTIVE IS MY MIDDLE NAME.

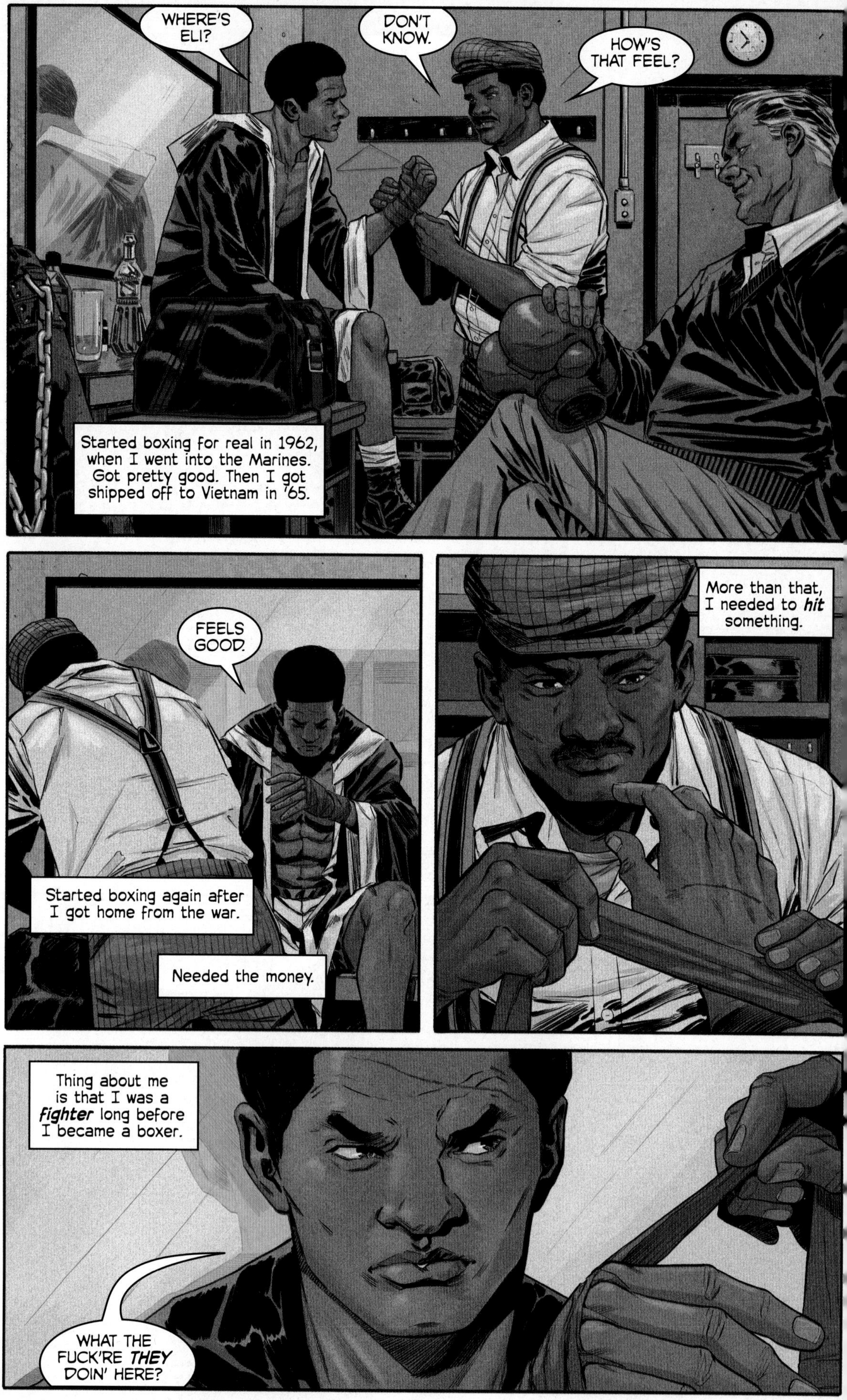
WHERE'S ELI?
DON'T KNOW.
HOW'S THAT FEEL?
Started boxing for real in 1962, when I went into the Marines. Got pretty good. Then I got shipped off to Vietnam in '65.
FEELS GOOD.
Started boxing again after I got home from the war.
Needed the money.
More than that, I needed to *hit* something.
Thing about me is that I was a *fighter* long before I became a boxer.
WHAT THE FUCK'RE *THEY* DOIN' HERE?

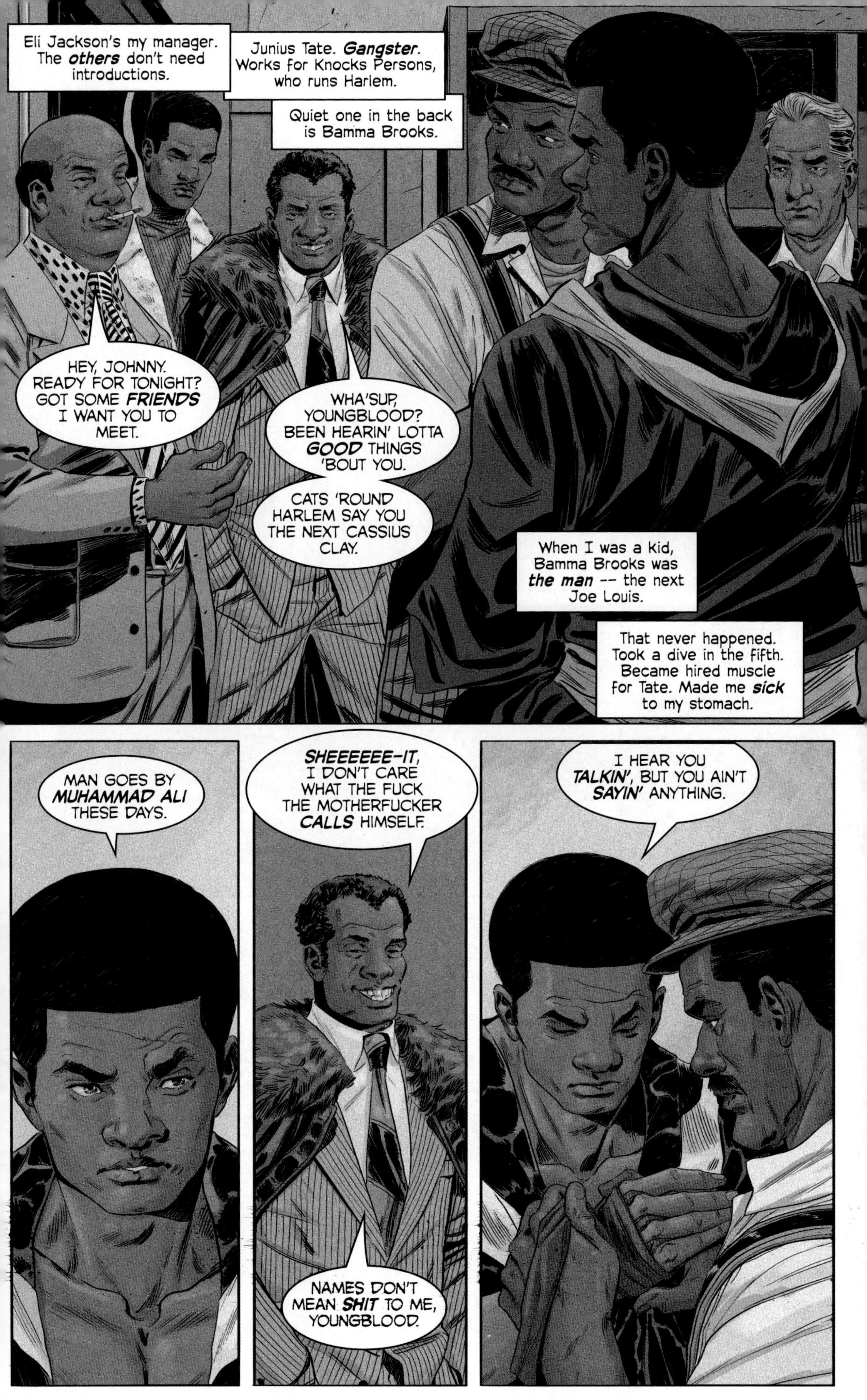

Eli Jackson's my manager. The *others* don't need introductions.
Junius Tate. *Gangster*. Works for Knocks Persons, who runs Harlem.
Quiet one in the back is Bamma Brooks.
HEY, JOHNNY. READY FOR TONIGHT? GOT SOME *FRIENDS* I WANT YOU TO MEET.
WHA'SUP, YOUNGBLOOD? BEEN HEARIN' LOTTA *GOOD* THINGS 'BOUT YOU.
CATS 'ROUND HARLEM SAY YOU THE NEXT CASSIUS CLAY.
When I was a kid, Bamma Brooks was *the man* -- the next Joe Louis.
That never happened. Took a dive in the fifth. Became hired muscle for Tate. Made me *sick* to my stomach.
MAN GOES BY *MUHAMMAD ALI* THESE DAYS.
SHEEEEEE-IT, I DON'T CARE WHAT THE FUCK THE MOTHERFUCKER *CALLS* HIMSELF.
NAMES DON'T MEAN *SHIT* TO ME, YOUNGBLOOD.
I HEAR YOU *TALKIN'*, BUT YOU AIN'T *SAYIN'* ANYTHING.

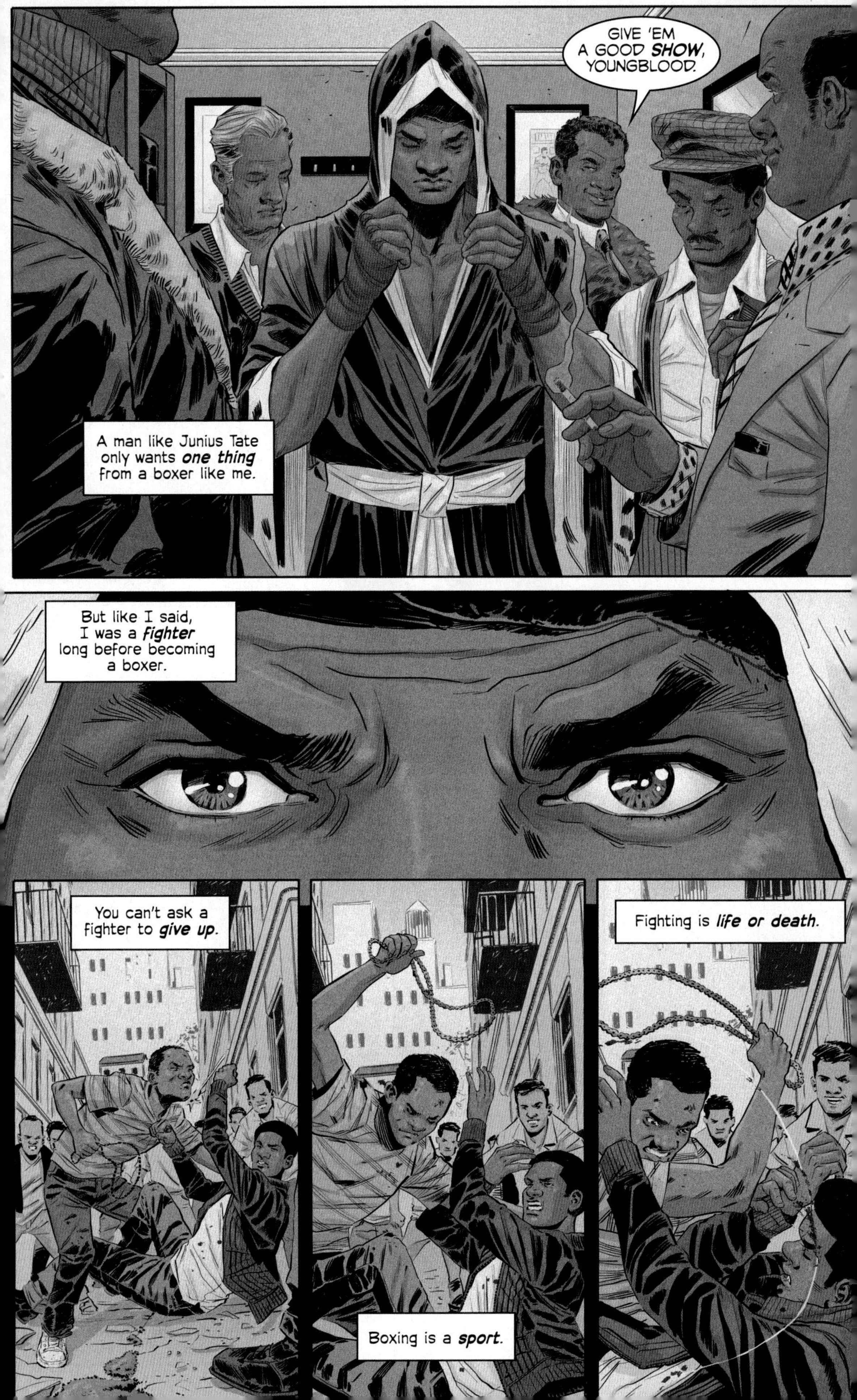
GIVE 'EM A GOOD **SHOW**, YOUNGBLOOD.
A man like Junius Tate only wants ***one thing*** from a boxer like me.
But like I said, I was a ***fighter*** long before becoming a boxer.
You can't ask a fighter to ***give up***.
Boxing is a ***sport***.
Fighting is ***life or death***.

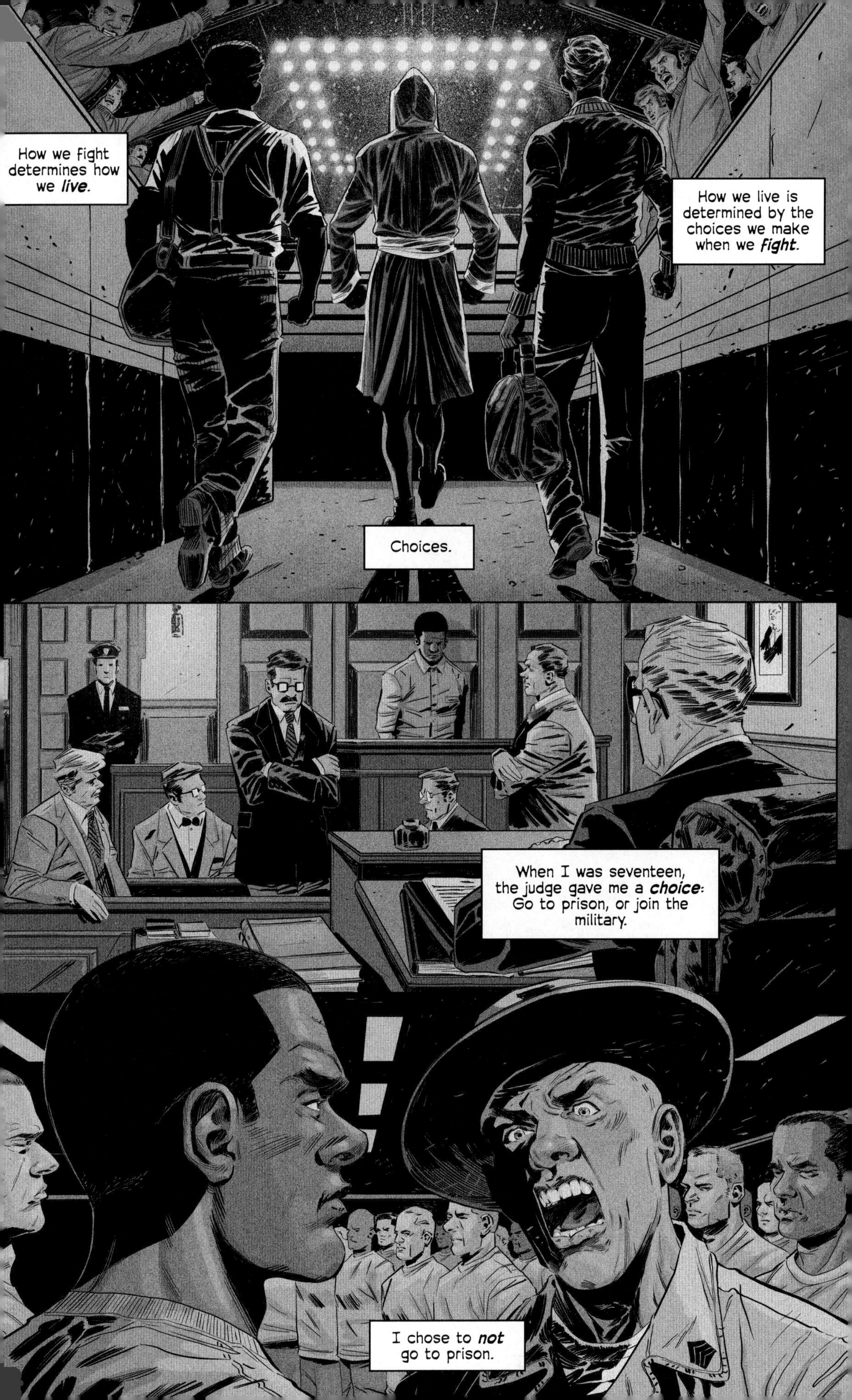
How we fight determines how we *live.*
How we live is determined by the choices we make when we ***fight.***
Choices.
When I was seventeen, the judge gave me a ***choice:*** Go to prison, or join the military.
I chose to ***not*** go to prison.

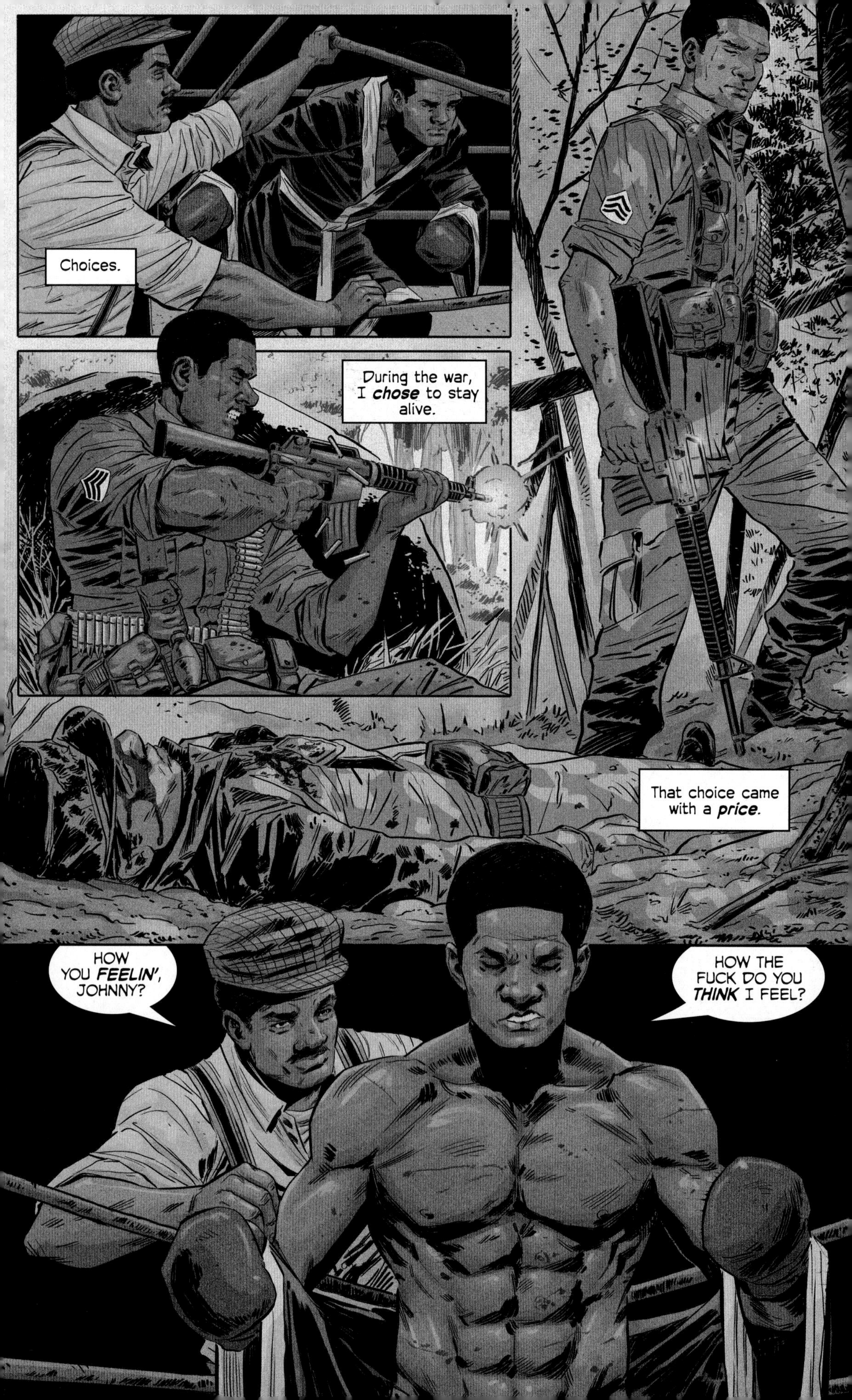
Choices.
During the war, I *chose* to stay alive.
That choice came with a *price*.
HOW YOU *FEELIN'*, JOHNNY?
HOW THE FUCK DO YOU *THINK* I FEEL?

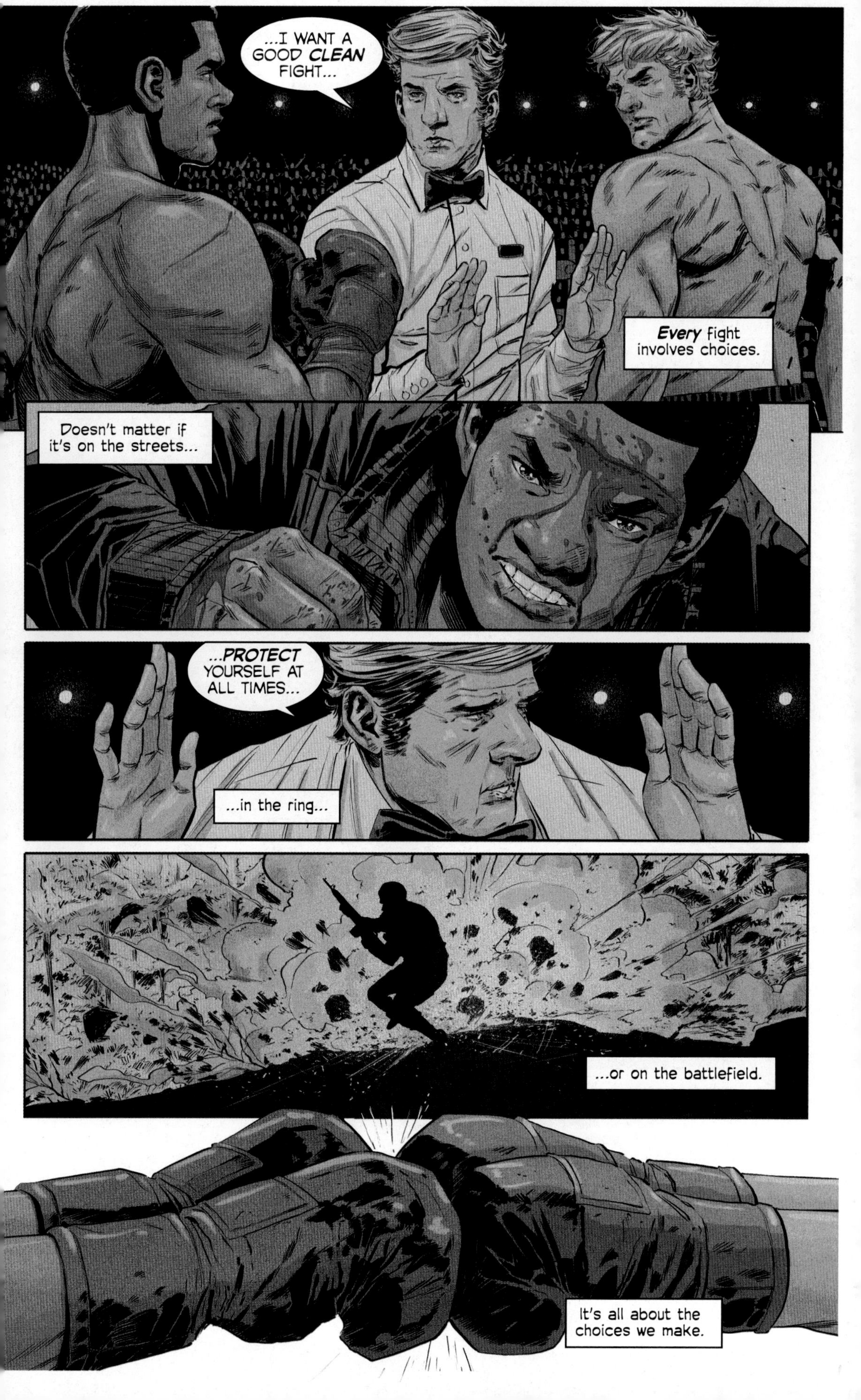
...I WANT A GOOD CLEAN FIGHT...
Every fight involves choices.
Doesn't matter if it's on the streets...
...PROTECT YOURSELF AT ALL TIMES...
...in the ring...
...or on the battlefield.
It's all about the choices we make.

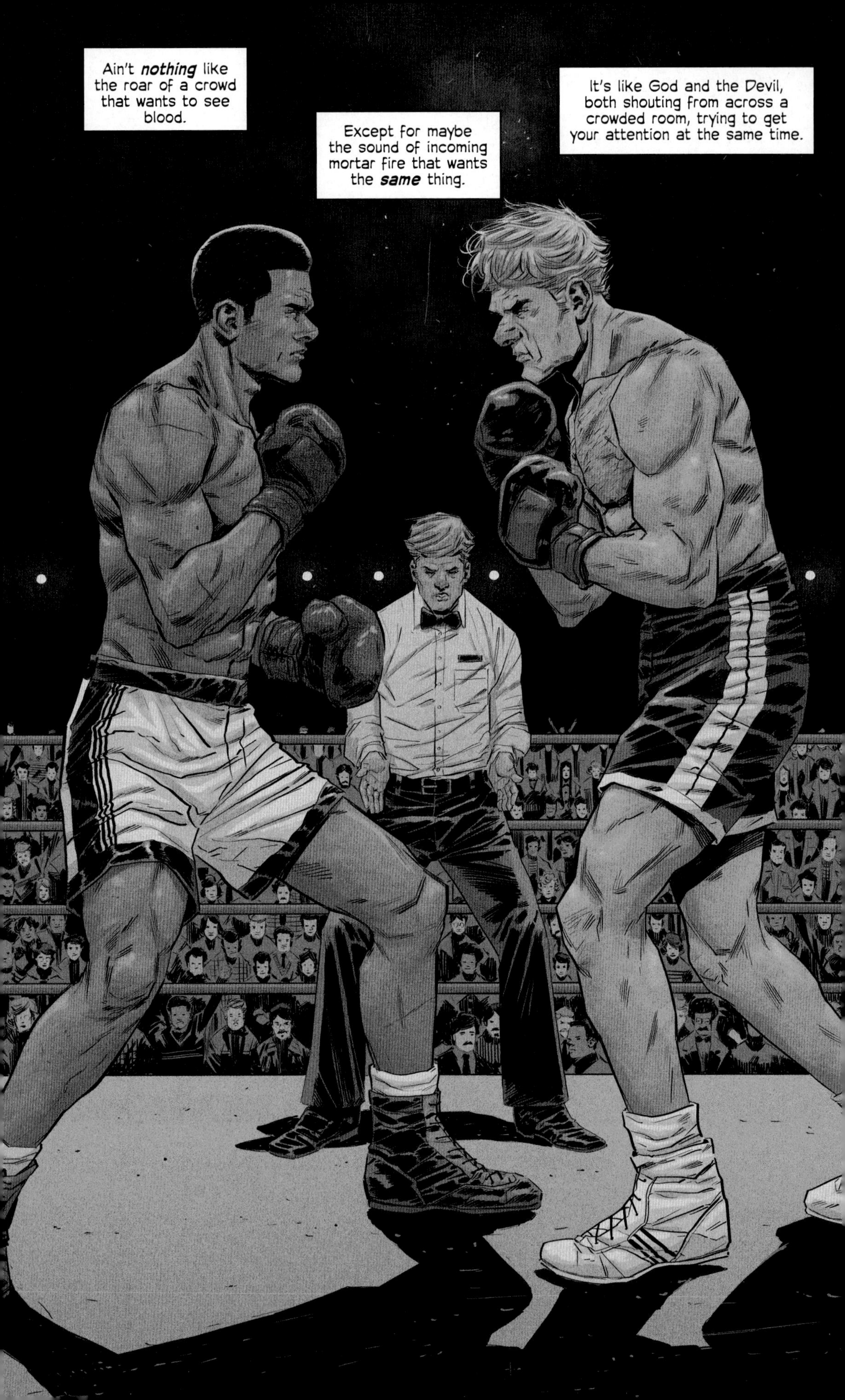
Ain't *nothing* like the roar of a crowd that wants to see blood.
Except for maybe the sound of incoming mortar fire that wants the *same* thing.
It's like God and the Devil, both shouting from across a crowded room, trying to get your attention at the same time.

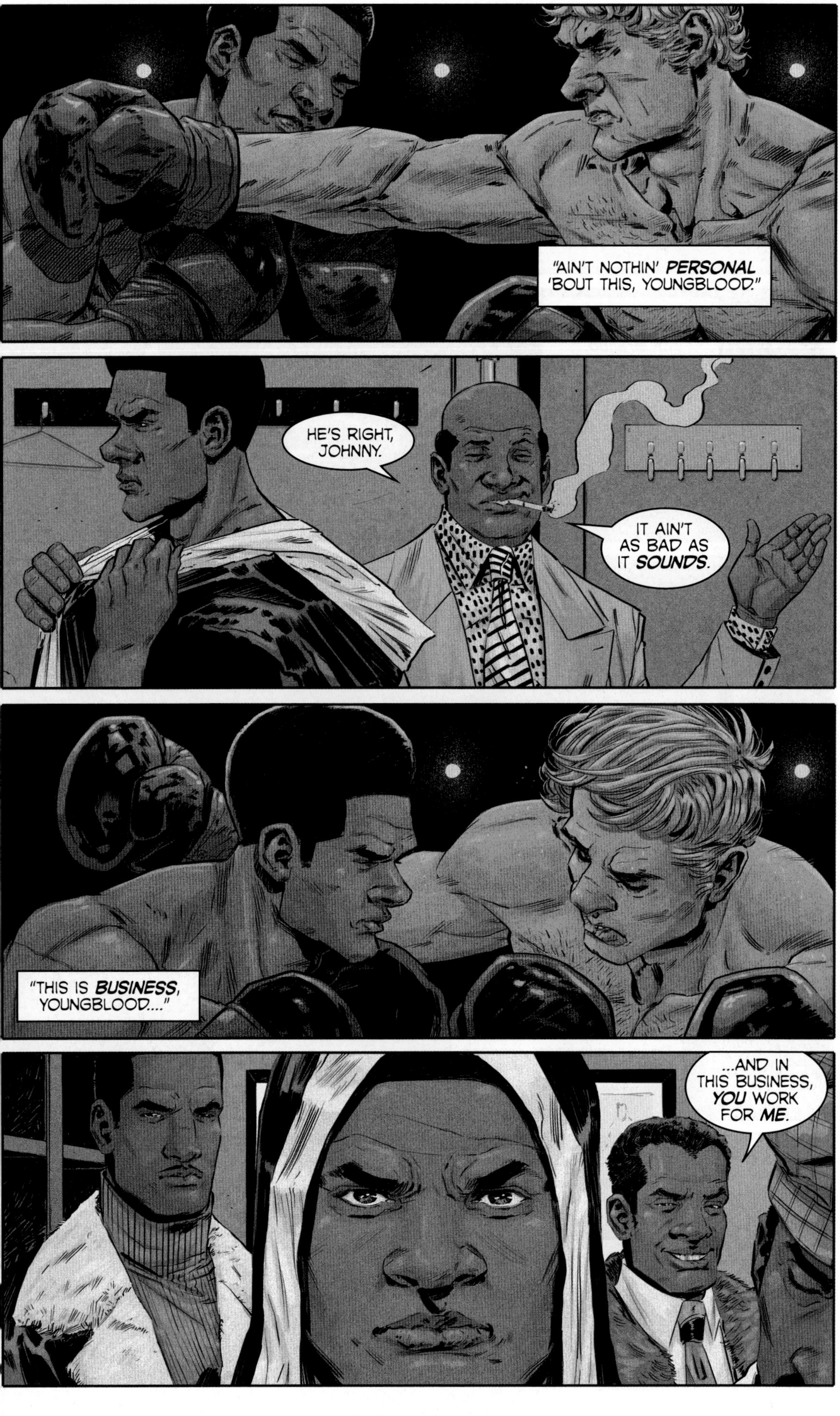
"AIN'T NOTHIN' PERSONAL 'BOUT THIS, YOUNGBLOOD."
HE'S RIGHT, JOHNNY.
IT AIN'T AS BAD AS IT SOUNDS.
"THIS IS BUSINESS, YOUNGBLOOD..."
...AND IN THIS BUSINESS, YOU WORK FOR ME.

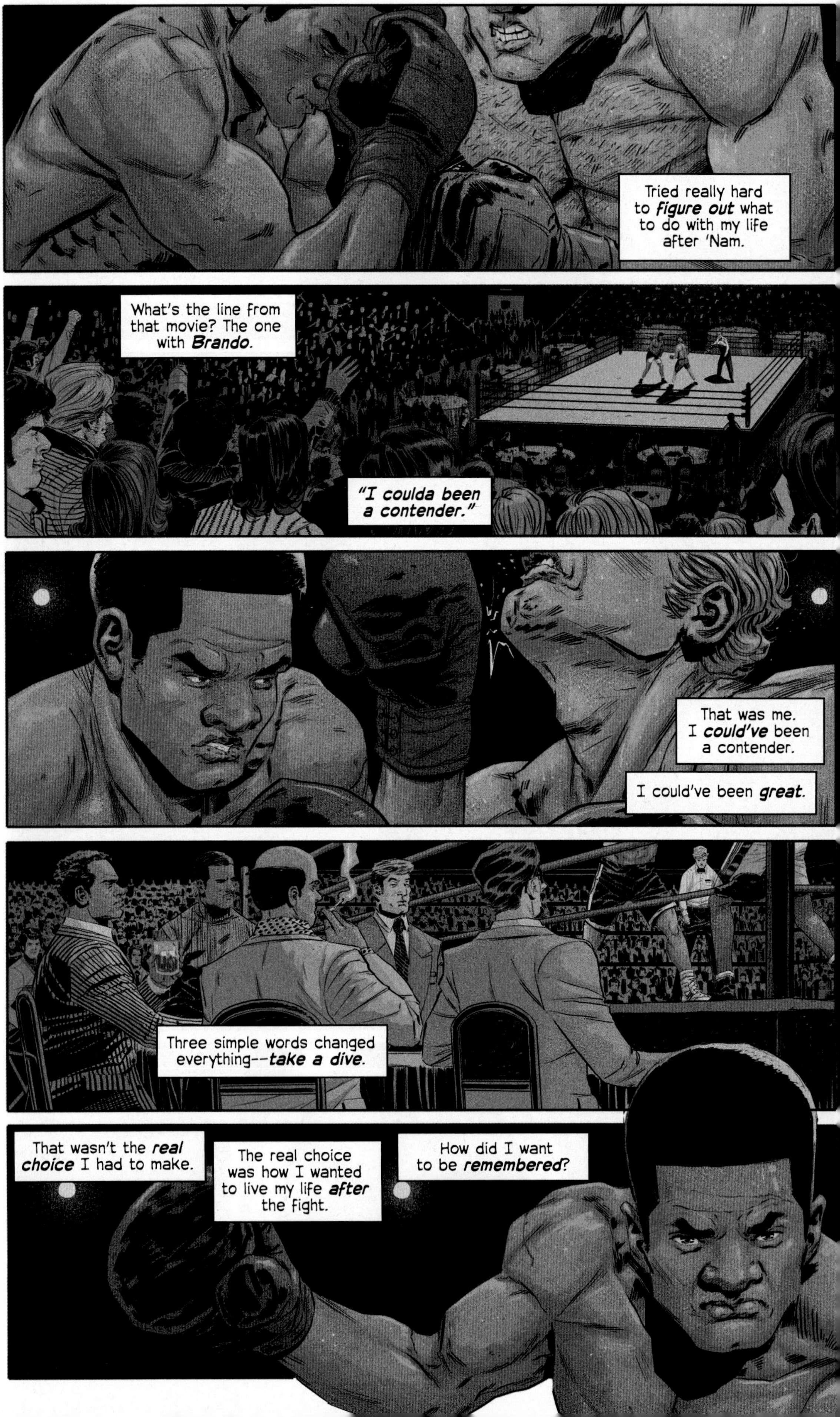
Tried really hard to *figure out* what to do with my life after 'Nam.
What's the line from that movie? The one with *Brando*.
"I coulda been a contender."
That was me. I *could've* been a contender.
I could've been *great*.
Three simple words changed everything--*take a dive*.
That wasn't the *real choice* I had to make.
The real choice was how I wanted to live my life *after* the fight.
How did I want to be *remembered*?

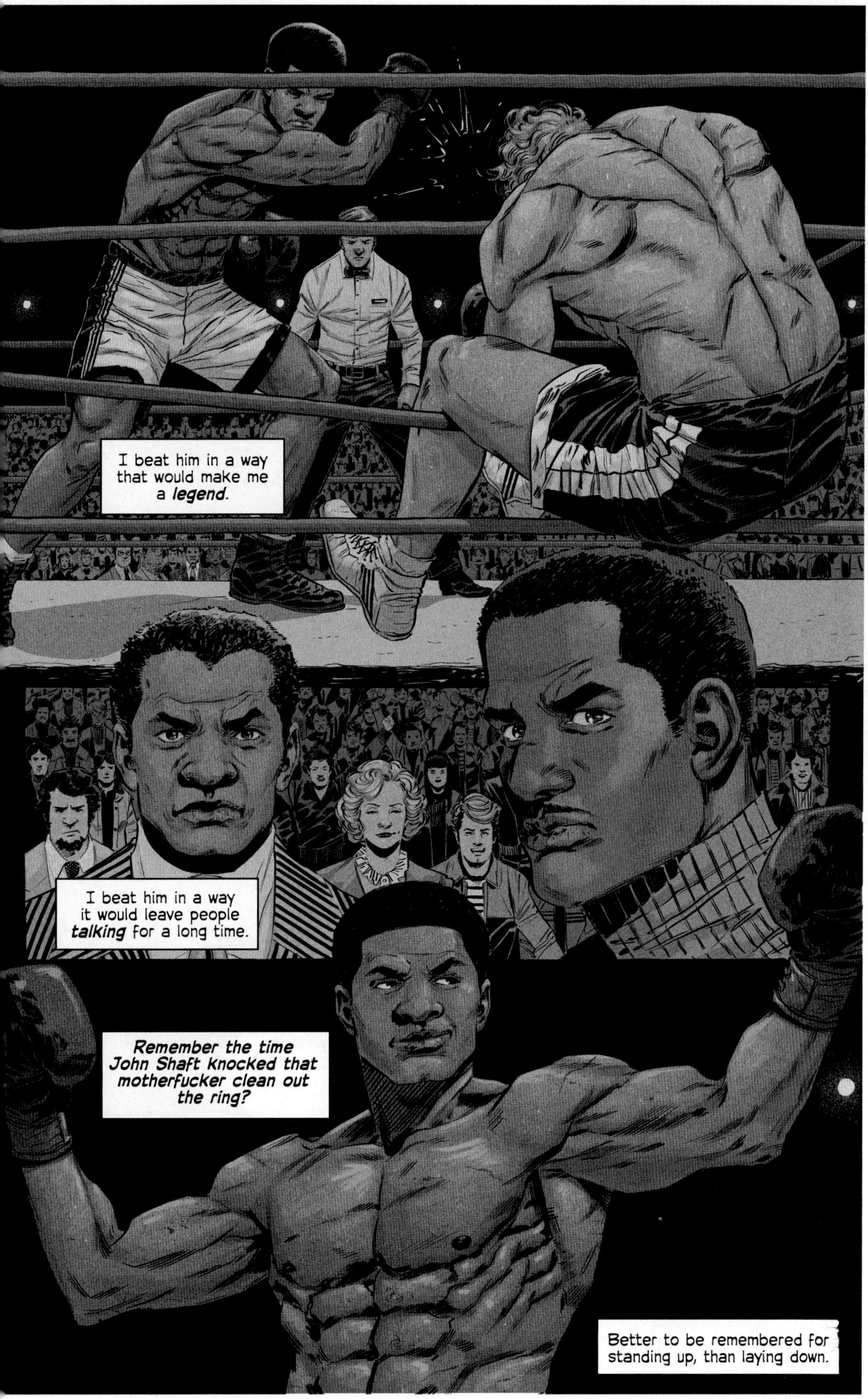
I beat him in a way that would make me a *legend*.
I beat him in a way it would leave people *talking* for a long time.
Remember the time John Shaft knocked that motherfucker clean out the ring?
Better to be remembered for standing up, than laying down.

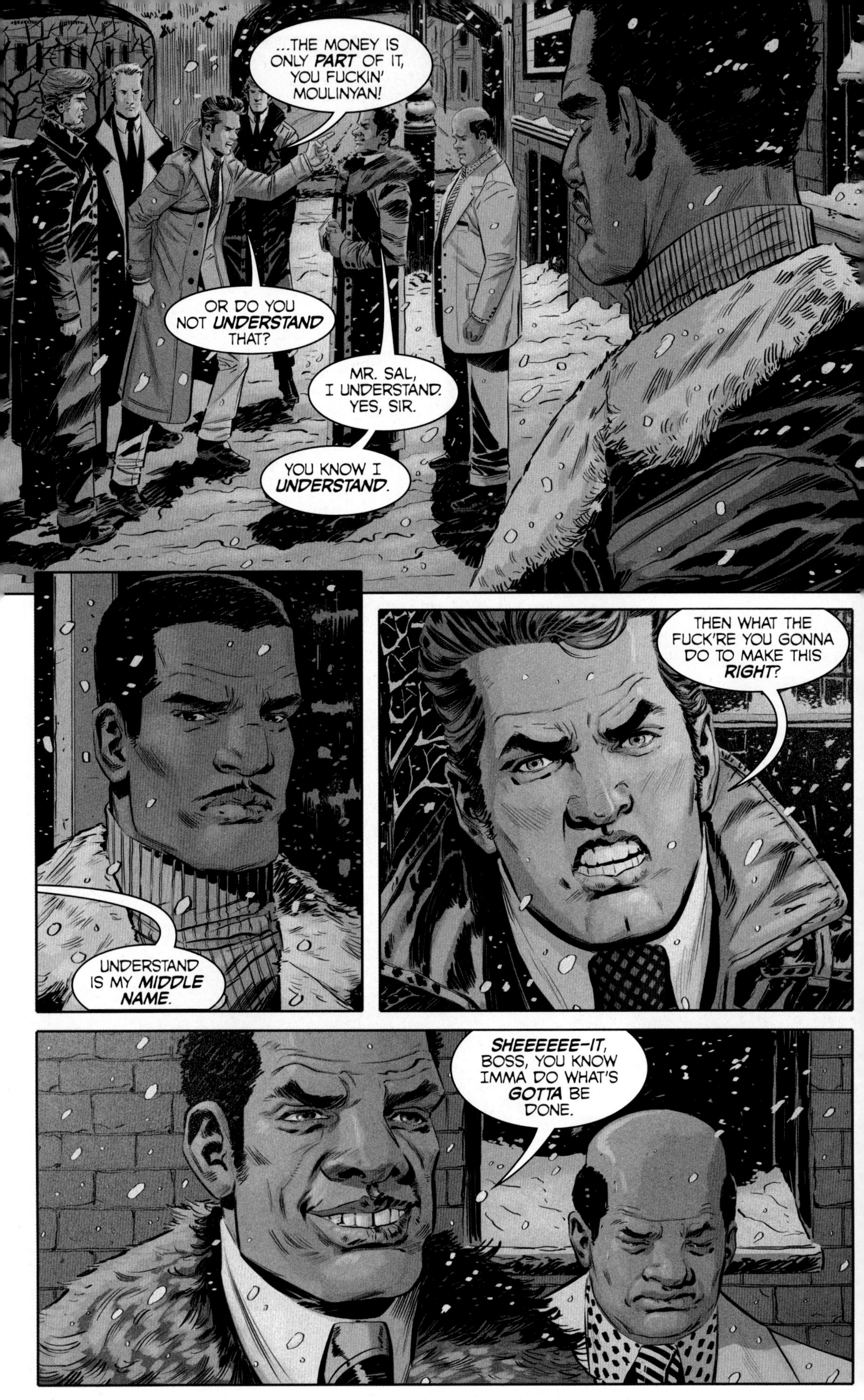
...THE MONEY IS ONLY PART OF IT, YOU FUCKIN' MOULINYAN!
OR DO YOU NOT UNDERSTAND THAT?
MR. SAL, I UNDERSTAND. YES, SIR.
YOU KNOW I UNDERSTAND.
UNDERSTAND IS MY MIDDLE NAME.
THEN WHAT THE FUCK'RE YOU GONNA DO TO MAKE THIS RIGHT?
SHEEEEEE-IT, BOSS, YOU KNOW IMMA DO WHAT'S GOTTA BE DONE.

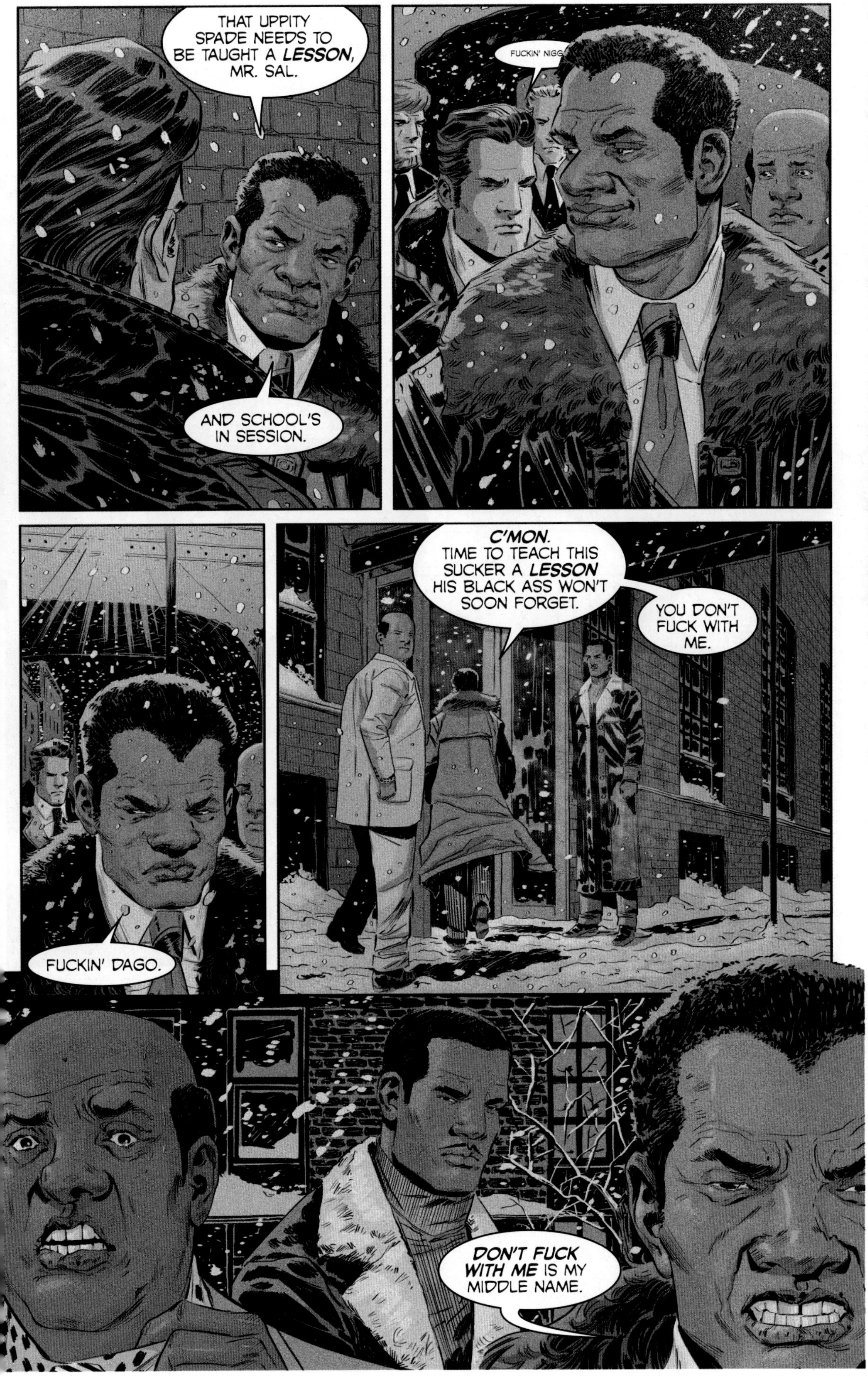
THAT UPPITY SPADE NEEDS TO BE TAUGHT A LESSON, MR. SAL.
AND SCHOOL'S IN SESSION.
FUCKIN' NIGG
FUCKIN' DAGO.
C'MON. TIME TO TEACH THIS SUCKER A LESSON HIS BLACK ASS WON'T SOON FORGET.
YOU DON'T FUCK WITH ME.
DON'T FUCK WITH ME IS MY MIDDLE NAME.

WHAT'RE YOU DOING JUST HANGING AROUND?

YOU GOTTA GET THE HELL *OUTTA* HERE.

DO I LOOK LIKE I *GIVE* A SHIT?

YOU THINK JUNIUS TATE IS GONNA LET THIS *SLIDE*?

ANY SECOND, HE'S GONNA COME THROUGH THAT DOOR...

DOC CAN JUST *STITCH* ME BACK TOGETHER. AIN'T THAT RIGHT, DOC?

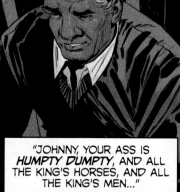

I'LL DO MY BEST, KID.

"JOHNNY, YOUR ASS IS *HUMPTY DUMPTY*, AND ALL THE KING'S HORSES, AND ALL THE KING'S MEN..."

...AIN'T GONNA BE ABLE TO PUT *YOU* BACK TOGETHER AGAIN.

YOU GOT *THAT* RIGHT.

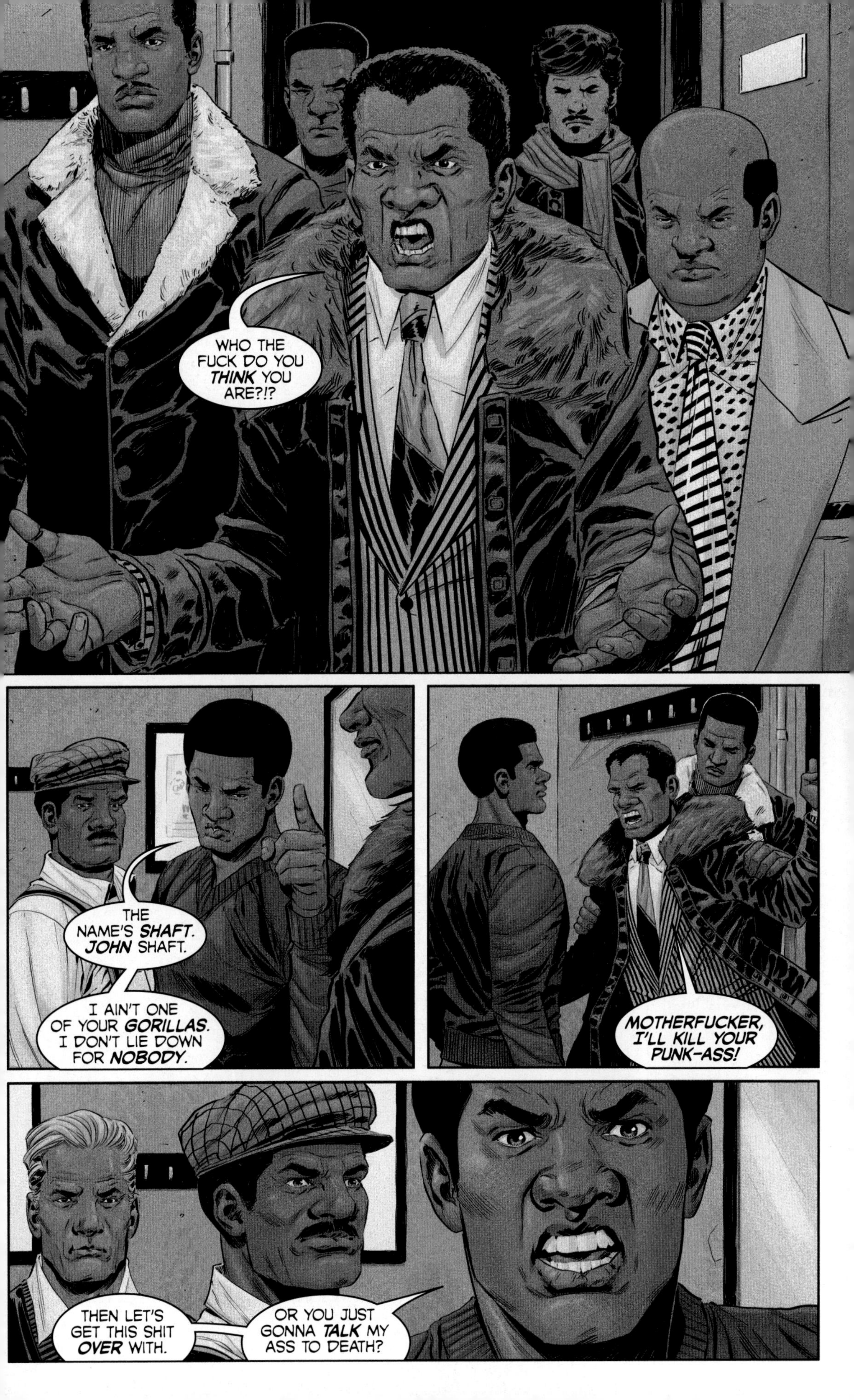
WHO THE FUCK DO YOU *THINK* YOU ARE?!?
THE NAME'S *SHAFT*. *JOHN* SHAFT.
I AIN'T ONE OF YOUR *GORILLAS*. I DON'T LIE DOWN FOR *NOBODY*.
MOTHERFUCKER, I'LL KILL YOUR PUNK-ASS!
THEN LET'S GET THIS SHIT *OVER* WITH.
OR YOU JUST GONNA *TALK* MY ASS TO DEATH?

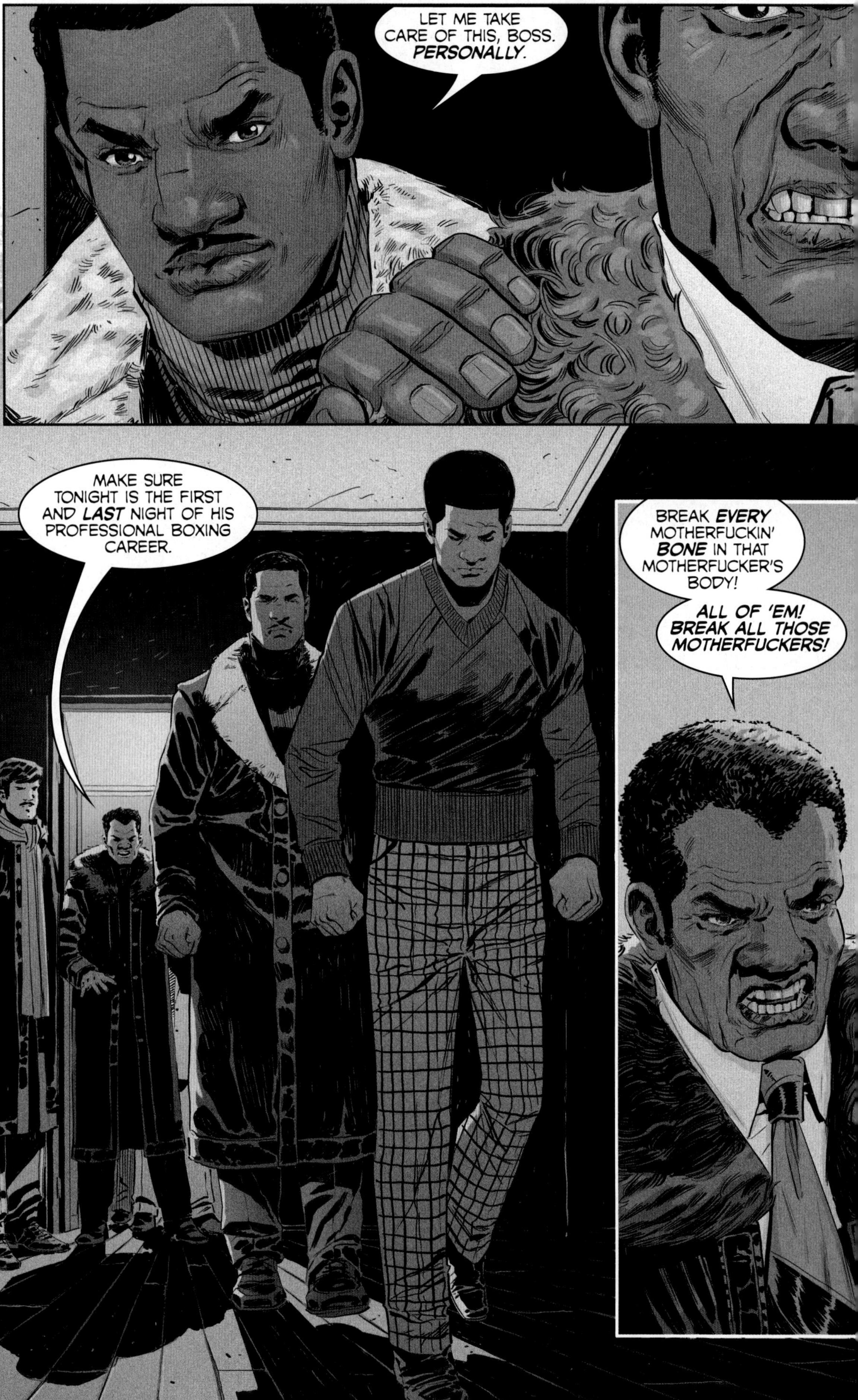
LET ME TAKE CARE OF THIS, BOSS. PERSONALLY.
MAKE SURE TONIGHT IS THE FIRST AND LAST NIGHT OF HIS PROFESSIONAL BOXING CAREER.
BREAK EVERY MOTHERFUCKIN' BONE IN THAT MOTHERFUCKER'S BODY!
ALL OF 'EM! BREAK ALL THOSE MOTHERFUCKERS!

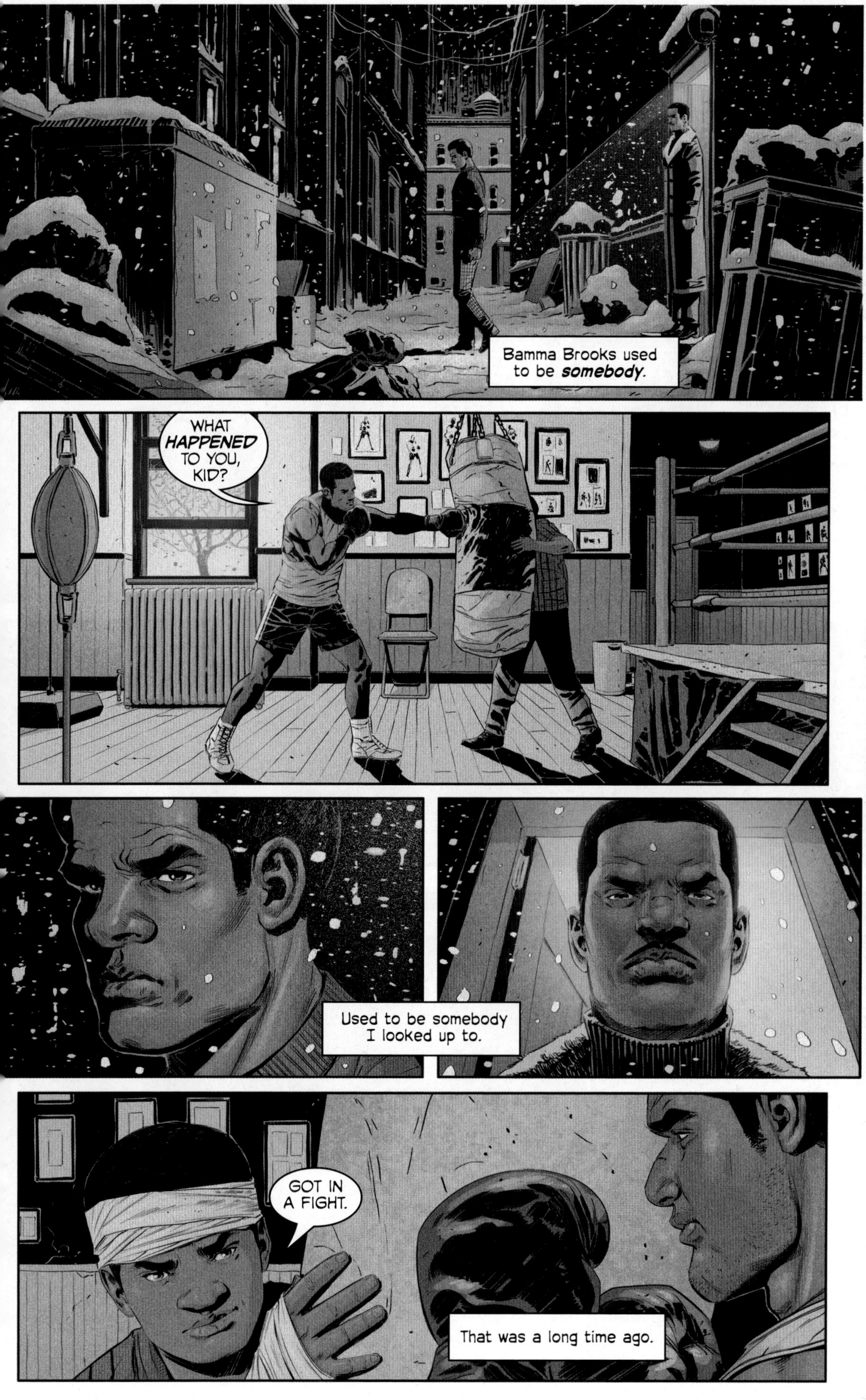
Bamma Brooks used to be *somebody*.
WHAT *HAPPENED* TO YOU, KID?
Used to be somebody I looked up to.
GOT IN A FIGHT.
That was a long time ago.

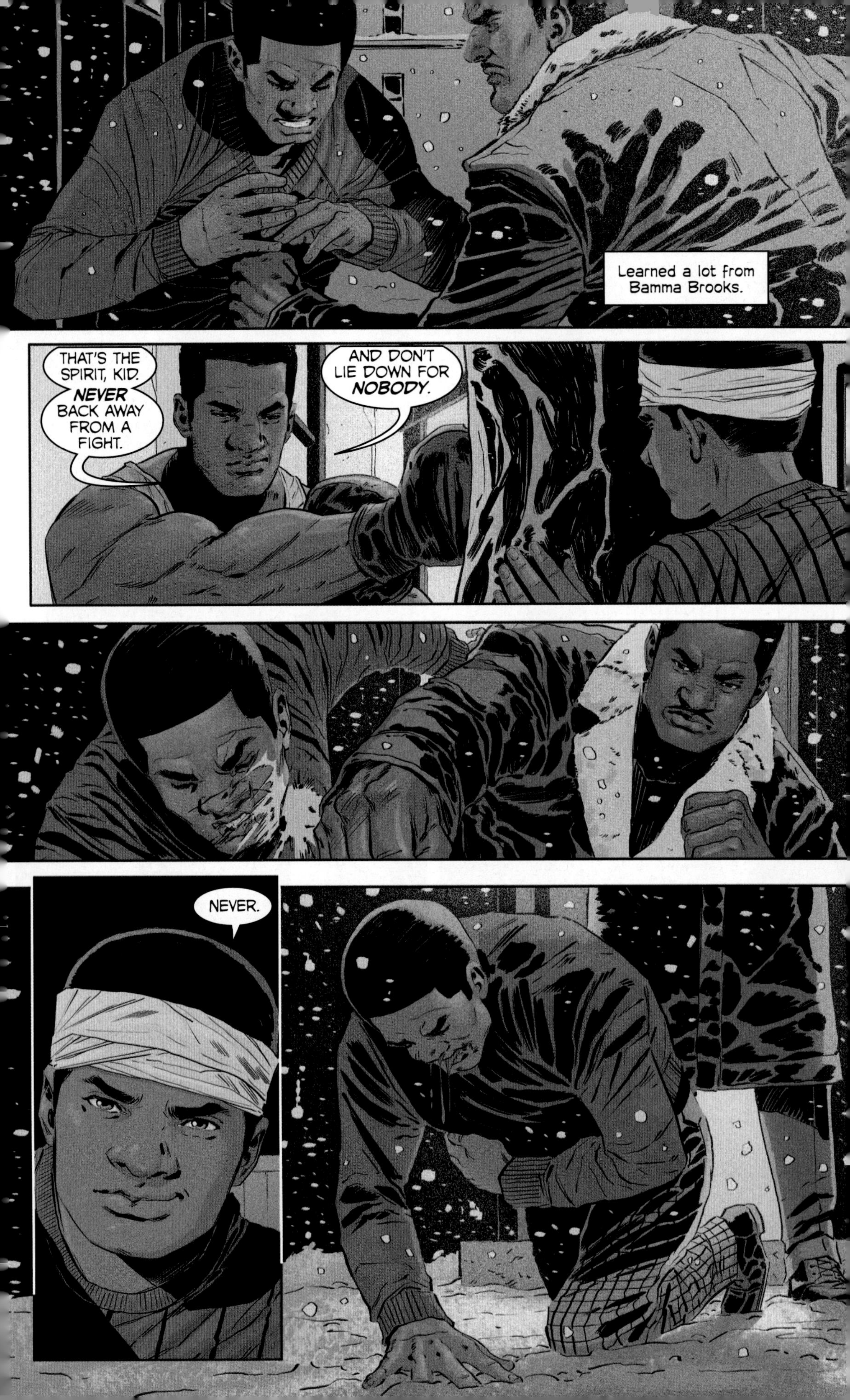

Learned a lot from Bamma Brooks.
THAT'S THE SPIRIT, KID. NEVER BACK AWAY FROM A FIGHT.
AND DON'T LIE DOWN FOR NOBODY.
NEVER.

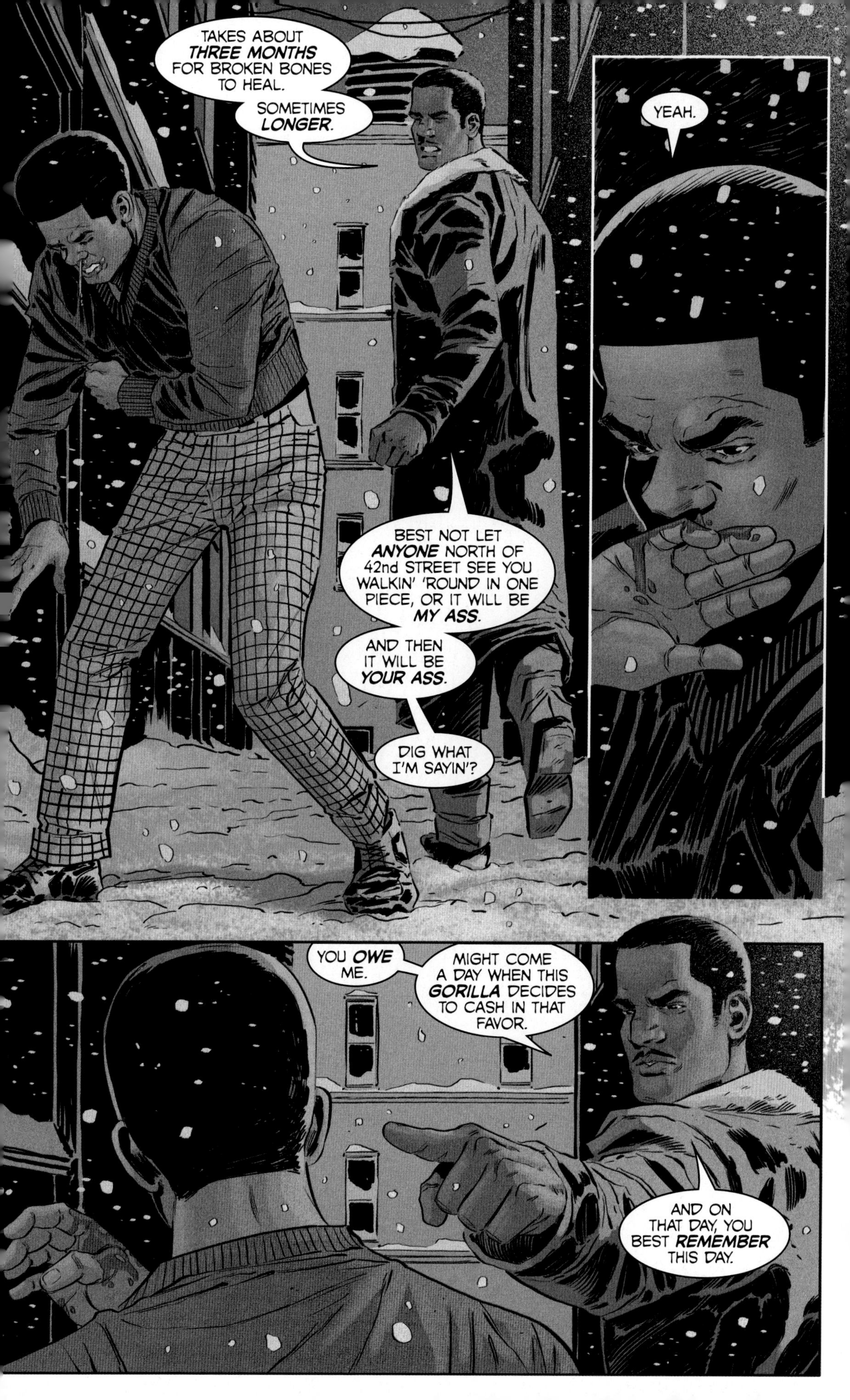
TAKES ABOUT *THREE MONTHS* FOR BROKEN BONES TO HEAL.
SOMETIMES *LONGER*.
YEAH.
BEST NOT LET *ANYONE* NORTH OF 42nd STREET SEE YOU WALKIN' 'ROUND IN ONE PIECE, OR IT WILL BE *MY ASS*.
AND THEN IT WILL BE *YOUR ASS*.
DIG WHAT I'M SAYIN'?
YOU *OWE* ME.
MIGHT COME A DAY WHEN THIS *GORILLA* DECIDES TO CASH IN THAT FAVOR.
AND ON THAT DAY, YOU BEST *REMEMBER* THIS DAY.

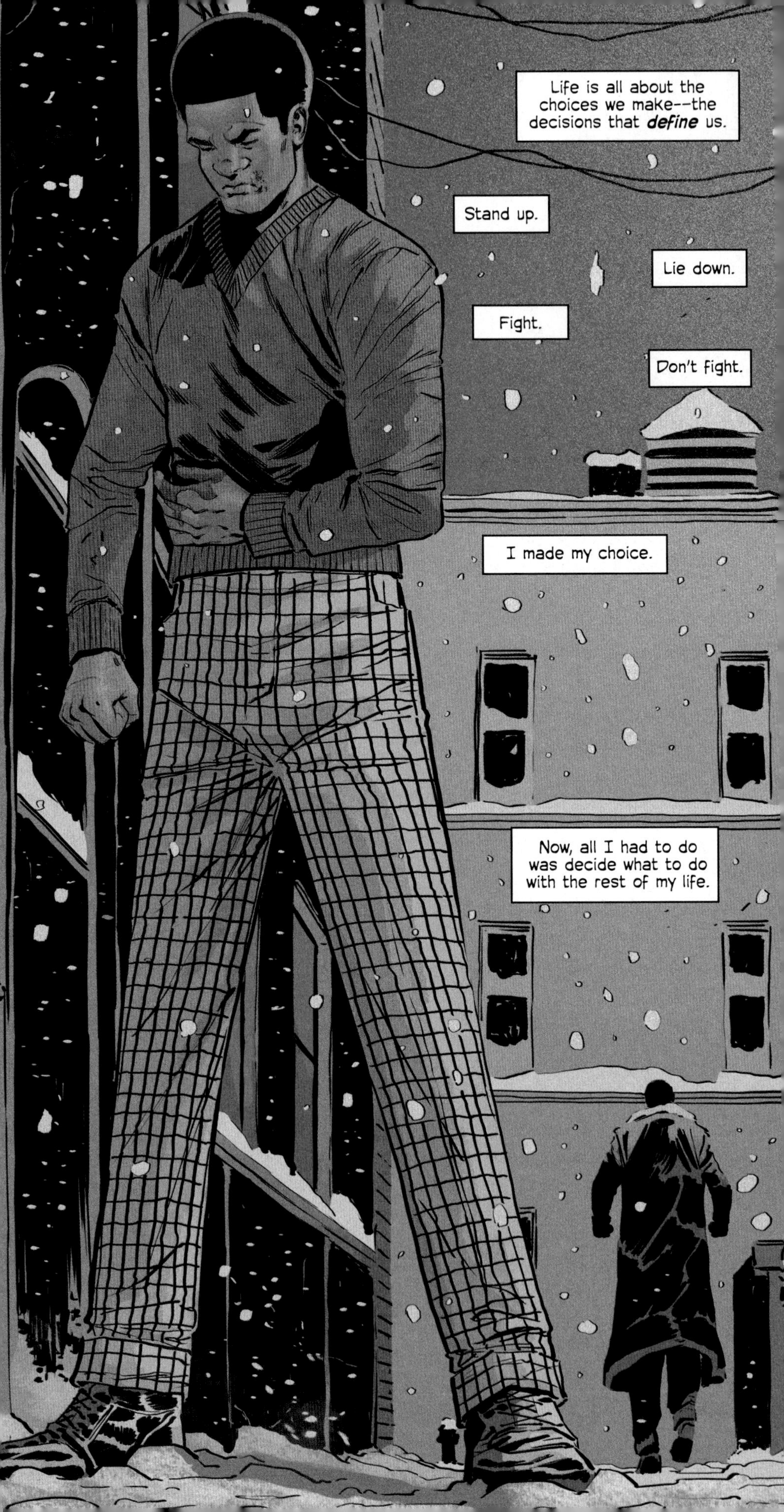
Life is all about the choices we make--the decisions that *define* us.
Stand up.
Lie down.
Fight.
Don't fight.
I made my choice.
Now, all I had to do was decide what to do with the rest of my life.

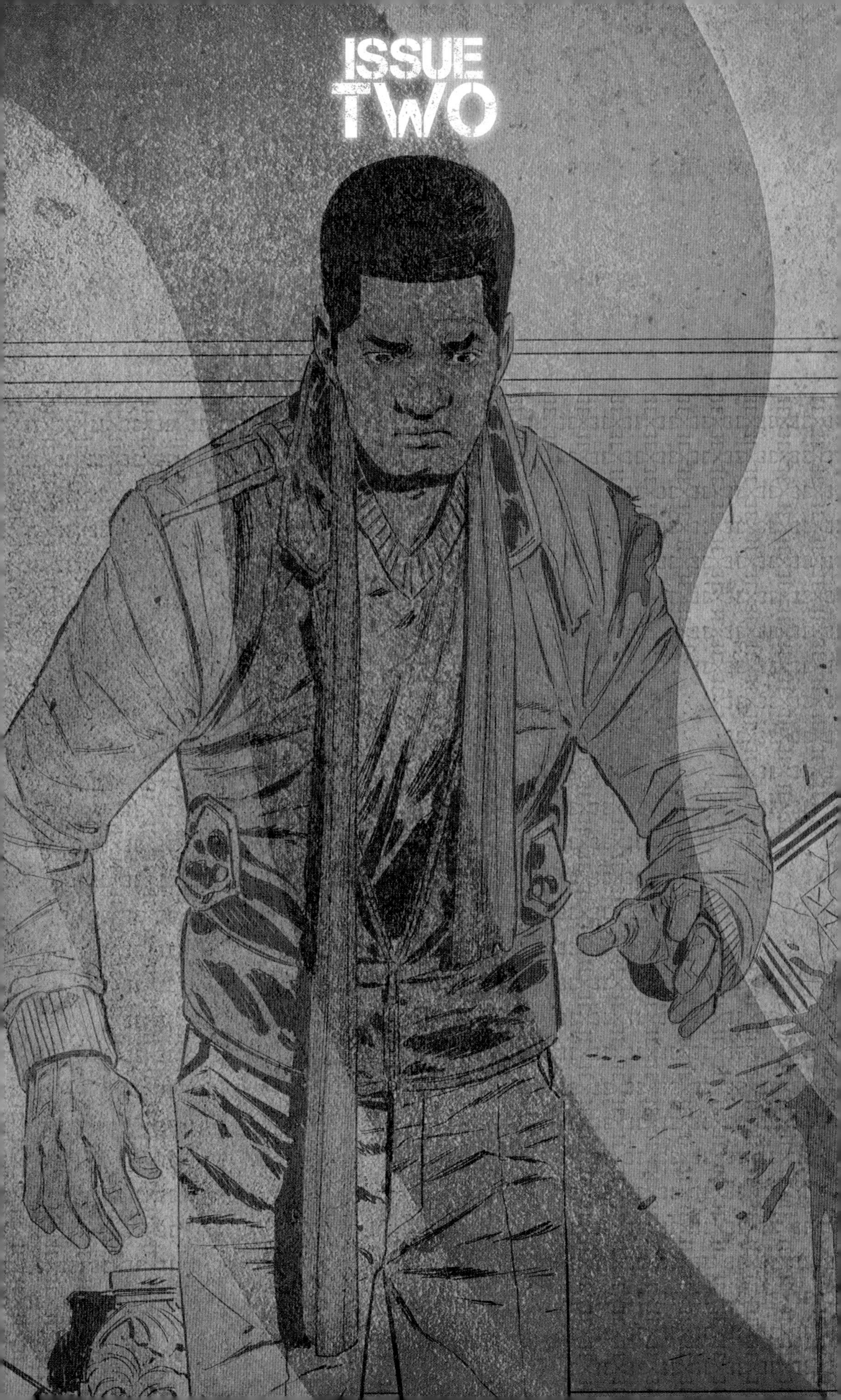
ISSUE
TWO

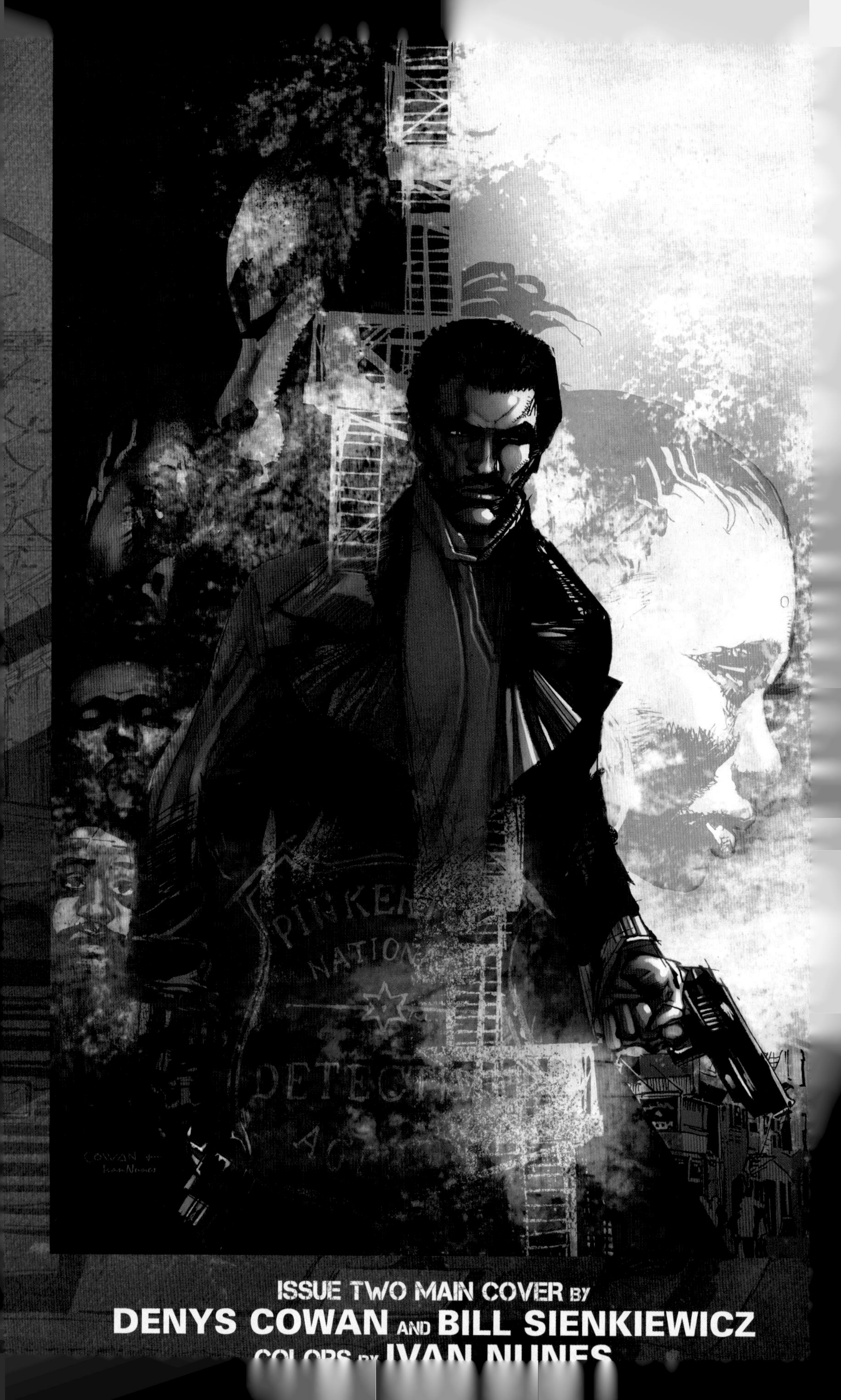

ISSUE TWO MAIN COVER BY
DENYS COWAN AND BILL SIENKIEWICZ
COLORS BY IVAN NUNES

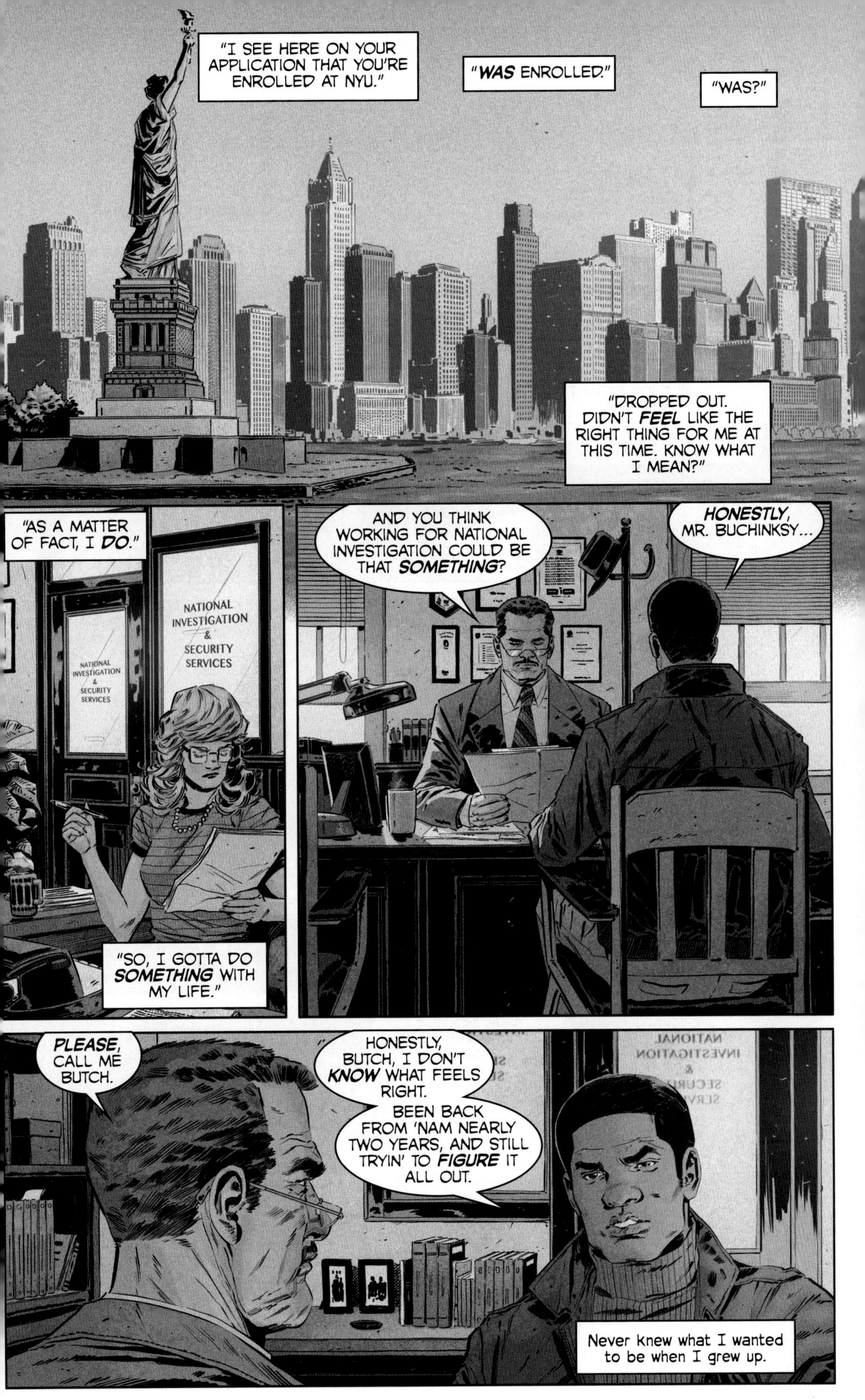
"I SEE HERE ON YOUR APPLICATION THAT YOU'RE ENROLLED AT NYU."
"WAS ENROLLED."
"WAS?"
"DROPPED OUT. DIDN'T FEEL LIKE THE RIGHT THING FOR ME AT THIS TIME. KNOW WHAT I MEAN?"
"AS A MATTER OF FACT, I DO."
NATIONAL INVESTIGATION & SECURITY SERVICES
NATIONAL INVESTIGATION & SECURITY SERVICES
"SO, I GOTTA DO SOMETHING WITH MY LIFE."
AND YOU THINK WORKING FOR NATIONAL INVESTIGATION COULD BE THAT SOMETHING?
HONESTLY, MR. BUCHINKSY...
PLEASE, CALL ME BUTCH.
HONESTLY, BUTCH, I DON'T KNOW WHAT FEELS RIGHT.
BEEN BACK FROM 'NAM NEARLY TWO YEARS, AND STILL TRYIN' TO FIGURE IT ALL OUT.
Never knew what I wanted to be when I grew up.

FELT THE *SAME* WAY WHEN I GOT BACK FROM KOREA IN '52.

NOT SO MUCH WHEN I GOT BACK FROM GERMANY IN '45.

BUT *THOSE* WERE DIFFERENT WARS.

CAN'T EVEN *IMAGINE* WHAT IT'S LIKE IN VIETNAM.

Then again, never really *thought* about growing up.

Only thought about *not* dying.

For me, not dying and growing up were the *same* thing.

IT'S WAR.

PEOPLE *KILLING* OTHER PEOPLE OVER REAL ESTATE.

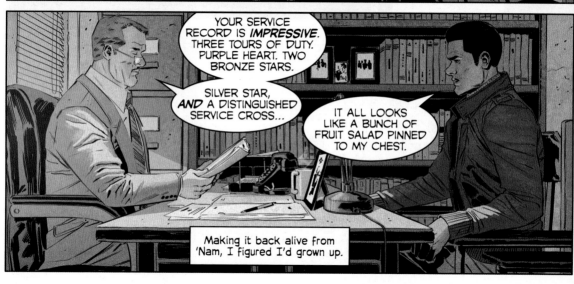

YOUR SERVICE RECORD IS *IMPRESSIVE*. THREE TOURS OF DUTY. PURPLE HEART. TWO BRONZE STARS.

SILVER STAR, *AND* A DISTINGUISHED SERVICE CROSS...

IT ALL LOOKS LIKE A BUNCH OF FRUIT SALAD PINNED TO MY CHEST.

Making it back alive from 'Nam, I figured I'd grown up.

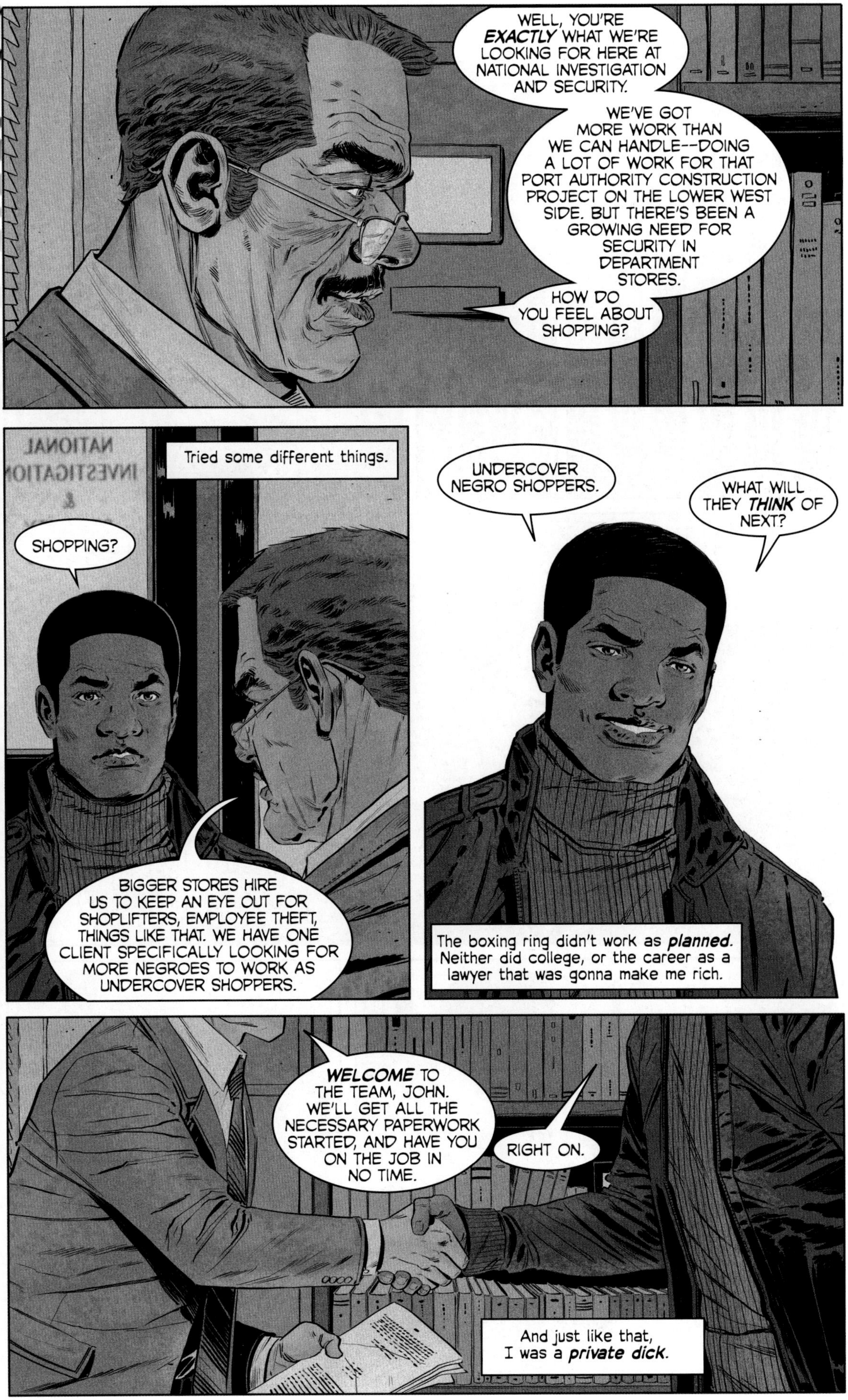

WELL, YOU'RE *EXACTLY* WHAT WE'RE LOOKING FOR HERE AT NATIONAL INVESTIGATION AND SECURITY.
WE'VE GOT MORE WORK THAN WE CAN HANDLE--DOING A LOT OF WORK FOR THAT PORT AUTHORITY CONSTRUCTION PROJECT ON THE LOWER WEST SIDE. BUT THERE'S BEEN A GROWING NEED FOR SECURITY IN DEPARTMENT STORES.
HOW DO YOU FEEL ABOUT SHOPPING?
Tried some different things.
SHOPPING?
BIGGER STORES HIRE US TO KEEP AN EYE OUT FOR SHOPLIFTERS, EMPLOYEE THEFT, THINGS LIKE THAT. WE HAVE ONE CLIENT SPECIFICALLY LOOKING FOR MORE NEGROES TO WORK AS UNDERCOVER SHOPPERS.
UNDERCOVER NEGRO SHOPPERS.
WHAT WILL THEY *THINK* OF NEXT?
The boxing ring didn't work as *planned*. Neither did college, or the career as a lawyer that was gonna make me rich.
WELCOME TO THE TEAM, JOHN. WE'LL GET ALL THE NECESSARY PAPERWORK STARTED, AND HAVE YOU ON THE JOB IN NO TIME.
RIGHT ON.
And just like that, I was a *private dick*.

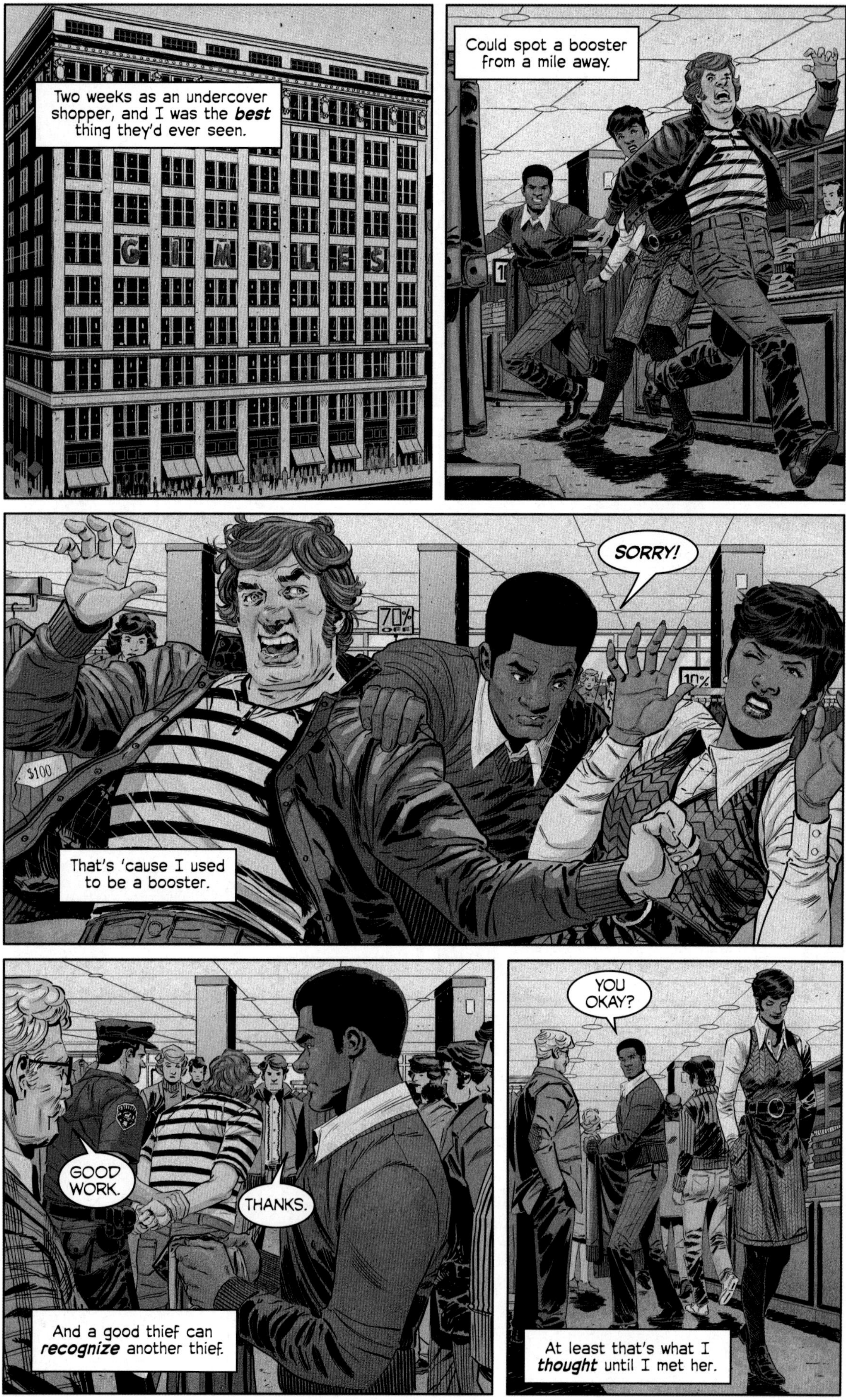

Two weeks as an undercover shopper, and I was the **best** thing they'd ever seen.
GIMBLES
Could spot a booster from a mile away.
SORRY!
70% OFF
10%
$100
That's 'cause I used to be a booster.
GOOD WORK.
THANKS.
And a good thief can **recognize** another thief.
YOU OKAY?
At least that's what I **thought** until I met her.

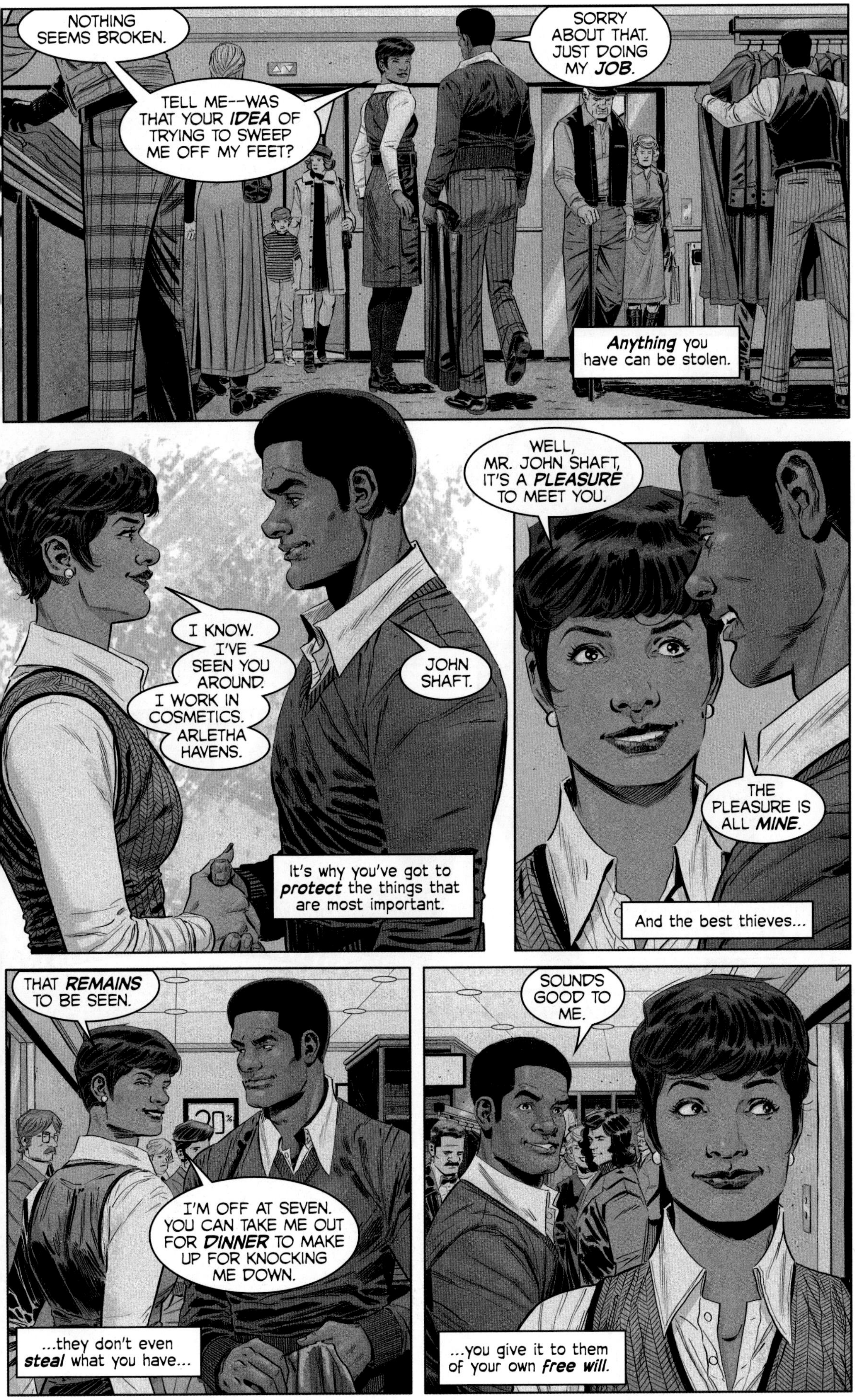
NOTHING SEEMS BROKEN.
TELL ME--WAS THAT YOUR IDEA OF TRYING TO SWEEP ME OFF MY FEET?
SORRY ABOUT THAT. JUST DOING MY JOB.
Anything you have can be stolen.
JOHN SHAFT.
I KNOW. I'VE SEEN YOU AROUND.
I WORK IN COSMETICS. ARLETHA HAVENS.
It's why you've got to protect the things that are most important.
WELL, MR. JOHN SHAFT, IT'S A PLEASURE TO MEET YOU.
THE PLEASURE IS ALL MINE.
And the best thieves...
THAT REMAINS TO BE SEEN.
I'M OFF AT SEVEN. YOU CAN TAKE ME OUT FOR DINNER TO MAKE UP FOR KNOCKING ME DOWN.
...they don't even steal what you have...
SOUNDS GOOD TO ME.
...you give it to them of your own free will.

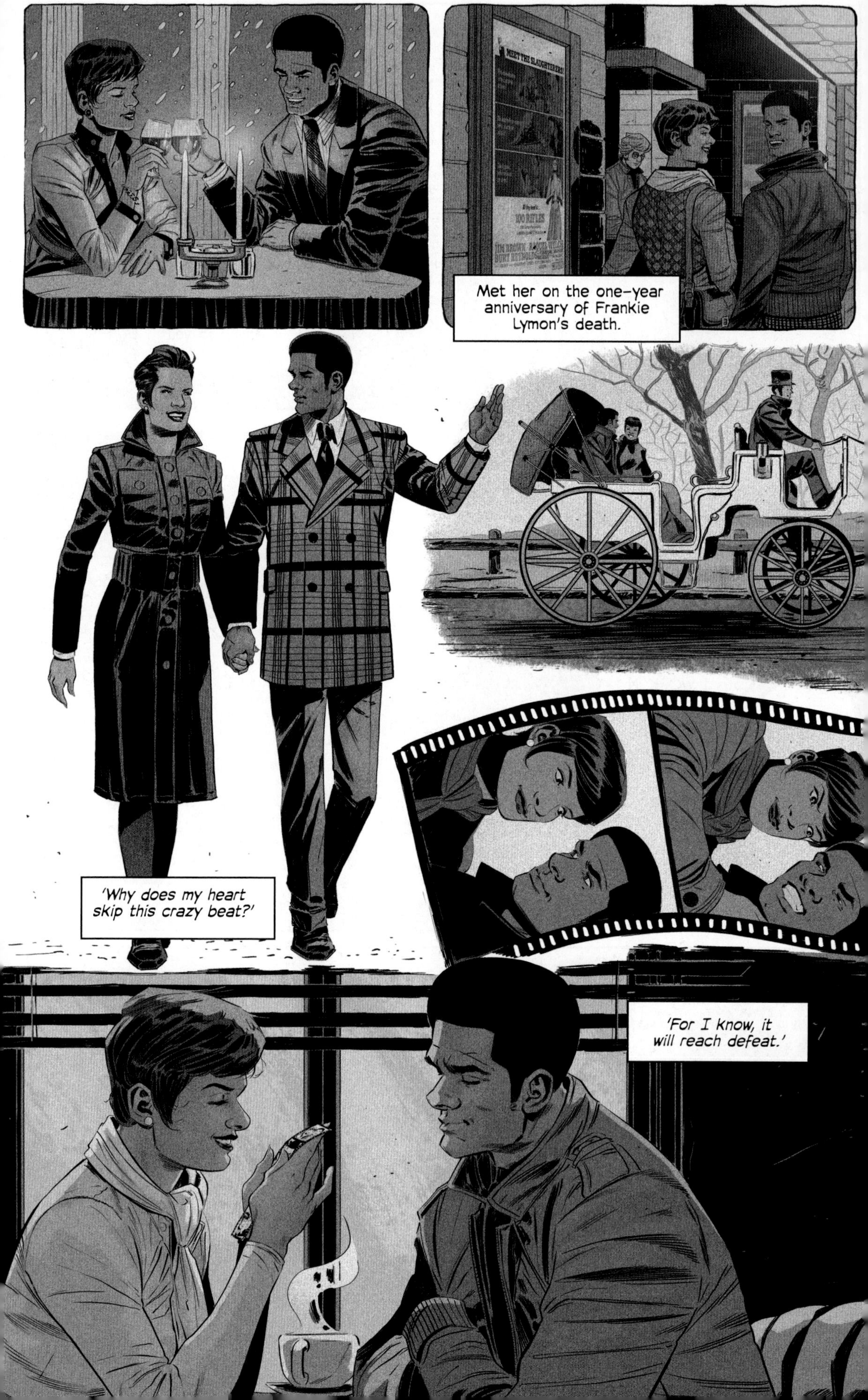
MEET THE SLAUGHTERERS
100 RIFLES
Met her on the one-year anniversary of Frankie Lymon's death.
'Why does my heart skip this crazy beat?'
'For I know, it will reach defeat.'

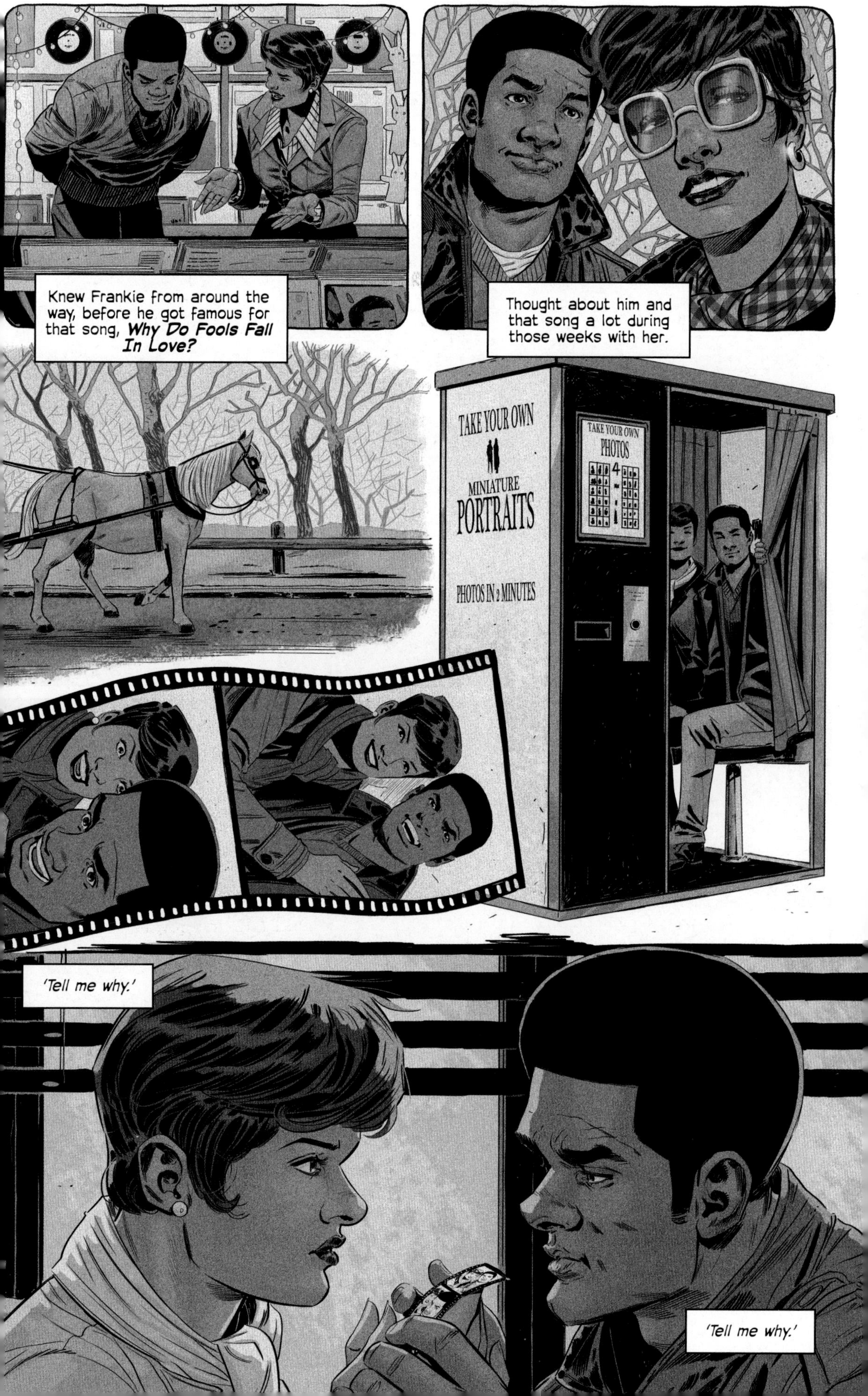
Knew Frankie from around the way, before he got famous for that song, ***Why Do Fools Fall In Love?***
Thought about him and that song a lot during those weeks with her.
TAKE YOUR OWN
MINIATURE
PORTRAITS
PHOTOS IN 2 MINUTES
TAKE YOUR OWN
PHOTOS
4
'Tell me why.'
'Tell me why.'

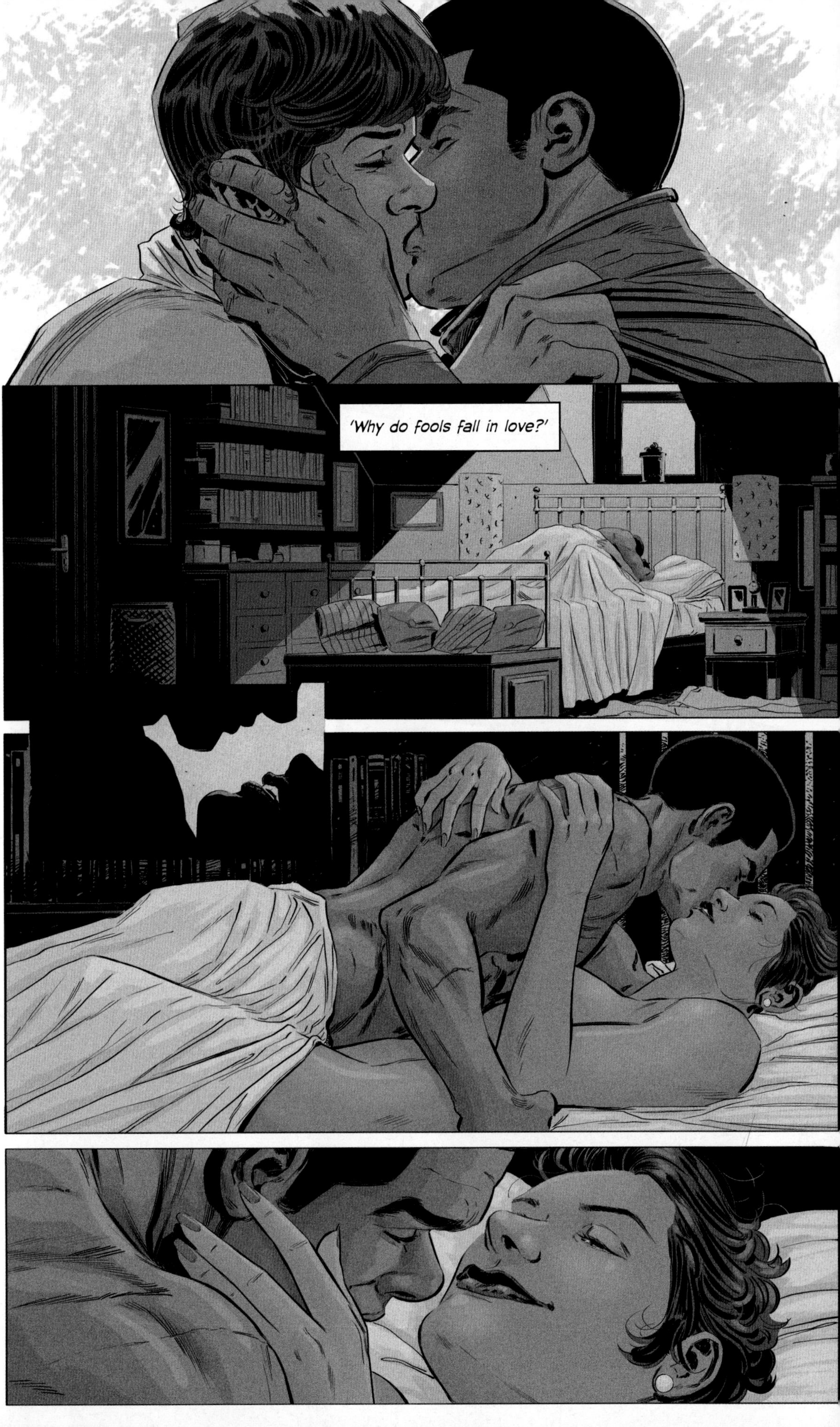
'Why do fools fall in love?'

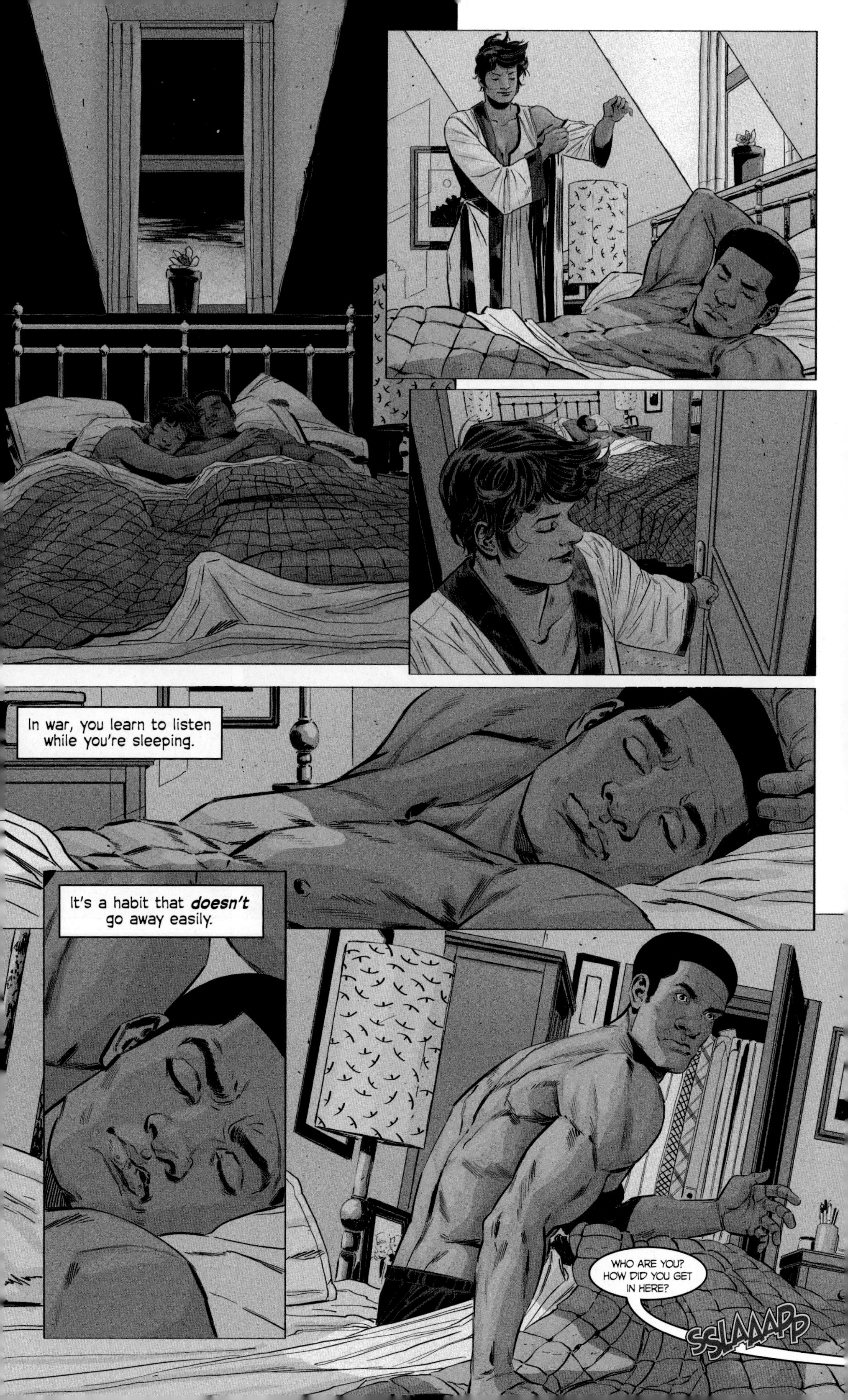
In war, you learn to listen while you're sleeping.
It's a habit that ***doesn't*** go away easily.
WHO ARE YOU? HOW DID YOU GET IN HERE?
SSLAAAPP

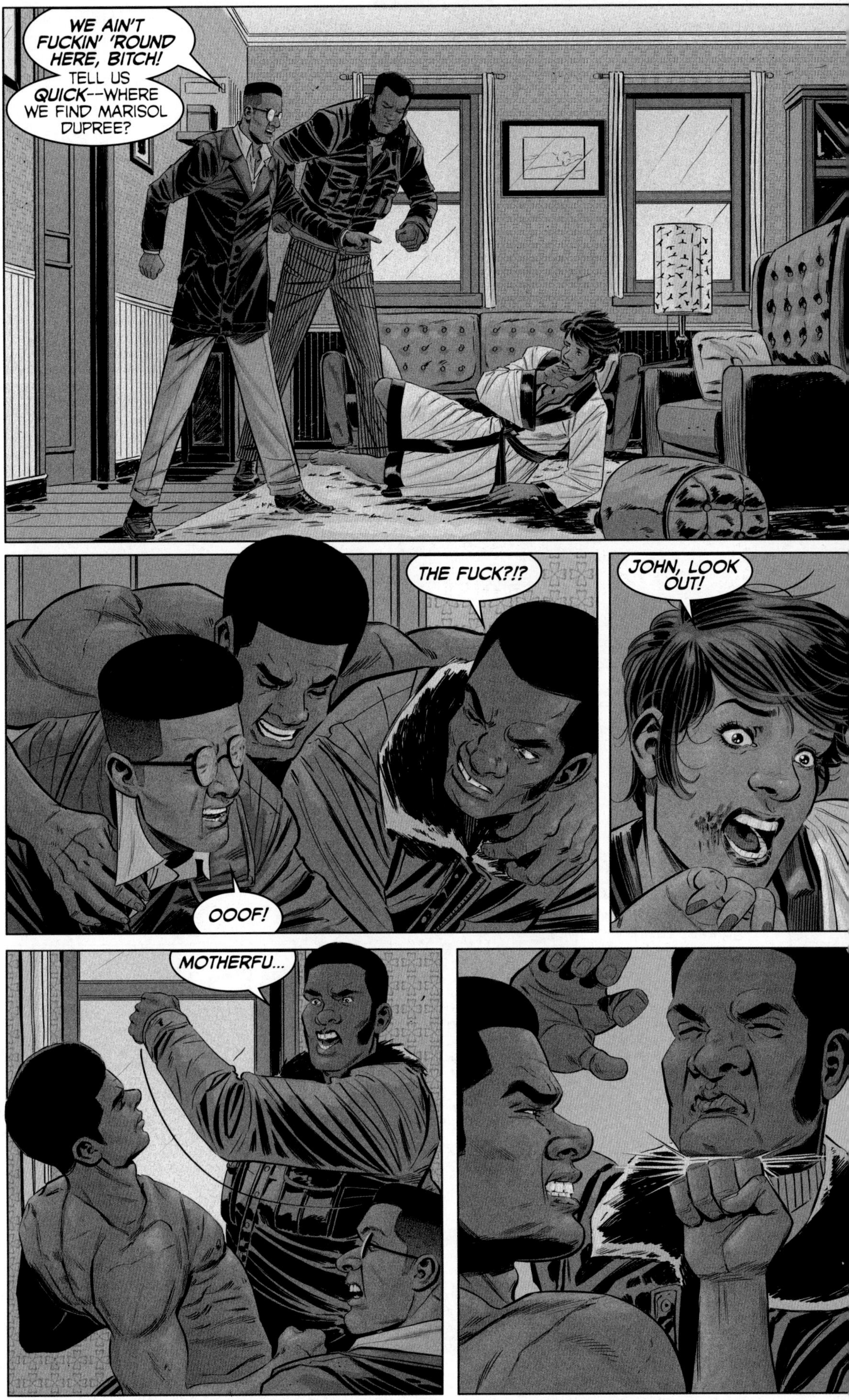
WE AIN'T FUCKIN' 'ROUND HERE, BITCH!
TELL US QUICK--WHERE WE FIND MARISOL DUPREE?
THE FUCK?!?
OOOF!
JOHN, LOOK OUT!
MOTHERFU...

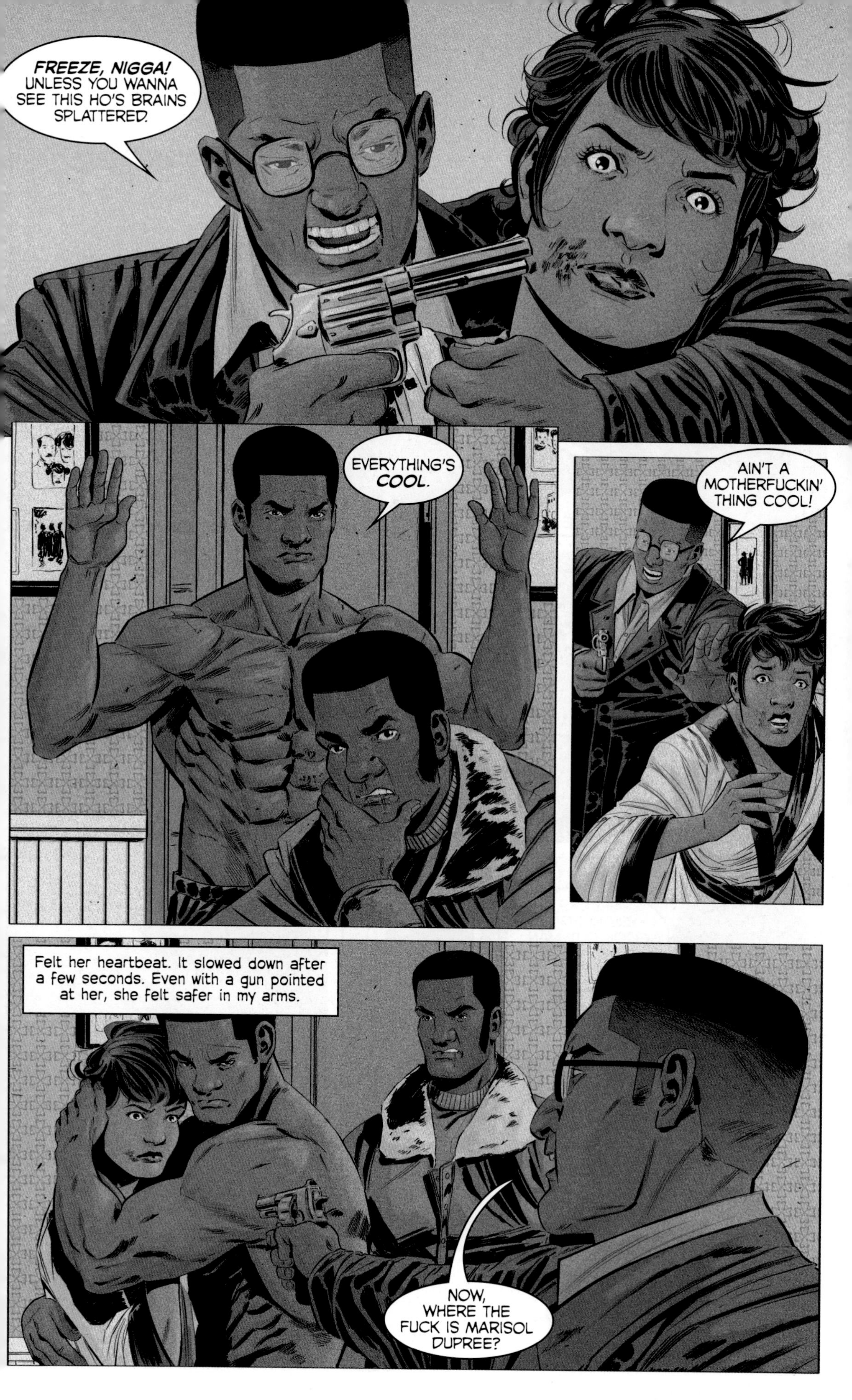

FREEZE, NIGGA! UNLESS YOU WANNA SEE THIS HO'S BRAINS SPLATTERED.
EVERYTHING'S COOL.
AIN'T A MOTHERFUCKIN' THING COOL!
Felt her heartbeat. It slowed down after a few seconds. Even with a gun pointed at her, she felt safer in my arms.
NOW, WHERE THE FUCK IS MARISOL DUPREE?

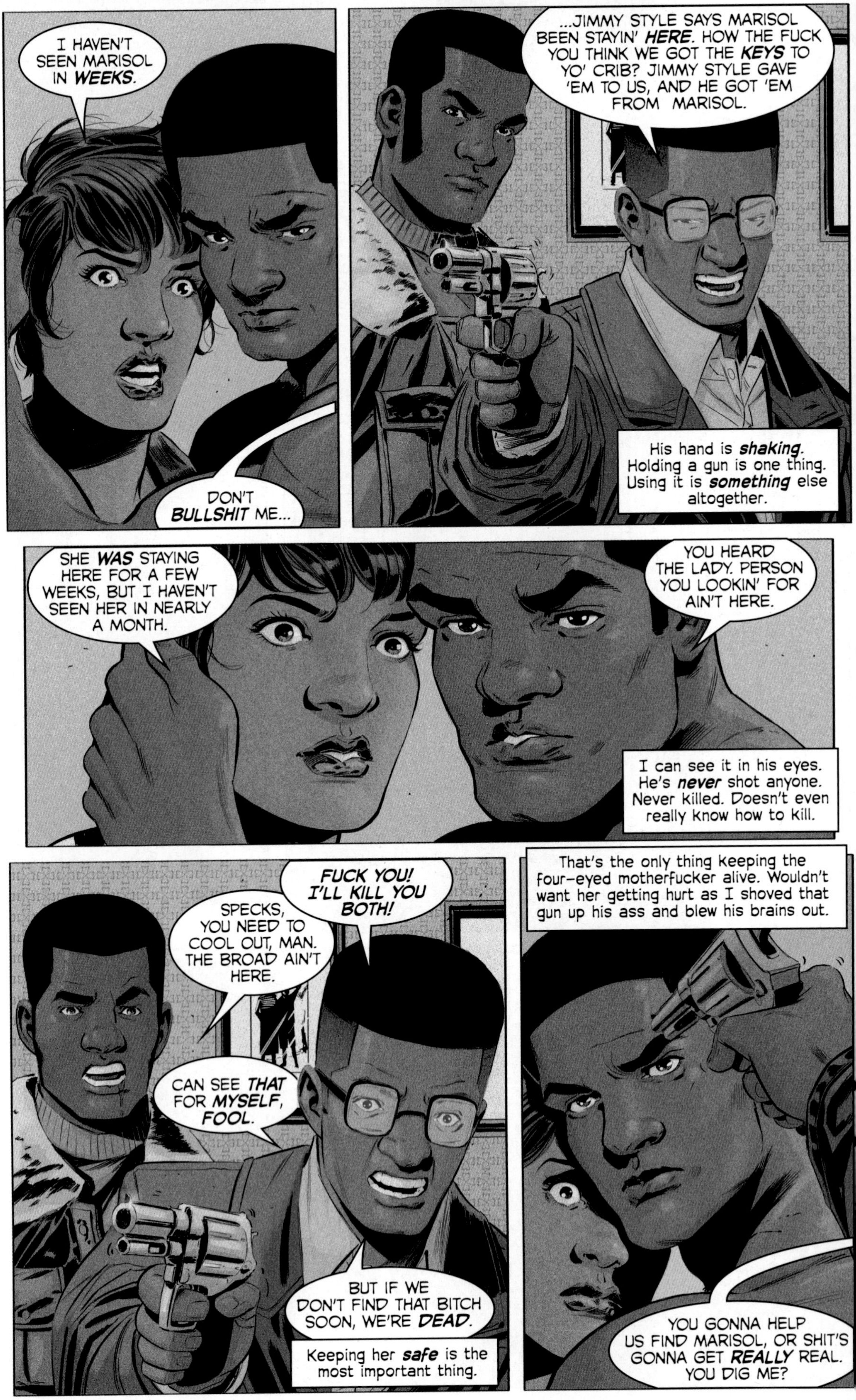

I HAVEN'T SEEN MARISOL IN WEEKS.
DON'T BULLSHIT ME...
...JIMMY STYLE SAYS MARISOL BEEN STAYIN' HERE. HOW THE FUCK YOU THINK WE GOT THE KEYS TO YO' CRIB? JIMMY STYLE GAVE 'EM TO US, AND HE GOT 'EM FROM MARISOL.
His hand is shaking. Holding a gun is one thing. Using it is something else altogether.
SHE WAS STAYING HERE FOR A FEW WEEKS, BUT I HAVEN'T SEEN HER IN NEARLY A MONTH.
YOU HEARD THE LADY. PERSON YOU LOOKIN' FOR AIN'T HERE.
I can see it in his eyes. He's never shot anyone. Never killed. Doesn't even really know how to kill.
SPECKS, YOU NEED TO COOL OUT, MAN. THE BROAD AIN'T HERE.
FUCK YOU! I'LL KILL YOU BOTH!
CAN SEE THAT FOR MYSELF, FOOL.
BUT IF WE DON'T FIND THAT BITCH SOON, WE'RE DEAD.
Keeping her safe is the most important thing.
That's the only thing keeping the four-eyed motherfucker alive. Wouldn't want her getting hurt as I shoved that gun up his ass and blew his brains out.
YOU GONNA HELP US FIND MARISOL, OR SHIT'S GONNA GET REALLY REAL. YOU DIG ME?

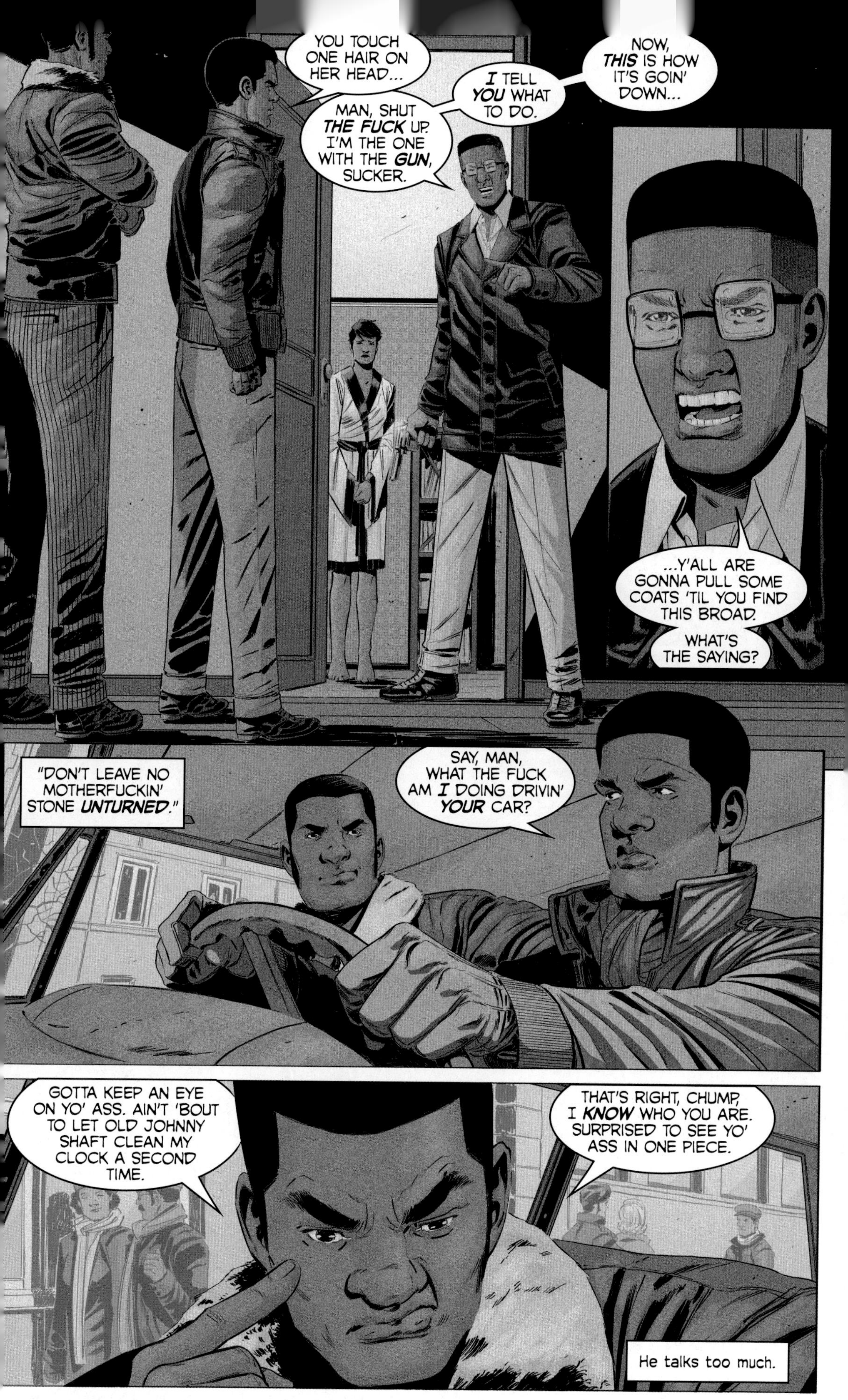
YOU TOUCH ONE HAIR ON HER HEAD...
MAN, SHUT THE FUCK UP. I'M THE ONE WITH THE GUN, SUCKER.
I TELL YOU WHAT TO DO.
NOW, THIS IS HOW IT'S GOIN' DOWN...
...Y'ALL ARE GONNA PULL SOME COATS 'TIL YOU FIND THIS BROAD.
WHAT'S THE SAYING?
"DON'T LEAVE NO MOTHERFUCKIN' STONE UNTURNED."
SAY, MAN, WHAT THE FUCK AM I DOING DRIVIN' YOUR CAR?
GOTTA KEEP AN EYE ON YO' ASS. AIN'T 'BOUT TO LET OLD JOHNNY SHAFT CLEAN MY CLOCK A SECOND TIME.
THAT'S RIGHT, CHUMP, I KNOW WHO YOU ARE. SURPRISED TO SEE YO' ASS IN ONE PIECE.
He talks too much.

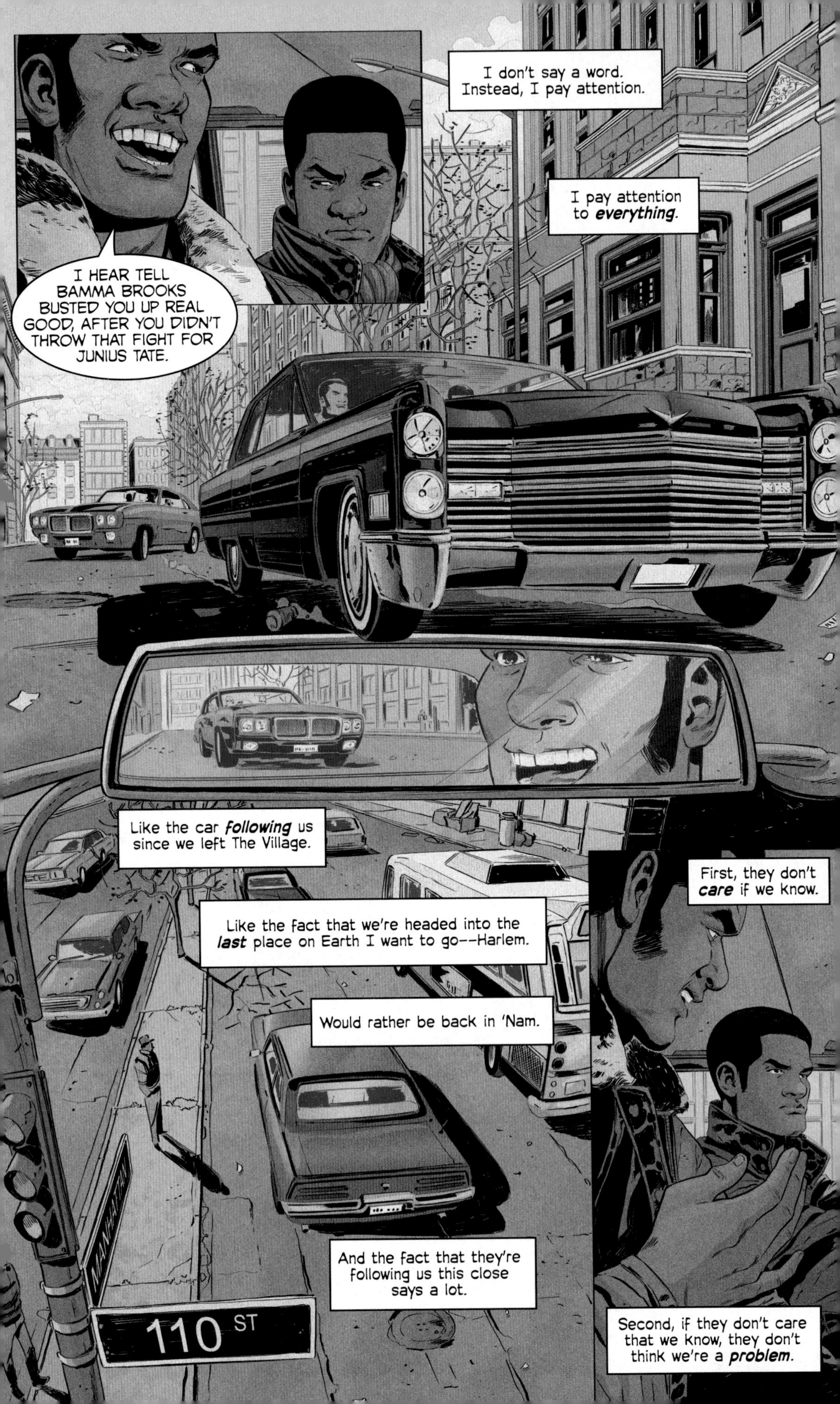
I HEAR TELL BAMMA BROOKS BUSTED YOU UP REAL GOOD, AFTER YOU DIDN'T THROW THAT FIGHT FOR JUNIUS TATE.
I don't say a word. Instead, I pay attention.
I pay attention to ***everything***.
Like the car ***following*** us since we left The Village.
Like the fact that we're headed into the ***last*** place on Earth I want to go--Harlem.
Would rather be back in 'Nam.
And the fact that they're following us this close says a lot.
110 ST
MANHATTAN
First, they don't ***care*** if we know.
Second, if they don't care that we know, they don't think we're a ***problem***.

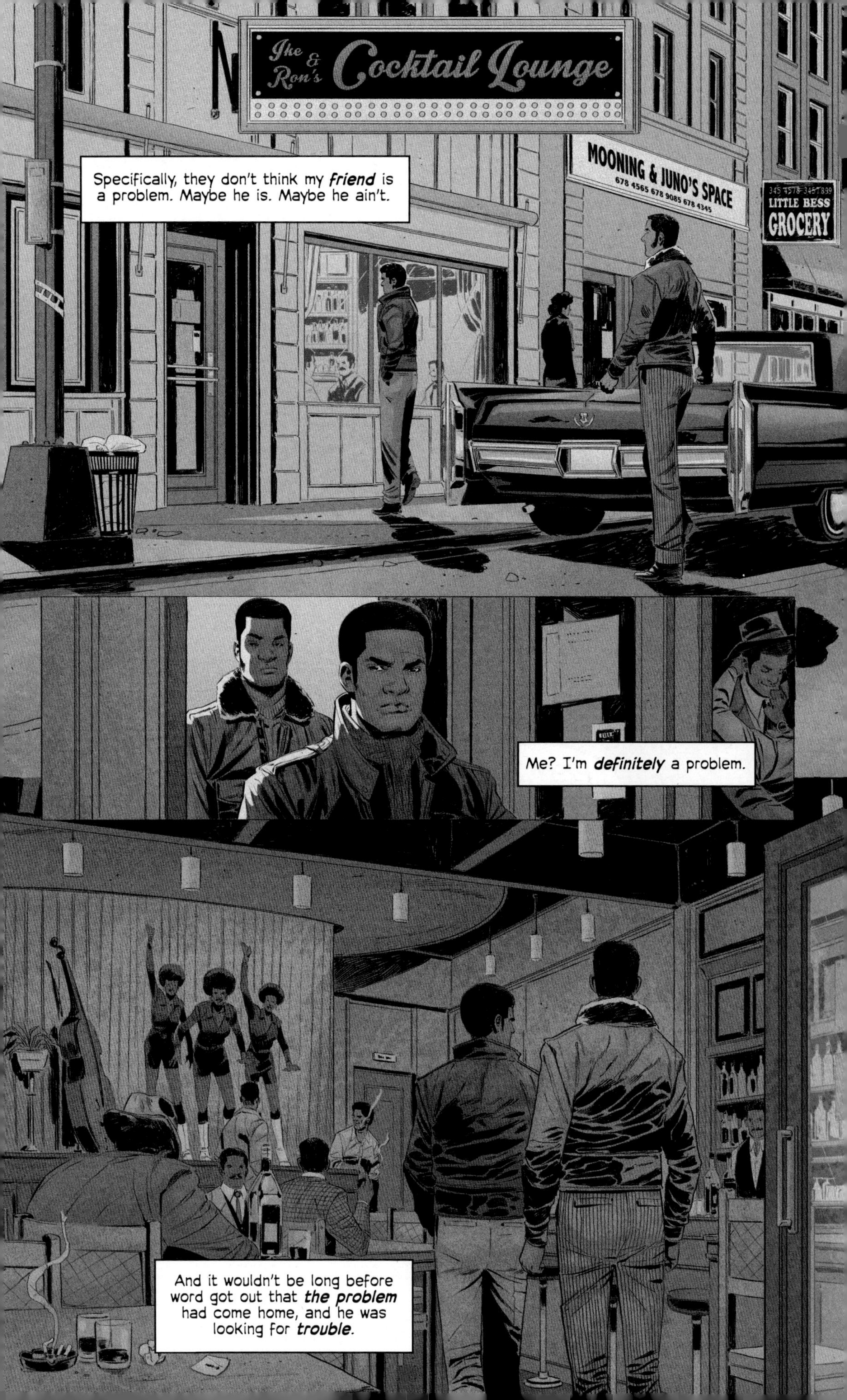
Ike & Ron's Cocktail Lounge
MOONING & JUNO'S SPACE
678 4565 678 9085 678 4345
LITTLE BESS GROCERY
Specifically, they don't think my *friend* is a problem. Maybe he is. Maybe he ain't.
Me? I'm *definitely* a problem.
And it wouldn't be long before word got out that *the problem* had come home, and he was looking for *trouble*.

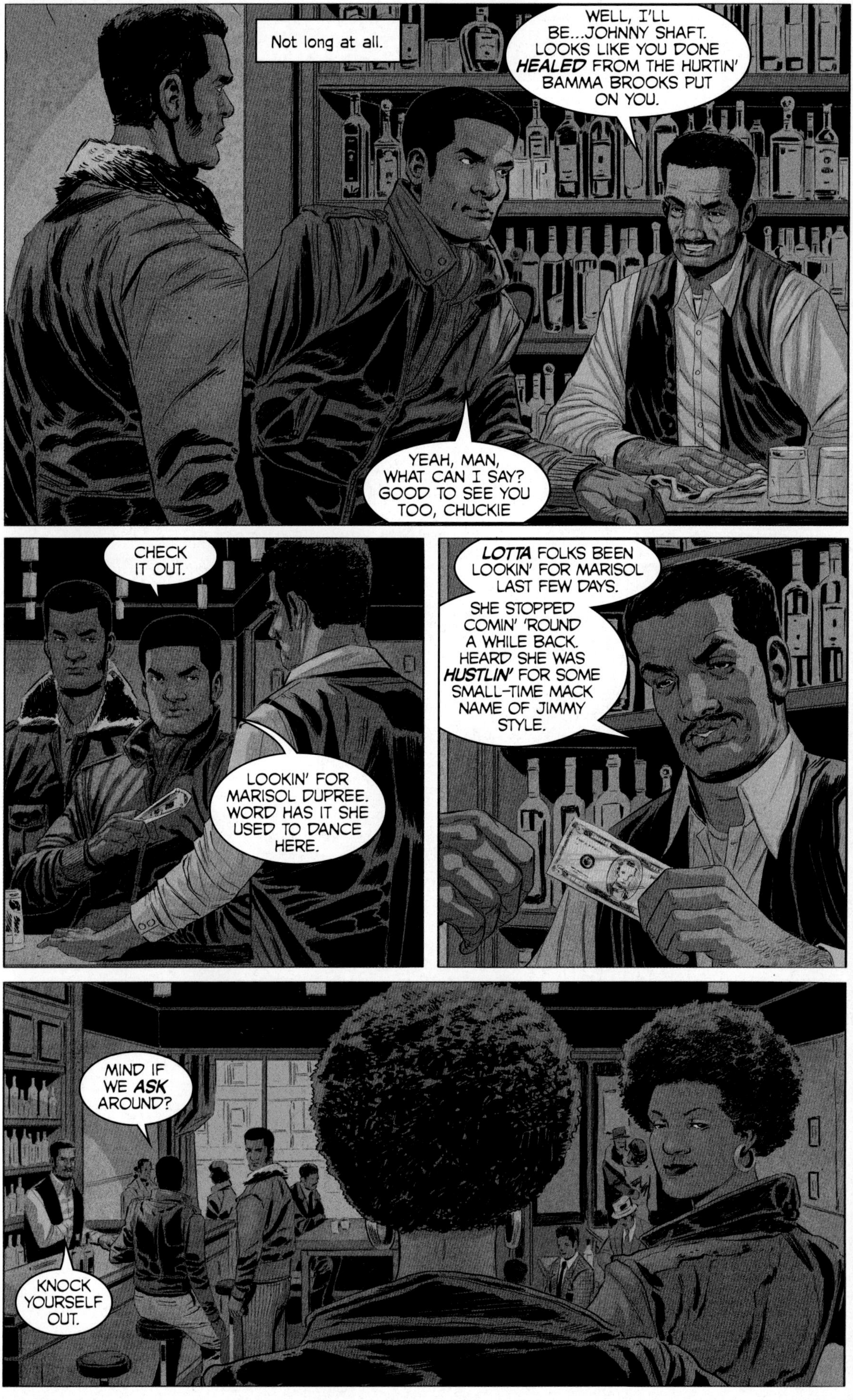
Not long at all.
WELL, I'LL BE...JOHNNY SHAFT. LOOKS LIKE YOU DONE HEALED FROM THE HURTIN' BAMMA BROOKS PUT ON YOU.
YEAH, MAN, WHAT CAN I SAY? GOOD TO SEE YOU TOO, CHUCKIE
CHECK IT OUT.
LOOKIN' FOR MARISOL DUPREE. WORD HAS IT SHE USED TO DANCE HERE.
LOTTA FOLKS BEEN LOOKIN' FOR MARISOL LAST FEW DAYS.
SHE STOPPED COMIN' 'ROUND A WHILE BACK. HEARD SHE WAS HUSTLIN' FOR SOME SMALL-TIME MACK NAME OF JIMMY STYLE.
MIND IF WE ASK AROUND?
KNOCK YOURSELF OUT.

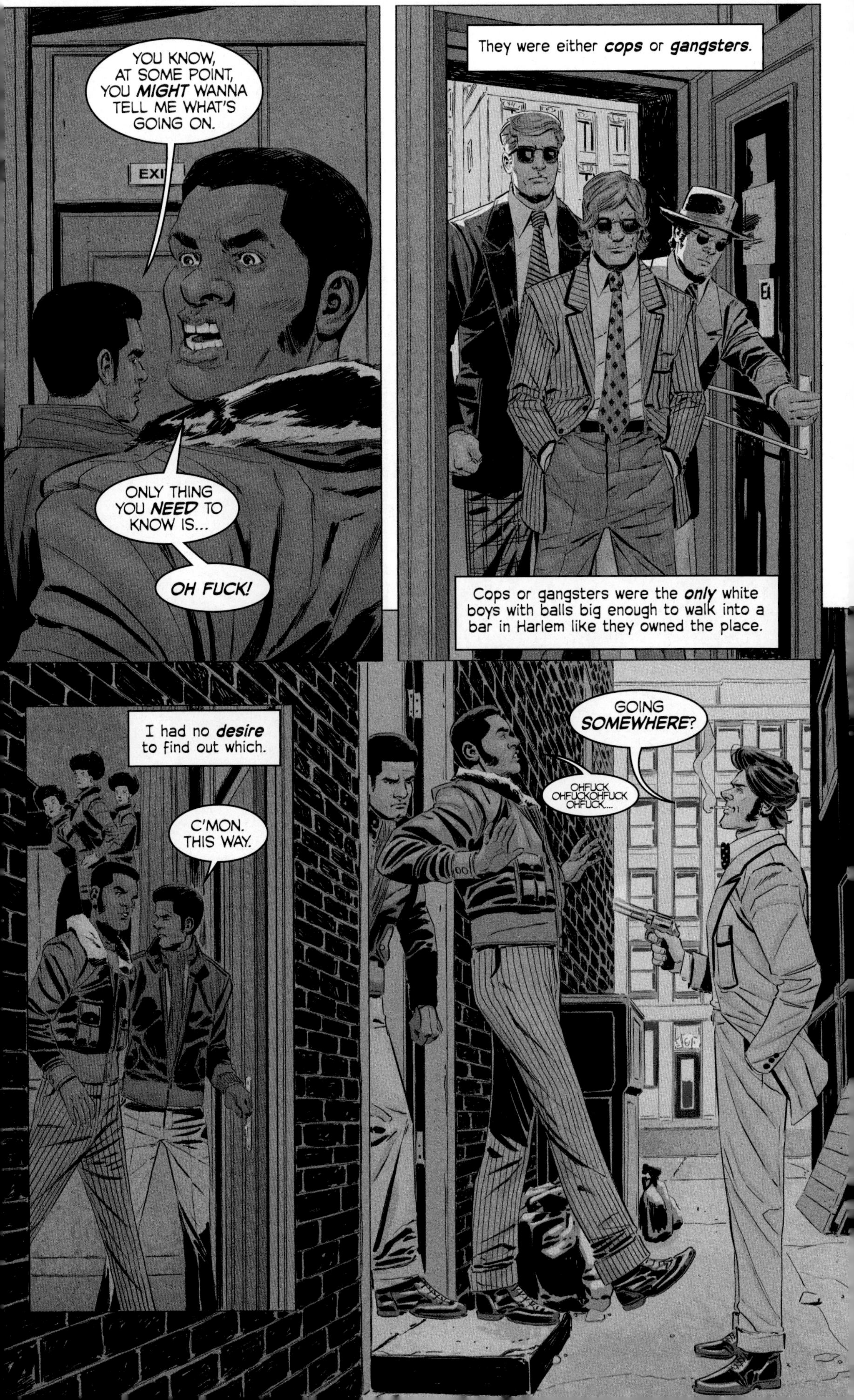

YOU KNOW, AT SOME POINT, YOU MIGHT WANNA TELL ME WHAT'S GOING ON.
EXIT
ONLY THING YOU NEED TO KNOW IS...
OH FUCK!
They were either cops or gangsters.
Cops or gangsters were the only white boys with balls big enough to walk into a bar in Harlem like they owned the place.
I had no desire to find out which.
C'MON. THIS WAY.
GOING SOMEWHERE?
OHFUCK OHFUCKOHFUCK OHFUCK....

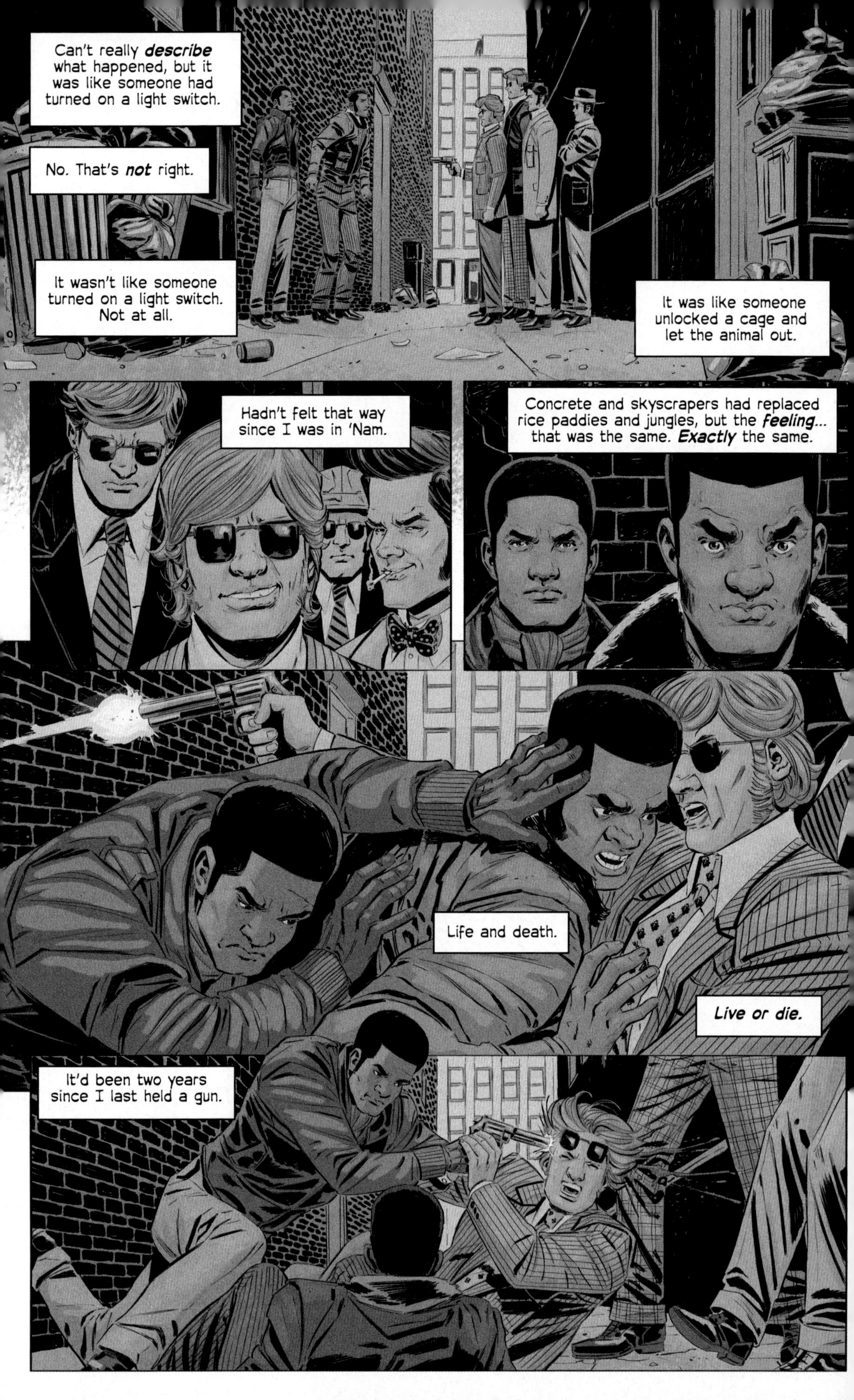
Can't really *describe* what happened, but it was like someone had turned on a light switch.
No. That's *not* right.
It wasn't like someone turned on a light switch. Not at all.
It was like someone unlocked a cage and let the animal out.
Hadn't felt that way since I was in 'Nam.
Concrete and skyscrapers had replaced rice paddies and jungles, but the *feeling*... that was the same. *Exactly* the same.
Life and death.
Live or die.
It'd been two years since I last held a gun.

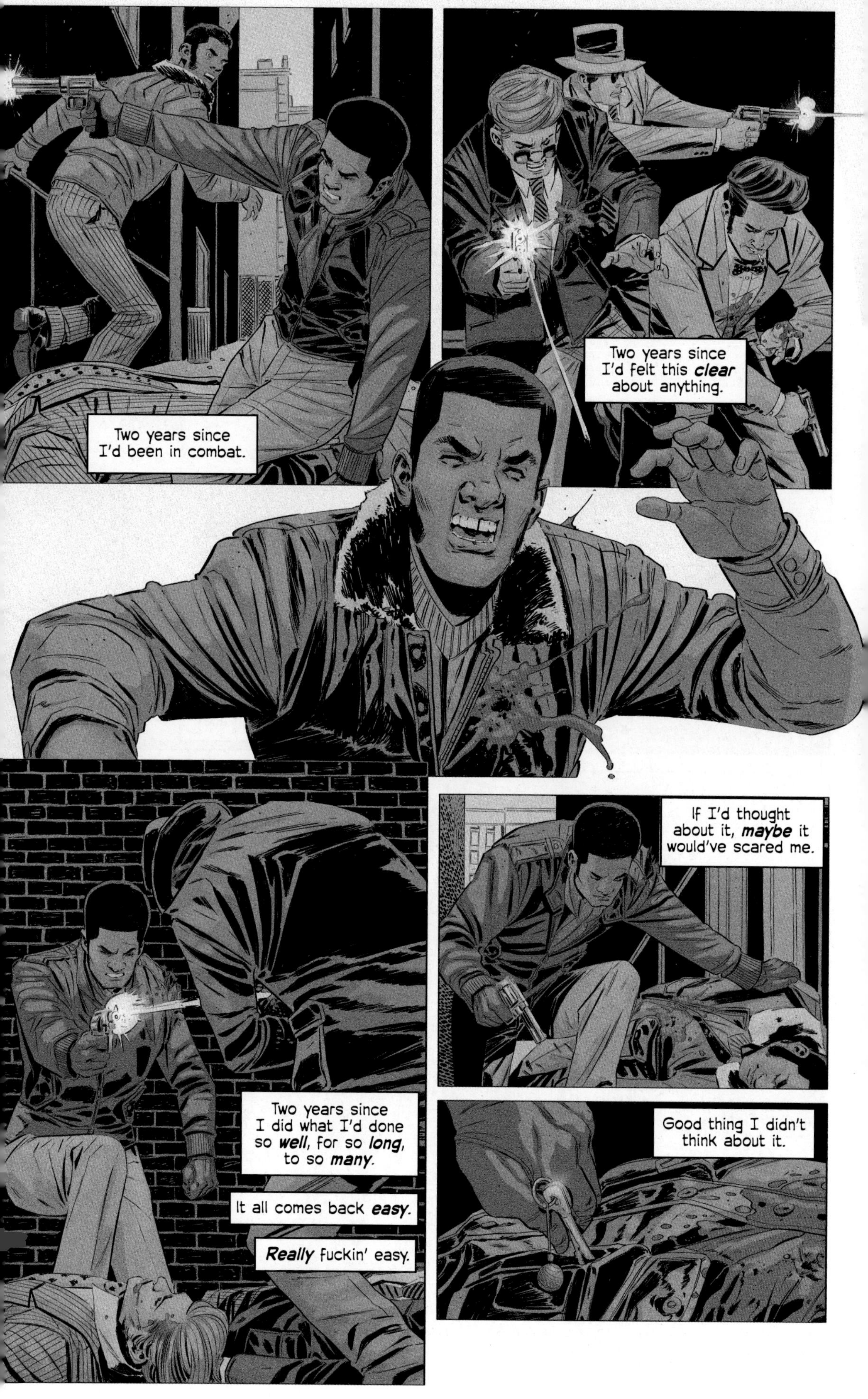
Two years since I'd been in combat.
Two years since I'd felt this *clear* about anything.
Two years since I did what I'd done so *well*, for so *long*, to so *many*.
It all comes back *easy*.
Really fuckin' easy.
If I'd thought about it, *maybe* it would've scared me.
Good thing I didn't think about it.

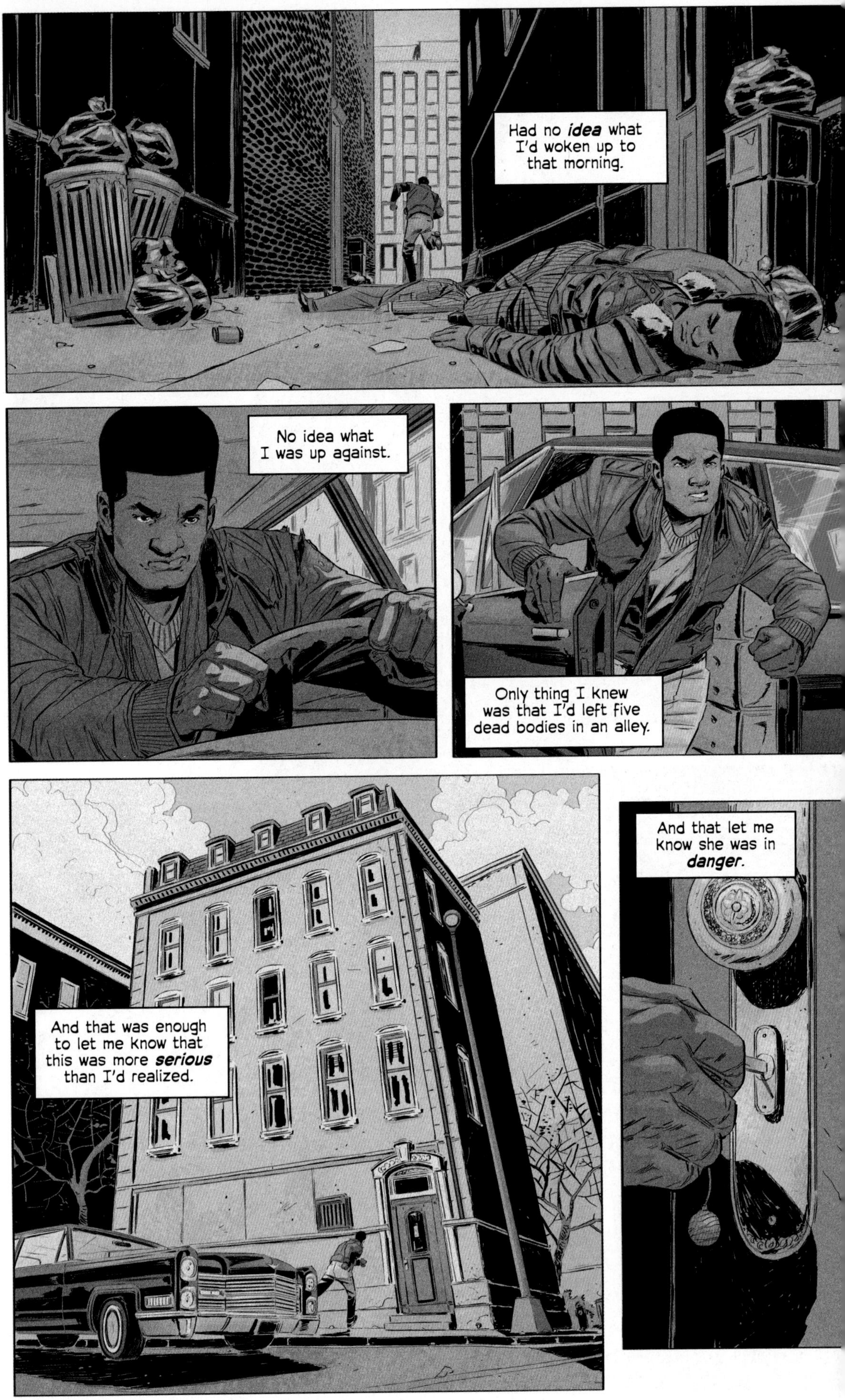
Had no *idea* what I'd woken up to that morning.
No idea what I was up against.
Only thing I knew was that I'd left five dead bodies in an alley.
And that was enough to let me know that this was more *serious* than I'd realized.
And that let me know she was in *danger*.

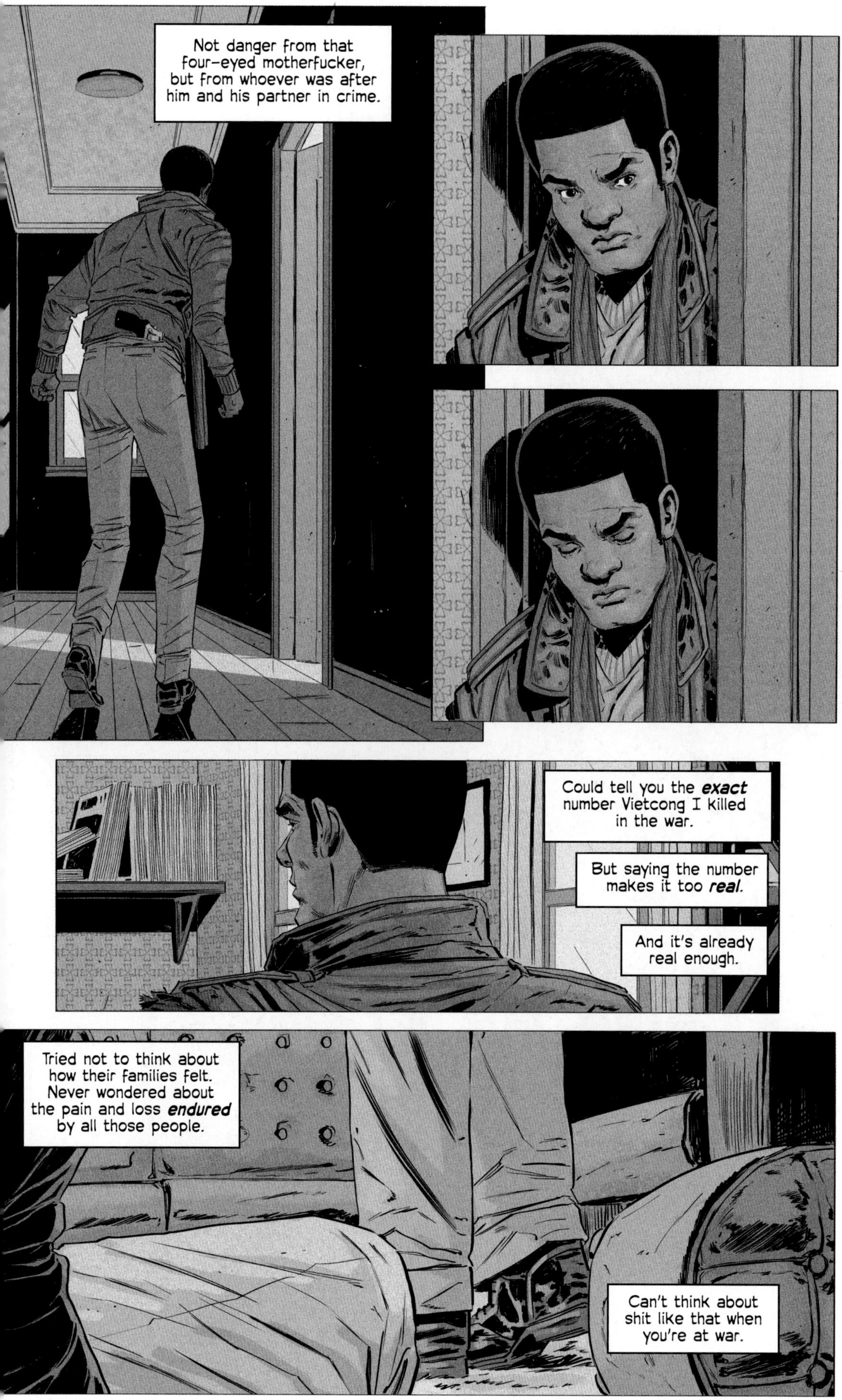
Not danger from that four-eyed motherfucker, but from whoever was after him and his partner in crime.
Could tell you the ***exact*** number Vietcong I killed in the war.
But saying the number makes it too ***real.***
And it's already real enough.
Tried not to think about how their families felt. Never wondered about the pain and loss ***endured*** by all those people.
Can't think about shit like that when you're at war.

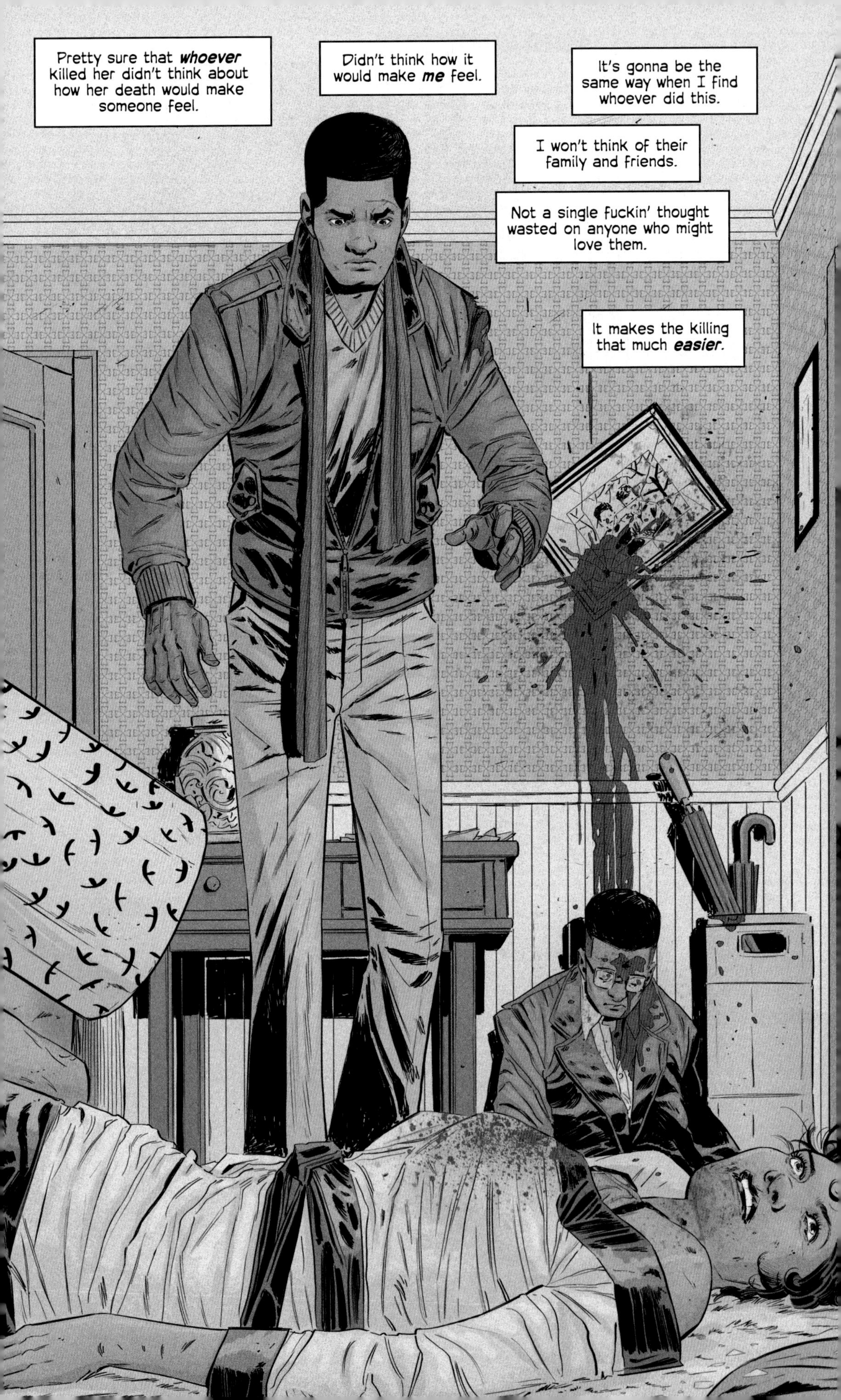

Pretty sure that *whoever* killed her didn't think about how her death would make someone feel.
Didn't think how it would make *me* feel.
It's gonna be the same way when I find whoever did this.
I won't think of their family and friends.
Not a single fuckin' thought wasted on anyone who might love them.
It makes the killing that much *easier*.

ISSUE THREE

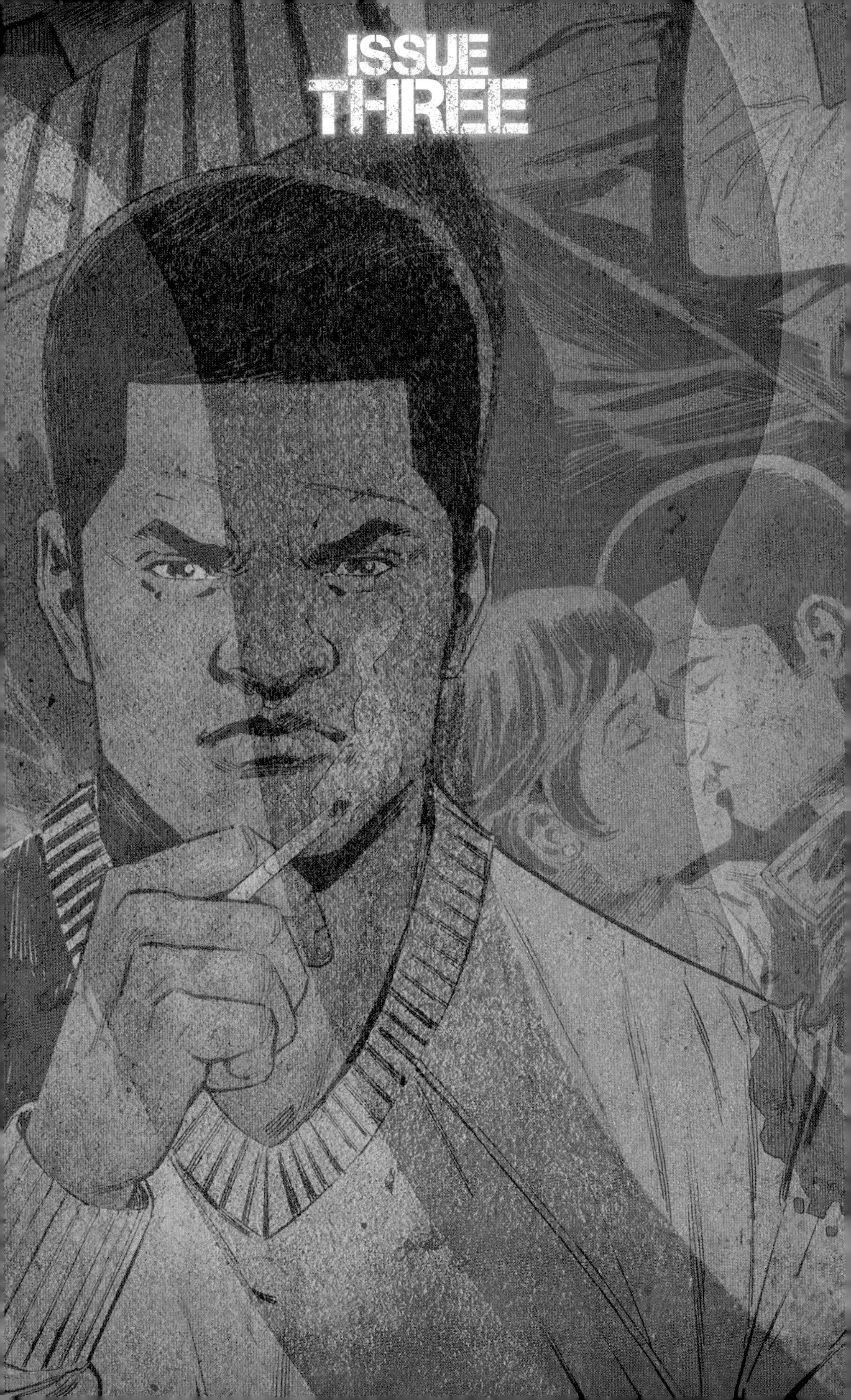

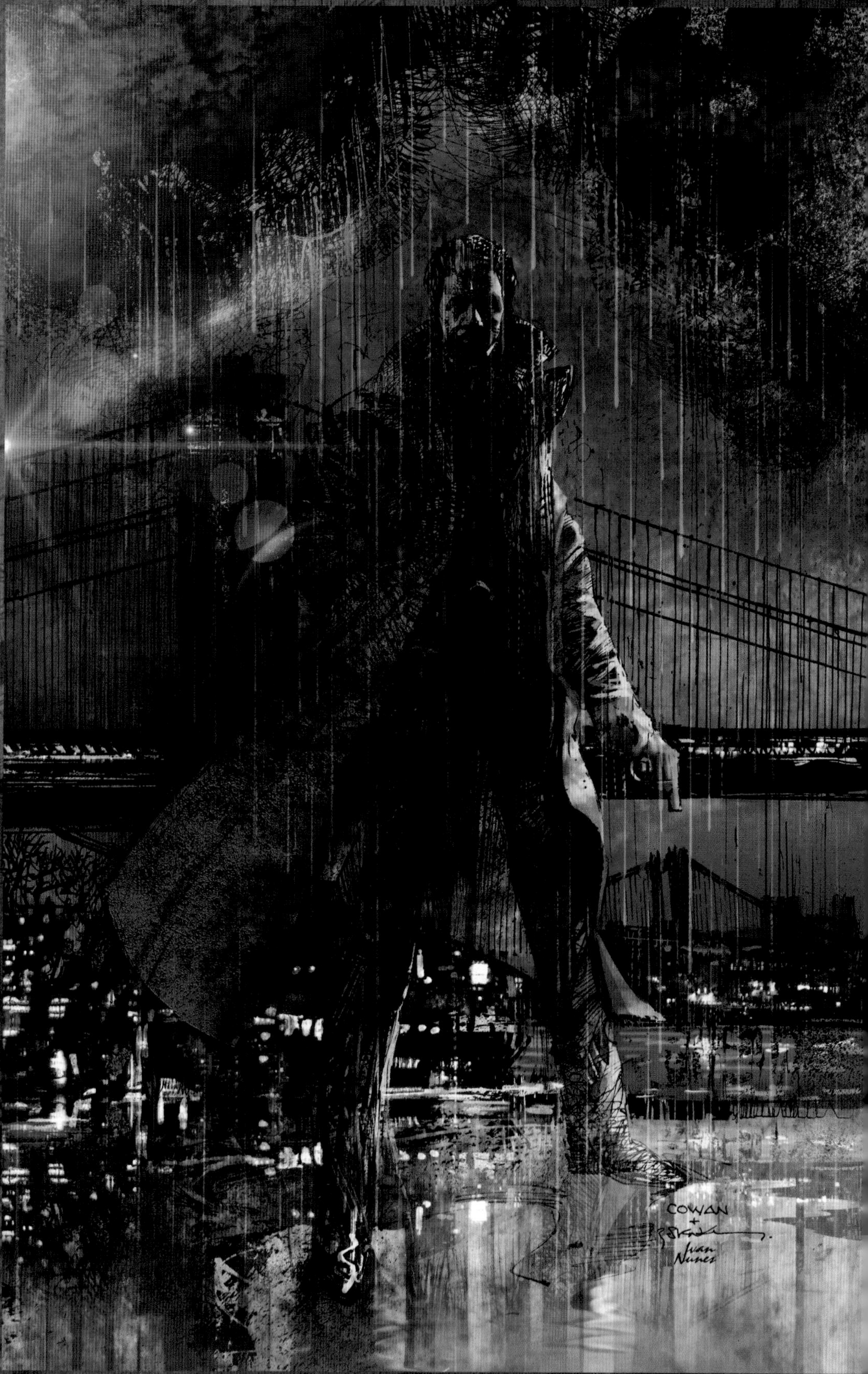
COWAN

ISSUE THREE MAIN COVER BY

DENYS COWAN AND BILL SIENKIEWICZ

COLORS IVAN NUNES

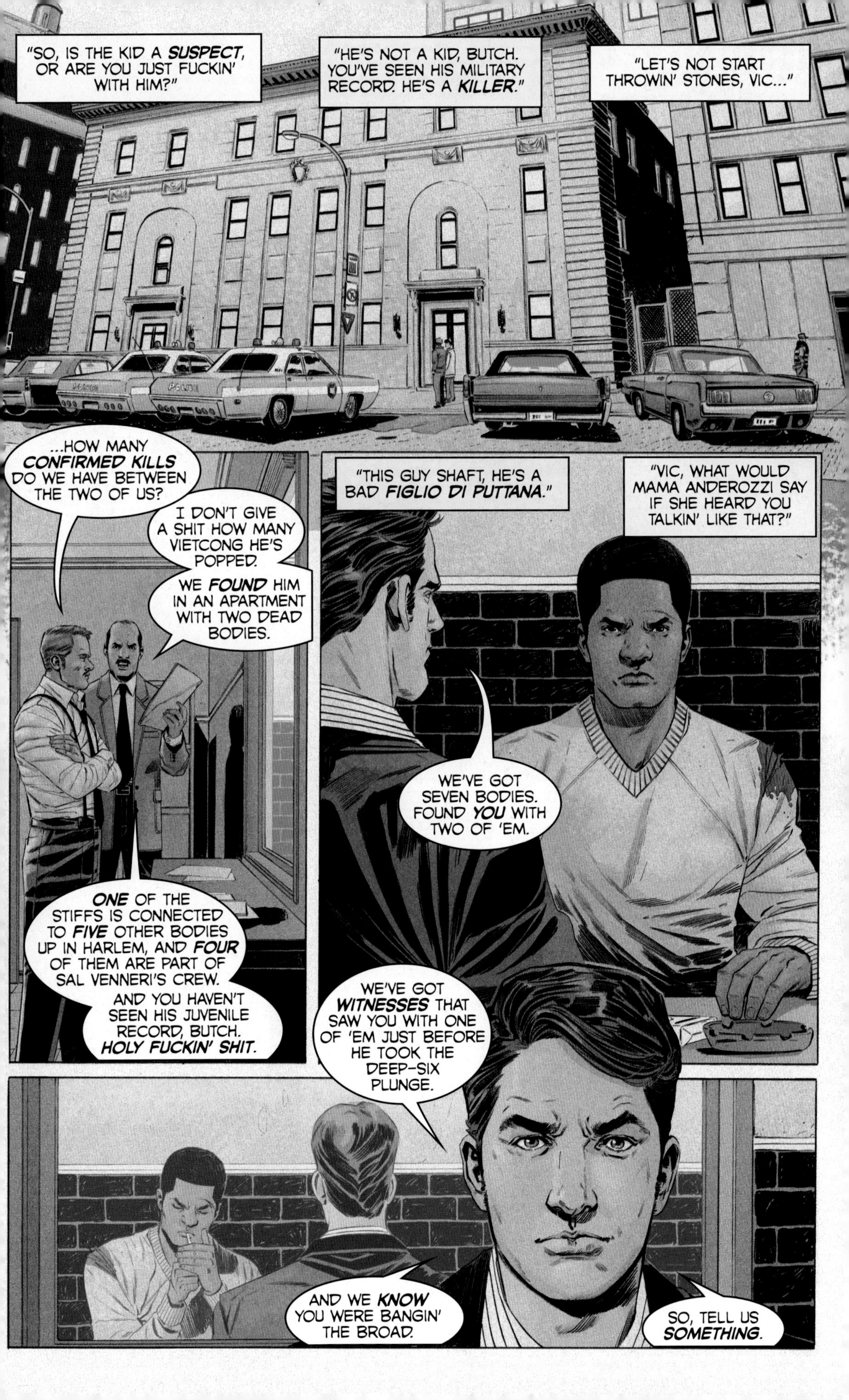

"SO, IS THE KID A SUSPECT, OR ARE YOU JUST FUCKIN' WITH HIM?"
"HE'S NOT A KID, BUTCH. YOU'VE SEEN HIS MILITARY RECORD. HE'S A KILLER."
"LET'S NOT START THROWIN' STONES, VIC..."
...HOW MANY CONFIRMED KILLS DO WE HAVE BETWEEN THE TWO OF US?
I DON'T GIVE A SHIT HOW MANY VIETCONG HE'S POPPED.
WE FOUND HIM IN AN APARTMENT WITH TWO DEAD BODIES.
ONE OF THE STIFFS IS CONNECTED TO FIVE OTHER BODIES UP IN HARLEM, AND FOUR OF THEM ARE PART OF SAL VENNERI'S CREW.
AND YOU HAVEN'T SEEN HIS JUVENILE RECORD, BUTCH. HOLY FUCKIN' SHIT.
"THIS GUY SHAFT, HE'S A BAD FIGLIO DI PUTTANA."
"VIC, WHAT WOULD MAMA ANDEROZZI SAY IF SHE HEARD YOU TALKIN' LIKE THAT?"
WE'VE GOT SEVEN BODIES. FOUND YOU WITH TWO OF 'EM.
WE'VE GOT WITNESSES THAT SAW YOU WITH ONE OF 'EM JUST BEFORE HE TOOK THE DEEP-SIX PLUNGE.
AND WE KNOW YOU WERE BANGIN' THE BROAD.
SO, TELL US SOMETHING.

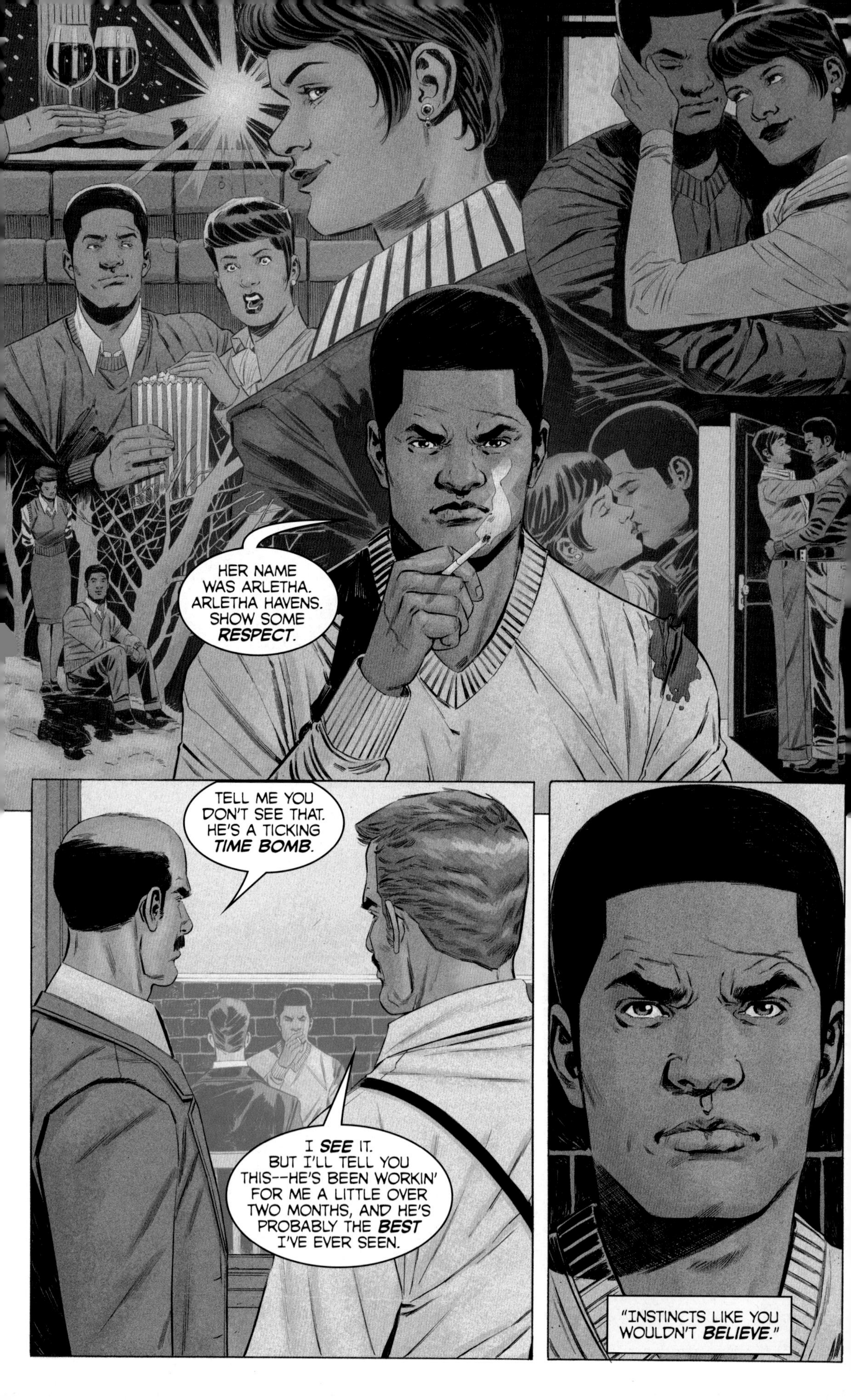
HER NAME WAS ARLETHA. ARLETHA HAVENS. SHOW SOME **RESPECT**.
TELL ME YOU DON'T SEE THAT. HE'S A TICKING **TIME BOMB**.
I **SEE** IT. BUT I'LL TELL YOU THIS--HE'S BEEN WORKIN' FOR ME A LITTLE OVER TWO MONTHS, AND HE'S PROBABLY THE **BEST** I'VE EVER SEEN.
"INSTINCTS LIKE YOU WOULDN'T **BELIEVE**."

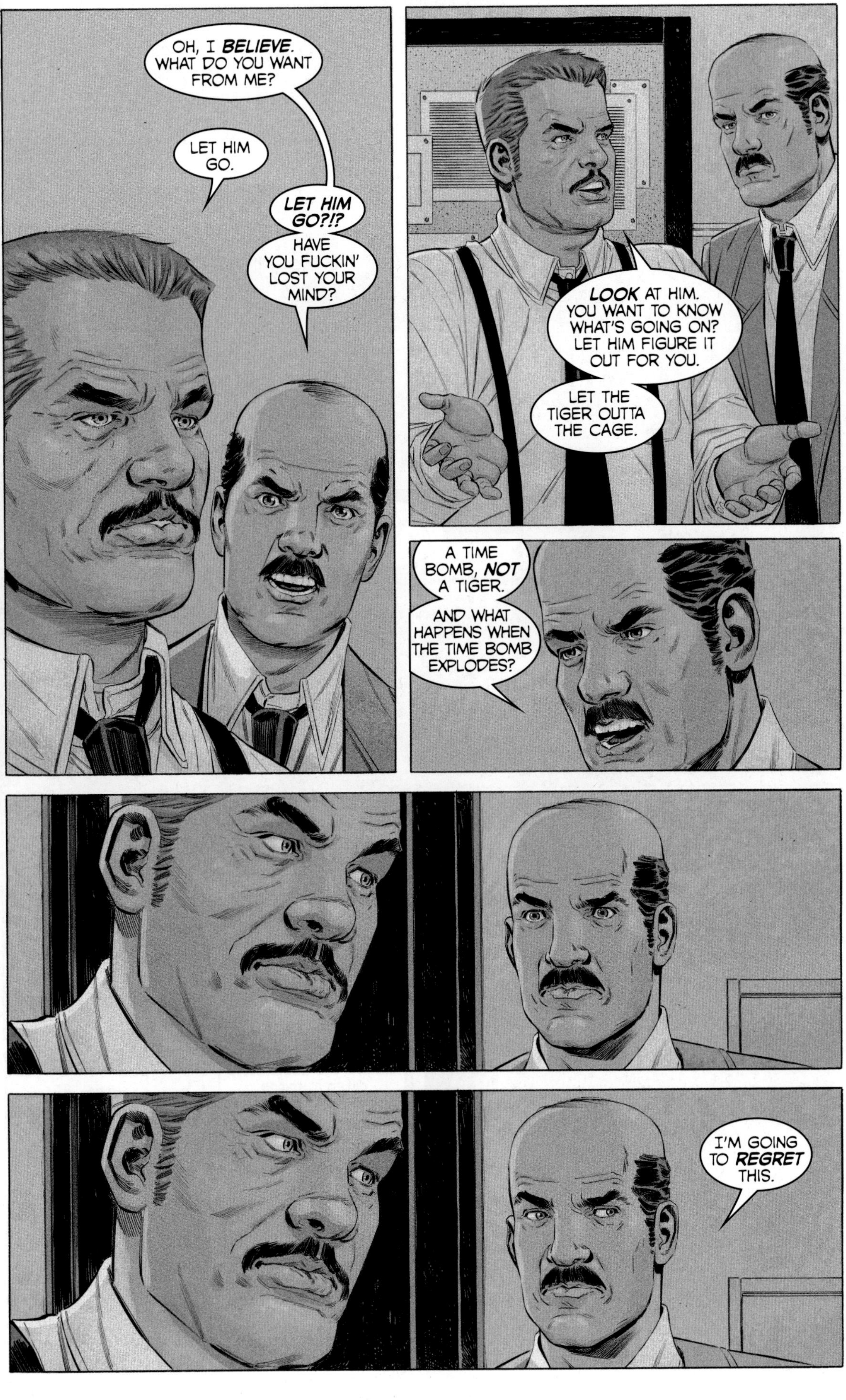
OH, I BELIEVE. WHAT DO YOU WANT FROM ME?
LET HIM GO.
LET HIM GO?!?
HAVE YOU FUCKIN' LOST YOUR MIND?
LOOK AT HIM. YOU WANT TO KNOW WHAT'S GOING ON? LET HIM FIGURE IT OUT FOR YOU.
LET THE TIGER OUTTA THE CAGE.
A TIME BOMB, NOT A TIGER.
AND WHAT HAPPENS WHEN THE TIME BOMB EXPLODES?
I'M GOING TO REGRET THIS.

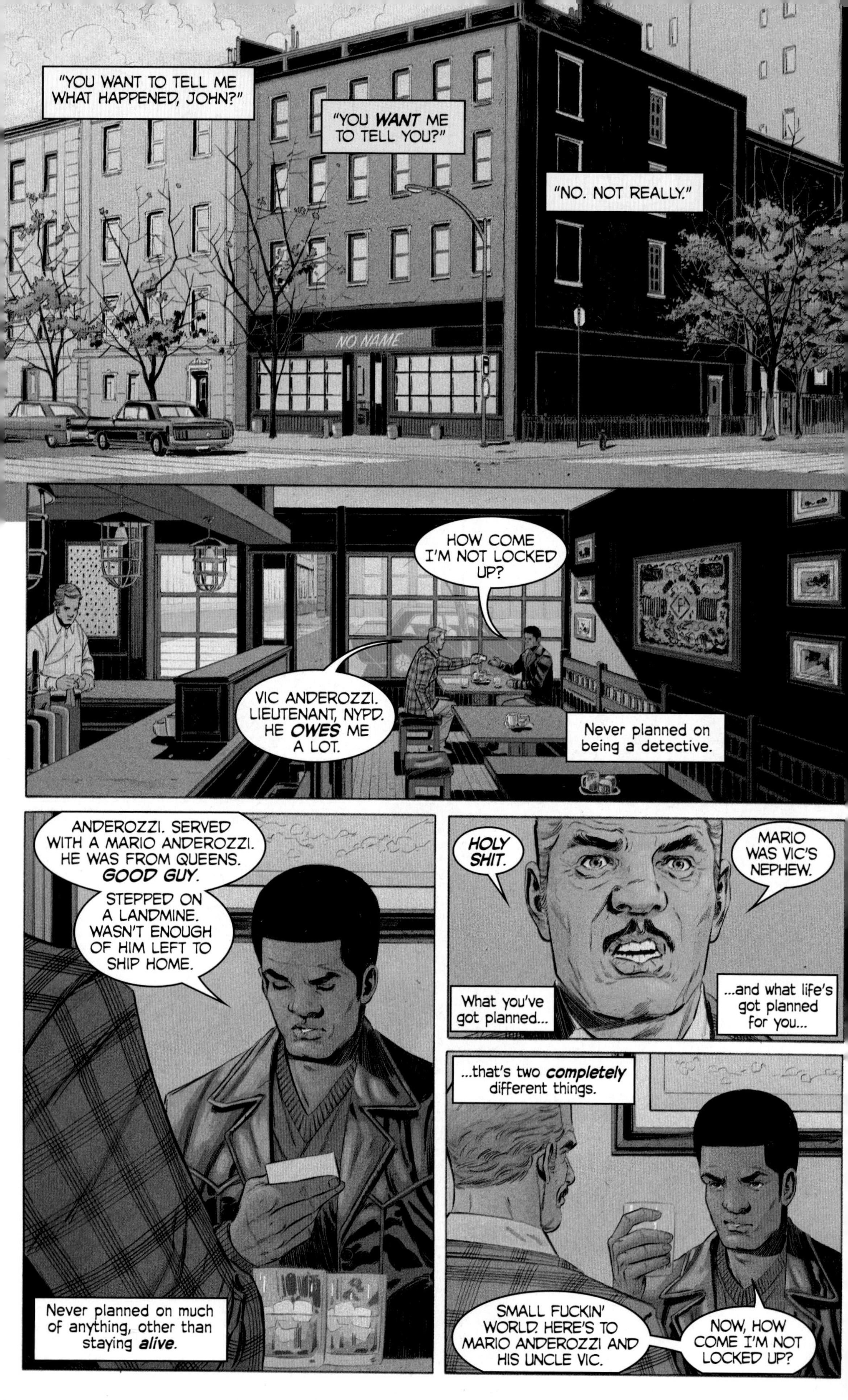
"YOU WANT TO TELL ME WHAT HAPPENED, JOHN?"
"YOU *WANT* ME TO TELL YOU?"
"NO. NOT REALLY."
NO NAME
HOW COME I'M NOT LOCKED UP?
VIC ANDEROZZI. LIEUTENANT, NYPD. HE *OWES* ME A LOT.
Never planned on being a detective.
ANDEROZZI. SERVED WITH A MARIO ANDEROZZI. HE WAS FROM QUEENS. *GOOD GUY*.
STEPPED ON A LANDMINE. WASN'T ENOUGH OF HIM LEFT TO SHIP HOME.
Never planned on much of anything, other than staying *alive*.
HOLY SHIT.
MARIO WAS VIC'S NEPHEW.
What you've got planned...
...and what life's got planned for you...
...that's two *completely* different things.
SMALL FUCKIN' WORLD. HERE'S TO MARIO ANDEROZZI AND HIS UNCLE VIC.
NOW, HOW COME I'M NOT LOCKED UP?

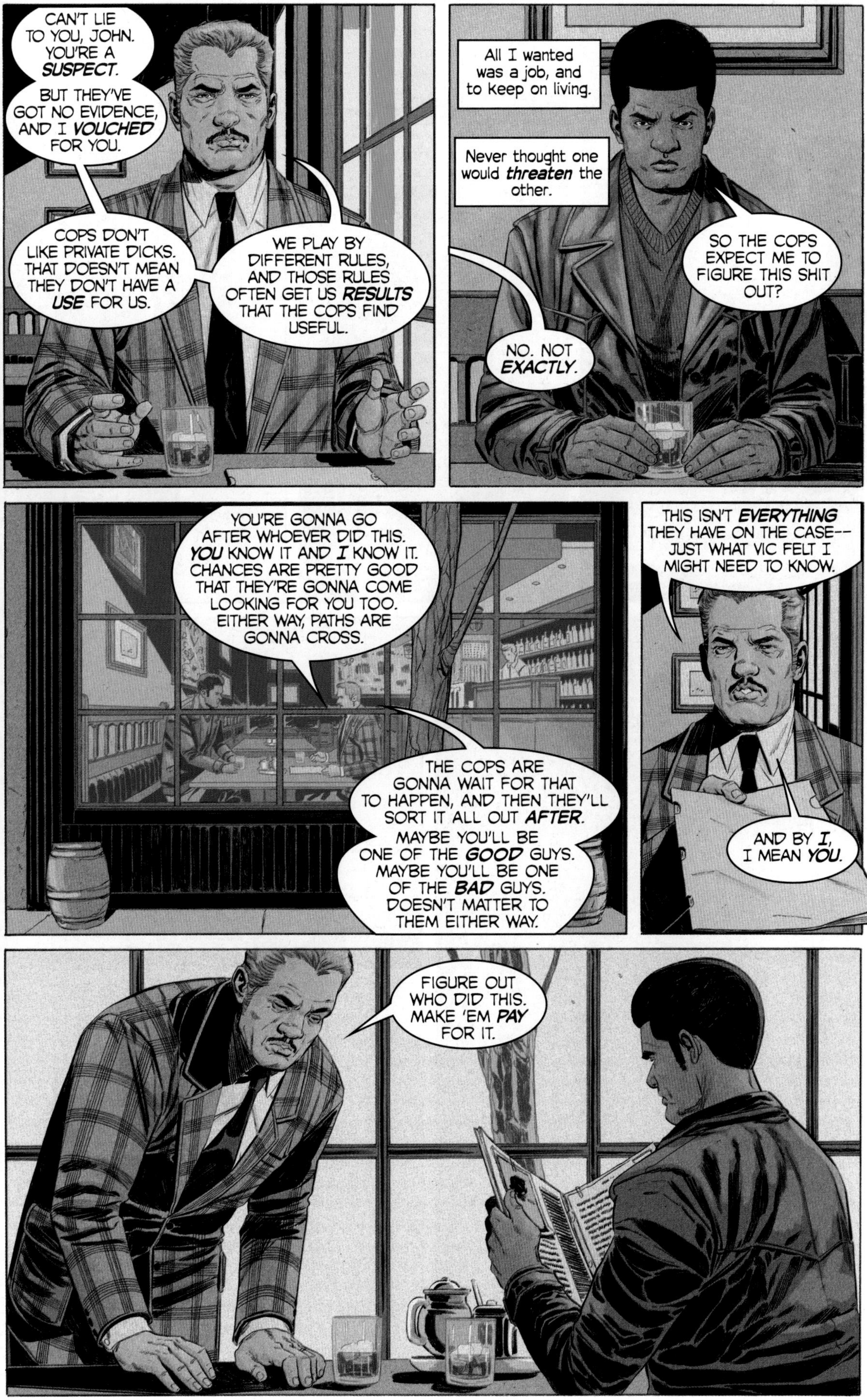
CAN'T LIE TO YOU, JOHN. YOU'RE A SUSPECT.
BUT THEY'VE GOT NO EVIDENCE, AND I VOUCHED FOR YOU.
COPS DON'T LIKE PRIVATE DICKS. THAT DOESN'T MEAN THEY DON'T HAVE A USE FOR US.
WE PLAY BY DIFFERENT RULES, AND THOSE RULES OFTEN GET US RESULTS THAT THE COPS FIND USEFUL.
All I wanted was a job, and to keep on living.
Never thought one would threaten the other.
SO THE COPS EXPECT ME TO FIGURE THIS SHIT OUT?
NO. NOT EXACTLY.
YOU'RE GONNA GO AFTER WHOEVER DID THIS. YOU KNOW IT AND I KNOW IT. CHANCES ARE PRETTY GOOD THAT THEY'RE GONNA COME LOOKING FOR YOU TOO. EITHER WAY, PATHS ARE GONNA CROSS.
THE COPS ARE GONNA WAIT FOR THAT TO HAPPEN, AND THEN THEY'LL SORT IT ALL OUT AFTER.
MAYBE YOU'LL BE ONE OF THE GOOD GUYS. MAYBE YOU'LL BE ONE OF THE BAD GUYS. DOESN'T MATTER TO THEM EITHER WAY.
THIS ISN'T EVERYTHING THEY HAVE ON THE CASE-- JUST WHAT VIC FELT I MIGHT NEED TO KNOW.
AND BY I, I MEAN YOU.
FIGURE OUT WHO DID THIS. MAKE 'EM PAY FOR IT.

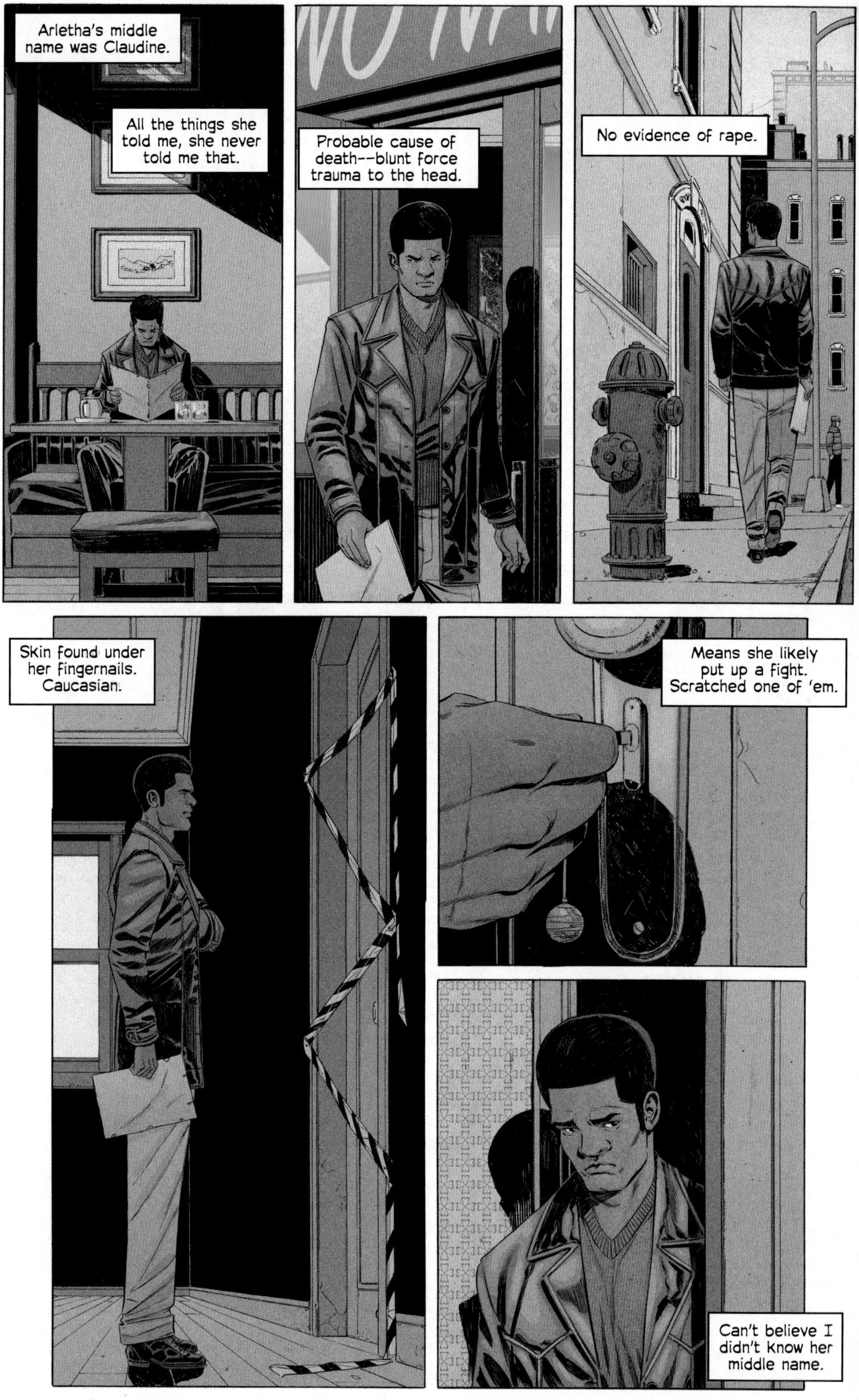
Arletha's middle name was Claudine.
All the things she told me, she never told me that.
Probable cause of death--blunt force trauma to the head.
No evidence of rape.
Skin found under her fingernails. Caucasian.
Means she likely put up a fight. Scratched one of 'em.
Can't believe I didn't know her middle name.

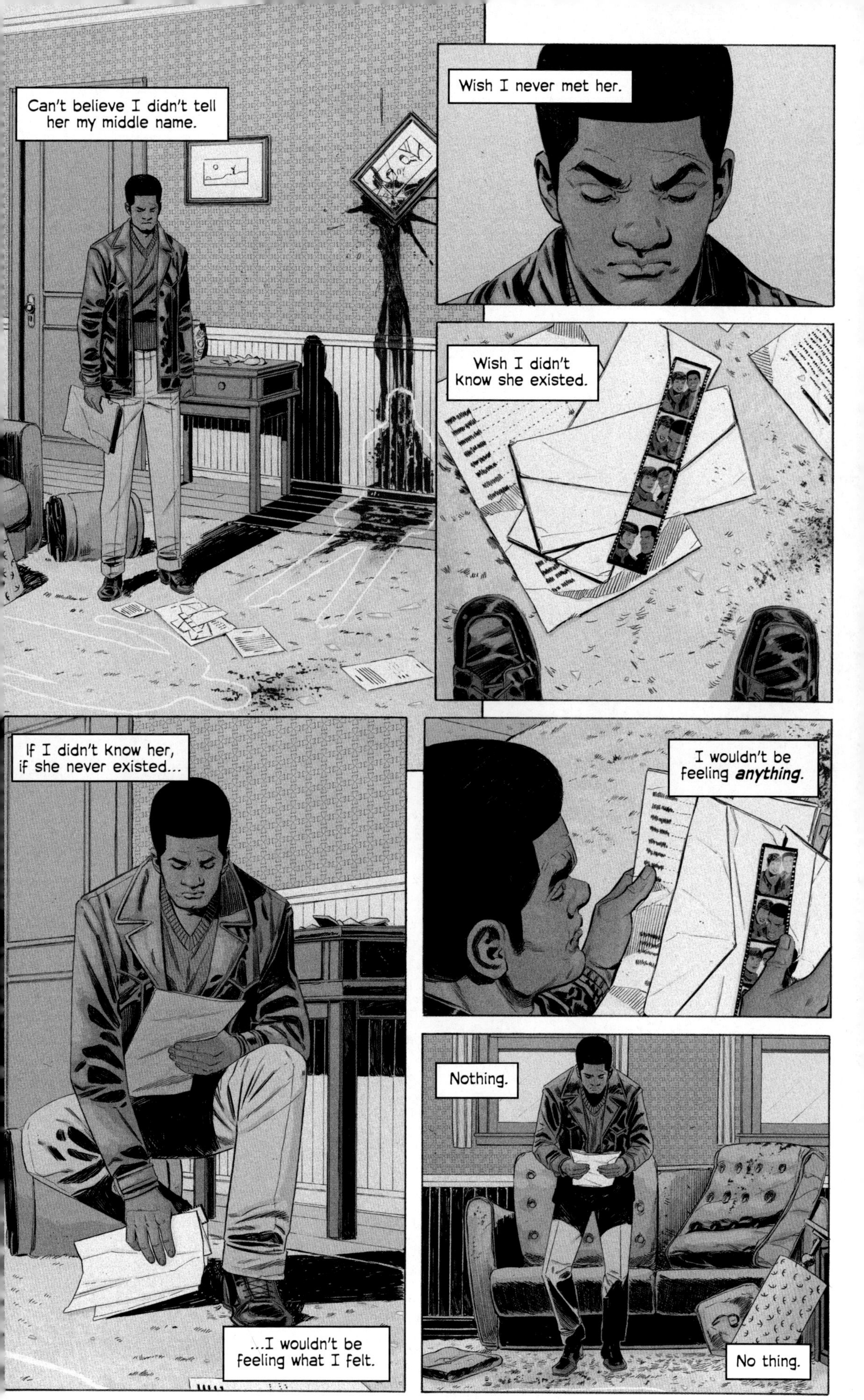
Can't believe I didn't tell her my middle name.
Wish I never met her.
Wish I didn't know she existed.
If I didn't know her, if she never existed...
...I wouldn't be feeling what I felt.
I wouldn't be feeling *anything*.
Nothing.
No thing.

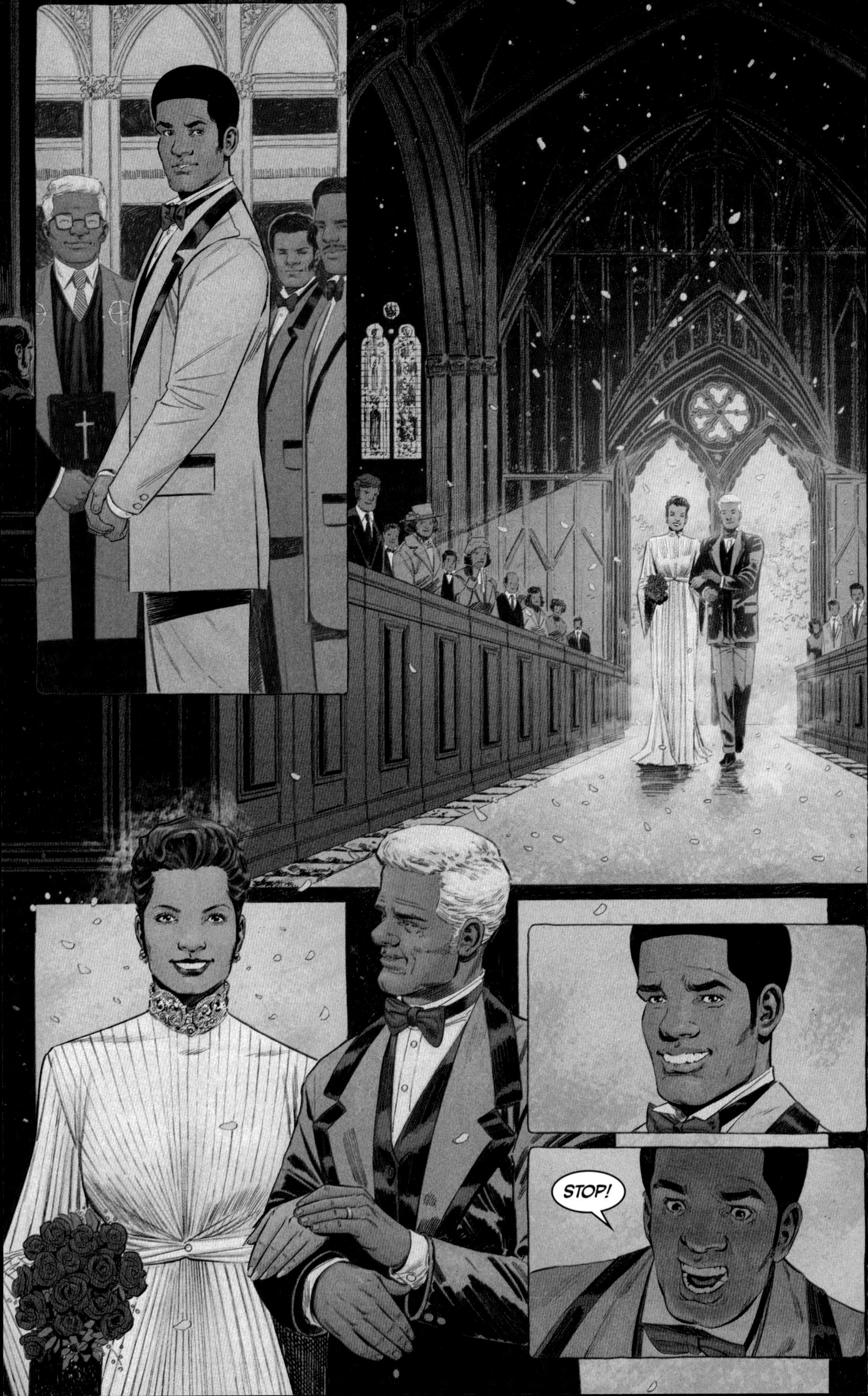
STOP!

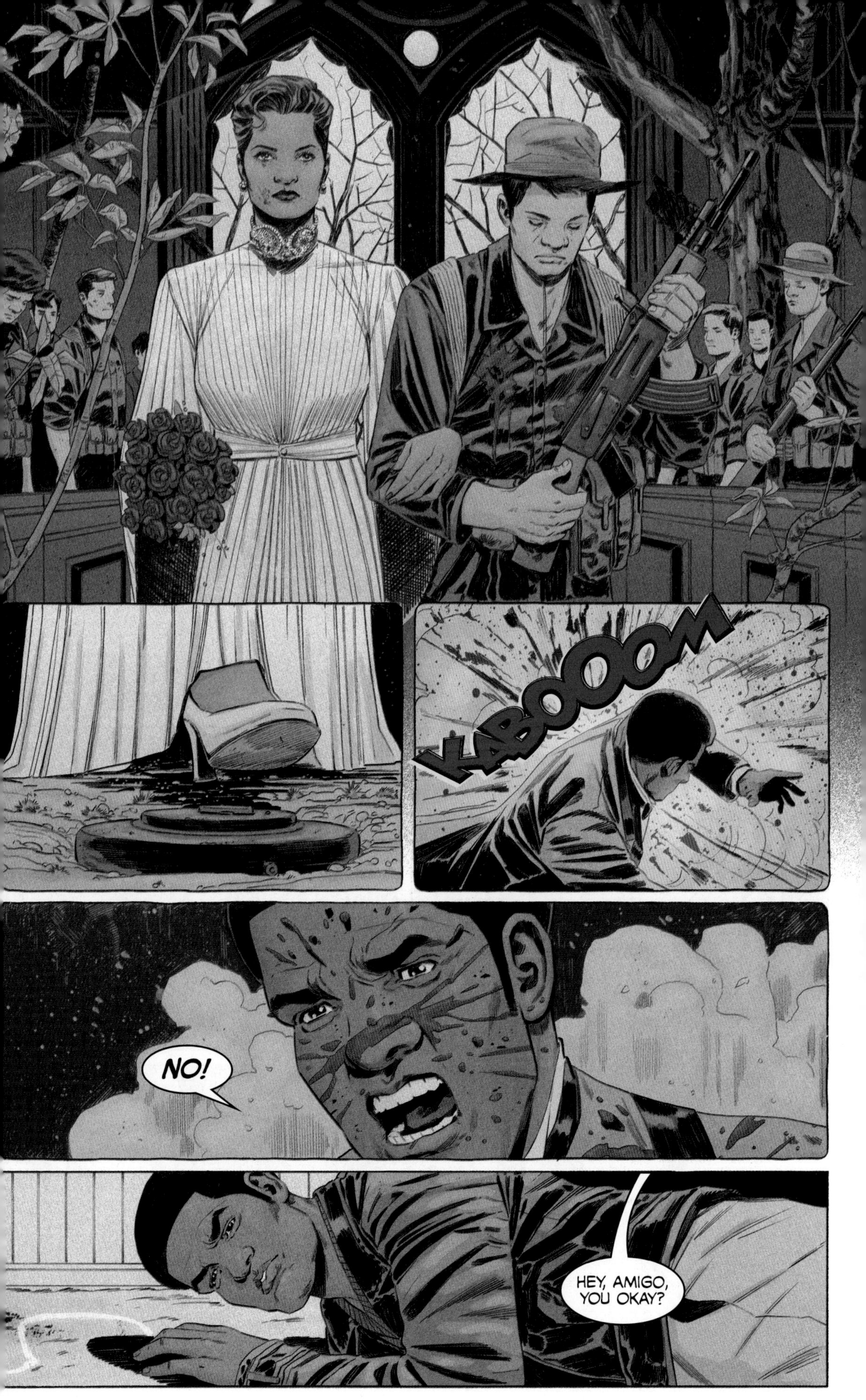
KABOOOM
NO!
HEY, AMIGO, YOU OKAY?

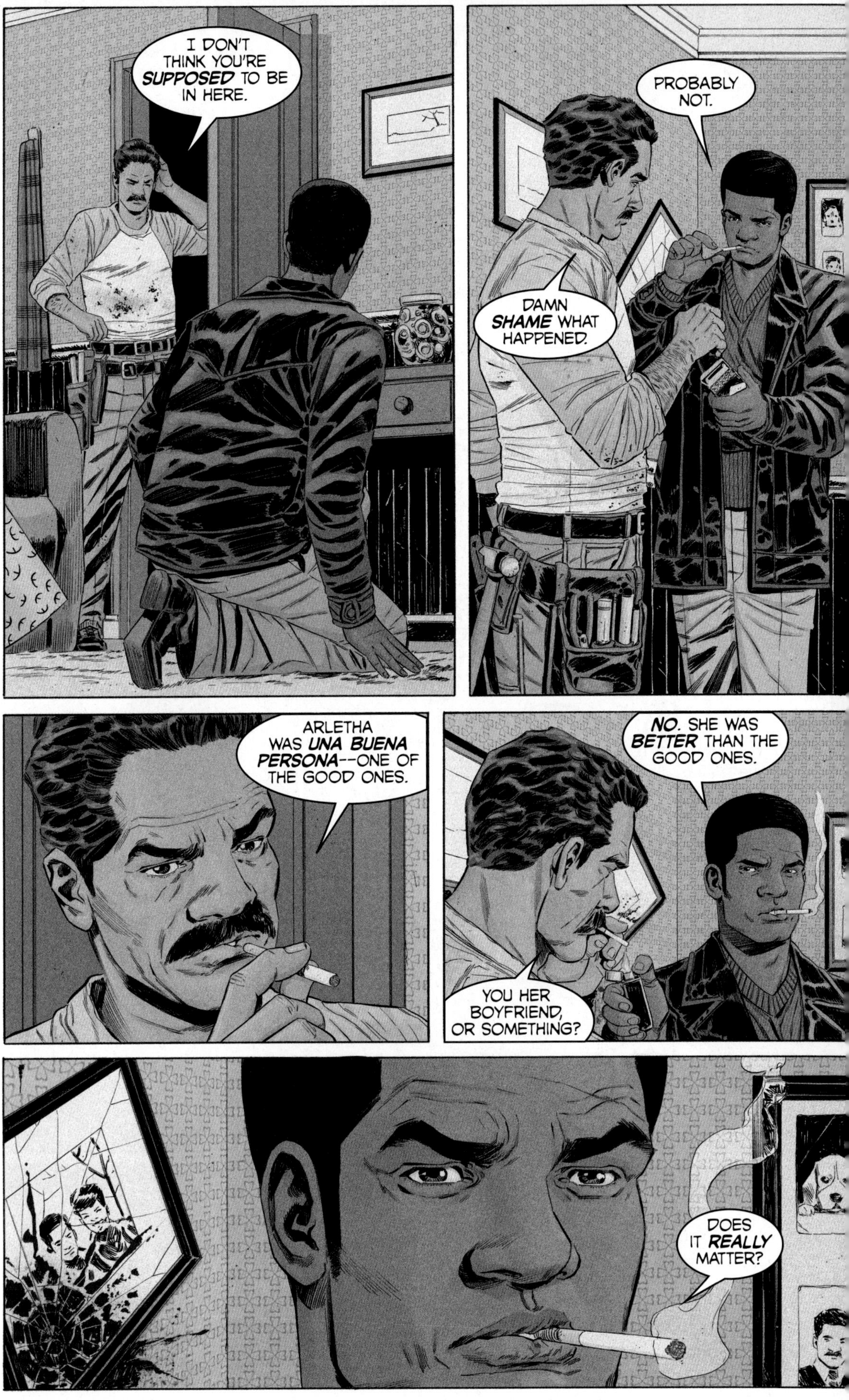
I DON'T THINK YOU'RE SUPPOSED TO BE IN HERE.
PROBABLY NOT.
DAMN SHAME WHAT HAPPENED.
ARLETHA WAS UNA BUENA PERSONA--ONE OF THE GOOD ONES.
NO. SHE WAS BETTER THAN THE GOOD ONES.
YOU HER BOYFRIEND, OR SOMETHING?
DOES IT REALLY MATTER?

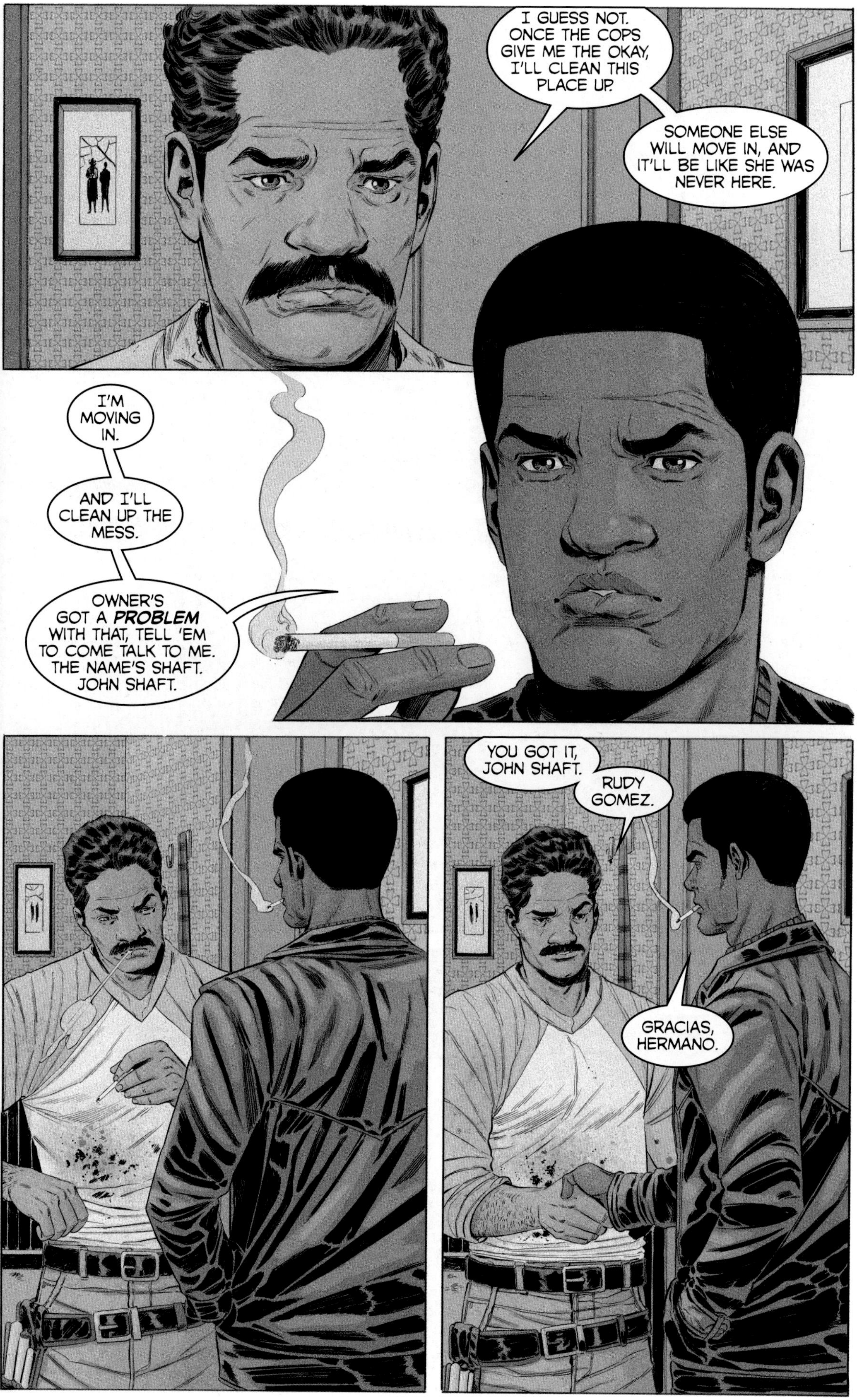
I GUESS NOT. ONCE THE COPS GIVE ME THE OKAY, I'LL CLEAN THIS PLACE UP.
SOMEONE ELSE WILL MOVE IN, AND IT'LL BE LIKE SHE WAS NEVER HERE.
I'M MOVING IN.
AND I'LL CLEAN UP THE MESS.
OWNER'S GOT A ***PROBLEM*** WITH THAT, TELL 'EM TO COME TALK TO ME. THE NAME'S SHAFT. JOHN SHAFT.
YOU GOT IT, JOHN SHAFT.
RUDY GOMEZ.
GRACIAS, HERMANO.

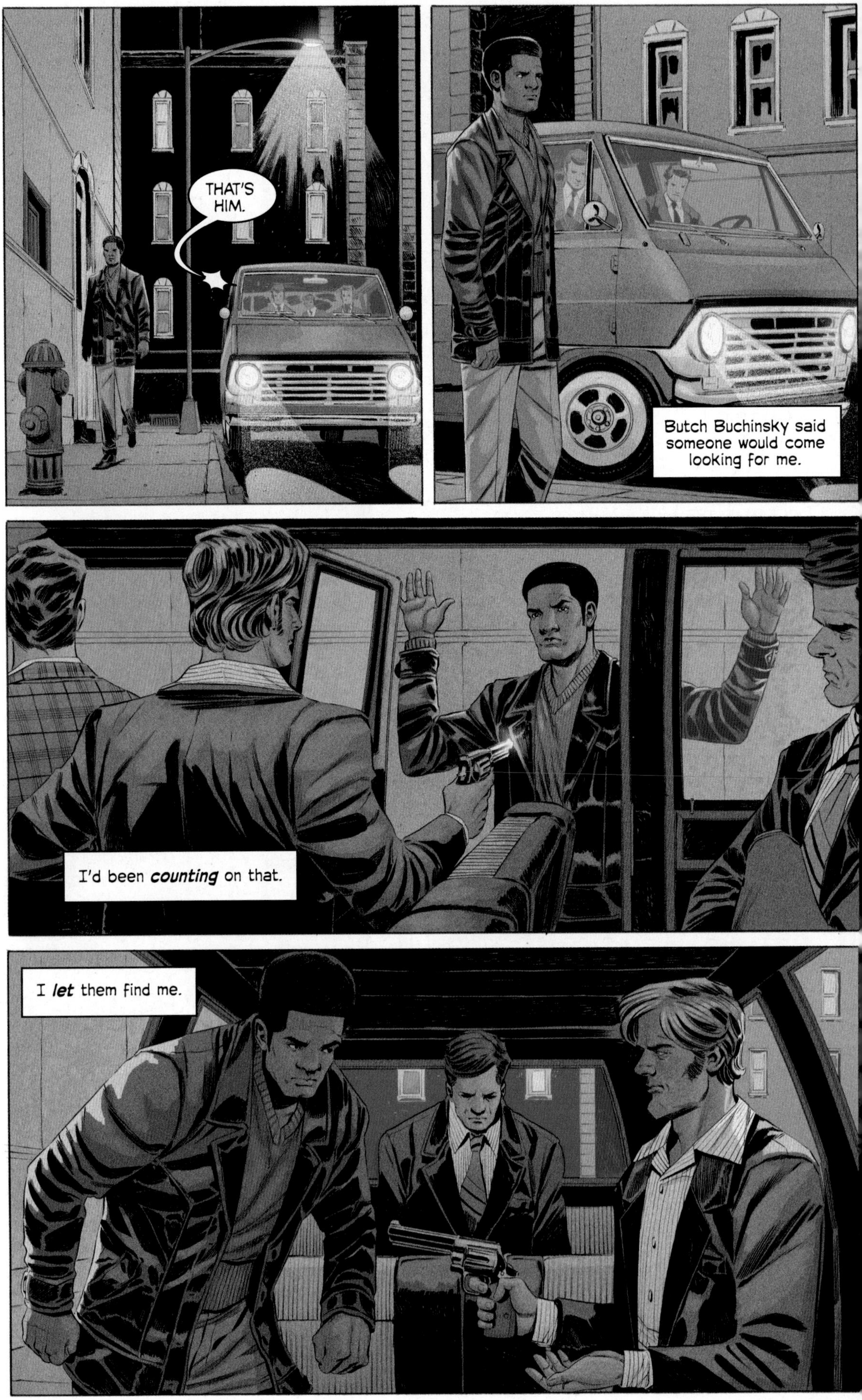
THAT'S HIM.
Butch Buchinsky said someone would come looking for me.
I'd been *counting* on that.
I *let* them find me.

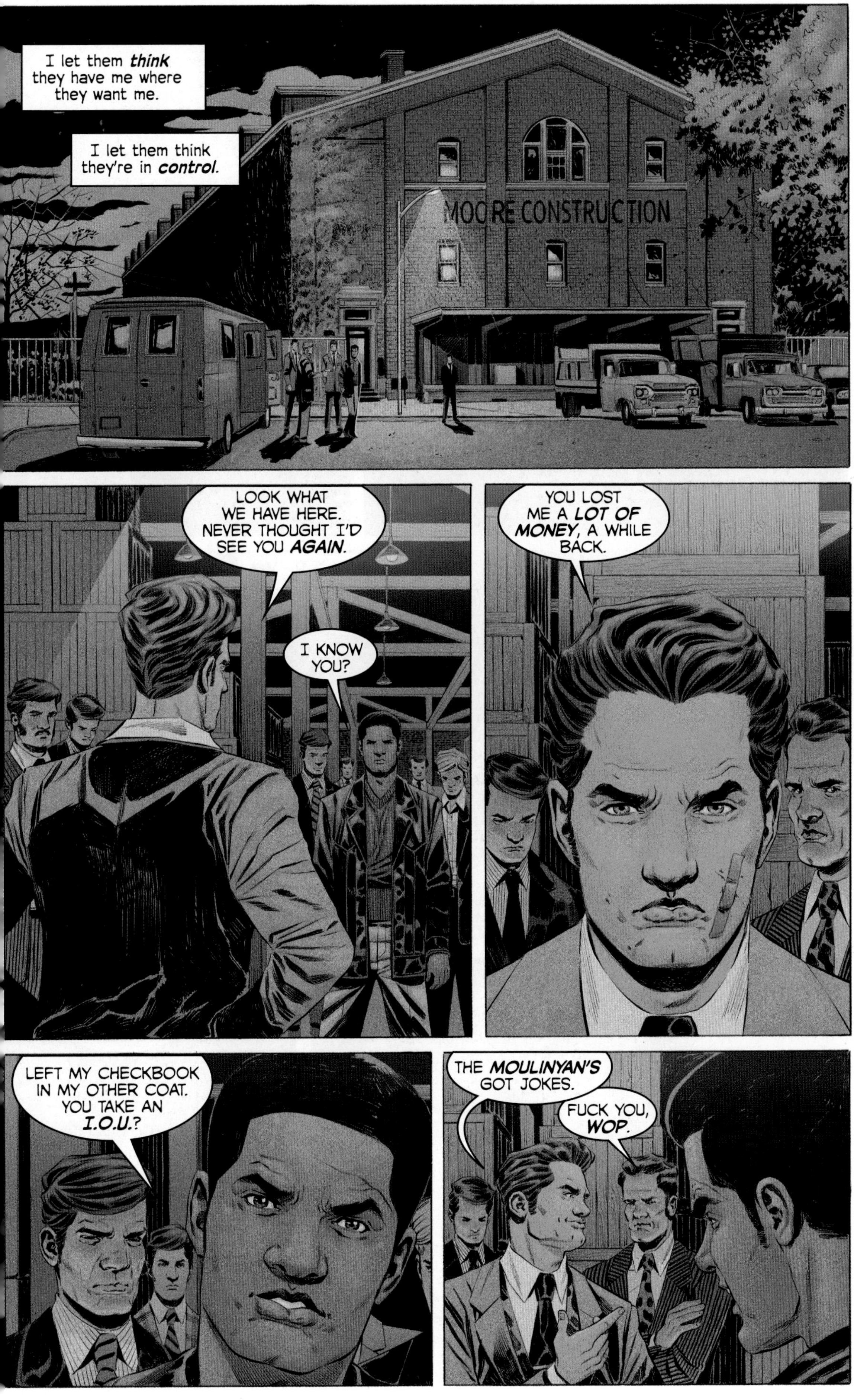

I let them *think* they have me where they want me.
I let them think they're in *control*.
MOORE CONSTRUCTION
LOOK WHAT WE HAVE HERE. NEVER THOUGHT I'D SEE YOU *AGAIN*.
I KNOW YOU?
YOU LOST ME A *LOT OF MONEY*, A WHILE BACK.
LEFT MY CHECKBOOK IN MY OTHER COAT. YOU TAKE AN *I.O.U.*?
THE *MOULINYAN'S* GOT JOKES.
FUCK YOU, *WOP*.

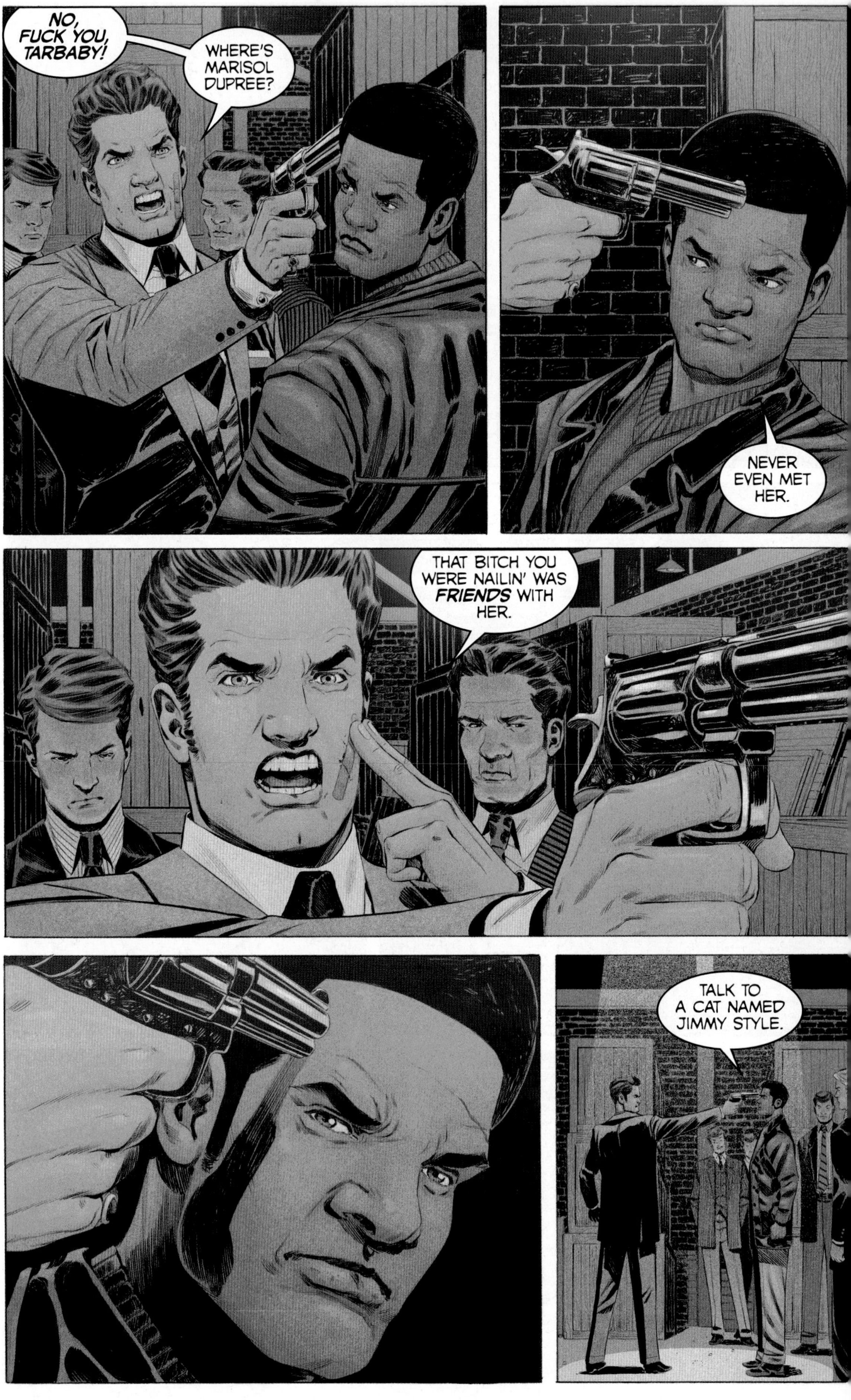
NO, FUCK YOU, TARBABY!
WHERE'S MARISOL DUPREE?
NEVER EVEN MET HER.
THAT BITCH YOU WERE NAILIN' WAS FRIENDS WITH HER.
TALK TO A CAT NAMED JIMMY STYLE.

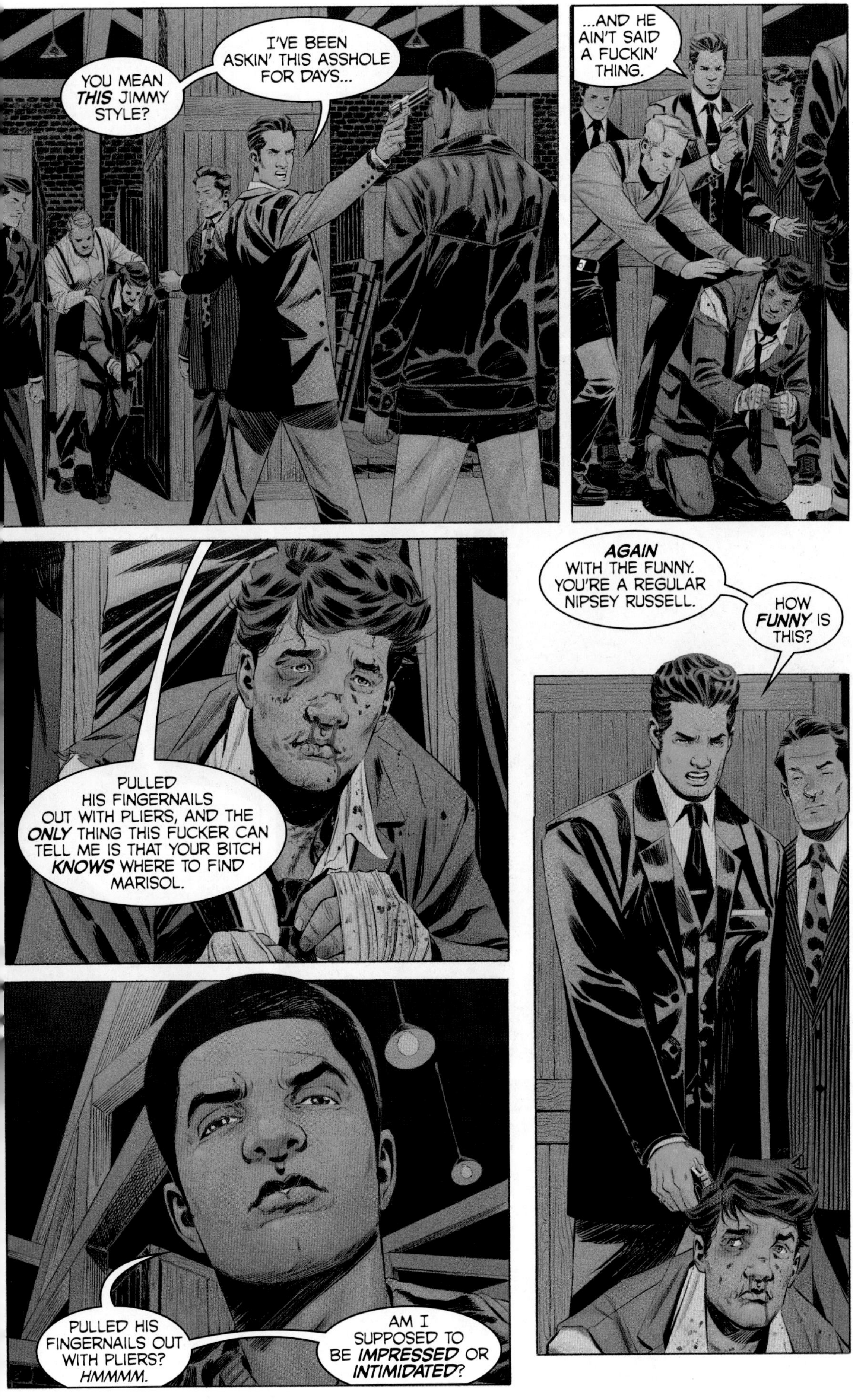

YOU MEAN THIS JIMMY STYLE?
I'VE BEEN ASKIN' THIS ASSHOLE FOR DAYS...
...AND HE AIN'T SAID A FUCKIN' THING.
PULLED HIS FINGERNAILS OUT WITH PLIERS, AND THE ONLY THING THIS FUCKER CAN TELL ME IS THAT YOUR BITCH KNOWS WHERE TO FIND MARISOL.
PULLED HIS FINGERNAILS OUT WITH PLIERS? HMMMM.
AM I SUPPOSED TO BE IMPRESSED OR INTIMIDATED?
AGAIN WITH THE FUNNY. YOU'RE A REGULAR NIPSEY RUSSELL.
HOW FUNNY IS THIS?

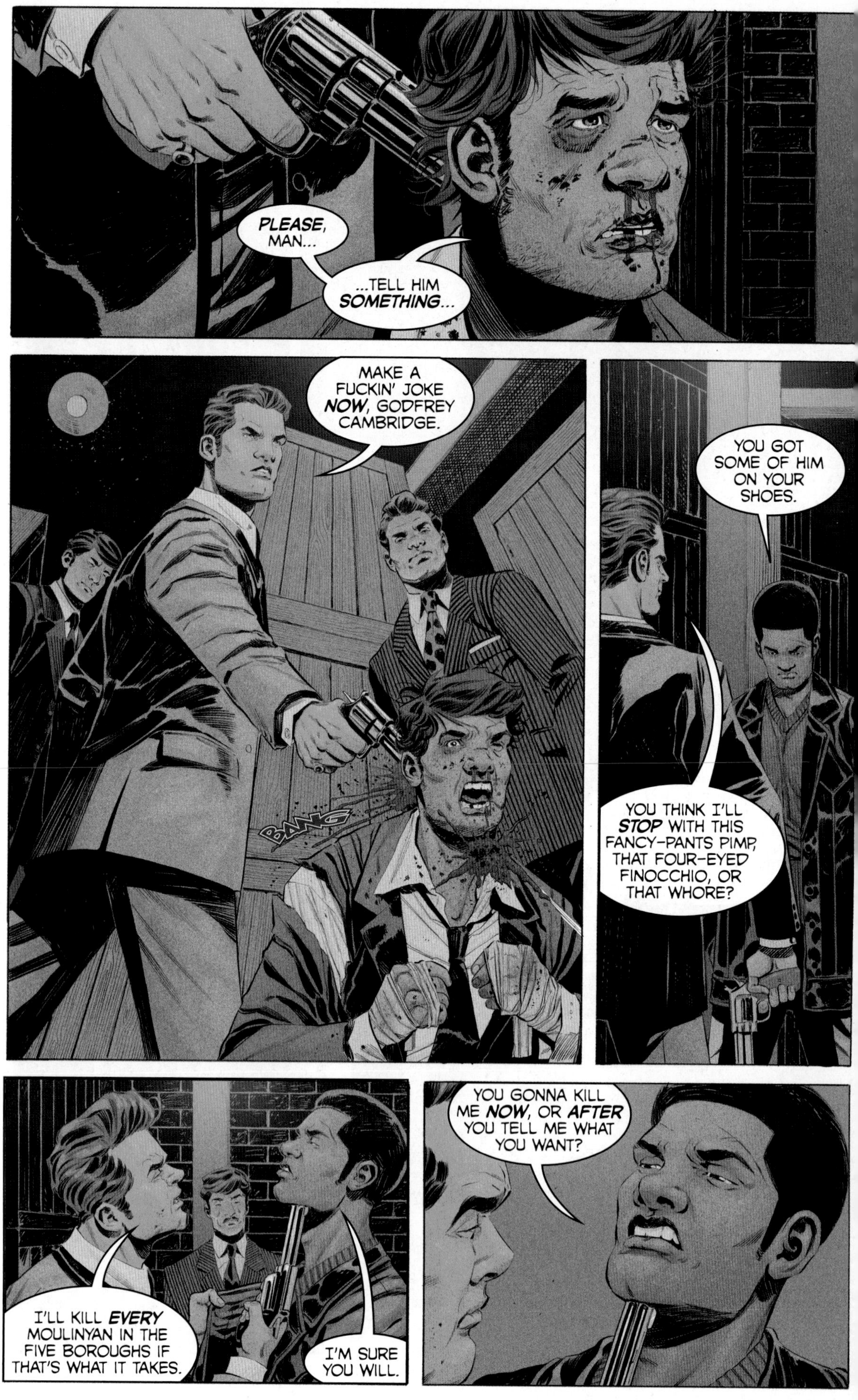
PLEASE, MAN...
...TELL HIM SOMETHING...
MAKE A FUCKIN' JOKE NOW, GODFREY CAMBRIDGE.
BANG
YOU GOT SOME OF HIM ON YOUR SHOES.
YOU THINK I'LL STOP WITH THIS FANCY-PANTS PIMP, THAT FOUR-EYED FINOCCHIO, OR THAT WHORE?
I'LL KILL EVERY MOULINYAN IN THE FIVE BOROUGHS IF THAT'S WHAT IT TAKES.
I'M SURE YOU WILL.
YOU GONNA KILL ME NOW, OR AFTER YOU TELL ME WHAT YOU WANT?

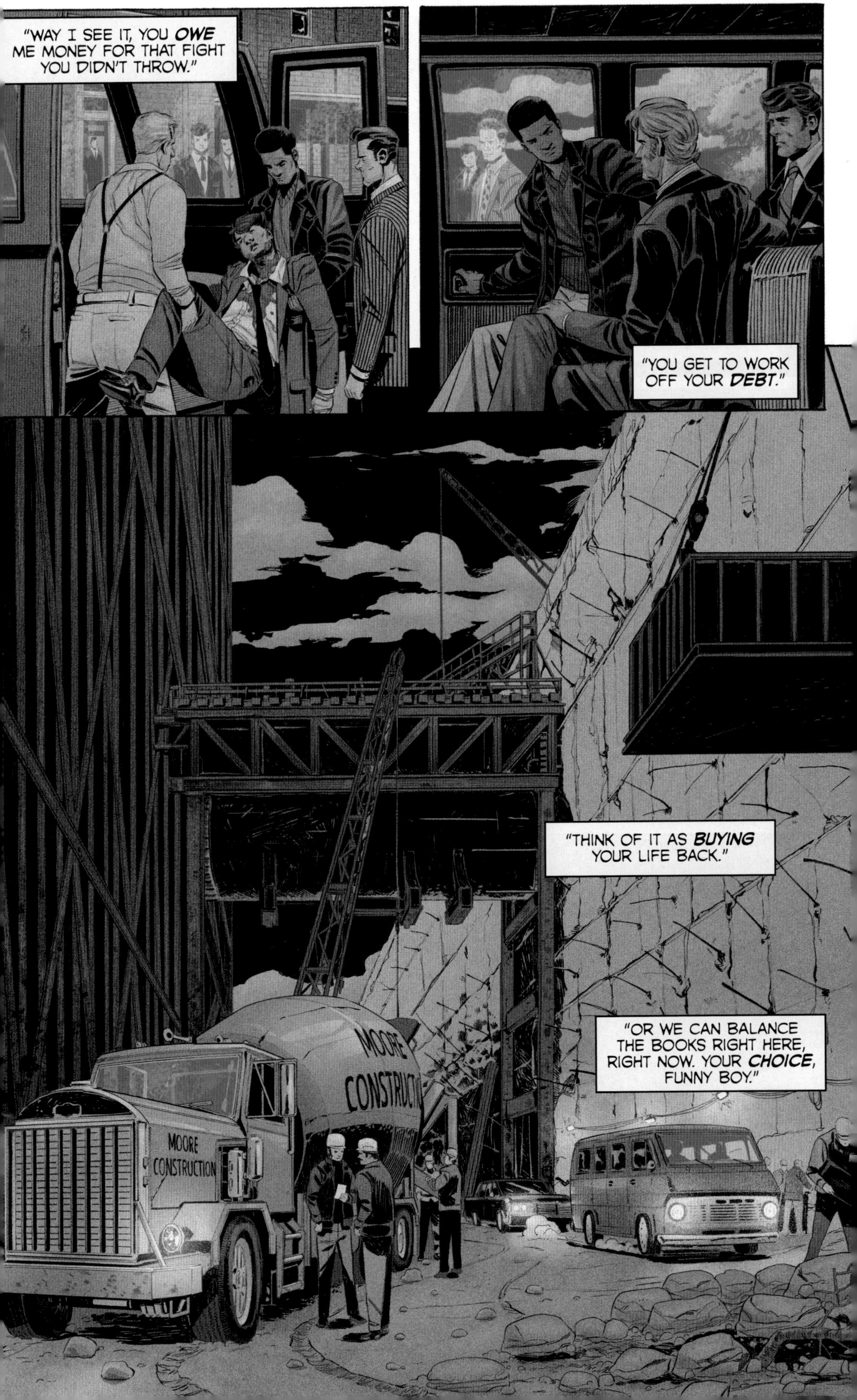
"WAY I SEE IT, YOU OWE ME MONEY FOR THAT FIGHT YOU DIDN'T THROW."
"YOU GET TO WORK OFF YOUR DEBT."
"THINK OF IT AS BUYING YOUR LIFE BACK."
"OR WE CAN BALANCE THE BOOKS RIGHT HERE, RIGHT NOW. YOUR CHOICE, FUNNY BOY."
MOORE CONSTRUCTION
MOORE CONSTRUCTION

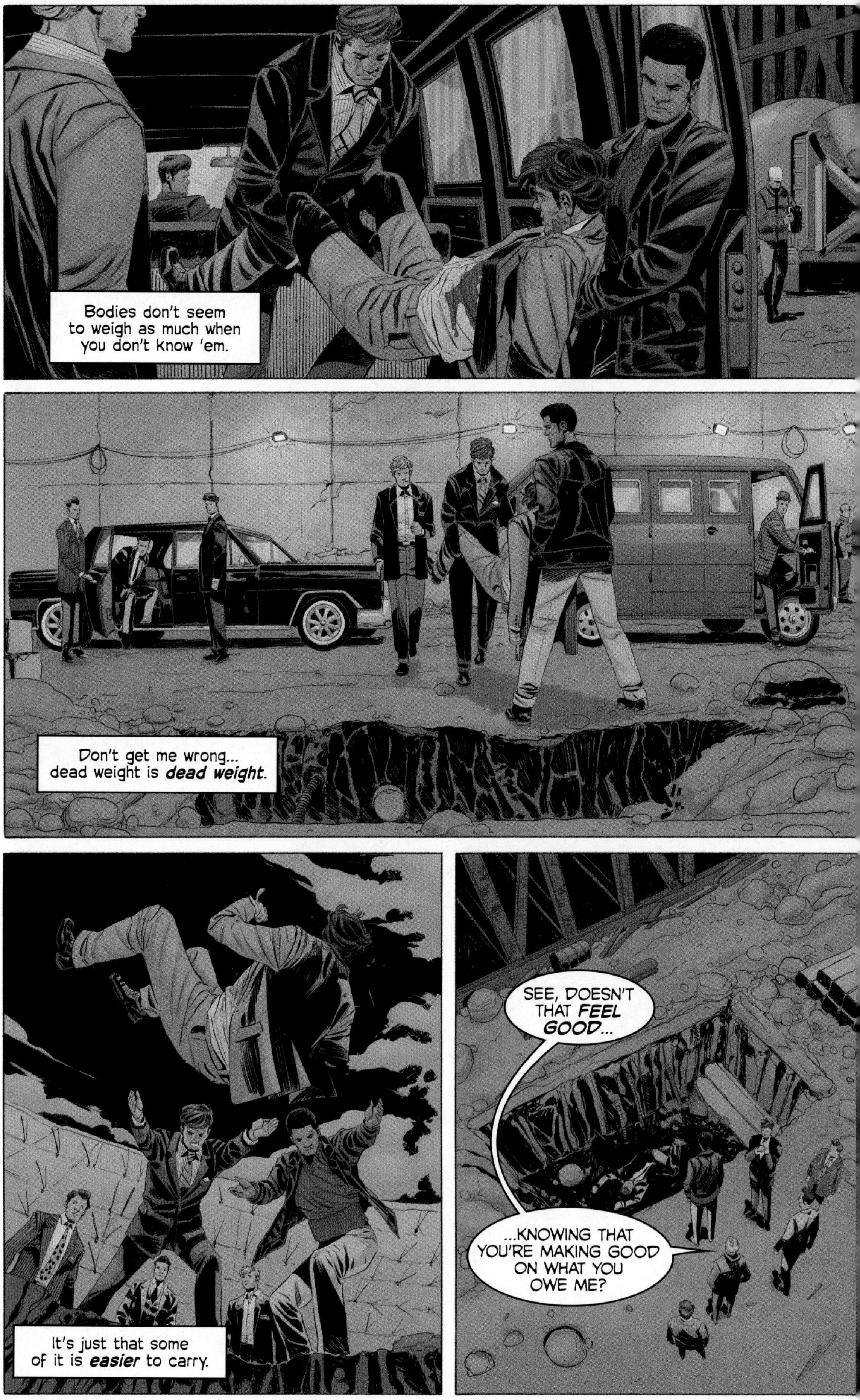
Bodies don't seem to weigh as much when you don't know 'em.
Don't get me wrong... dead weight is *dead weight*.
It's just that some of it is *easier* to carry.
SEE, DOESN'T THAT *FEEL GOOD*...
...KNOWING THAT YOU'RE MAKING GOOD ON WHAT YOU OWE ME?

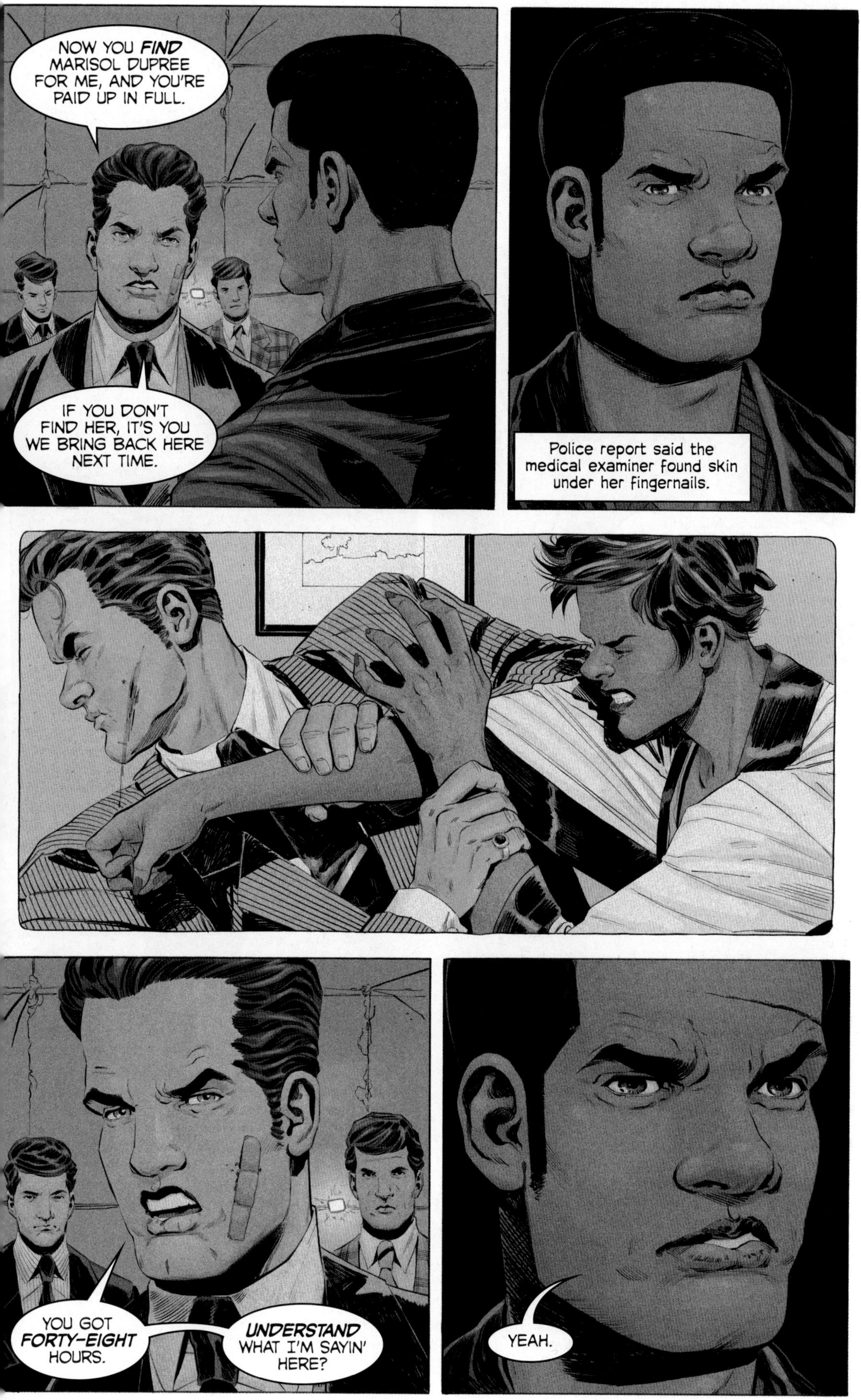
NOW YOU *FIND* MARISOL DUPREE FOR ME, AND YOU'RE PAID UP IN FULL.
IF YOU DON'T FIND HER, IT'S YOU WE BRING BACK HERE NEXT TIME.
Police report said the medical examiner found skin under her fingernails.
YOU GOT *FORTY-EIGHT* HOURS.
UNDERSTAND WHAT I'M SAYIN' HERE?
YEAH.

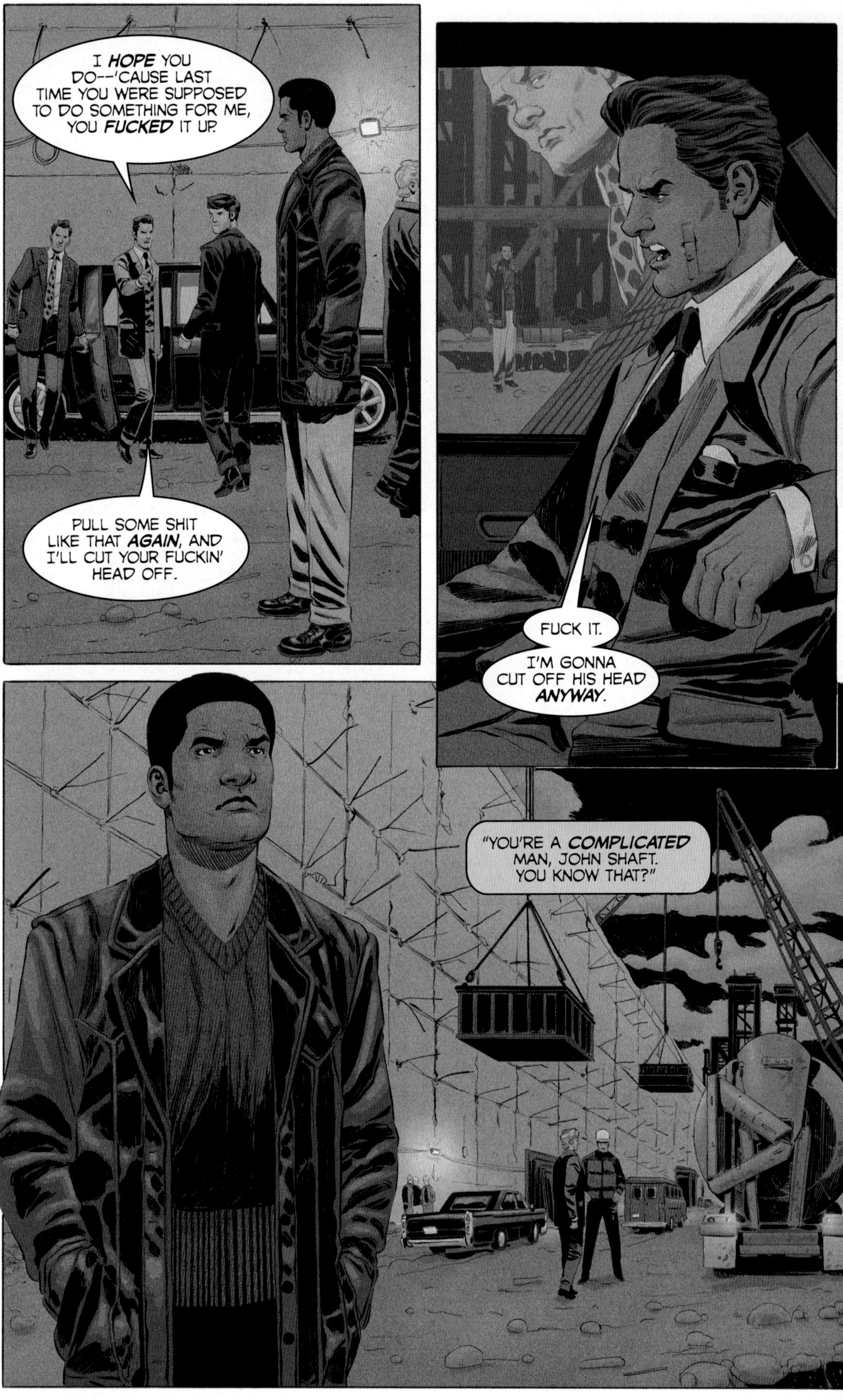
I HOPE YOU DO--'CAUSE LAST TIME YOU WERE SUPPOSED TO DO SOMETHING FOR ME, YOU FUCKED IT UP.
PULL SOME SHIT LIKE THAT AGAIN, AND I'LL CUT YOUR FUCKIN' HEAD OFF.
FUCK IT.
I'M GONNA CUT OFF HIS HEAD ANYWAY.
"YOU'RE A COMPLICATED MAN, JOHN SHAFT. YOU KNOW THAT?"

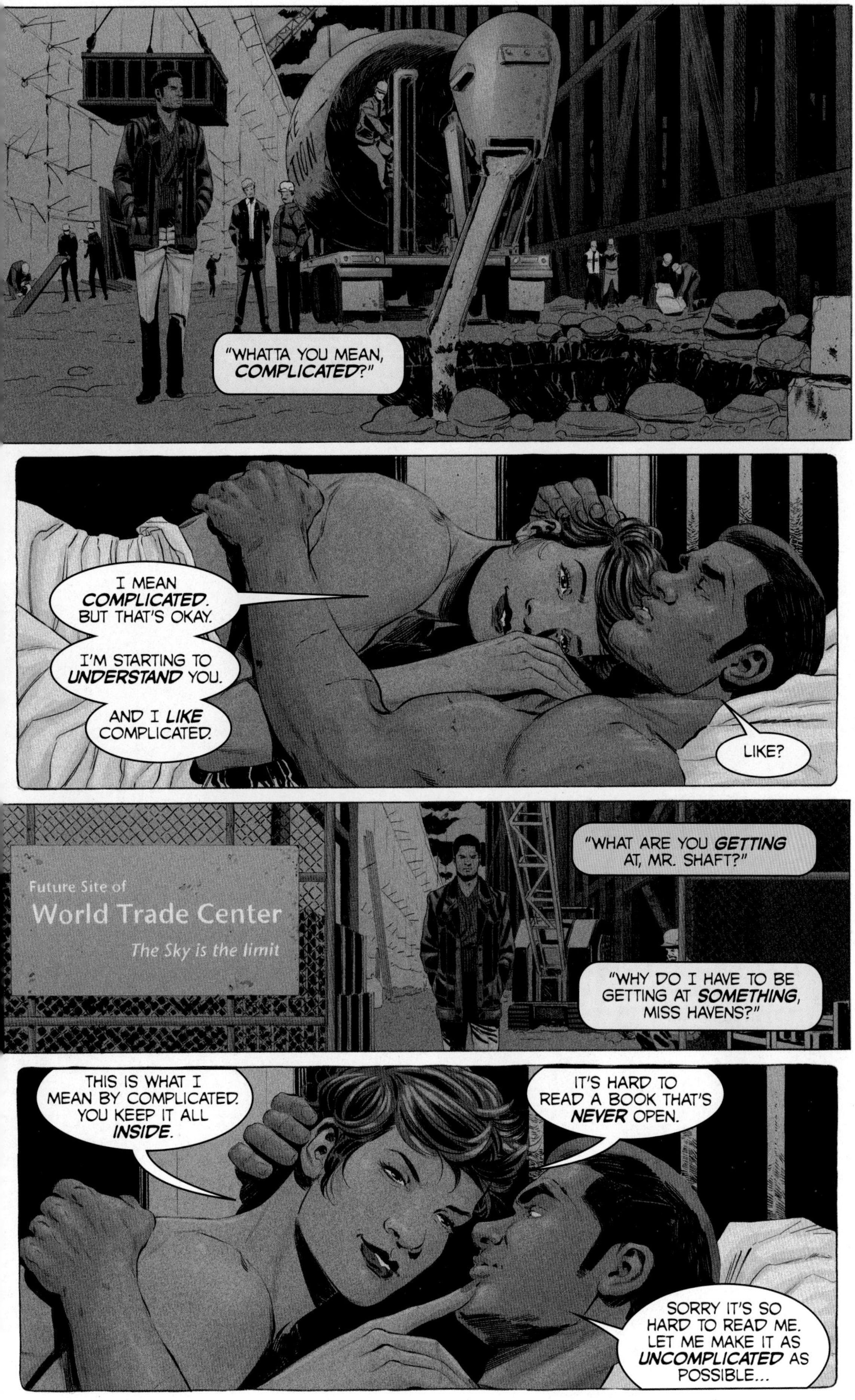

"WHATTA YOU MEAN, COMPLICATED?"
I MEAN COMPLICATED. BUT THAT'S OKAY.
I'M STARTING TO UNDERSTAND YOU.
AND I LIKE COMPLICATED.
LIKE?
Future Site of
World Trade Center
The Sky is the limit
"WHAT ARE YOU GETTING AT, MR. SHAFT?"
"WHY DO I HAVE TO BE GETTING AT SOMETHING, MISS HAVENS?"
THIS IS WHAT I MEAN BY COMPLICATED. YOU KEEP IT ALL INSIDE.
IT'S HARD TO READ A BOOK THAT'S NEVER OPEN.
SORRY IT'S SO HARD TO READ ME. LET ME MAKE IT AS UNCOMPLICATED AS POSSIBLE...

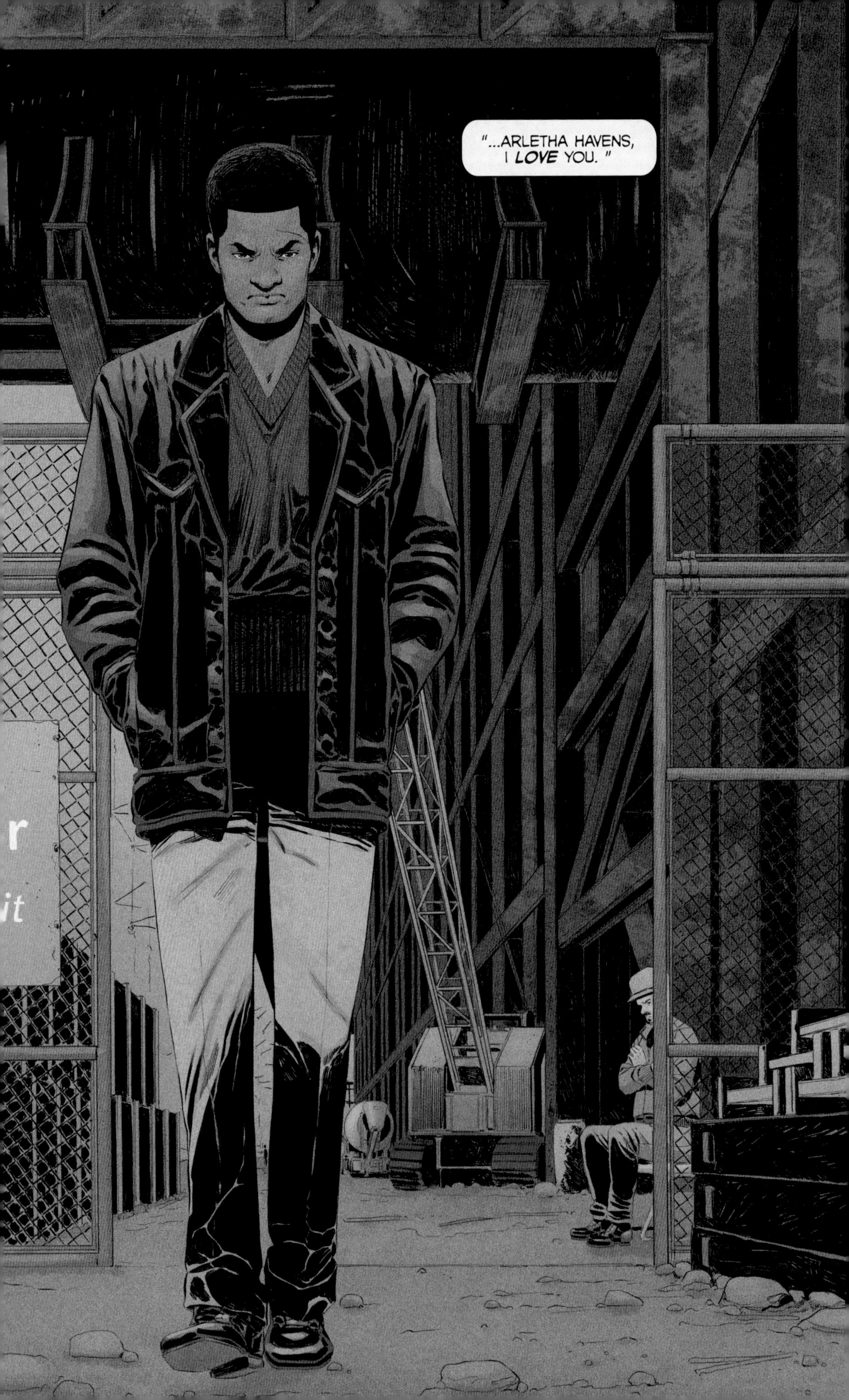
"...ARLETHA HAVENS, I LOVE YOU."

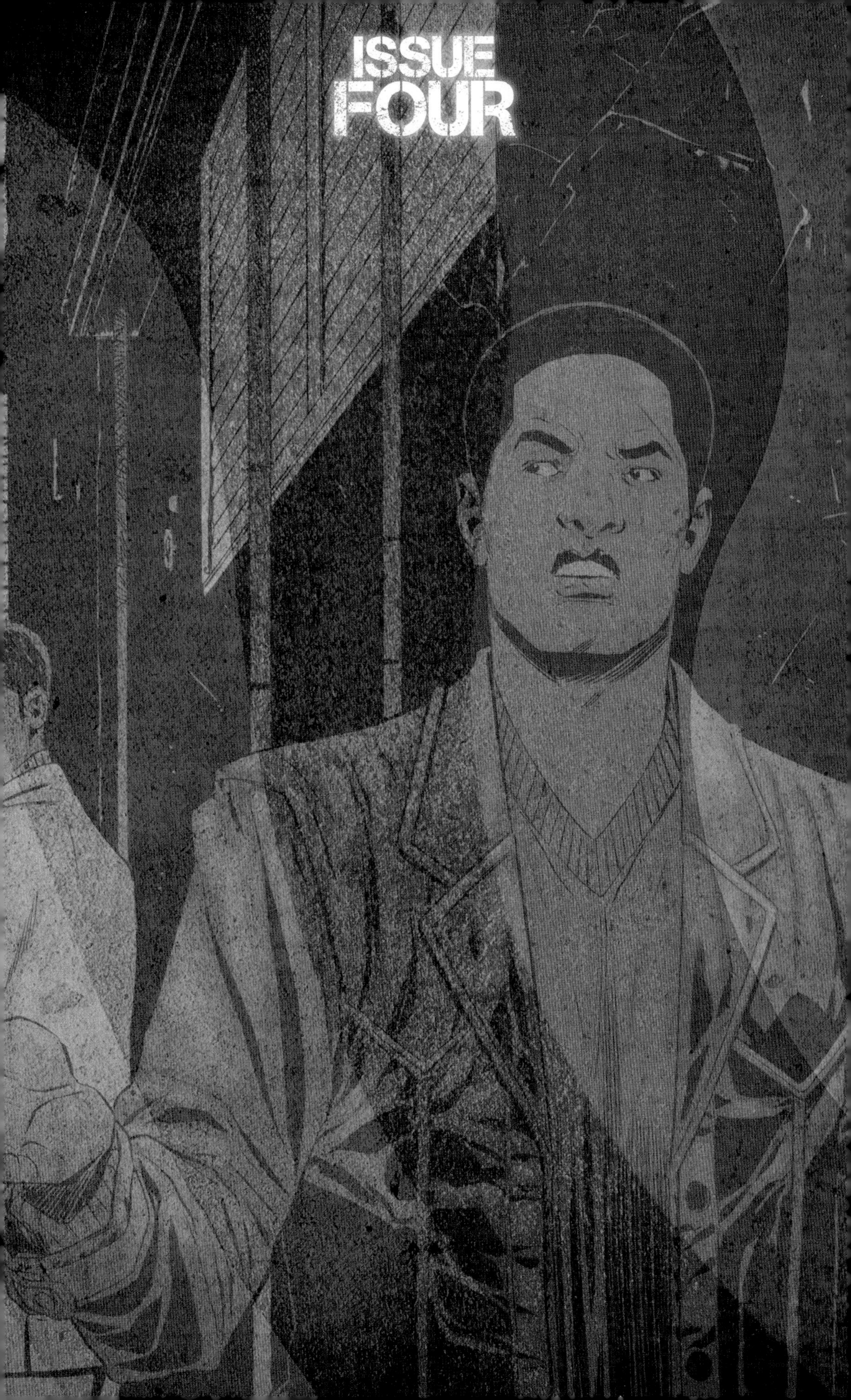
ISSUE
FOUR

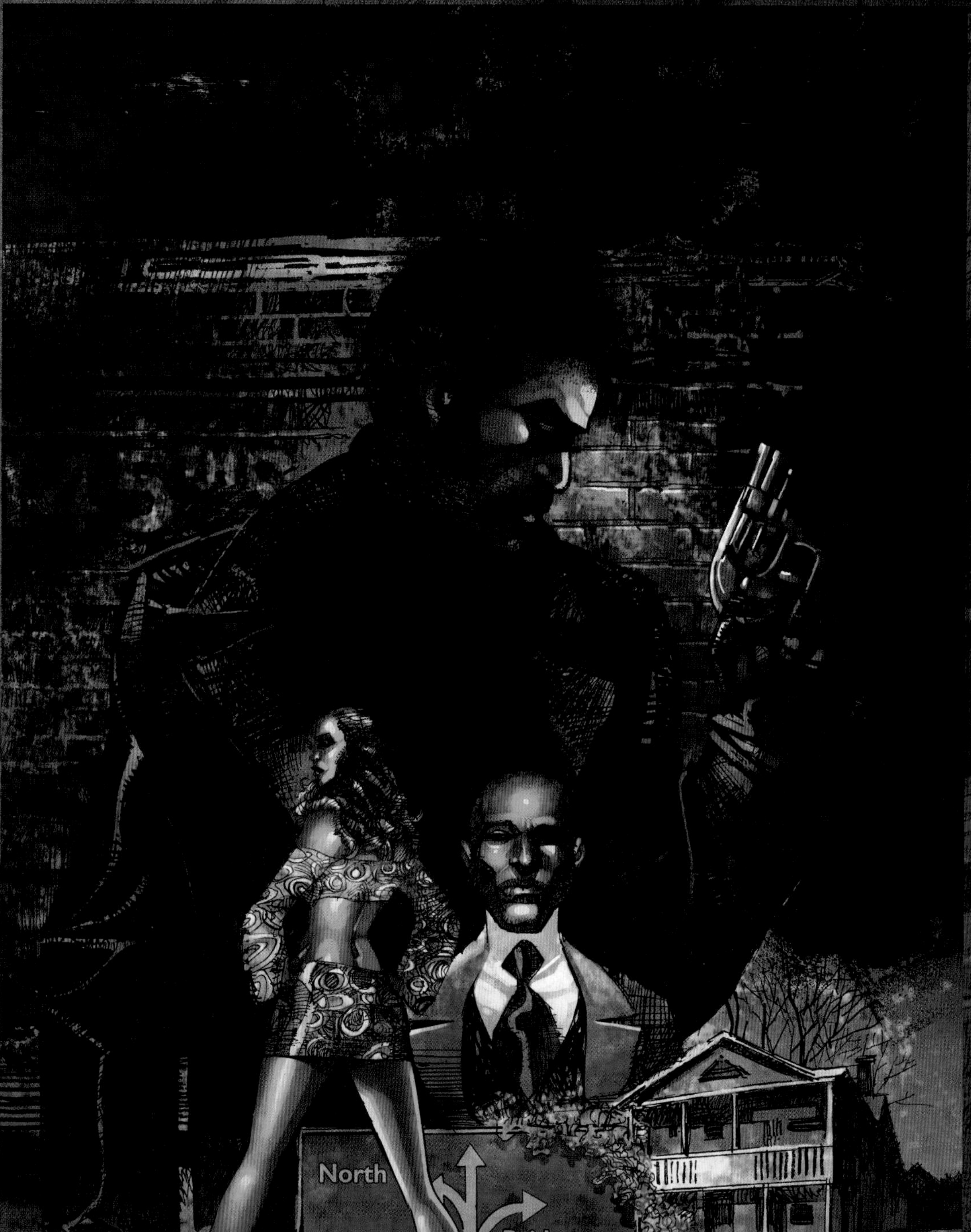
North
Torringto
Bridgeport
COWAN
Ivan Nunes

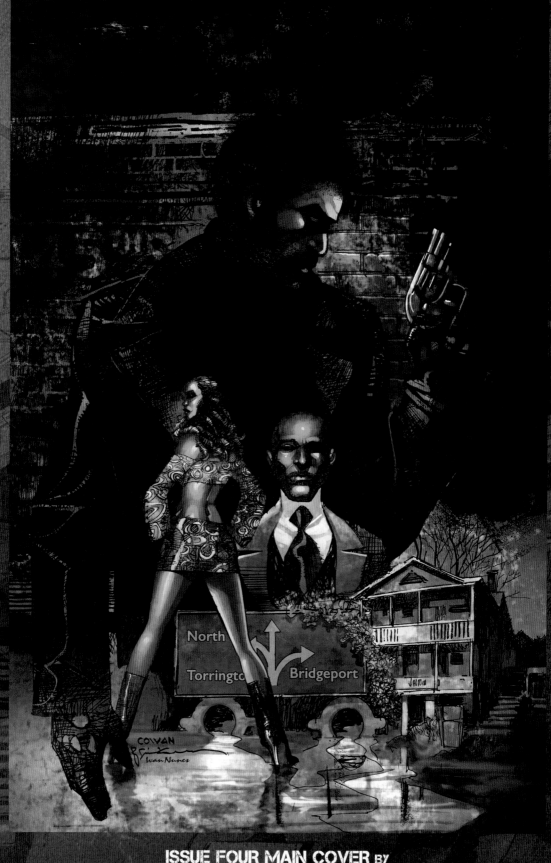

ISSUE FOUR MAIN COVER BY
DENYS COWAN AND BILL SIENKIEWICZ
COLORS BY IVAN NUNES

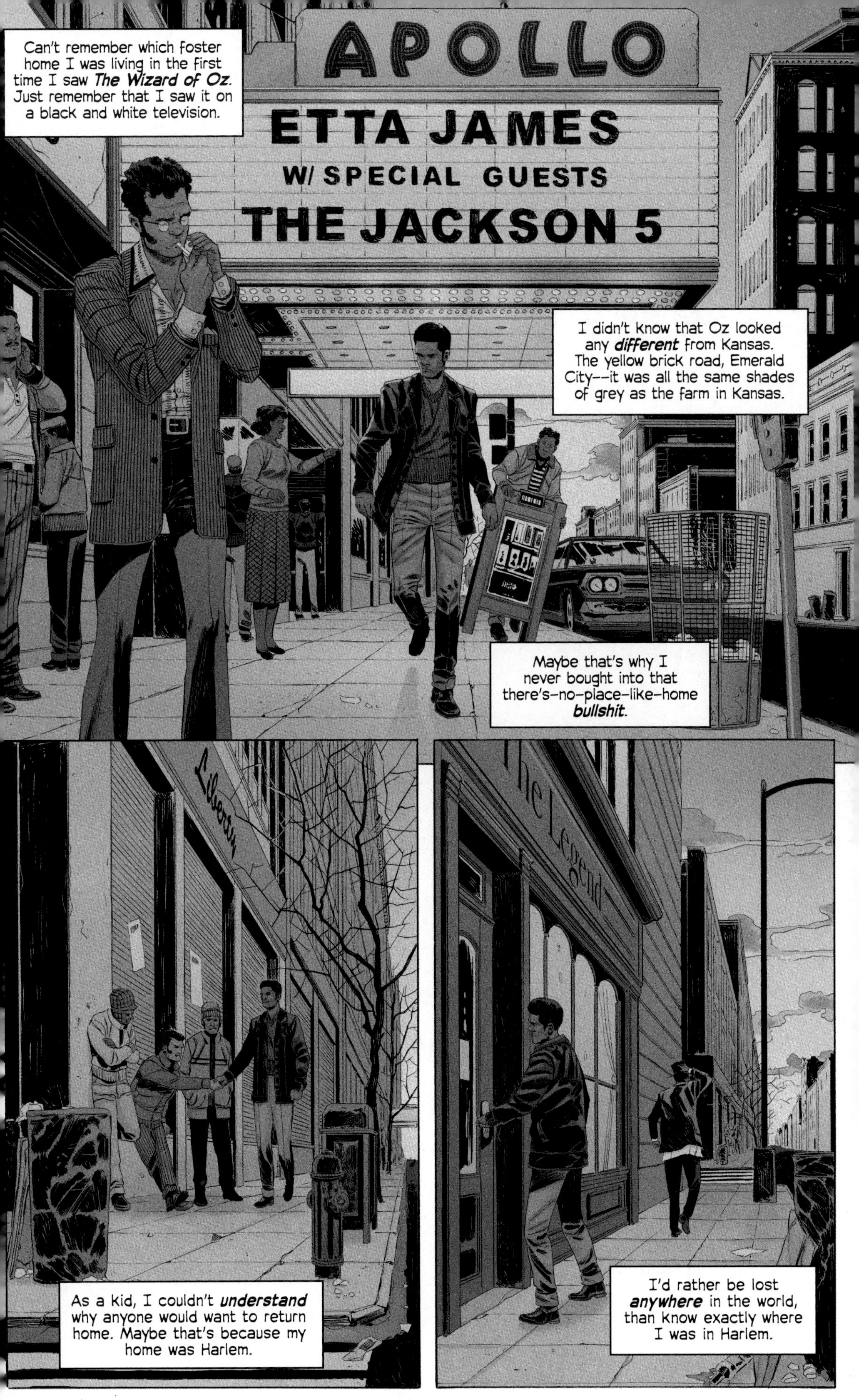
Can't remember which foster home I was living in the first time I saw *The Wizard of Oz*. Just remember that I saw it on a black and white television.
APOLLO
ETTA JAMES
W/ SPECIAL GUESTS
THE JACKSON 5
I didn't know that Oz looked any *different* from Kansas. The yellow brick road, Emerald City--it was all the same shades of grey as the farm in Kansas.
Maybe that's why I never bought into that there's-no-place-like-home *bullshit*.
Liberty
As a kid, I couldn't *understand* why anyone would want to return home. Maybe that's because my home was Harlem.
The Legend
I'd rather be lost *anywhere* in the world, than know exactly where I was in Harlem.

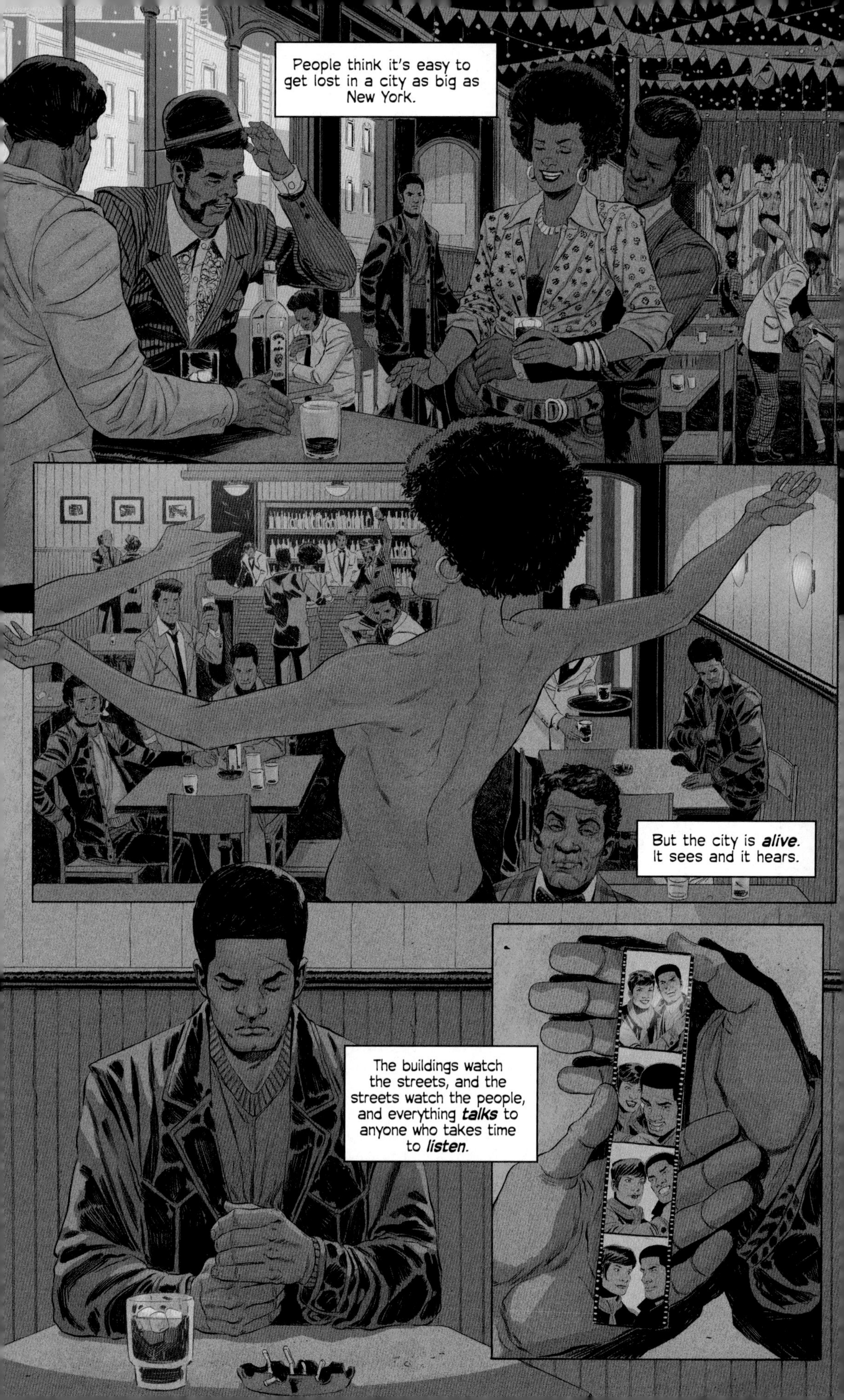

People think it's easy to get lost in a city as big as New York.
But the city is *alive*. It sees and it hears.
The buildings watch the streets, and the streets watch the people, and everything *talks* to anyone who takes time to *listen*.

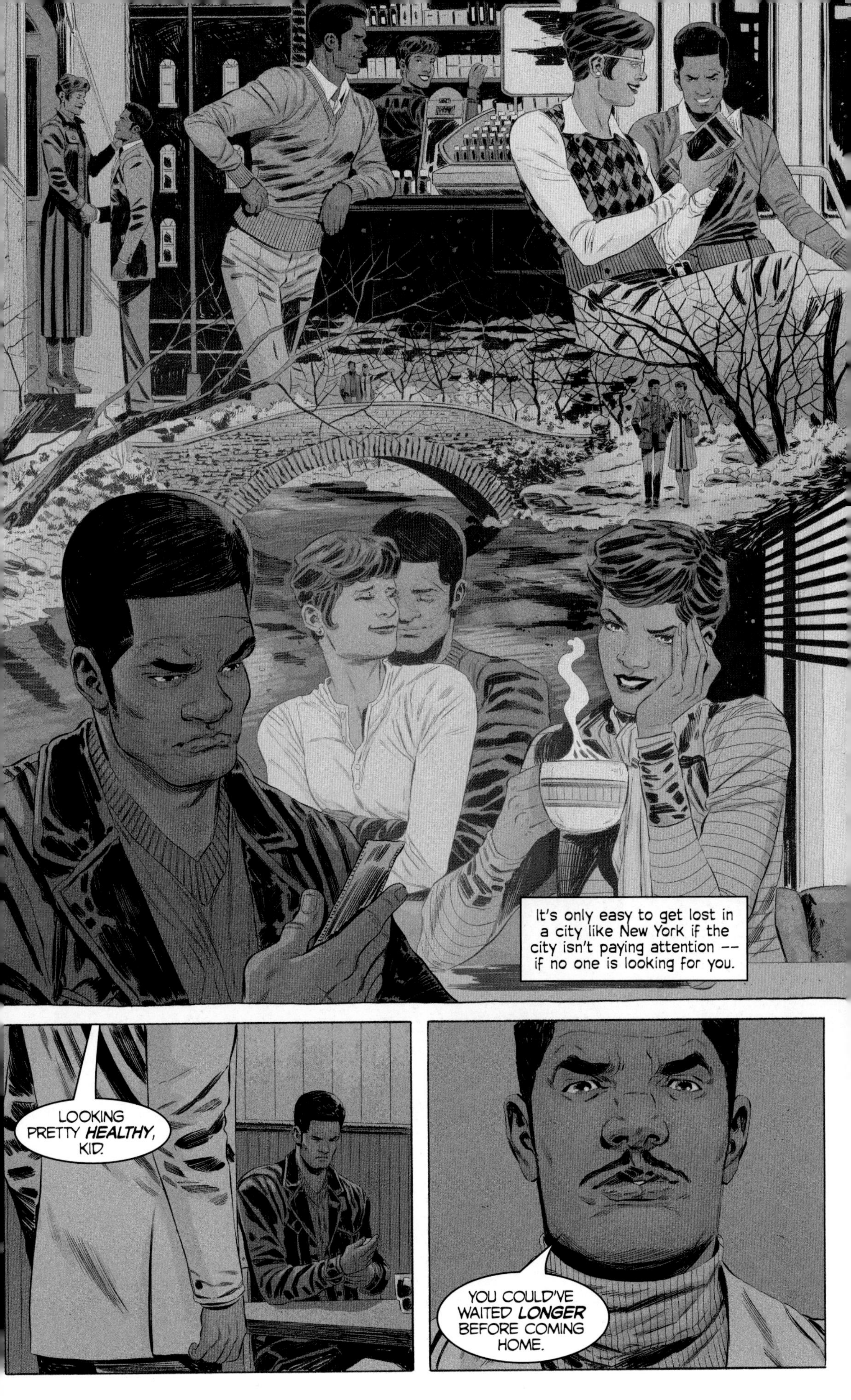
It's only easy to get lost in a city like New York if the city isn't paying attention -- if no one is looking for you.
LOOKING PRETTY **HEALTHY**, KID.
YOU COULD'VE WAITED **LONGER** BEFORE COMING HOME.

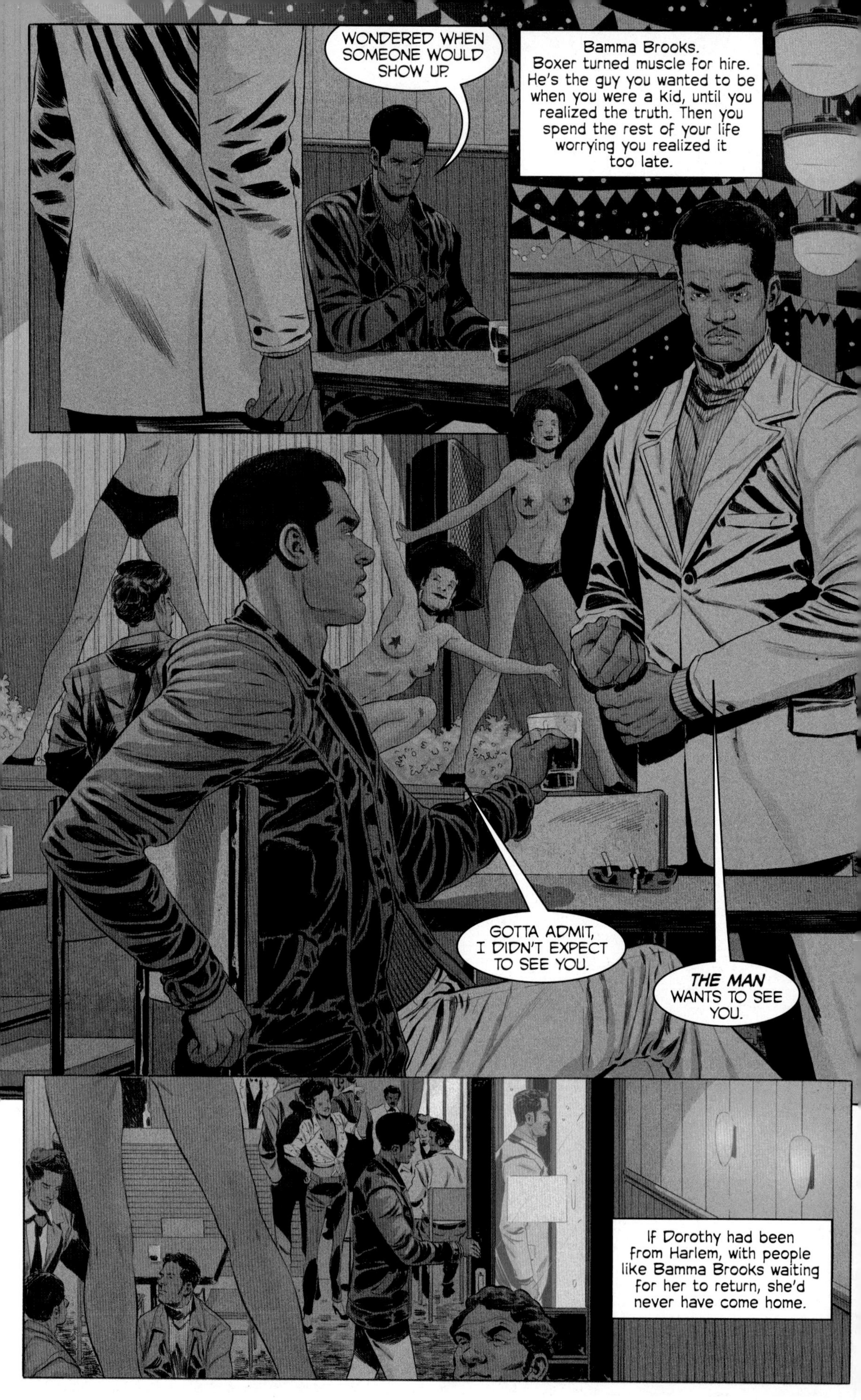
WONDERED WHEN SOMEONE WOULD SHOW UP.
Bamma Brooks. Boxer turned muscle for hire. He's the guy you wanted to be when you were a kid, until you realized the truth. Then you spend the rest of your life worrying you realized it too late.
GOTTA ADMIT, I DIDN'T EXPECT TO SEE YOU.
THE MAN WANTS TO SEE YOU.
If Dorothy had been from Harlem, with people like Bamma Brooks waiting for her to return, she'd never have come home.

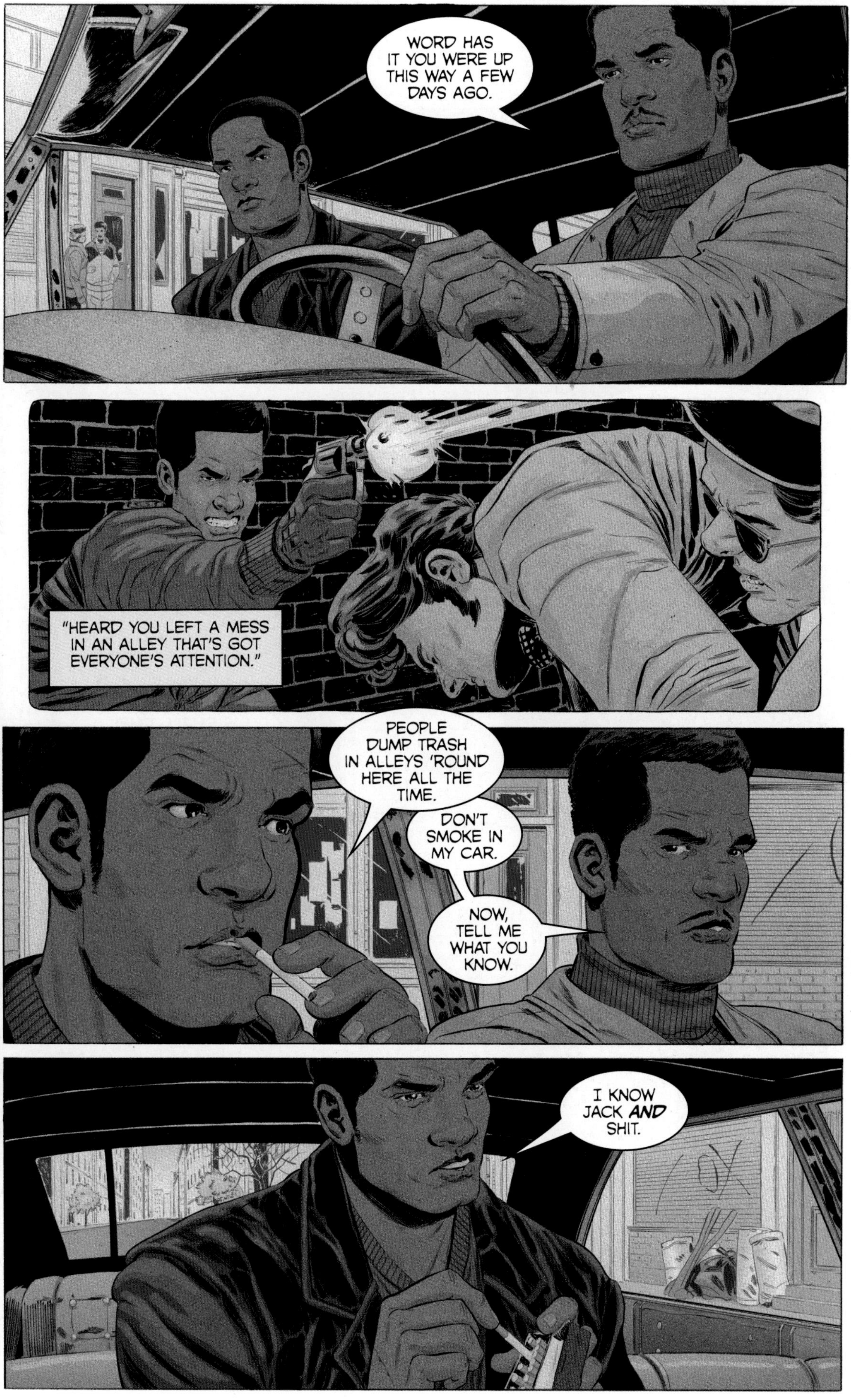

WORD HAS IT YOU WERE UP THIS WAY A FEW DAYS AGO.
"HEARD YOU LEFT A MESS IN AN ALLEY THAT'S GOT EVERYONE'S ATTENTION."
PEOPLE DUMP TRASH IN ALLEYS 'ROUND HERE ALL THE TIME.
DON'T SMOKE IN MY CAR.
NOW, TELL ME WHAT YOU KNOW.
I KNOW JACK AND SHIT.

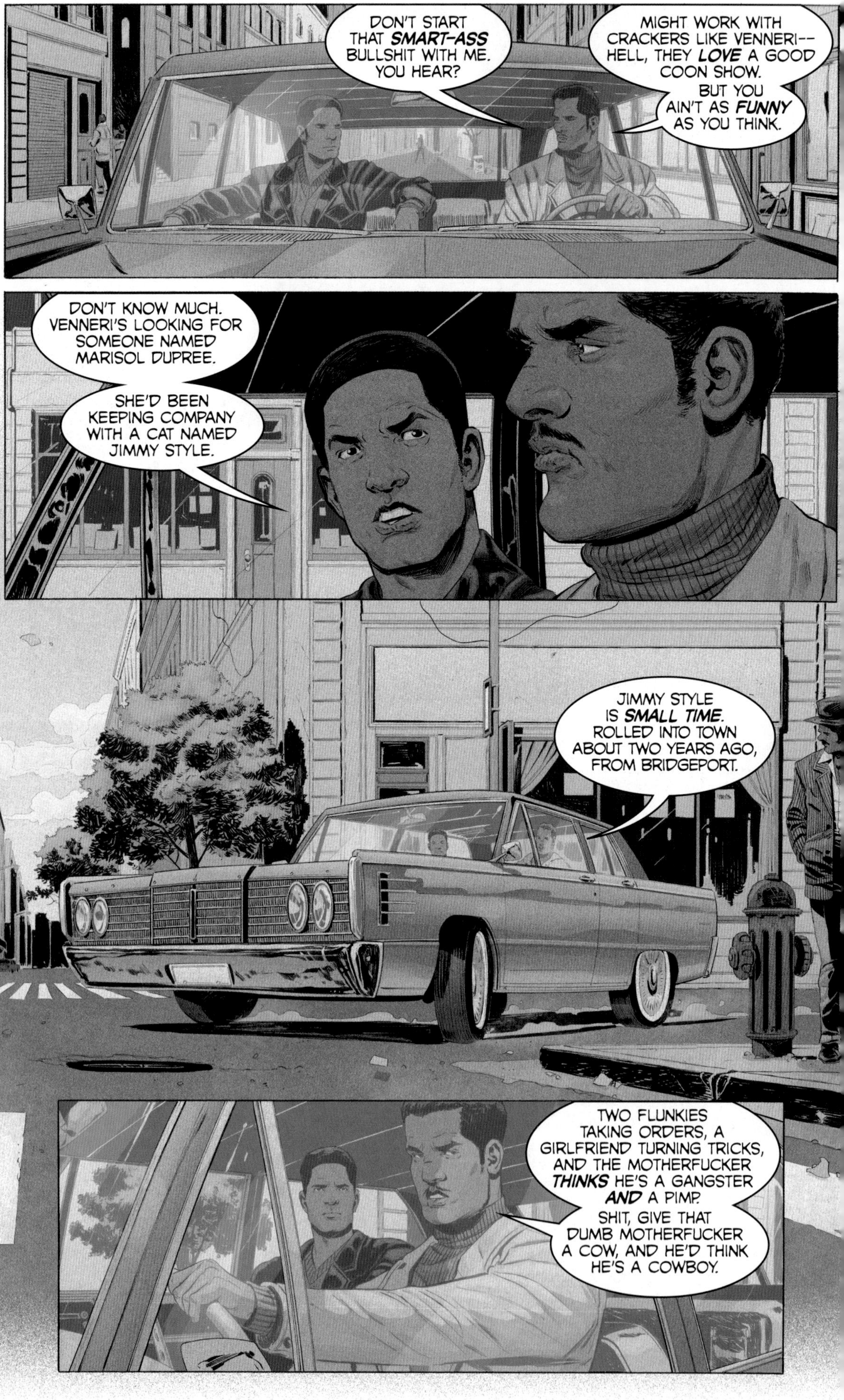
DON'T START THAT SMART-ASS BULLSHIT WITH ME. YOU HEAR?
MIGHT WORK WITH CRACKERS LIKE VENNERI-- HELL, THEY LOVE A GOOD COON SHOW.
BUT YOU AIN'T AS FUNNY AS YOU THINK.
DON'T KNOW MUCH. VENNERI'S LOOKING FOR SOMEONE NAMED MARISOL DUPREE.
SHE'D BEEN KEEPING COMPANY WITH A CAT NAMED JIMMY STYLE.
JIMMY STYLE IS SMALL TIME. ROLLED INTO TOWN ABOUT TWO YEARS AGO, FROM BRIDGEPORT.
TWO FLUNKIES TAKING ORDERS, A GIRLFRIEND TURNING TRICKS, AND THE MOTHERFUCKER THINKS HE'S A GANGSTER AND A PIMP.
SHIT, GIVE THAT DUMB MOTHERFUCKER A COW, AND HE'D THINK HE'S A COWBOY.

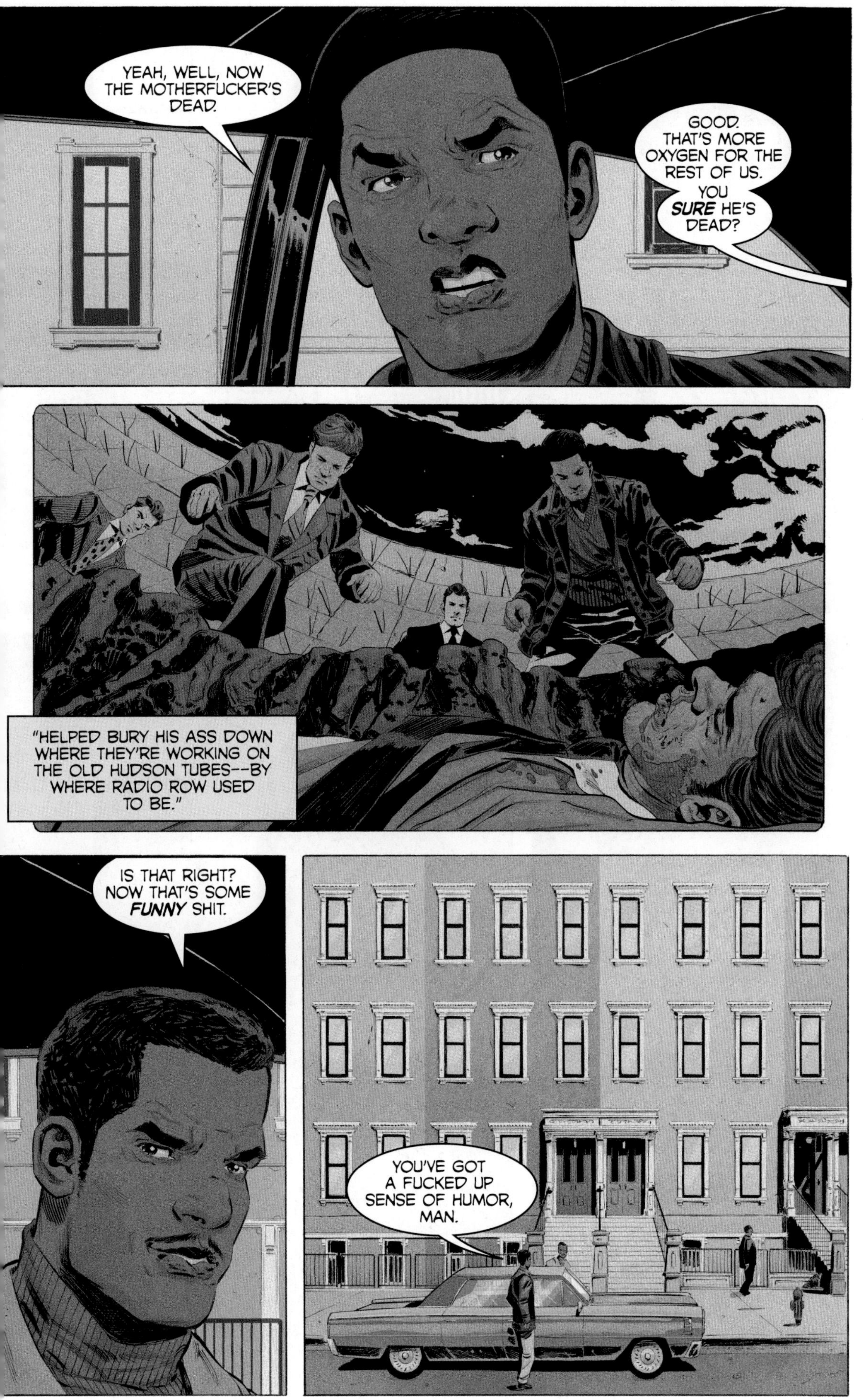
YEAH, WELL, NOW THE MOTHERFUCKER'S DEAD.
GOOD. THAT'S MORE OXYGEN FOR THE REST OF US.
YOU SURE HE'S DEAD?
"HELPED BURY HIS ASS DOWN WHERE THEY'RE WORKING ON THE OLD HUDSON TUBES--BY WHERE RADIO ROW USED TO BE."
IS THAT RIGHT? NOW THAT'S SOME FUNNY SHIT.
YOU'VE GOT A FUCKED UP SENSE OF HUMOR, MAN.

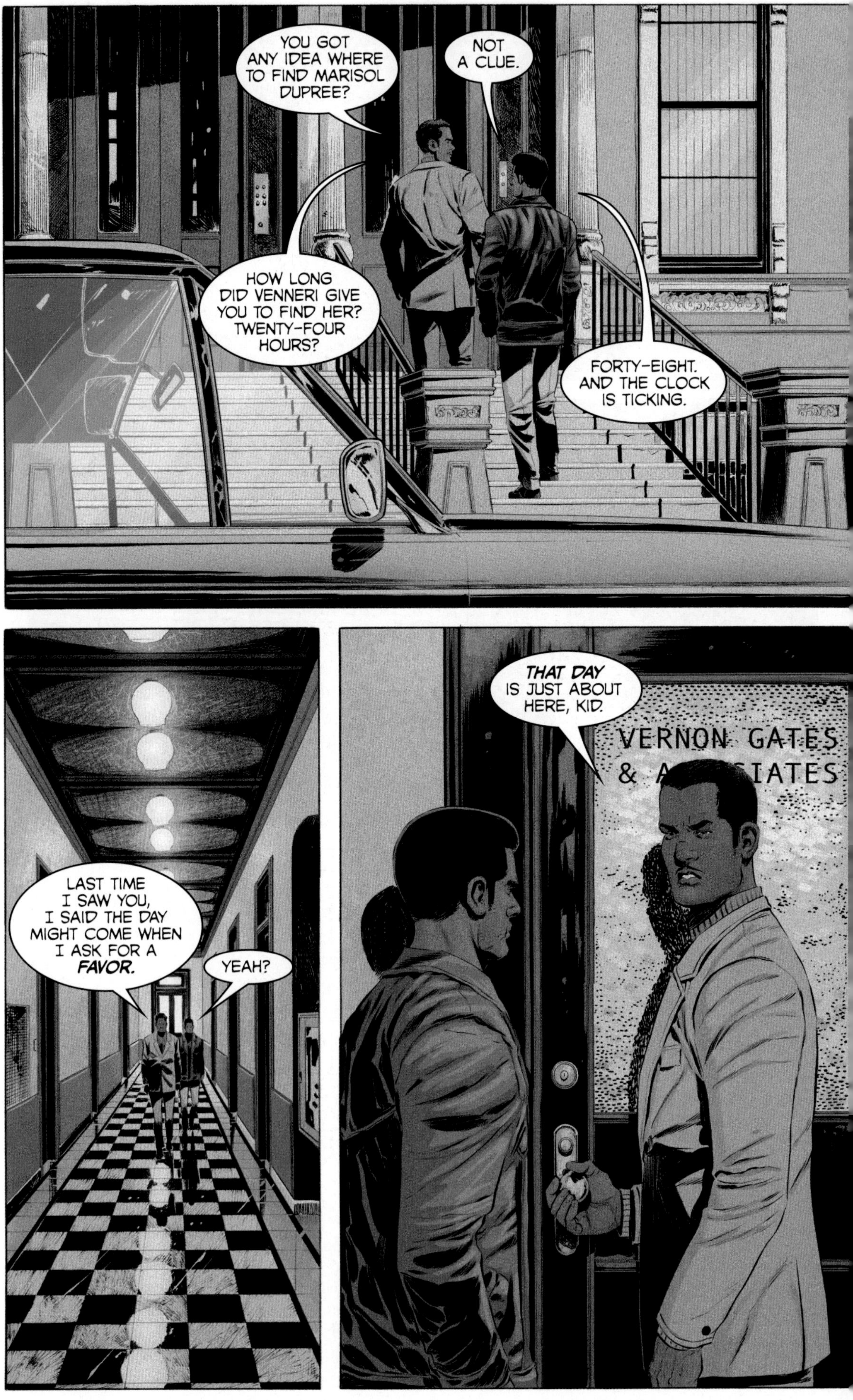
YOU GOT ANY IDEA WHERE TO FIND MARISOL DUPREE?
NOT A CLUE.
HOW LONG DID VENNERI GIVE YOU TO FIND HER? TWENTY-FOUR HOURS?
FORTY-EIGHT. AND THE CLOCK IS TICKING.
LAST TIME I SAW YOU, I SAID THE DAY MIGHT COME WHEN I ASK FOR A *FAVOR.*
YEAH?
THAT DAY IS JUST ABOUT HERE, KID.
VERNON GATES
& A SIATES

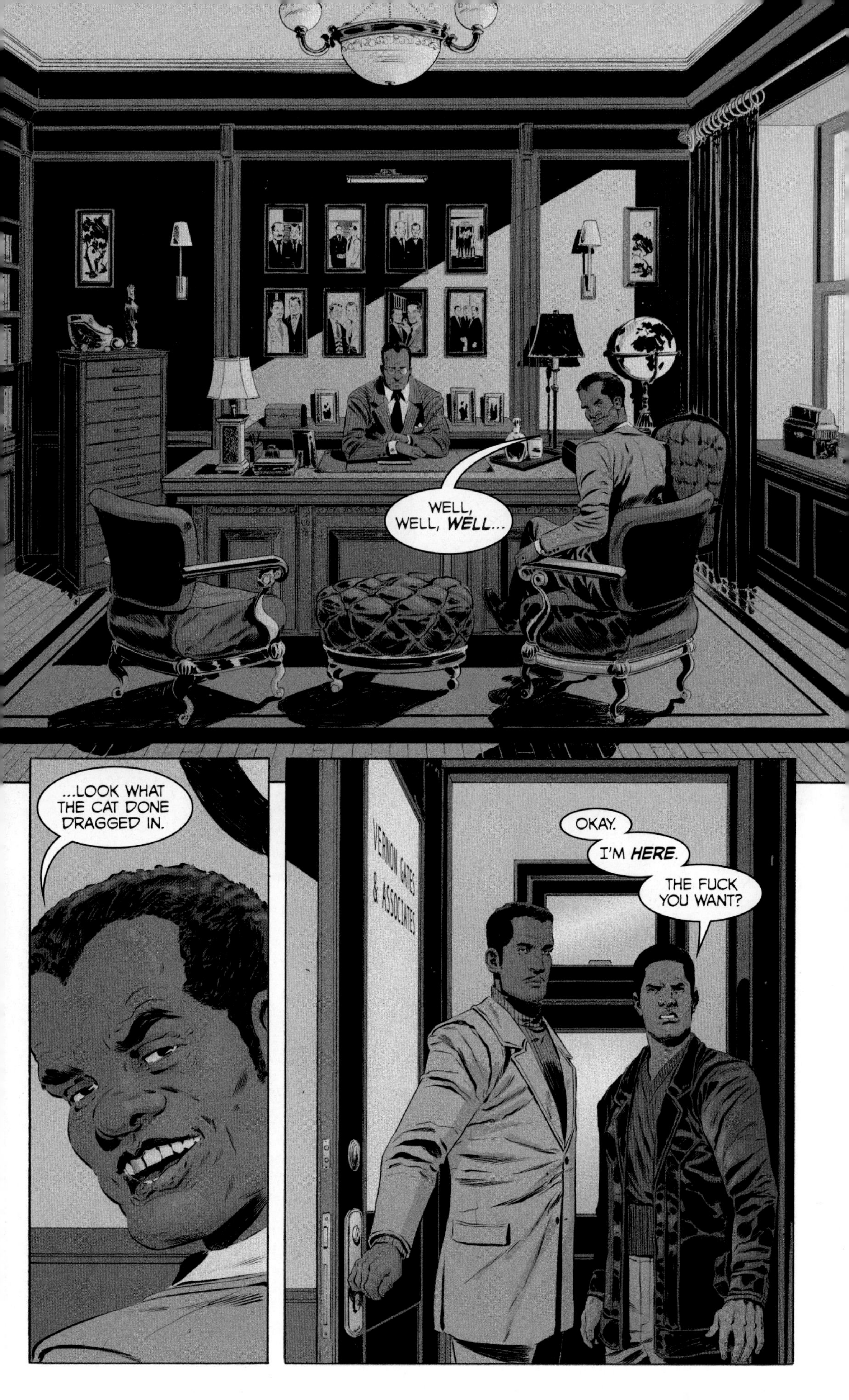
WELL, WELL, WELL...
...LOOK WHAT THE CAT DONE DRAGGED IN.
VERNON GATES & ASSOCIATES
OKAY.
I'M HERE.
THE FUCK YOU WANT?

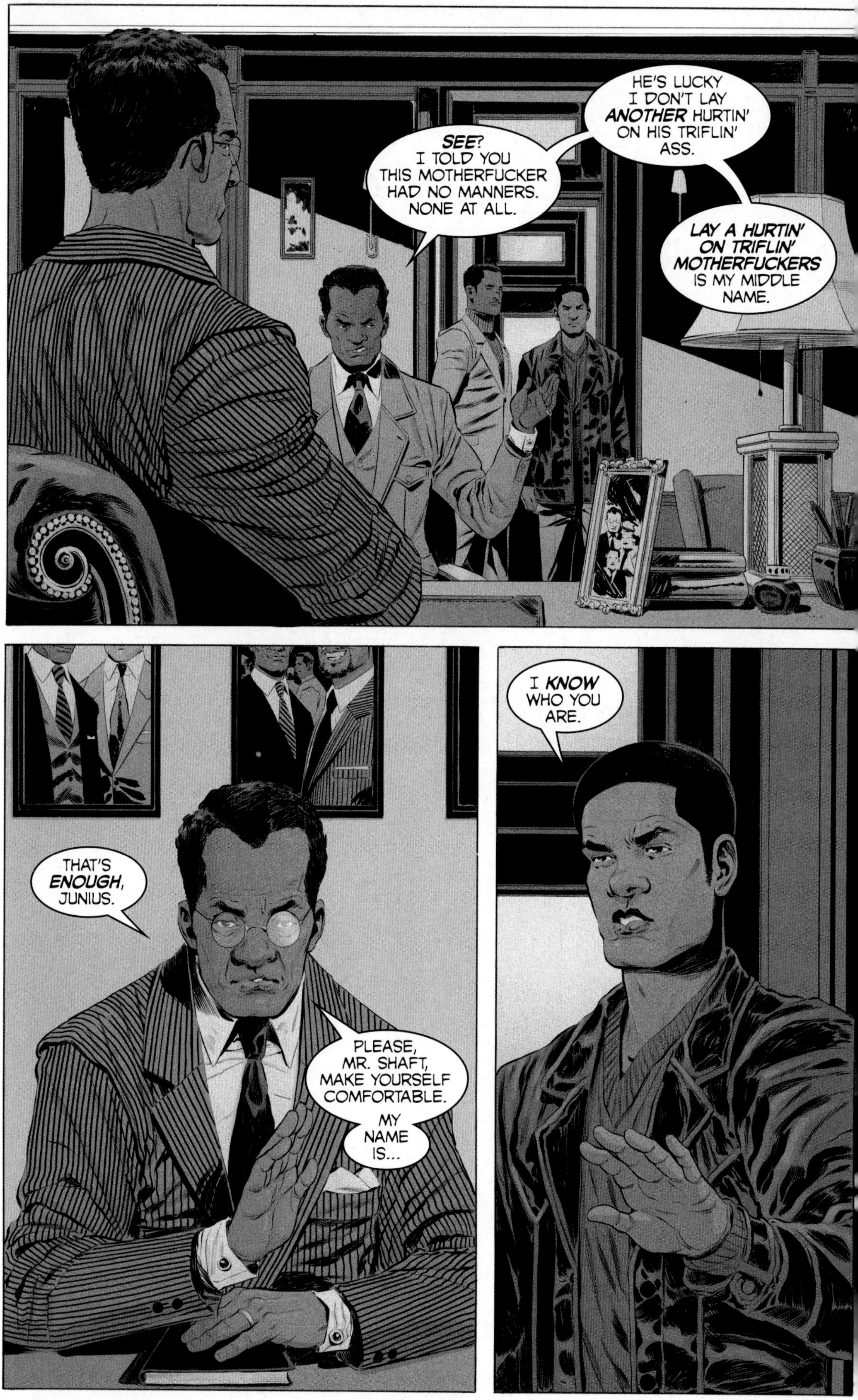
SEE? I TOLD YOU THIS MOTHERFUCKER HAD NO MANNERS. NONE AT ALL.
HE'S LUCKY I DON'T LAY ANOTHER HURTIN' ON HIS TRIFLIN' ASS.
LAY A HURTIN' ON TRIFLIN' MOTHERFUCKERS IS MY MIDDLE NAME.
THAT'S ENOUGH, JUNIUS.
PLEASE, MR. SHAFT, MAKE YOURSELF COMFORTABLE.
MY NAME IS...
I KNOW WHO YOU ARE.

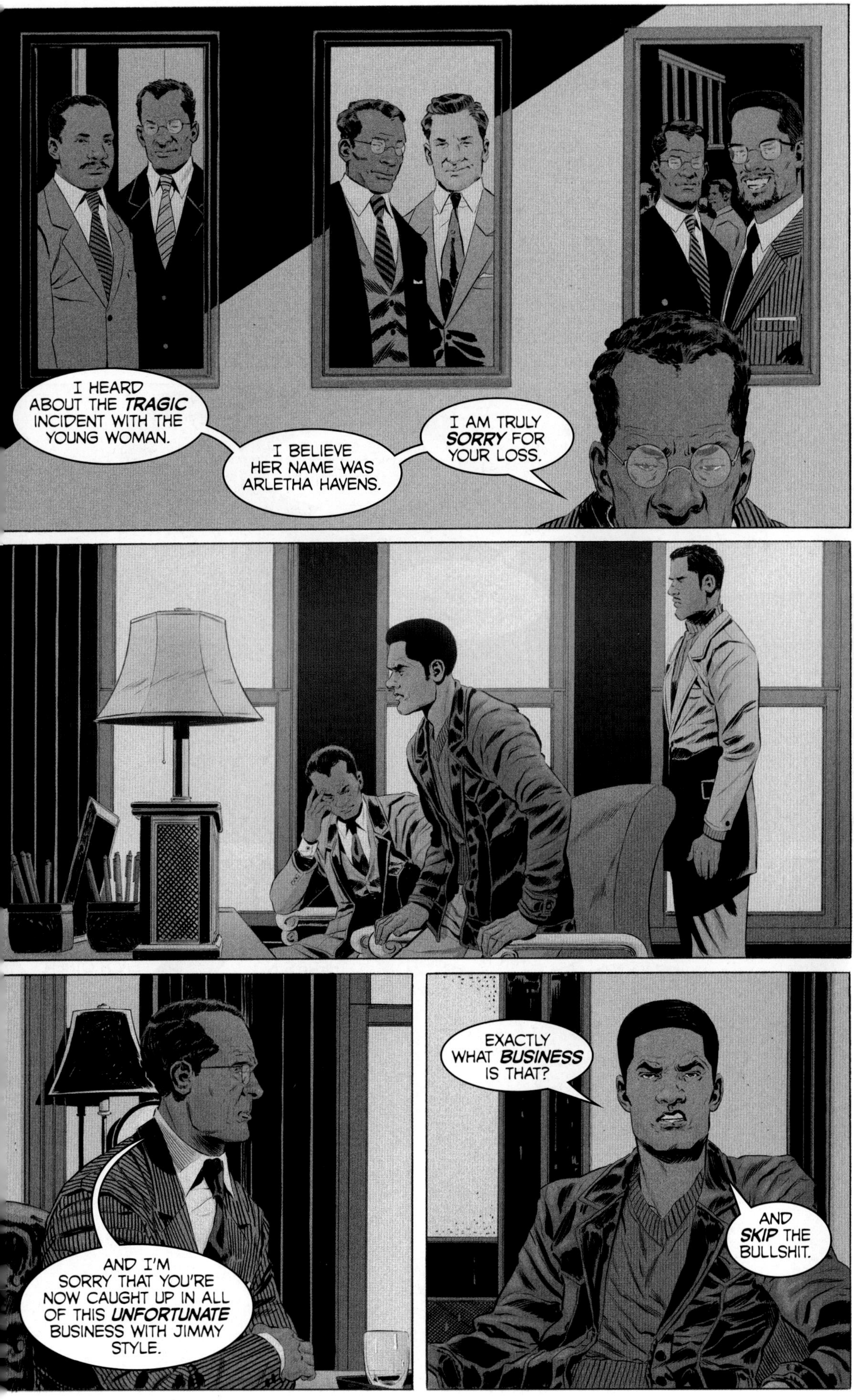
I HEARD ABOUT THE *TRAGIC* INCIDENT WITH THE YOUNG WOMAN.
I BELIEVE HER NAME WAS ARLETHA HAVENS.
I AM TRULY *SORRY* FOR YOUR LOSS.
AND I'M SORRY THAT YOU'RE NOW CAUGHT UP IN ALL OF THIS *UNFORTUNATE* BUSINESS WITH JIMMY STYLE.
EXACTLY WHAT *BUSINESS* IS THAT?
AND *SKIP* THE BULLSHIT.

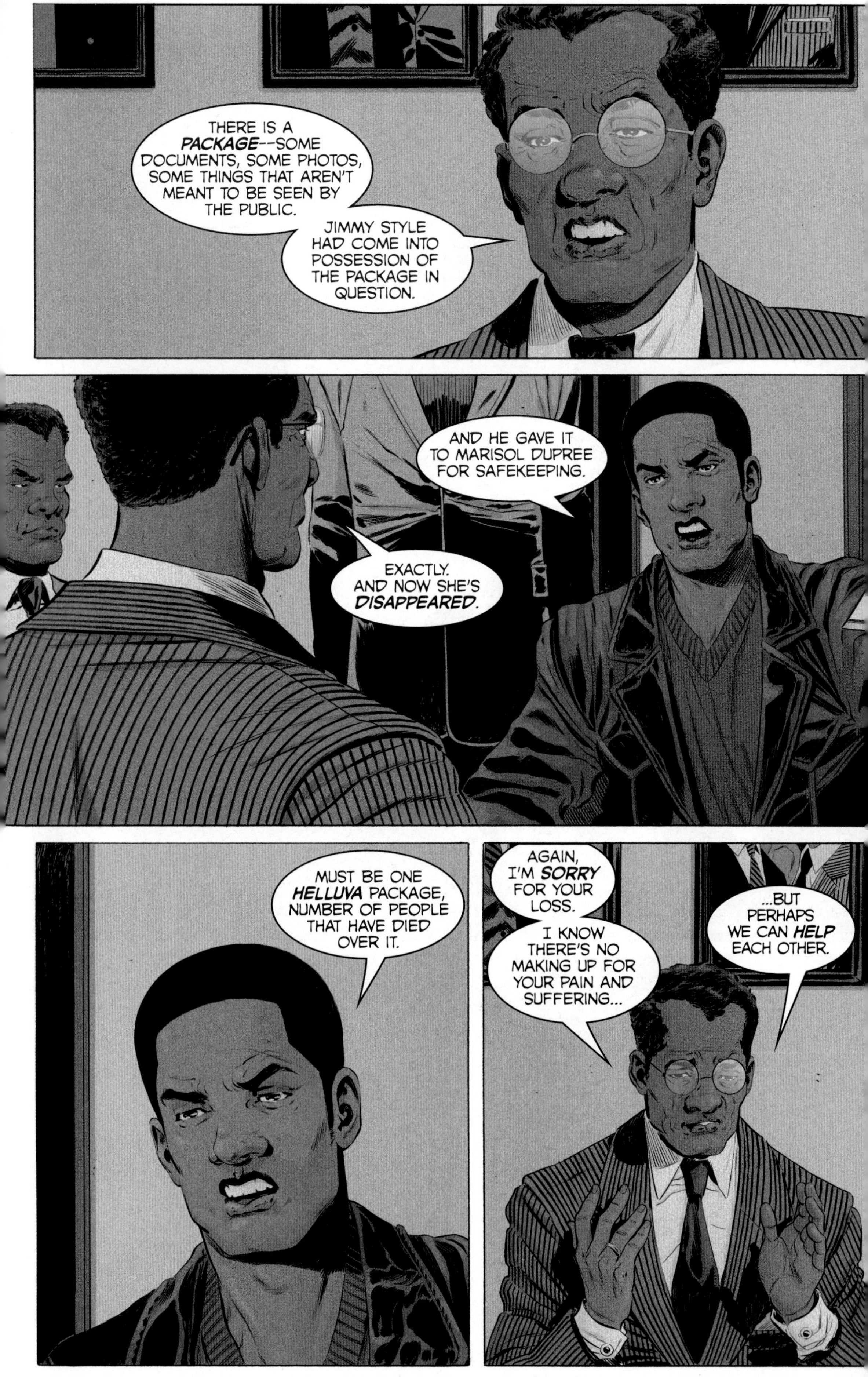
THERE IS A PACKAGE--SOME DOCUMENTS, SOME PHOTOS, SOME THINGS THAT AREN'T MEANT TO BE SEEN BY THE PUBLIC.
JIMMY STYLE HAD COME INTO POSSESSION OF THE PACKAGE IN QUESTION.
AND HE GAVE IT TO MARISOL DUPREE FOR SAFEKEEPING.
EXACTLY. AND NOW SHE'S DISAPPEARED.
MUST BE ONE HELLUVA PACKAGE, NUMBER OF PEOPLE THAT HAVE DIED OVER IT.
AGAIN, I'M SORRY FOR YOUR LOSS.
I KNOW THERE'S NO MAKING UP FOR YOUR PAIN AND SUFFERING...
...BUT PERHAPS WE CAN HELP EACH OTHER.

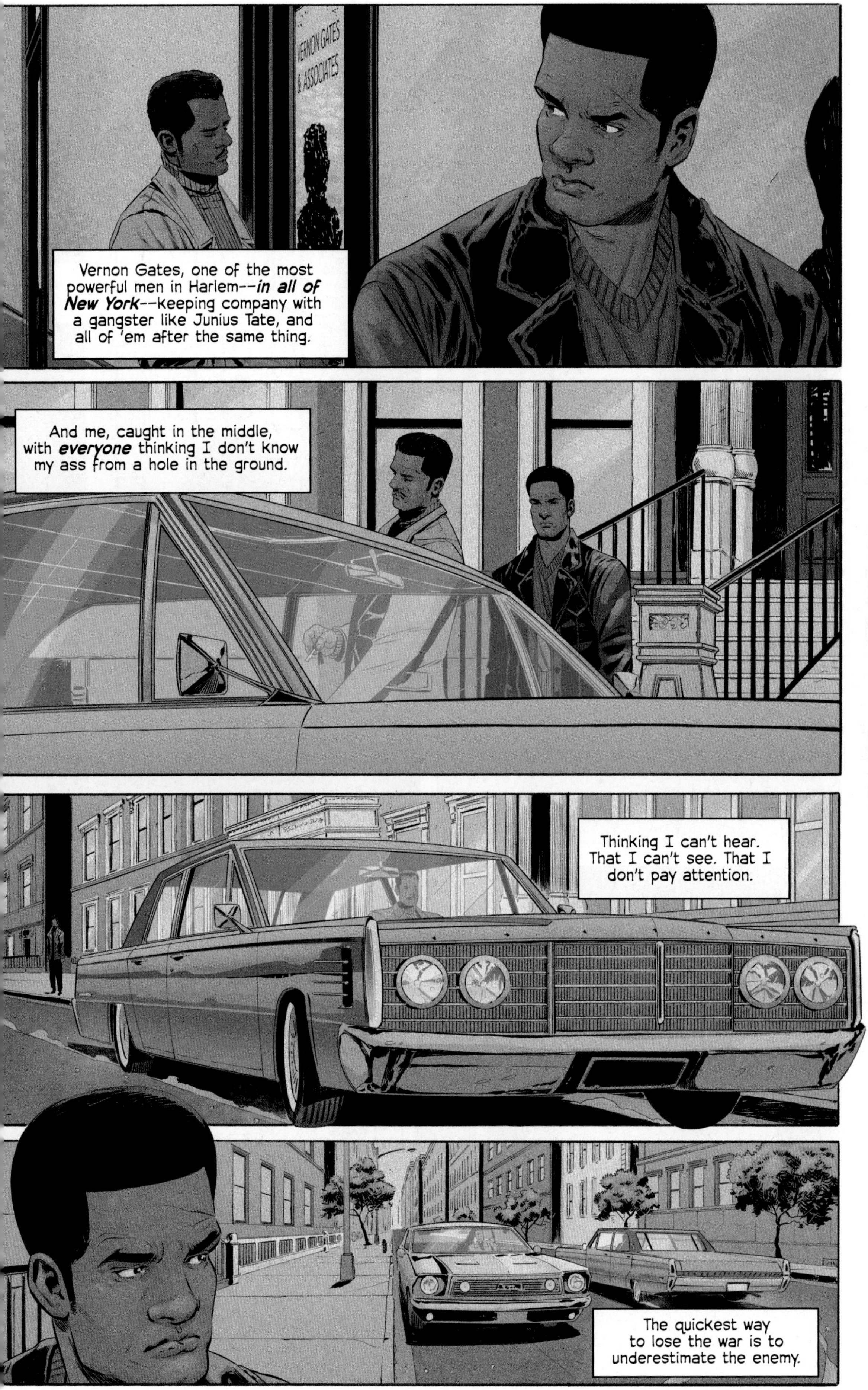
VERNON GATES & ASSOCIATES
Vernon Gates, one of the most powerful men in Harlem--*in all of New York*--keeping company with a gangster like Junius Tate, and all of 'em after the same thing.
And me, caught in the middle, with *everyone* thinking I don't know my ass from a hole in the ground.
Thinking I can't hear. That I can't see. That I don't pay attention.
The quickest way to lose the war is to underestimate the enemy.

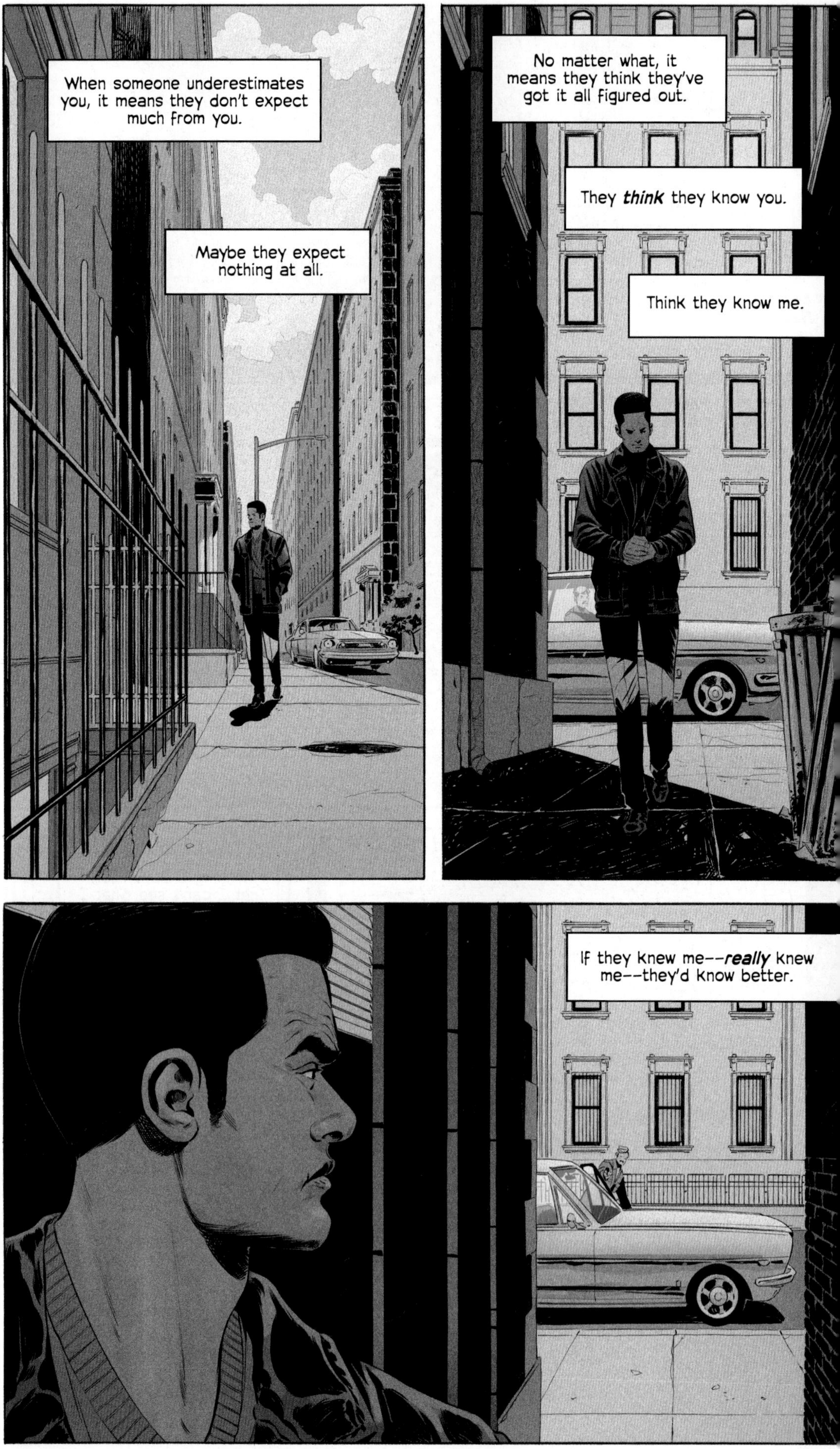
When someone underestimates you, it means they don't expect much from you.
Maybe they expect nothing at all.
No matter what, it means they think they've got it all figured out.
They *think* they know you.
Think they know me.
If they knew me--*really* knew me--they'd know better.

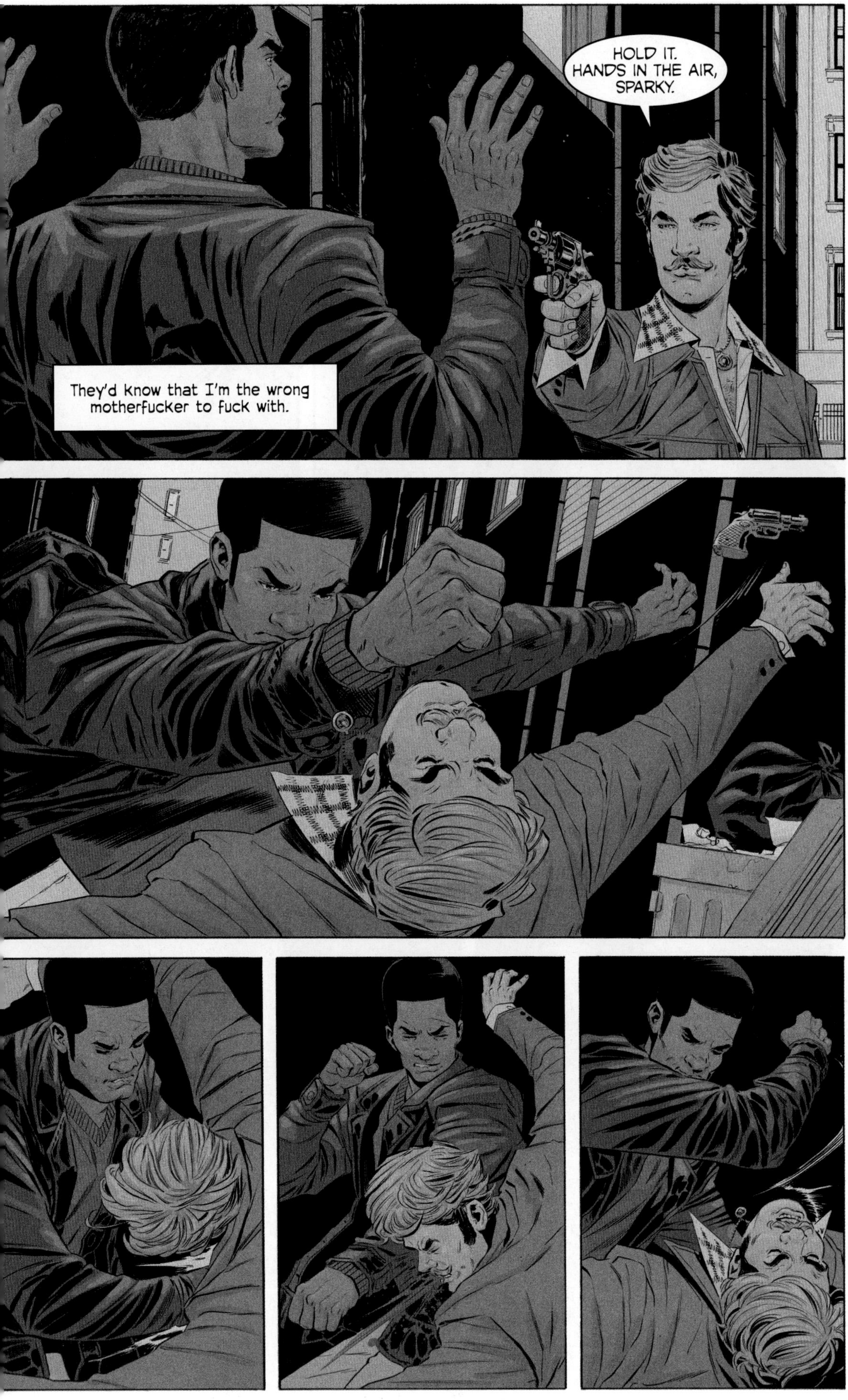
HOLD IT. HANDS IN THE AIR, SPARKY.
They'd know that I'm the wrong motherfucker to fuck with.

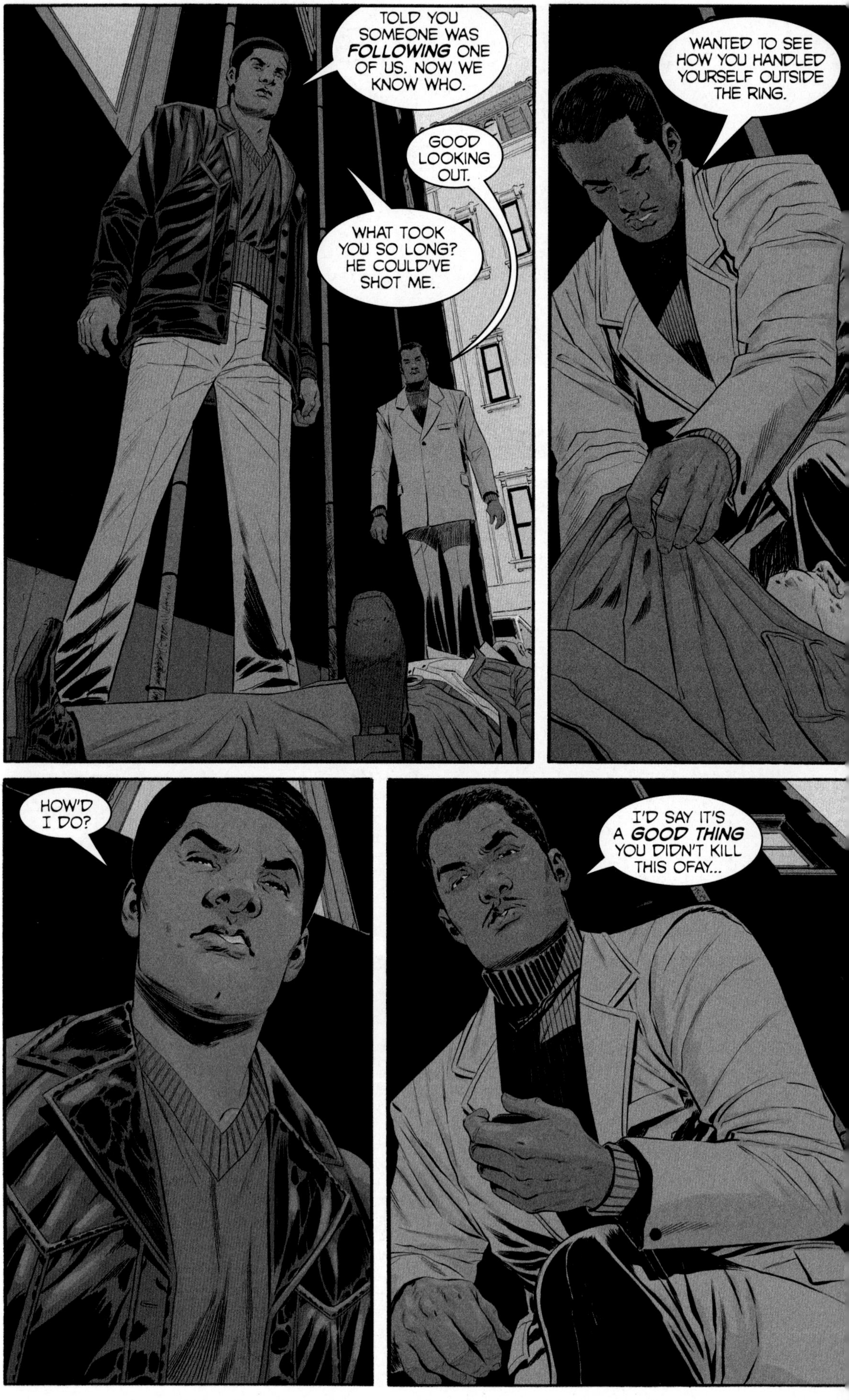
TOLD YOU SOMEONE WAS *FOLLOWING* ONE OF US. NOW WE KNOW WHO.
GOOD LOOKING OUT.
WHAT TOOK YOU SO LONG? HE COULD'VE SHOT ME.
WANTED TO SEE HOW YOU HANDLED YOURSELF OUTSIDE THE RING.
HOW'D I DO?
I'D SAY IT'S A *GOOD THING* YOU DIDN'T KILL THIS OFAY...

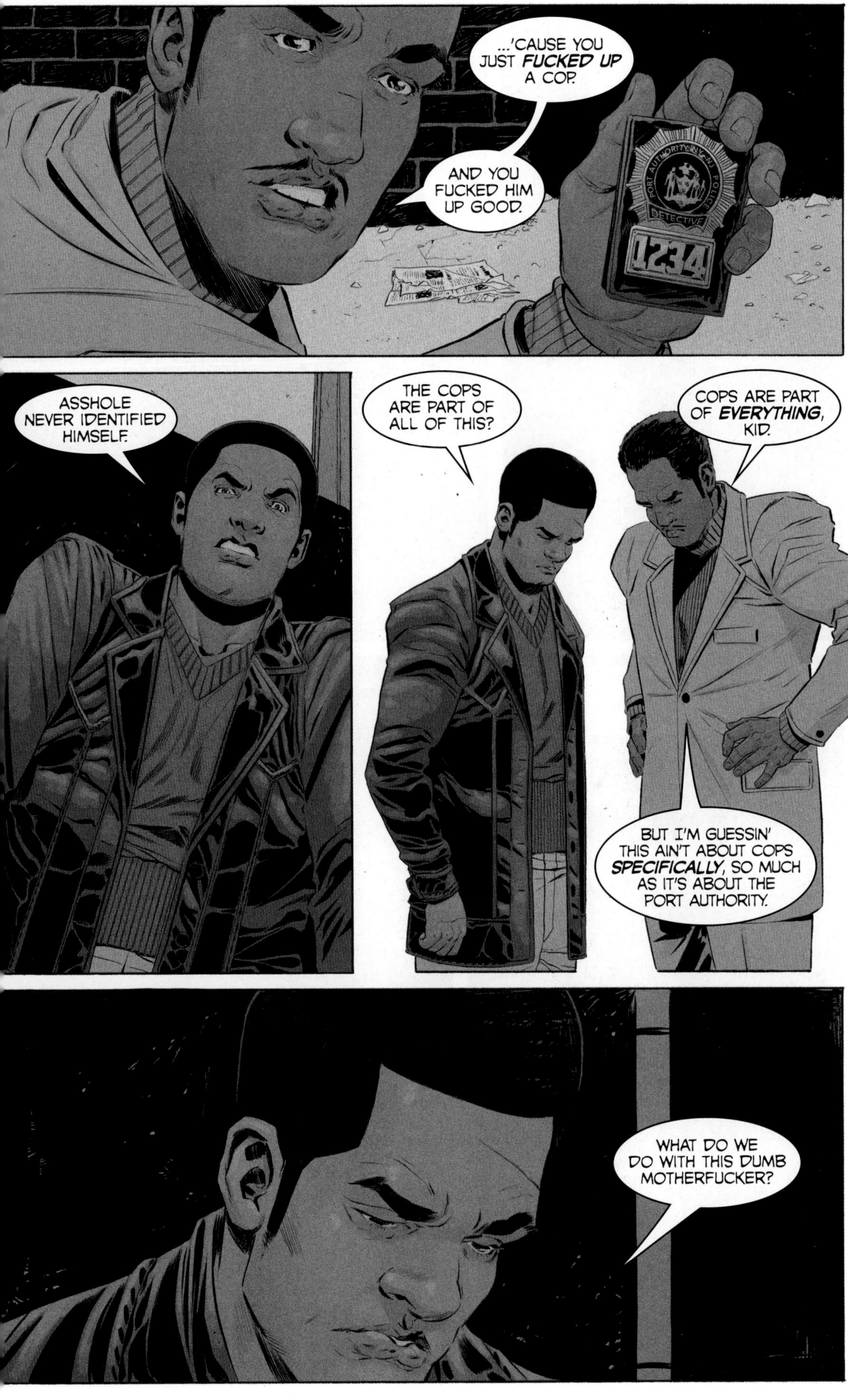
...'CAUSE YOU JUST FUCKED UP A COP.
AND YOU FUCKED HIM UP GOOD.
DETECTIVE
1234
ASSHOLE NEVER IDENTIFIED HIMSELF.
THE COPS ARE PART OF ALL OF THIS?
COPS ARE PART OF EVERYTHING, KID.
BUT I'M GUESSIN' THIS AIN'T ABOUT COPS SPECIFICALLY, SO MUCH AS IT'S ABOUT THE PORT AUTHORITY.
WHAT DO WE DO WITH THIS DUMB MOTHERFUCKER?

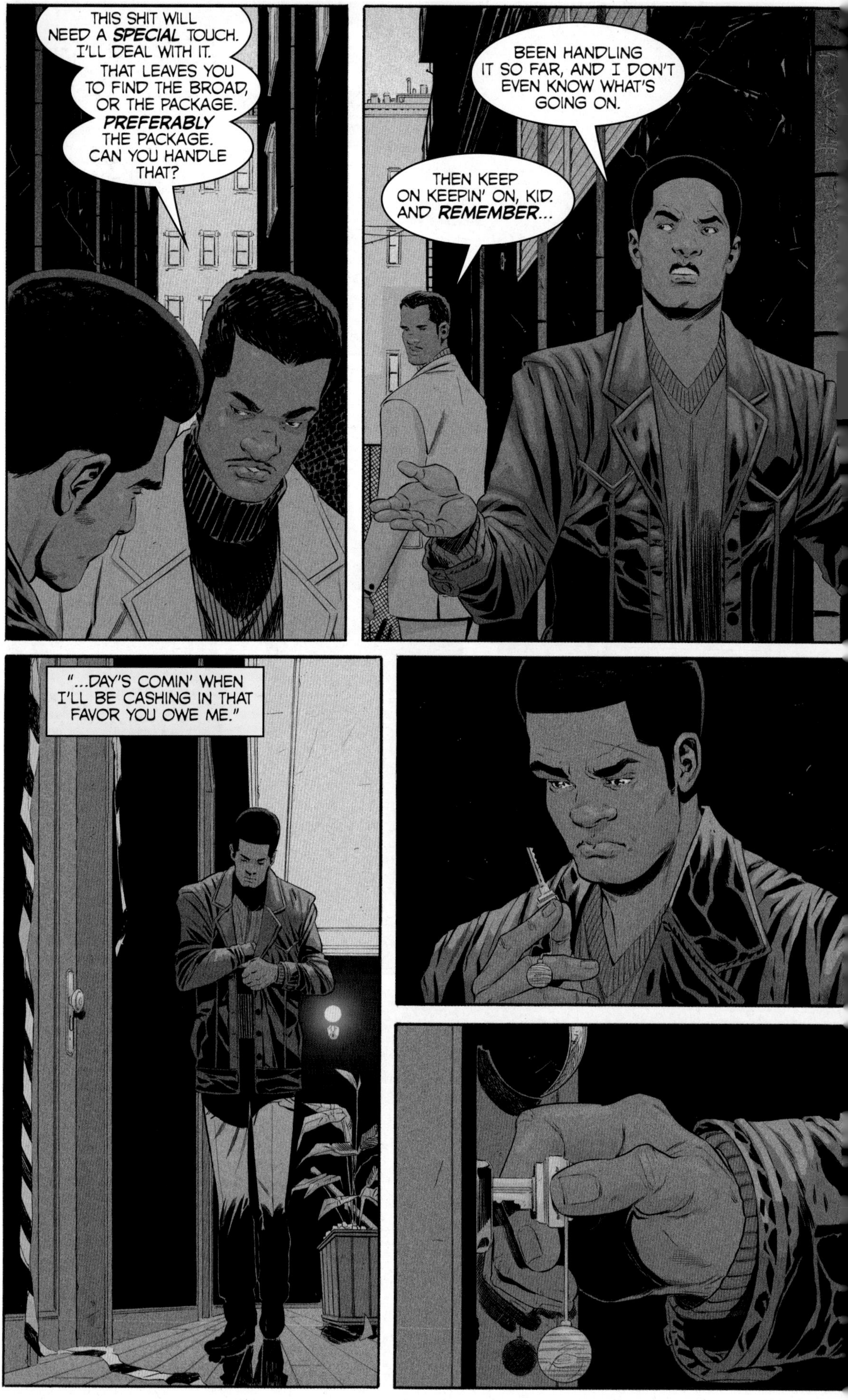
THIS SHIT WILL NEED A *SPECIAL* TOUCH. I'LL DEAL WITH IT.
THAT LEAVES YOU TO FIND THE BROAD, OR THE PACKAGE.
PREFERABLY THE PACKAGE. CAN YOU HANDLE THAT?
BEEN HANDLING IT SO FAR, AND I DON'T EVEN KNOW WHAT'S GOING ON.
THEN KEEP ON KEEPIN' ON, KID. AND *REMEMBER*...
"...DAY'S COMIN' WHEN I'LL BE CASHING IN THAT FAVOR YOU OWE ME."

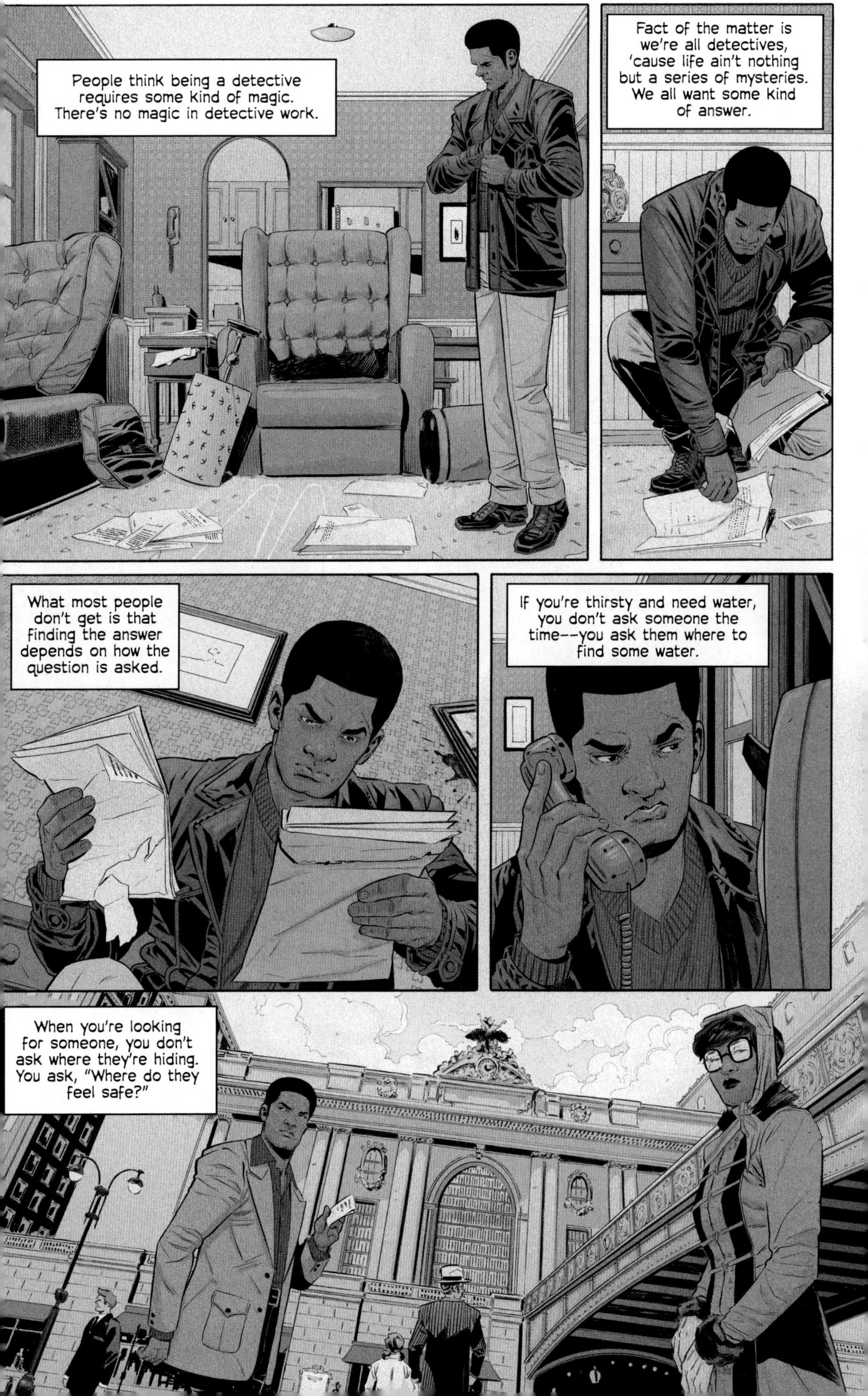
People think being a detective requires some kind of magic. There's no magic in detective work.
Fact of the matter is we're all detectives, 'cause life ain't nothing but a series of mysteries. We all want some kind of answer.
What most people don't get is that finding the answer depends on how the question is asked.
If you're thirsty and need water, you don't ask someone the time--you ask them where to find some water.
When you're looking for someone, you don't ask where they're hiding. You ask, "Where do they feel safe?"

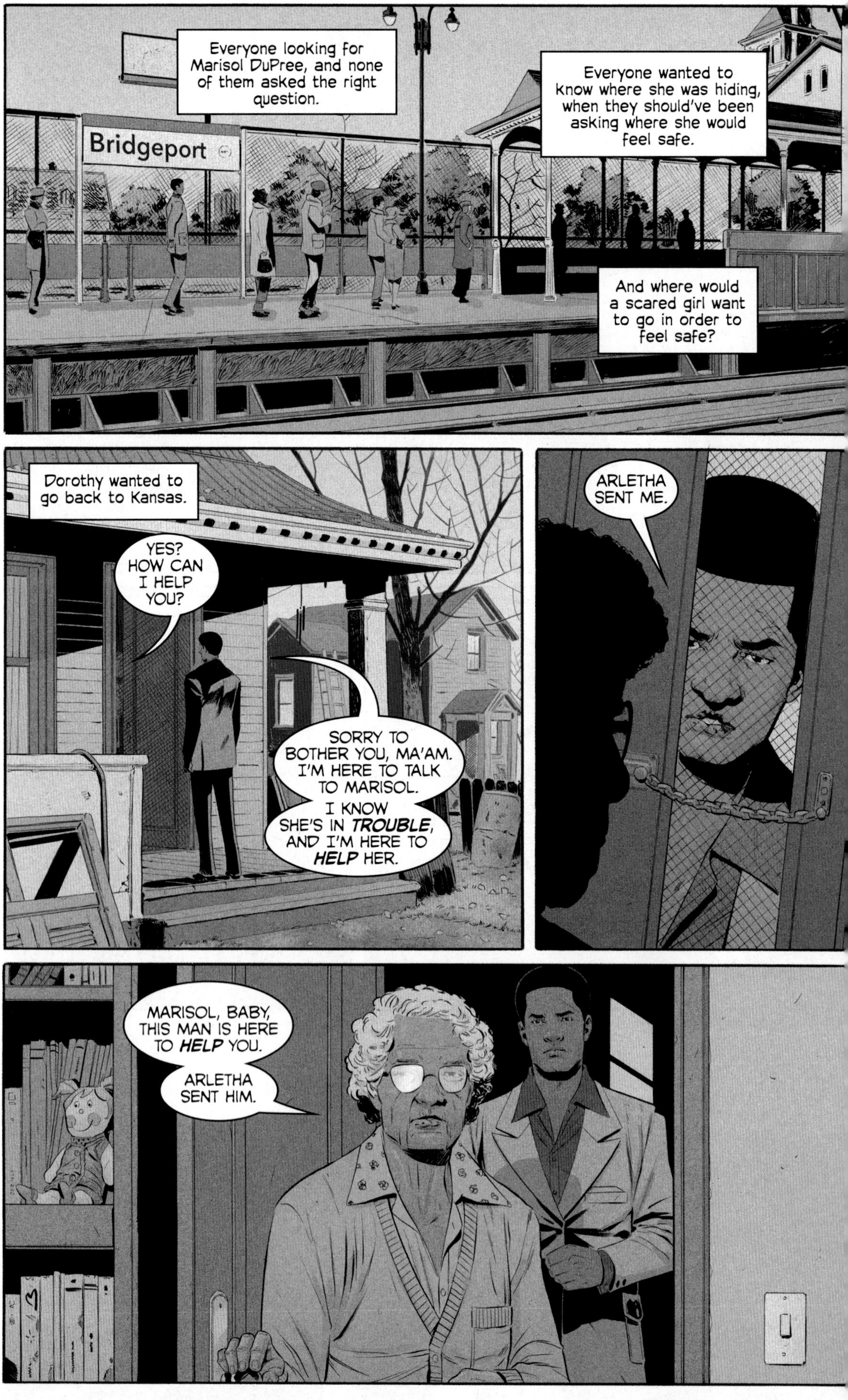
Everyone looking for Marisol DuPree, and none of them asked the right question.
Bridgeport
Everyone wanted to know where she was hiding, when they should've been asking where she would feel safe.
And where would a scared girl want to go in order to feel safe?
Dorothy wanted to go back to Kansas.
YES? HOW CAN I HELP YOU?
SORRY TO BOTHER YOU, MA'AM. I'M HERE TO TALK TO MARISOL.
I KNOW SHE'S IN *TROUBLE*, AND I'M HERE TO *HELP* HER.
ARLETHA SENT ME.
MARISOL, BABY, THIS MAN IS HERE TO *HELP* YOU.
ARLETHA SENT HIM.

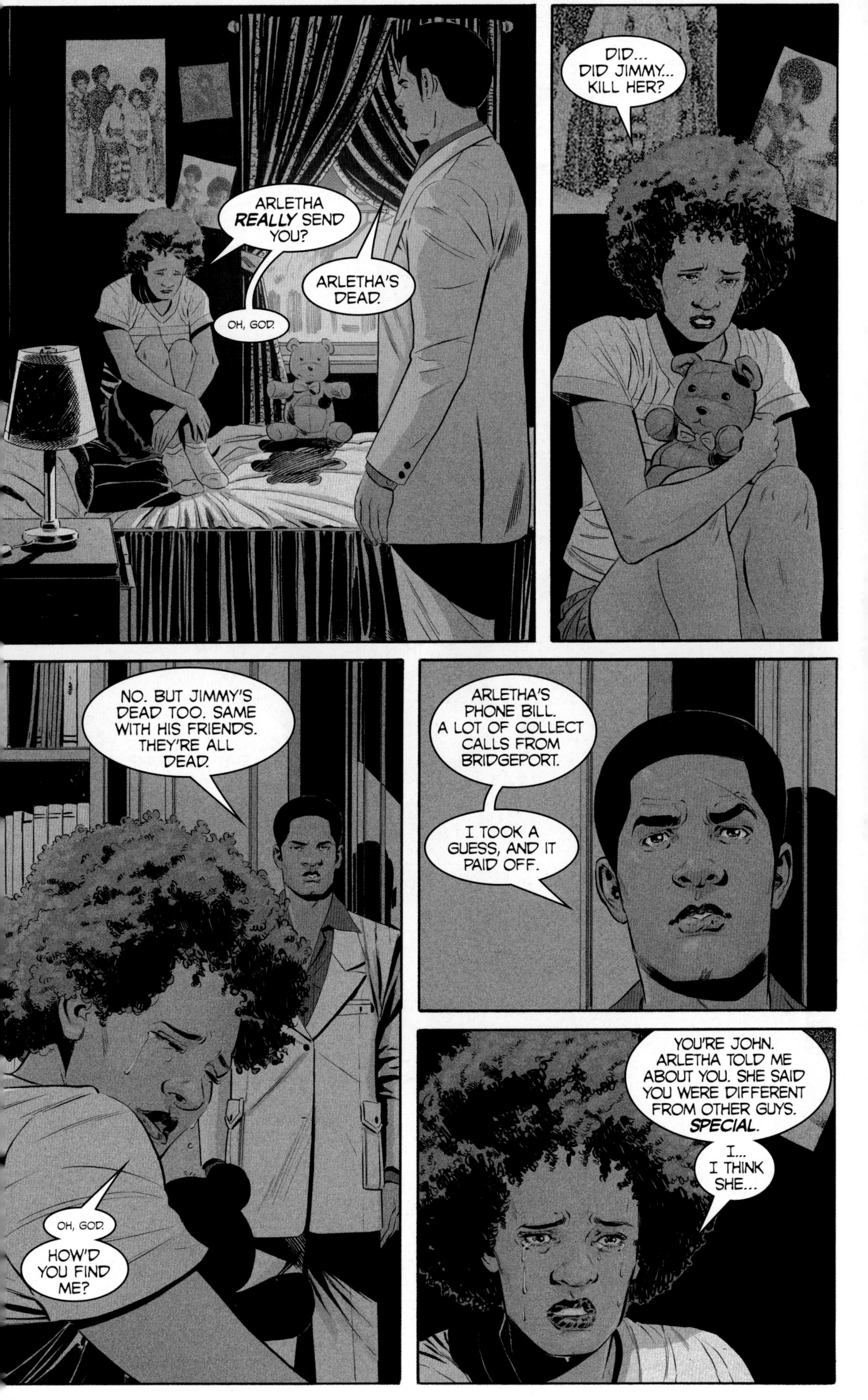
ARLETHA REALLY SEND YOU?
ARLETHA'S DEAD.
OH, GOD.
DID... DID JIMMY... KILL HER?
NO. BUT JIMMY'S DEAD TOO. SAME WITH HIS FRIENDS. THEY'RE ALL DEAD.
OH, GOD.
HOW'D YOU FIND ME?
ARLETHA'S PHONE BILL. A LOT OF COLLECT CALLS FROM BRIDGEPORT.
I TOOK A GUESS, AND IT PAID OFF.
YOU'RE JOHN. ARLETHA TOLD ME ABOUT YOU. SHE SAID YOU WERE DIFFERENT FROM OTHER GUYS. SPECIAL.
I... I THINK SHE...

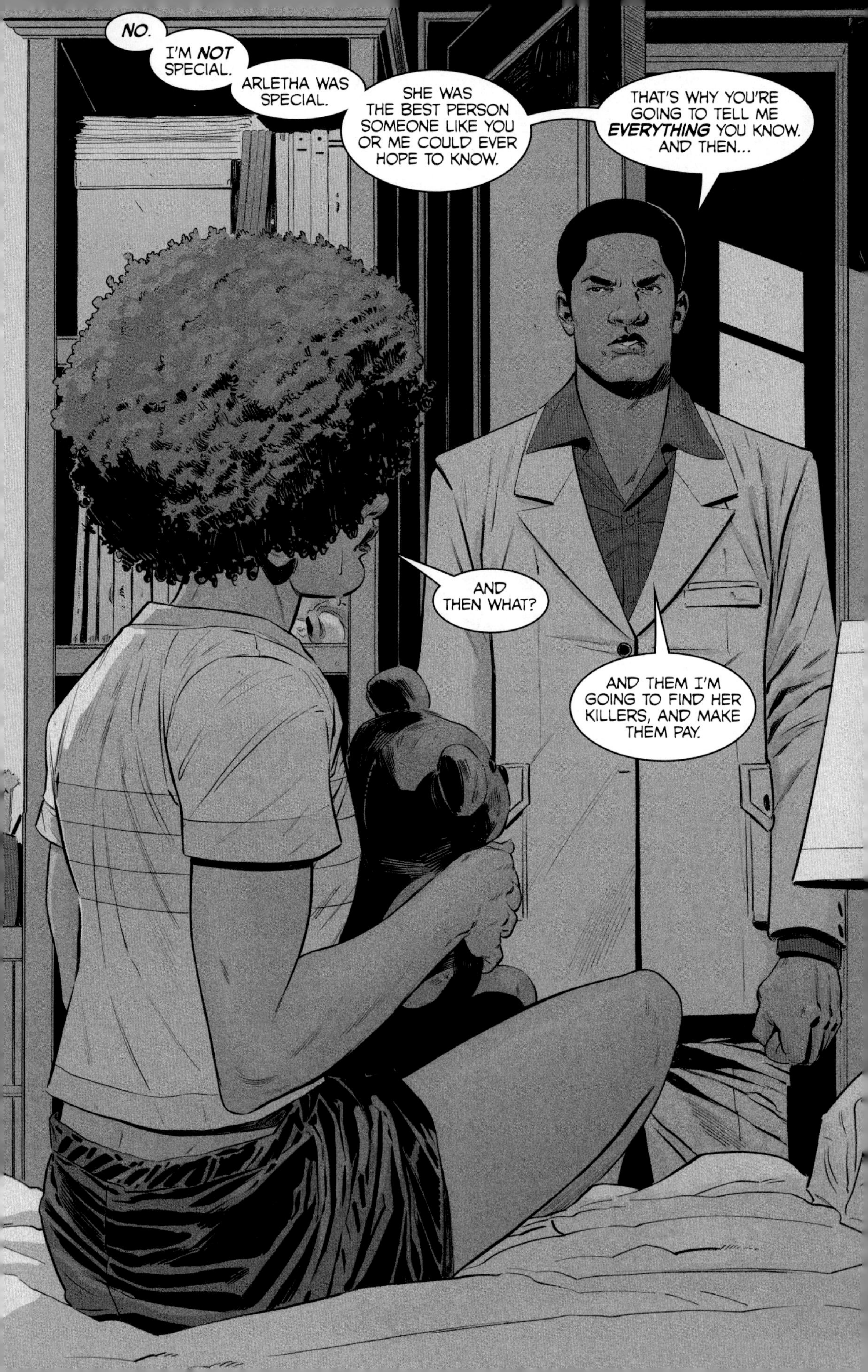
NO.
I'M *NOT* SPECIAL.
ARLETHA WAS SPECIAL.
SHE WAS THE BEST PERSON SOMEONE LIKE YOU OR ME COULD EVER HOPE TO KNOW.
THAT'S WHY YOU'RE GOING TO TELL ME *EVERYTHING* YOU KNOW. AND THEN...
AND THEN WHAT?
AND THEM I'M GOING TO FIND HER KILLERS, AND MAKE THEM PAY.

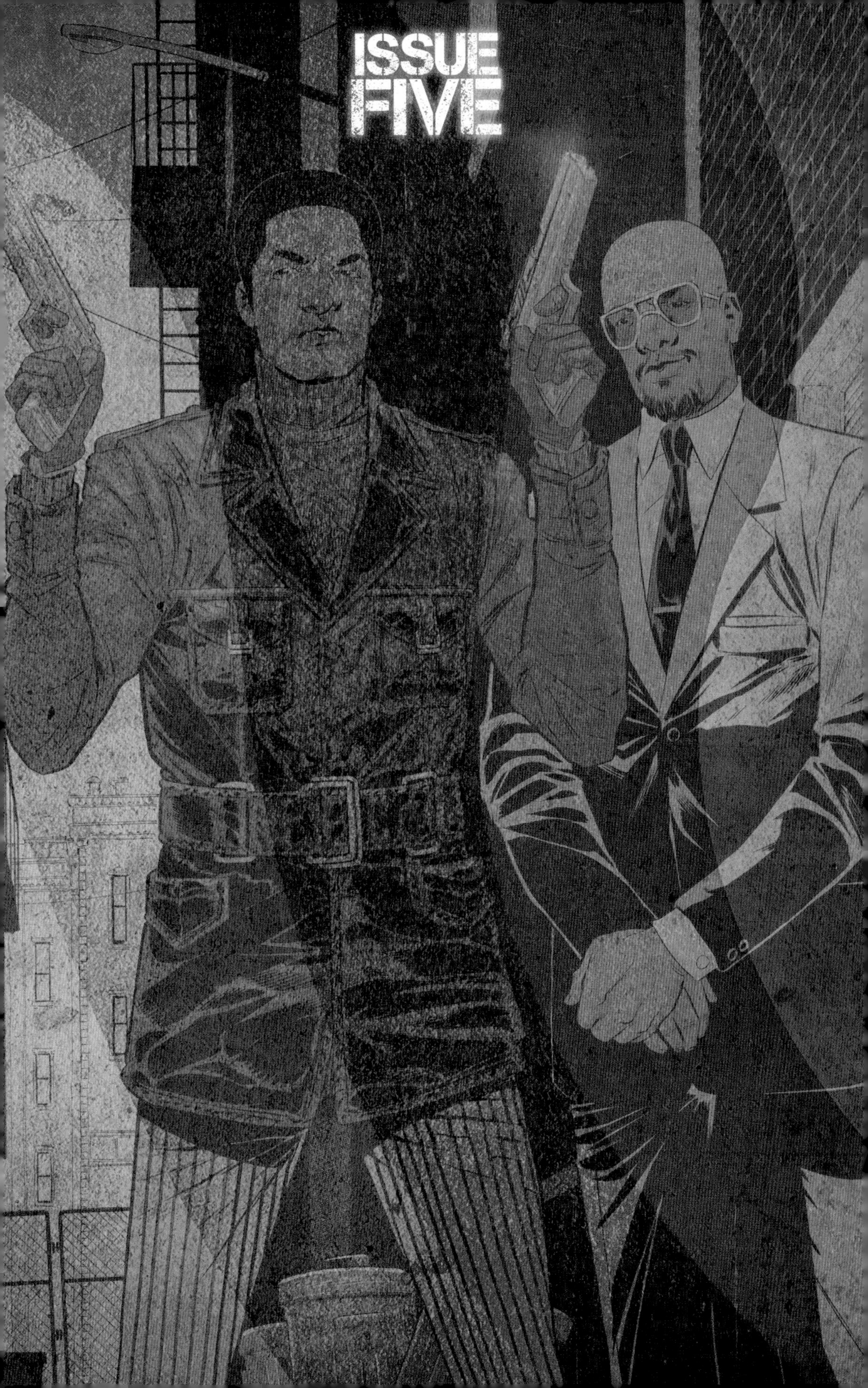
ISSUE
FIVE

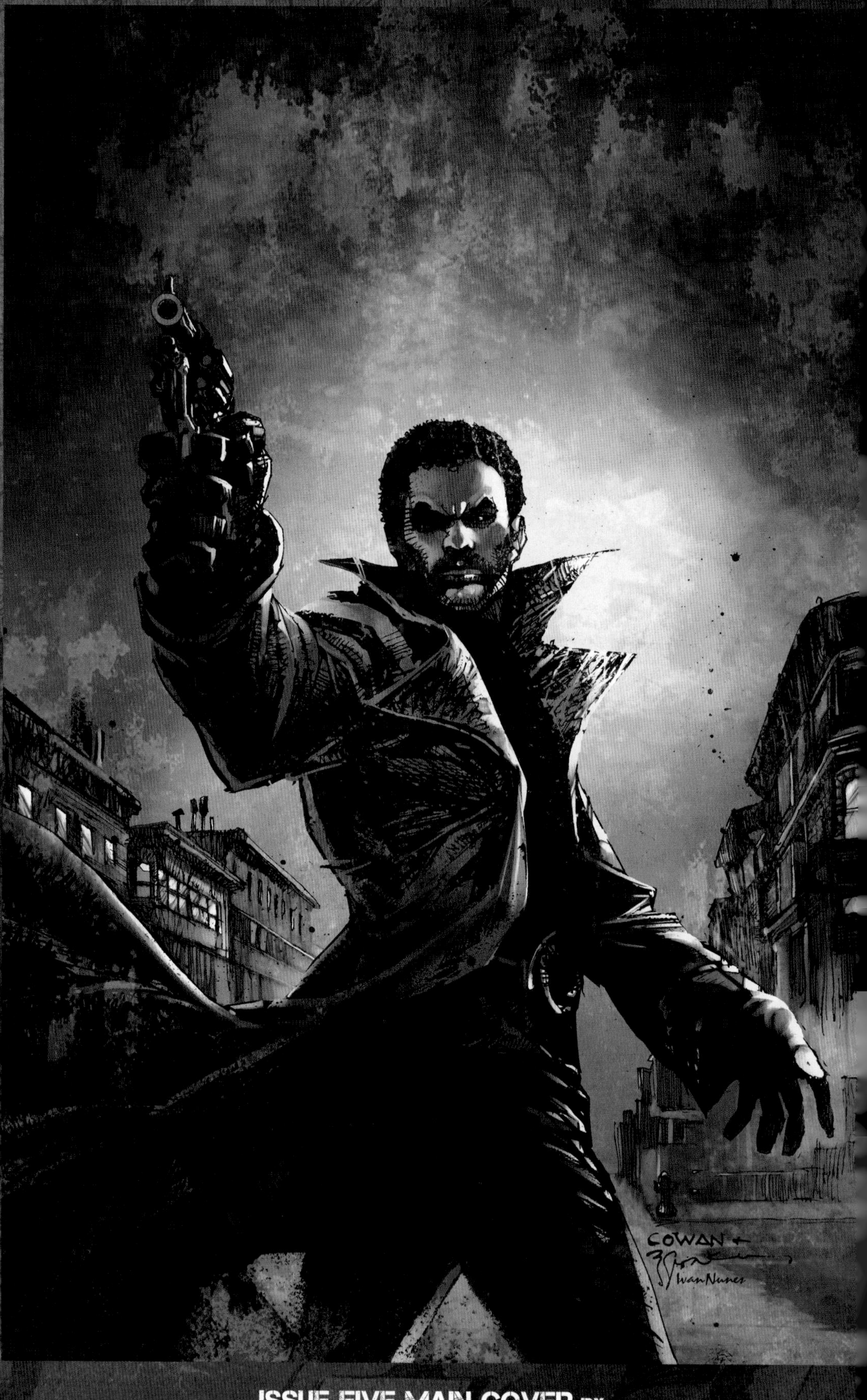
COWAN +
Ivan Nunes

ISSUE FIVE MAIN COVER BY
DENYS COWAN AND BILL SIENKIEWICZ
COLORS BY IVAN NUNES

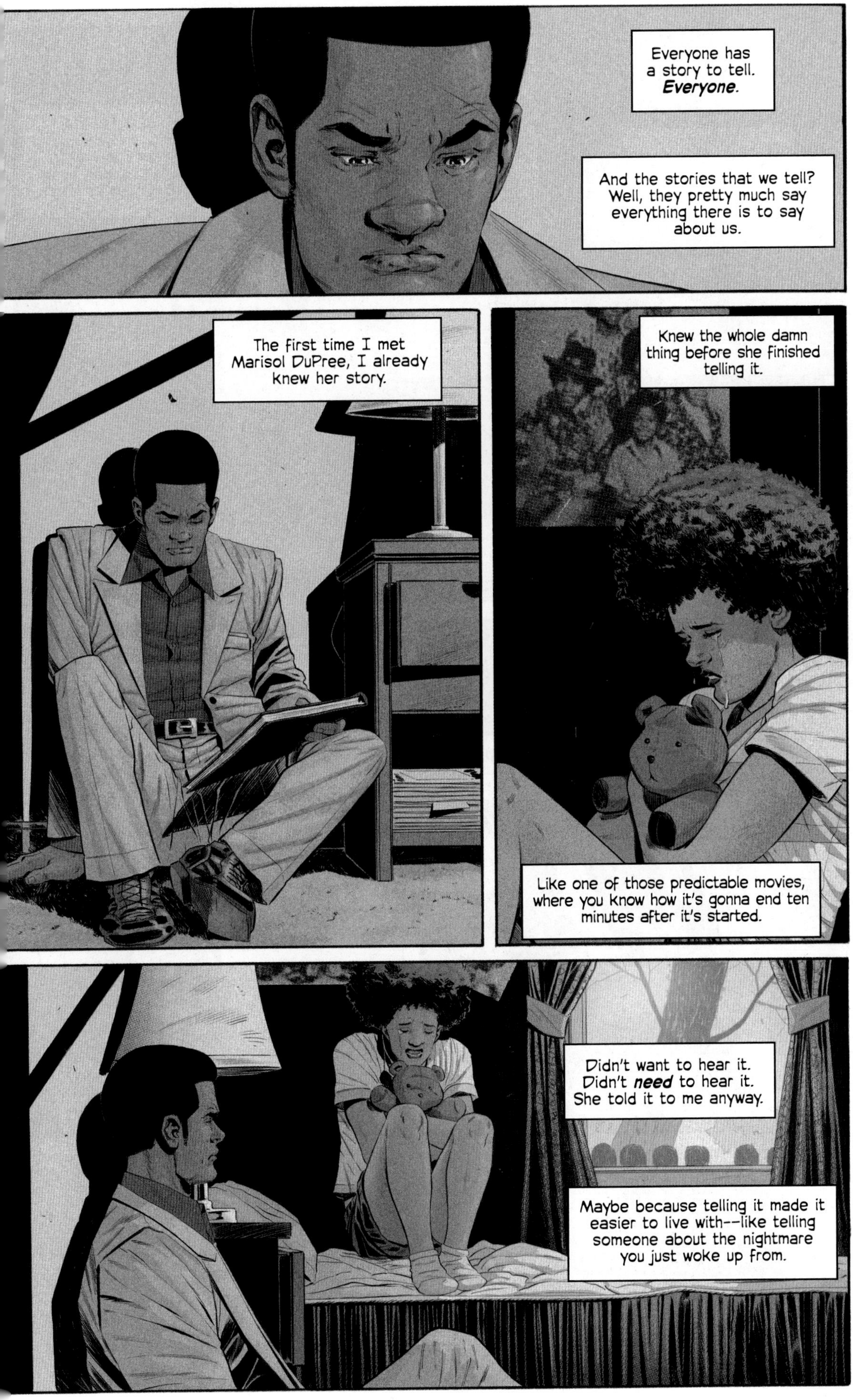
Everyone has a story to tell. *Everyone*.
And the stories that we tell? Well, they pretty much say everything there is to say about us.
The first time I met Marisol DuPree, I already knew her story.
Knew the whole damn thing before she finished telling it.
Like one of those predictable movies, where you know how it's gonna end ten minutes after it's started.
Didn't want to hear it. Didn't *need* to hear it. She told it to me anyway.
Maybe because telling it made it easier to live with--like telling someone about the nightmare you just woke up from.

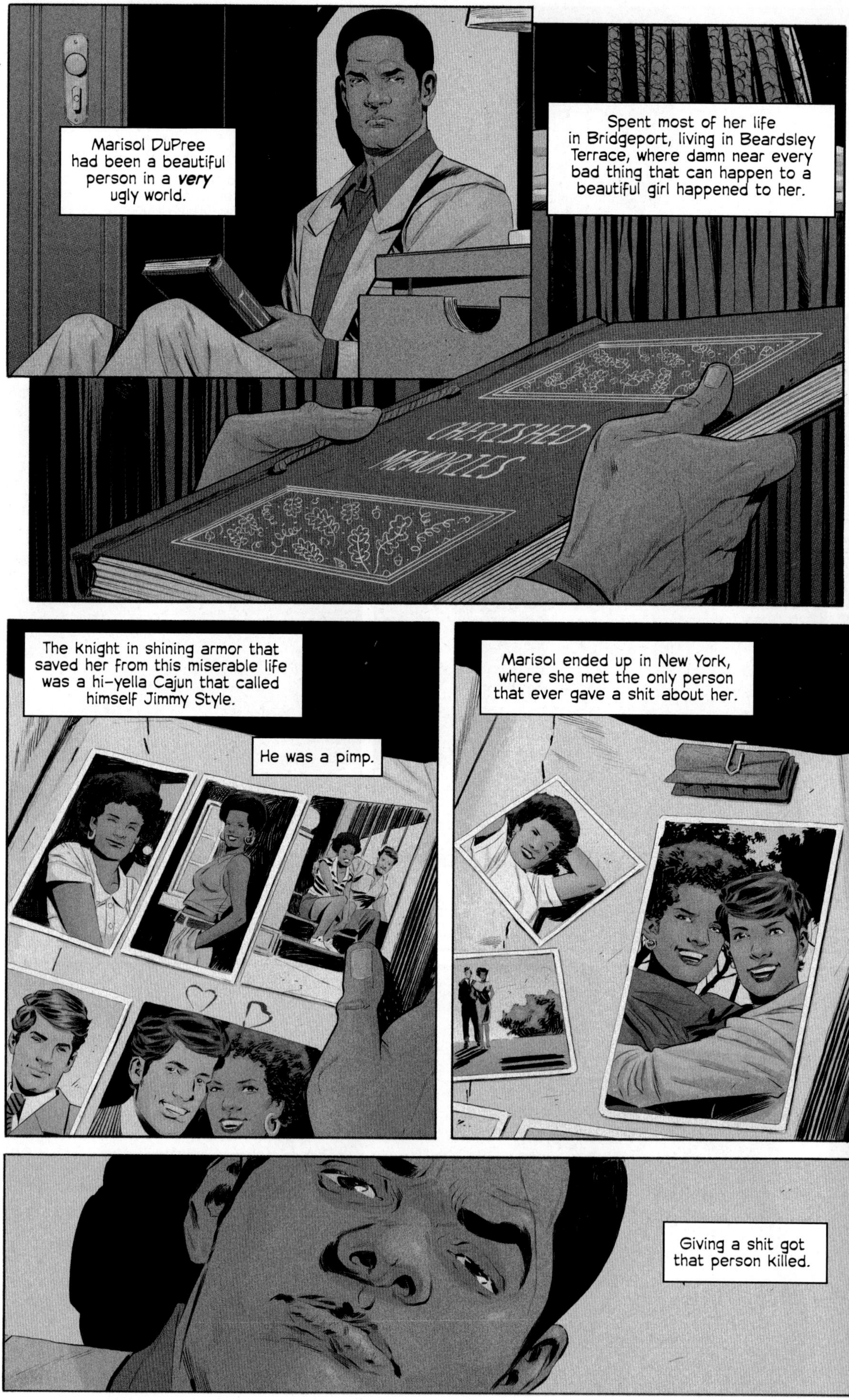
Marisol DuPree had been a beautiful person in a *very* ugly world.
Spent most of her life in Bridgeport, living in Beardsley Terrace, where damn near every bad thing that can happen to a beautiful girl happened to her.
CHERISHED MEMORIES
The knight in shining armor that saved her from this miserable life was a hi-yella Cajun that called himself Jimmy Style.
He was a pimp.
Marisol ended up in New York, where she met the only person that ever gave a shit about her.
Giving a shit got that person killed.

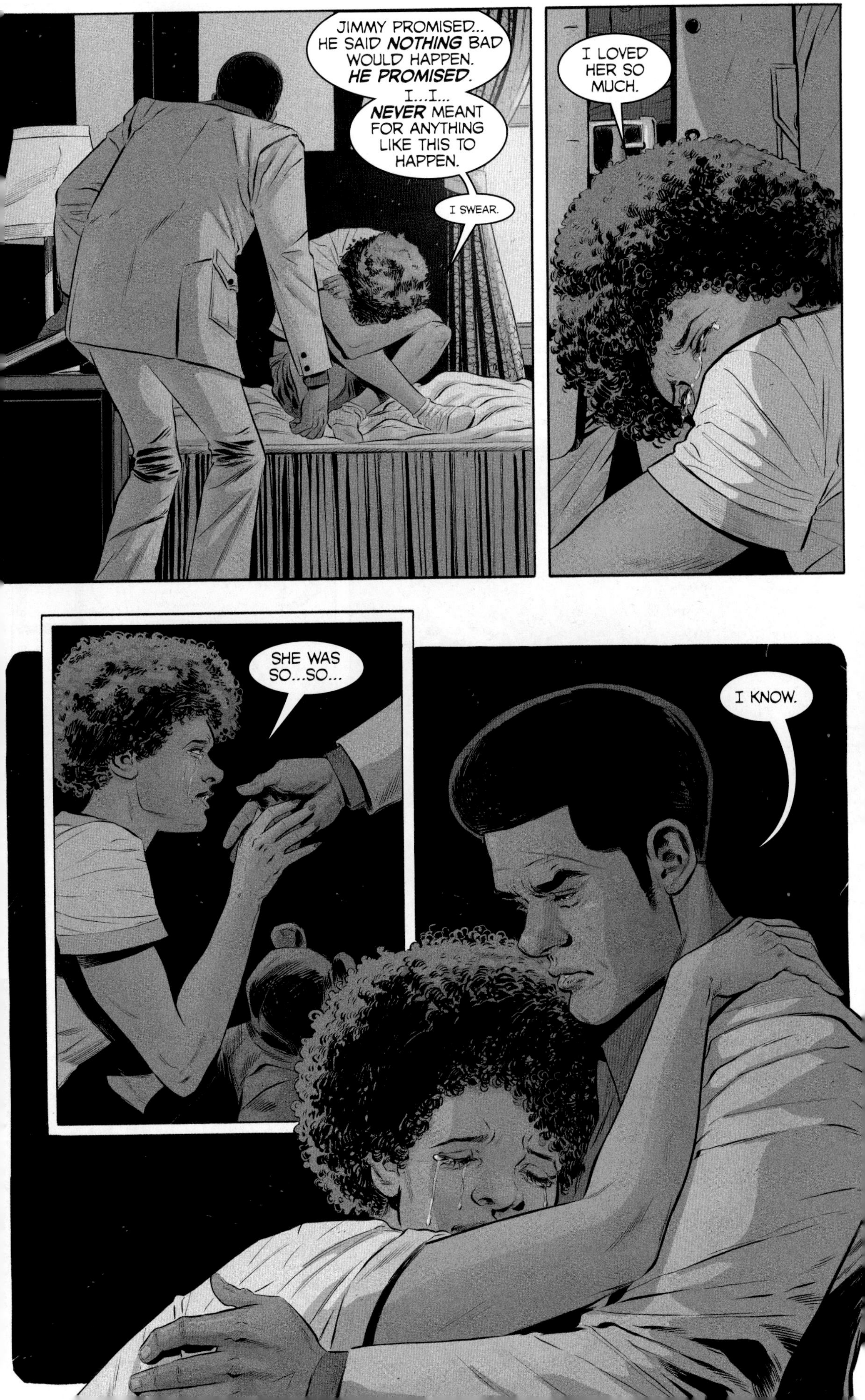
JIMMY PROMISED... HE SAID NOTHING BAD WOULD HAPPEN. HE PROMISED.
I...I... NEVER MEANT FOR ANYTHING LIKE THIS TO HAPPEN.
I SWEAR.
I LOVED HER SO MUCH.
SHE WAS SO...SO...
I KNOW.

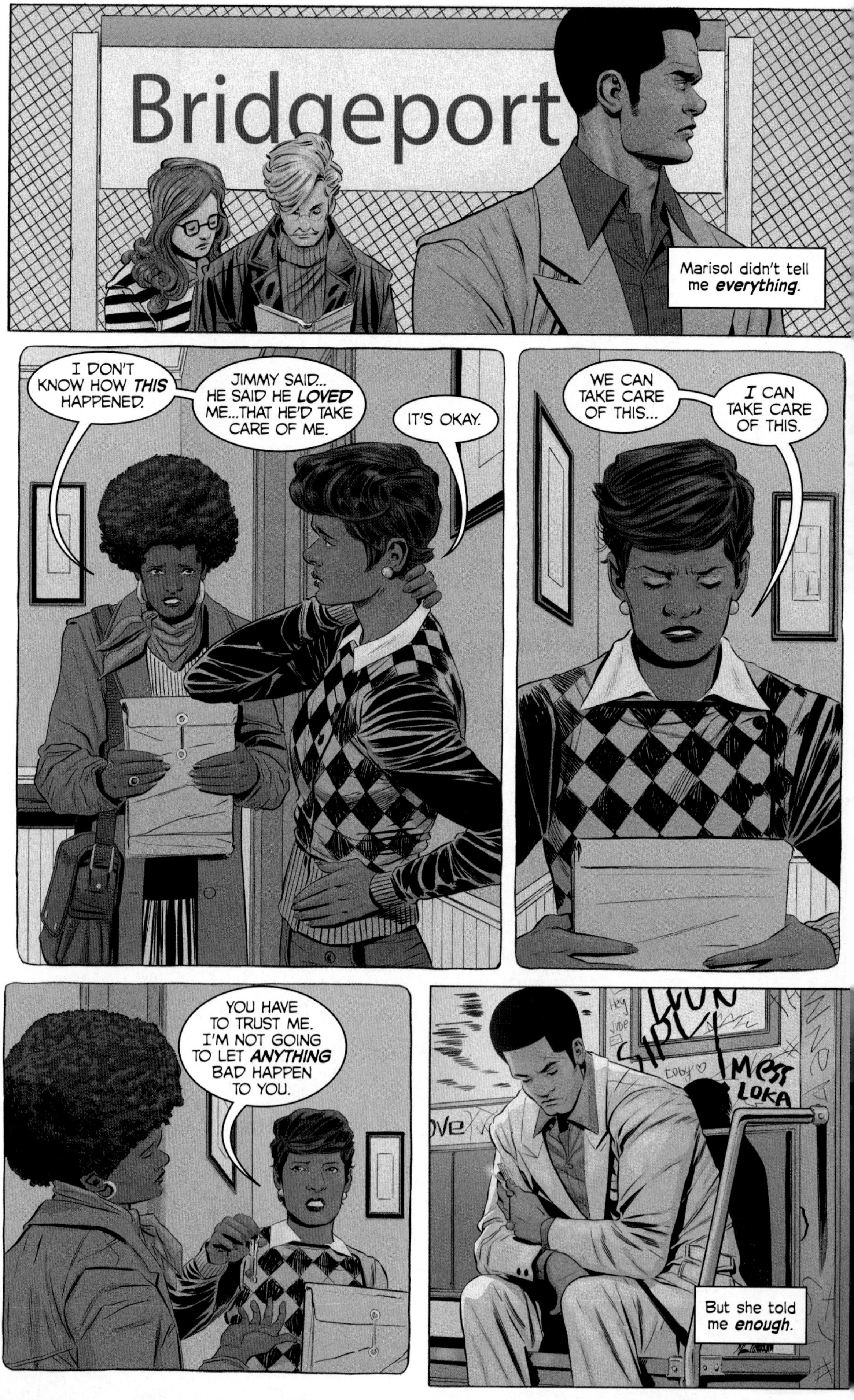
Bridgeport
Marisol didn't tell me *everything*.
I DON'T KNOW HOW *THIS* HAPPENED.
JIMMY SAID... HE SAID HE *LOVED* ME...THAT HE'D TAKE CARE OF ME.
IT'S OKAY.
WE CAN TAKE CARE OF THIS...
I CAN TAKE CARE OF THIS.
YOU HAVE TO TRUST ME. I'M NOT GOING TO LET *ANYTHING* BAD HAPPEN TO YOU.
But she told me *enough*.

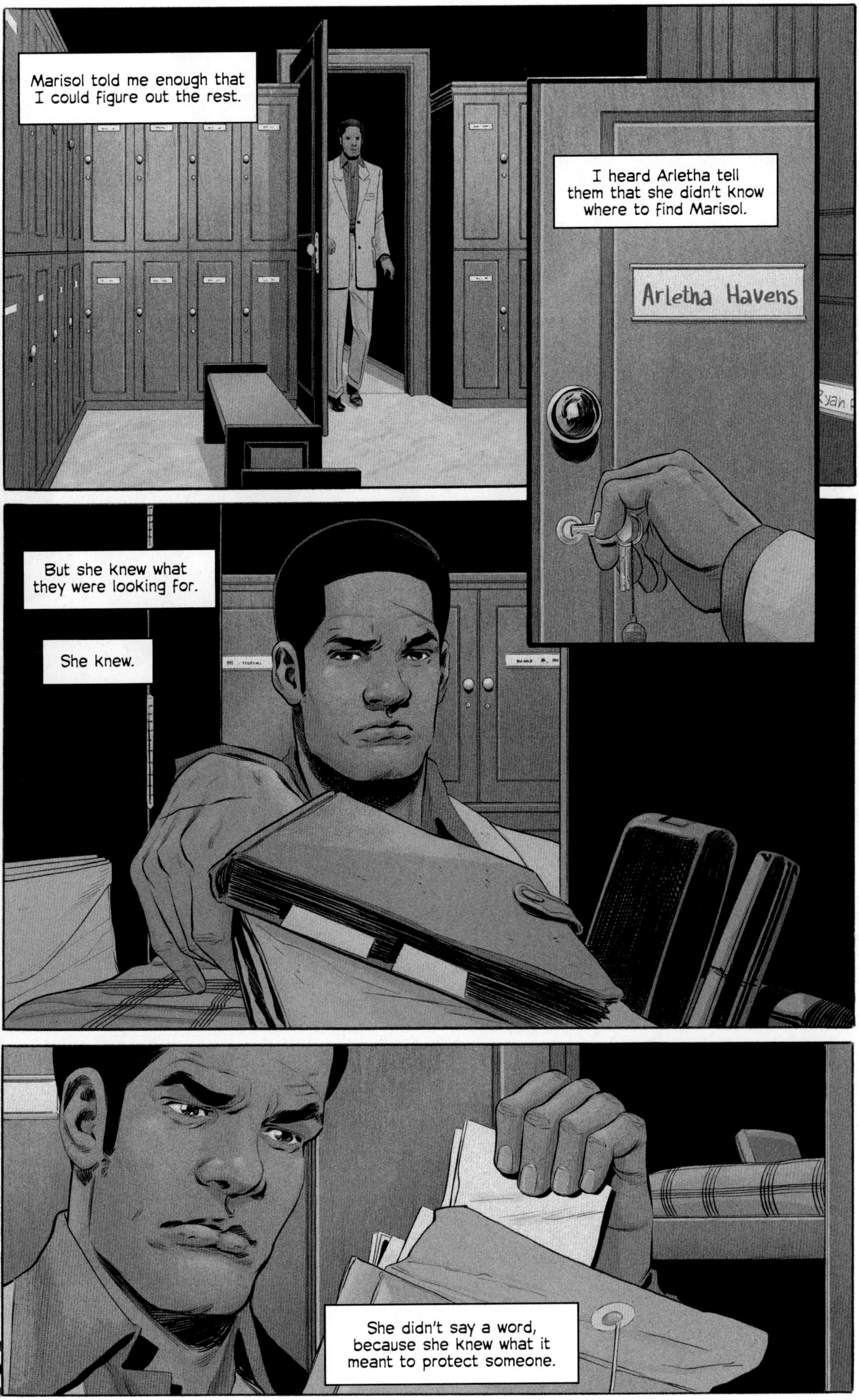
Marisol told me enough that I could figure out the rest.
I heard Arletha tell them that she didn't know where to find Marisol.
Arletha Havens
But she knew what they were looking for.
She knew.
She didn't say a word, because she knew what it meant to protect someone.

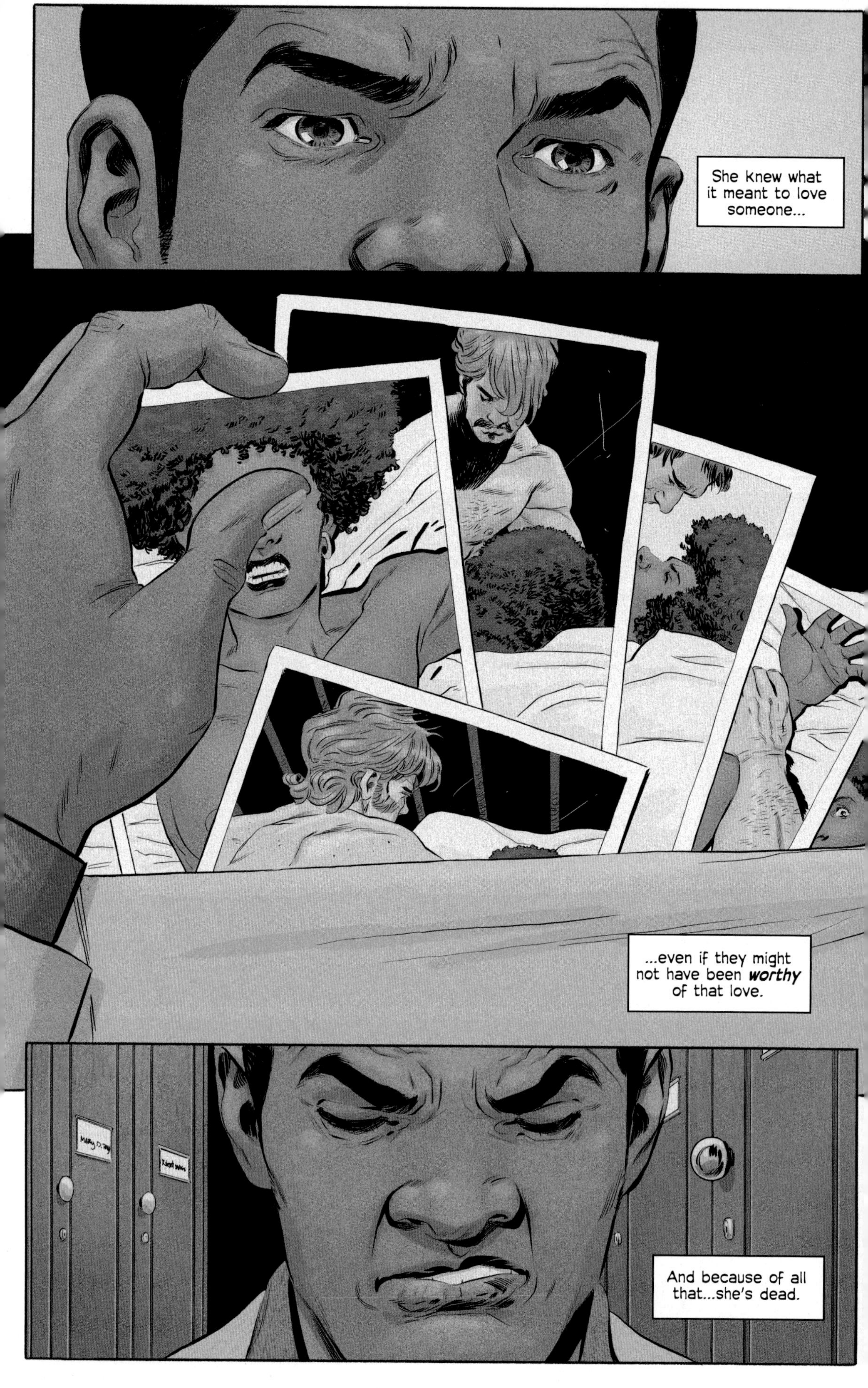
She knew what it meant to love someone...
...even if they might not have been *worthy* of that love.
And because of all that...she's dead.

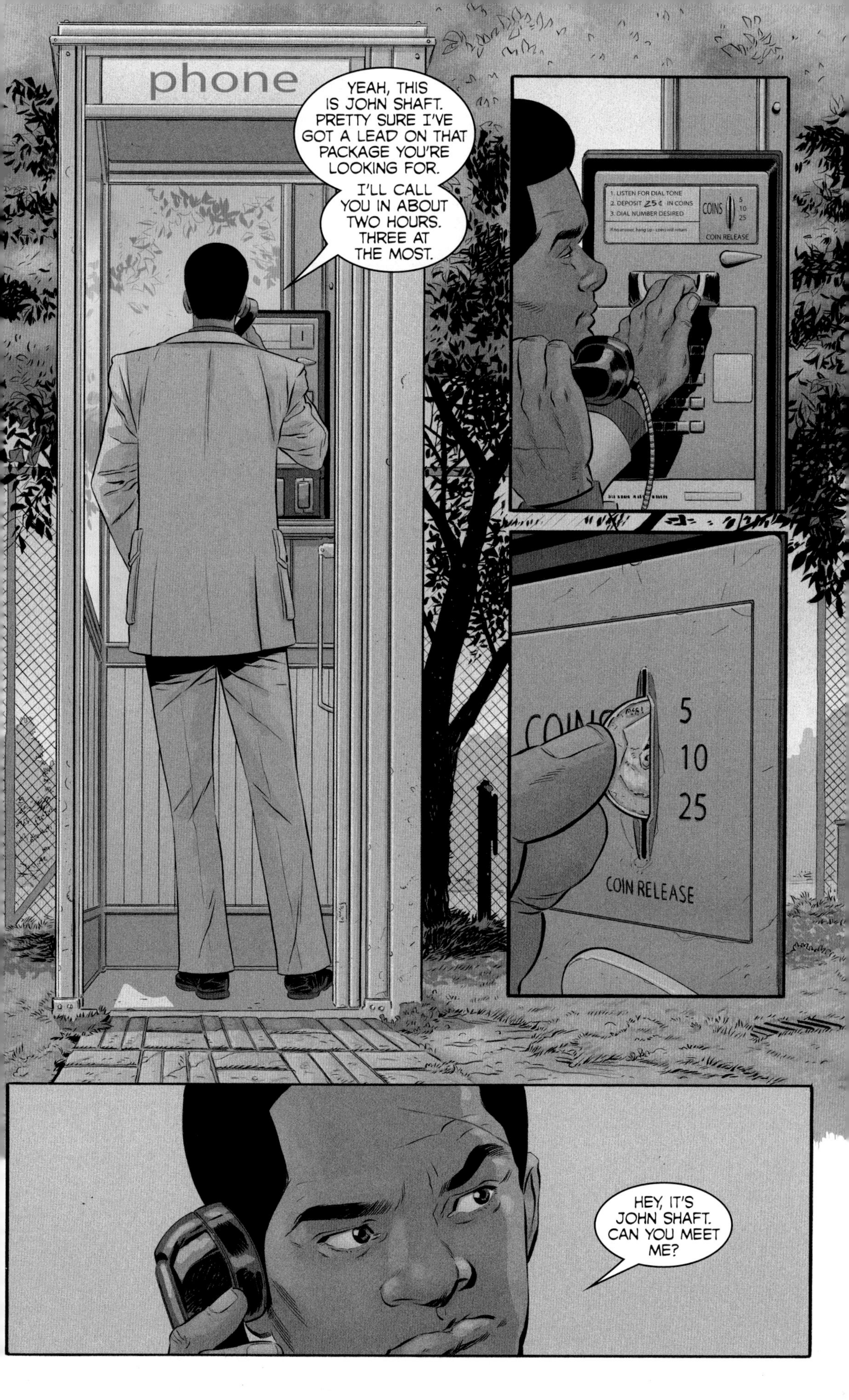
phone
YEAH, THIS IS JOHN SHAFT. PRETTY SURE I'VE GOT A LEAD ON THAT PACKAGE YOU'RE LOOKING FOR.
I'LL CALL YOU IN ABOUT TWO HOURS. THREE AT THE MOST.
1. LISTEN FOR DIAL TONE
2. DEPOSIT 25¢ IN COINS
3. DIAL NUMBER DESIRED
COINS 5 10 25
COIN RELEASE
COINS 5 10 25
COIN RELEASE
HEY, IT'S JOHN SHAFT. CAN YOU MEET ME?

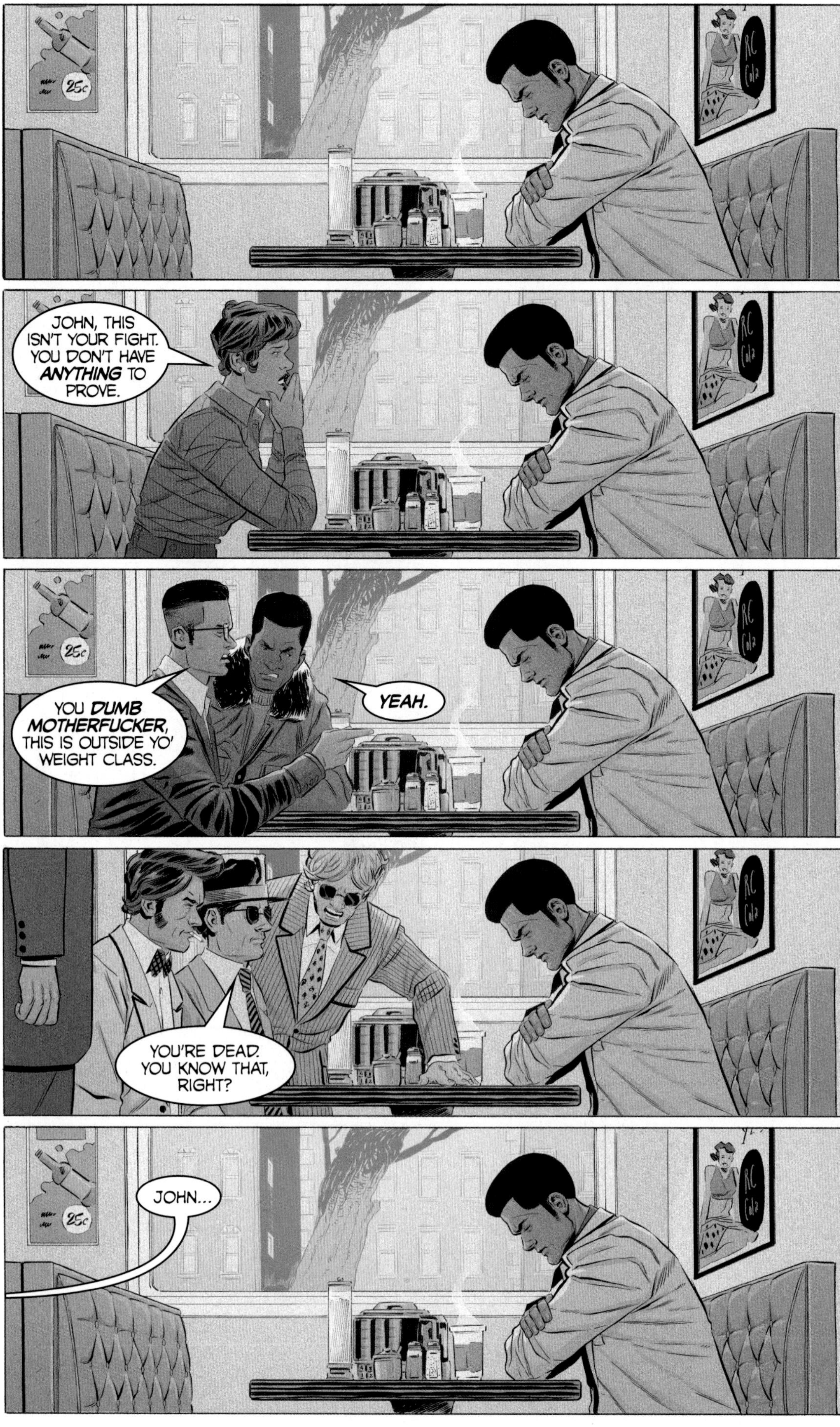
JOHN, THIS ISN'T YOUR FIGHT. YOU DON'T HAVE *ANYTHING* TO PROVE.
25¢
RC Cola
YOU *DUMB MOTHERFUCKER*, THIS IS OUTSIDE YO' WEIGHT CLASS.
YEAH.
YOU'RE DEAD. YOU KNOW THAT, RIGHT?
JOHN...

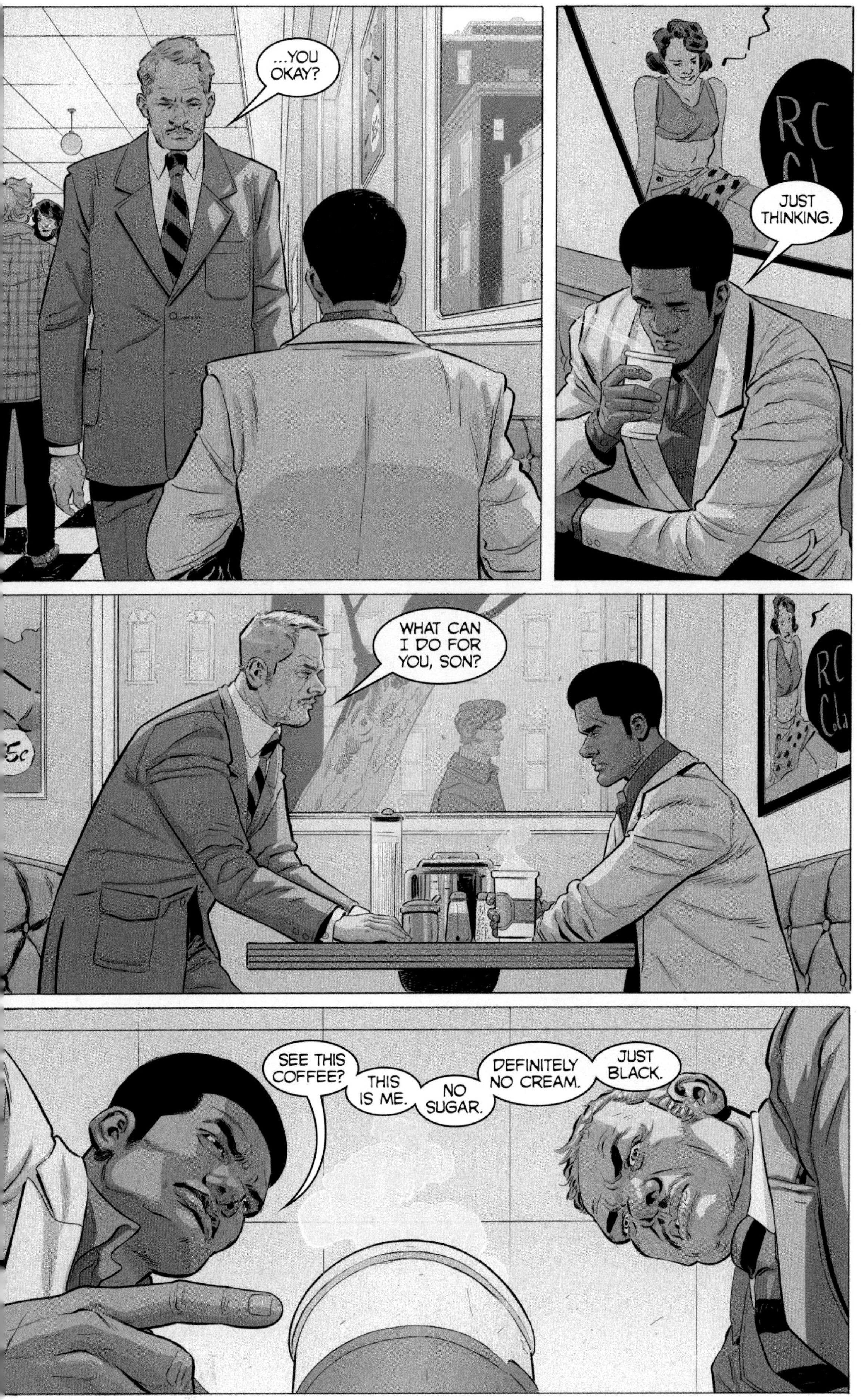
...YOU OKAY?
JUST THINKING.
RC Cola
WHAT CAN I DO FOR YOU, SON?
SEE THIS COFFEE?
THIS IS ME.
NO SUGAR.
DEFINITELY NO CREAM.
JUST BLACK.

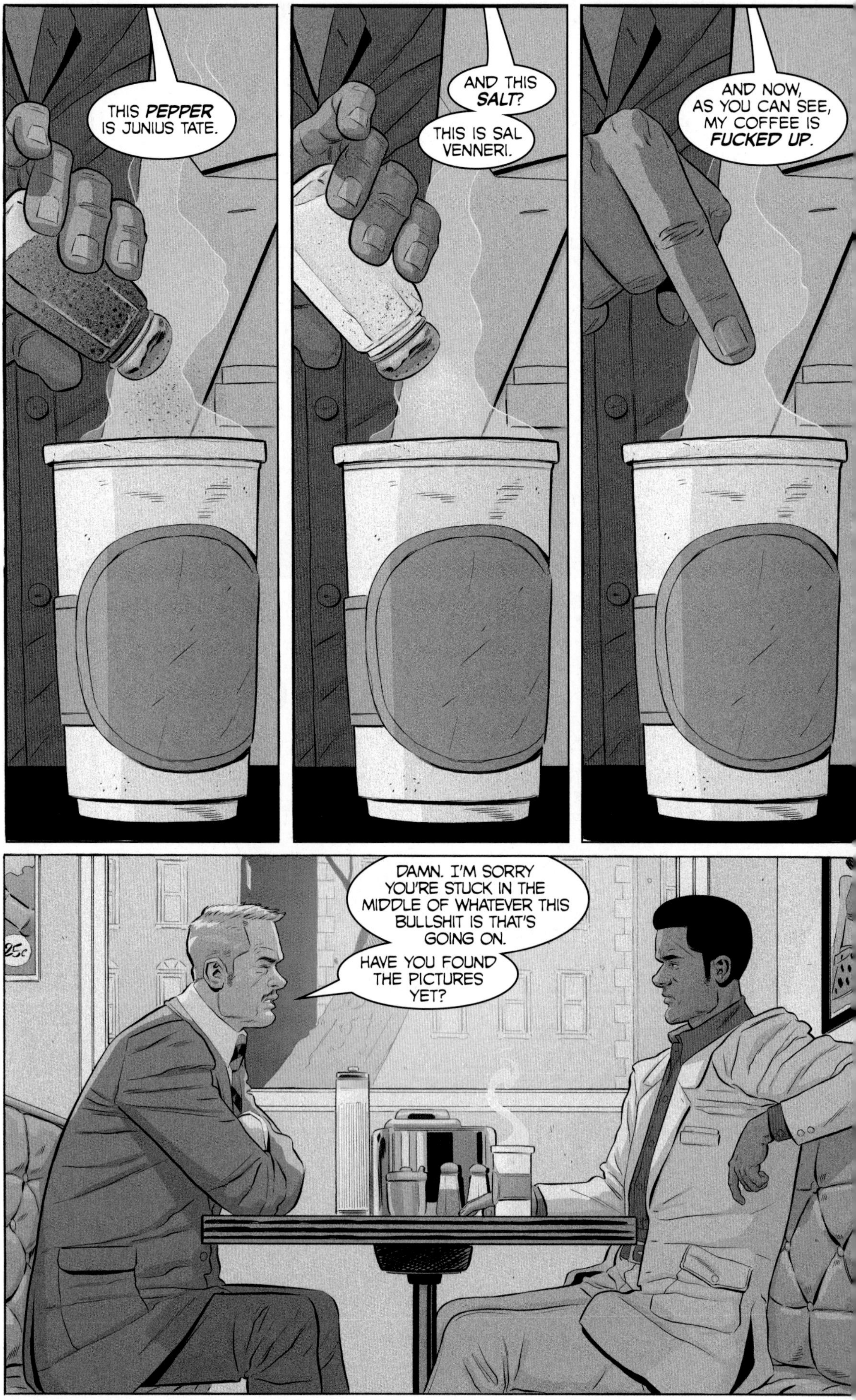
THIS PEPPER IS JUNIUS TATE.
AND THIS SALT?
THIS IS SAL VENNERI.
AND NOW, AS YOU CAN SEE, MY COFFEE IS FUCKED UP.
DAMN. I'M SORRY YOU'RE STUCK IN THE MIDDLE OF WHATEVER THIS BULLSHIT IS THAT'S GOING ON.
HAVE YOU FOUND THE PICTURES YET?
25¢

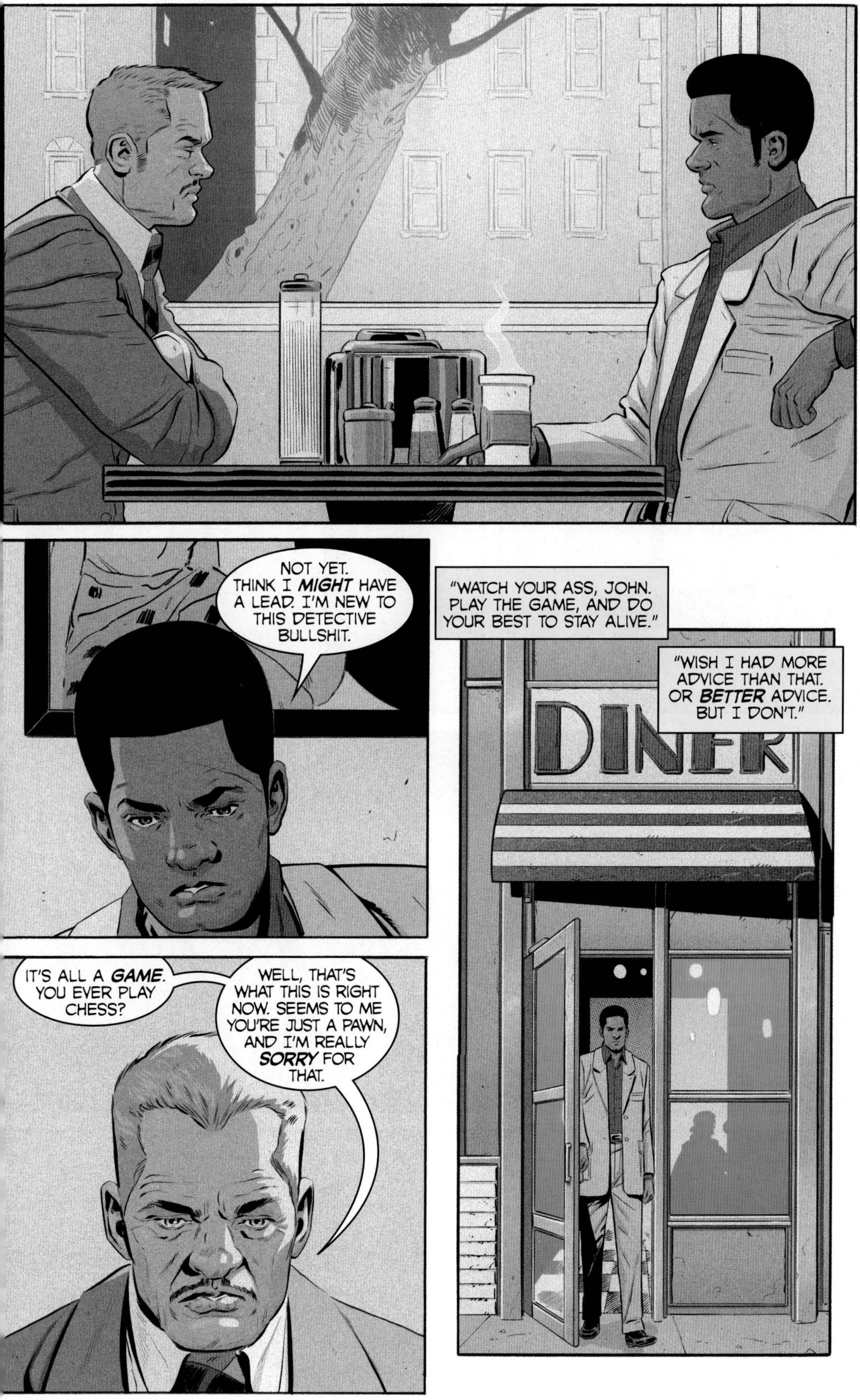
NOT YET. THINK I MIGHT HAVE A LEAD. I'M NEW TO THIS DETECTIVE BULLSHIT.
IT'S ALL A GAME. YOU EVER PLAY CHESS?
WELL, THAT'S WHAT THIS IS RIGHT NOW. SEEMS TO ME YOU'RE JUST A PAWN, AND I'M REALLY SORRY FOR THAT.
"WATCH YOUR ASS, JOHN. PLAY THE GAME, AND DO YOUR BEST TO STAY ALIVE."
"WISH I HAD MORE ADVICE THAN THAT. OR BETTER ADVICE. BUT I DON'T."
DINER

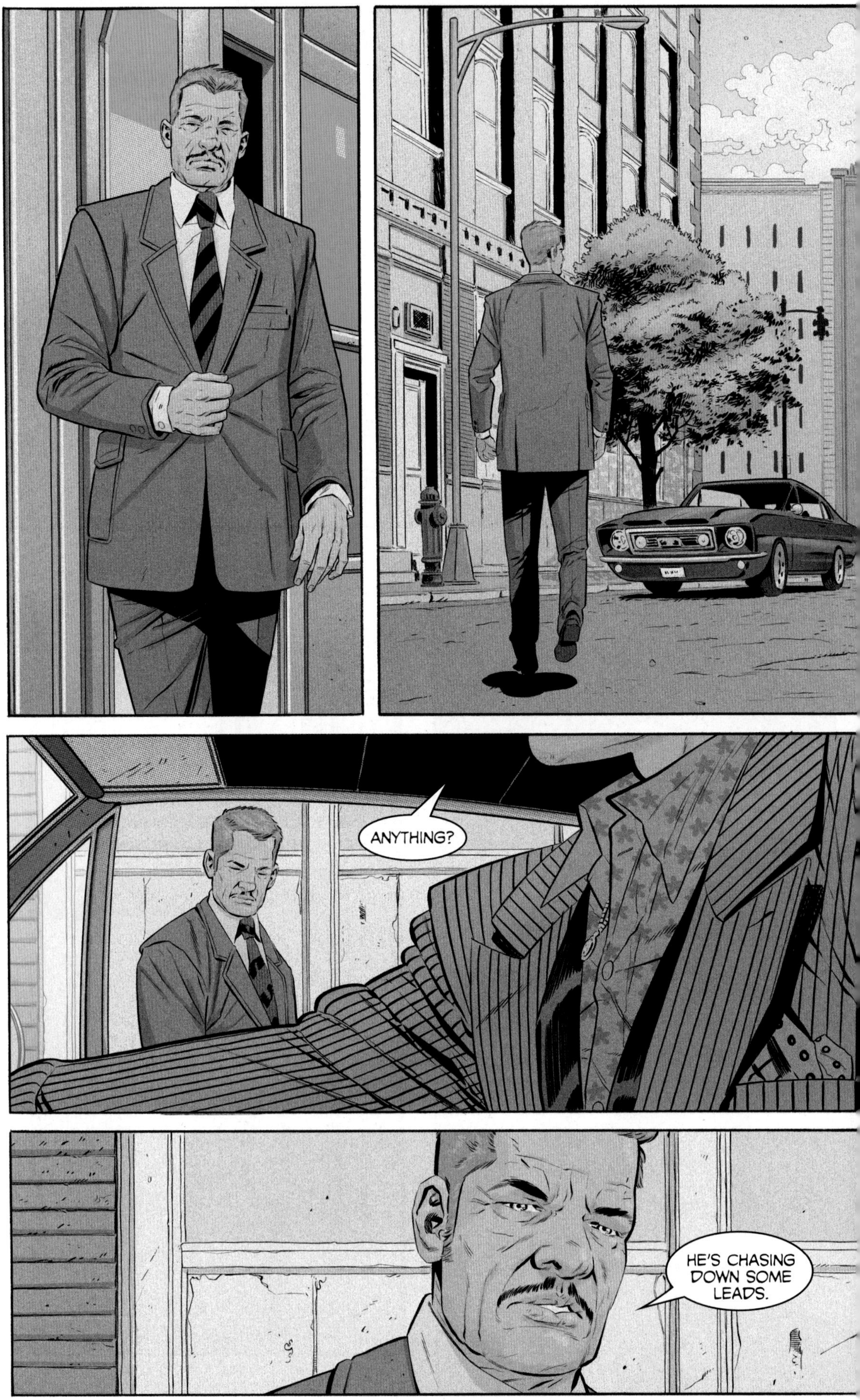
ANYTHING?
HE'S CHASING DOWN SOME LEADS.

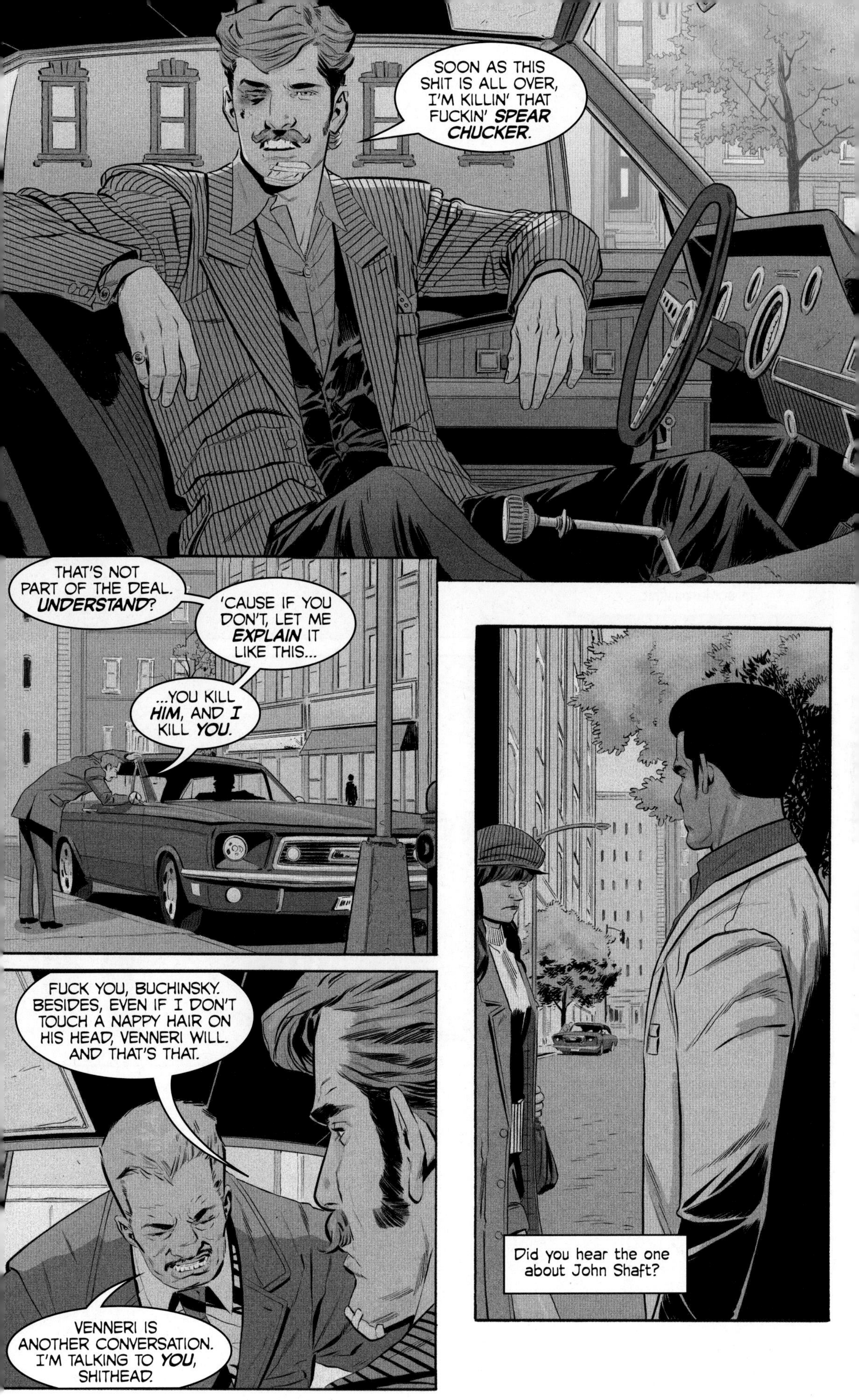
SOON AS THIS SHIT IS ALL OVER, I'M KILLIN' THAT FUCKIN' SPEAR CHUCKER.
THAT'S NOT PART OF THE DEAL. UNDERSTAND?
'CAUSE IF YOU DON'T, LET ME EXPLAIN IT LIKE THIS...
...YOU KILL HIM, AND I KILL YOU.
FUCK YOU, BUCHINSKY. BESIDES, EVEN IF I DON'T TOUCH A NAPPY HAIR ON HIS HEAD, VENNERI WILL. AND THAT'S THAT.
VENNERI IS ANOTHER CONVERSATION. I'M TALKING TO YOU, SHITHEAD.
Did you hear the one about John Shaft?

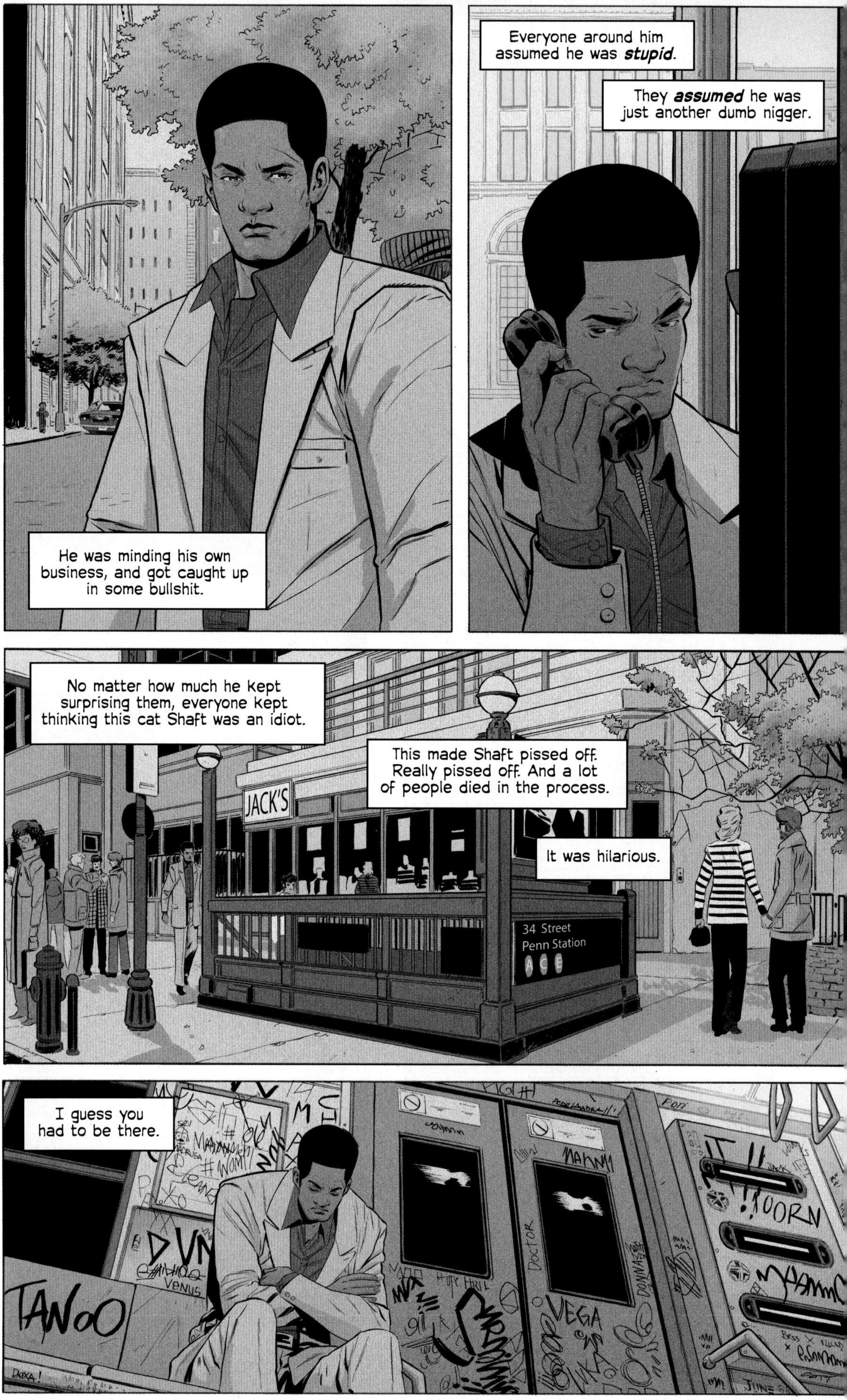
He was minding his own business, and got caught up in some bullshit.
Everyone around him assumed he was *stupid.*
They ***assumed*** he was just another dumb nigger.
No matter how much he kept surprising them, everyone kept thinking this cat Shaft was an idiot.
JACK'S
This made Shaft pissed off. Really pissed off. And a lot of people died in the process.
It was hilarious.
34 Street
Penn Station
A C E
I guess you had to be there.

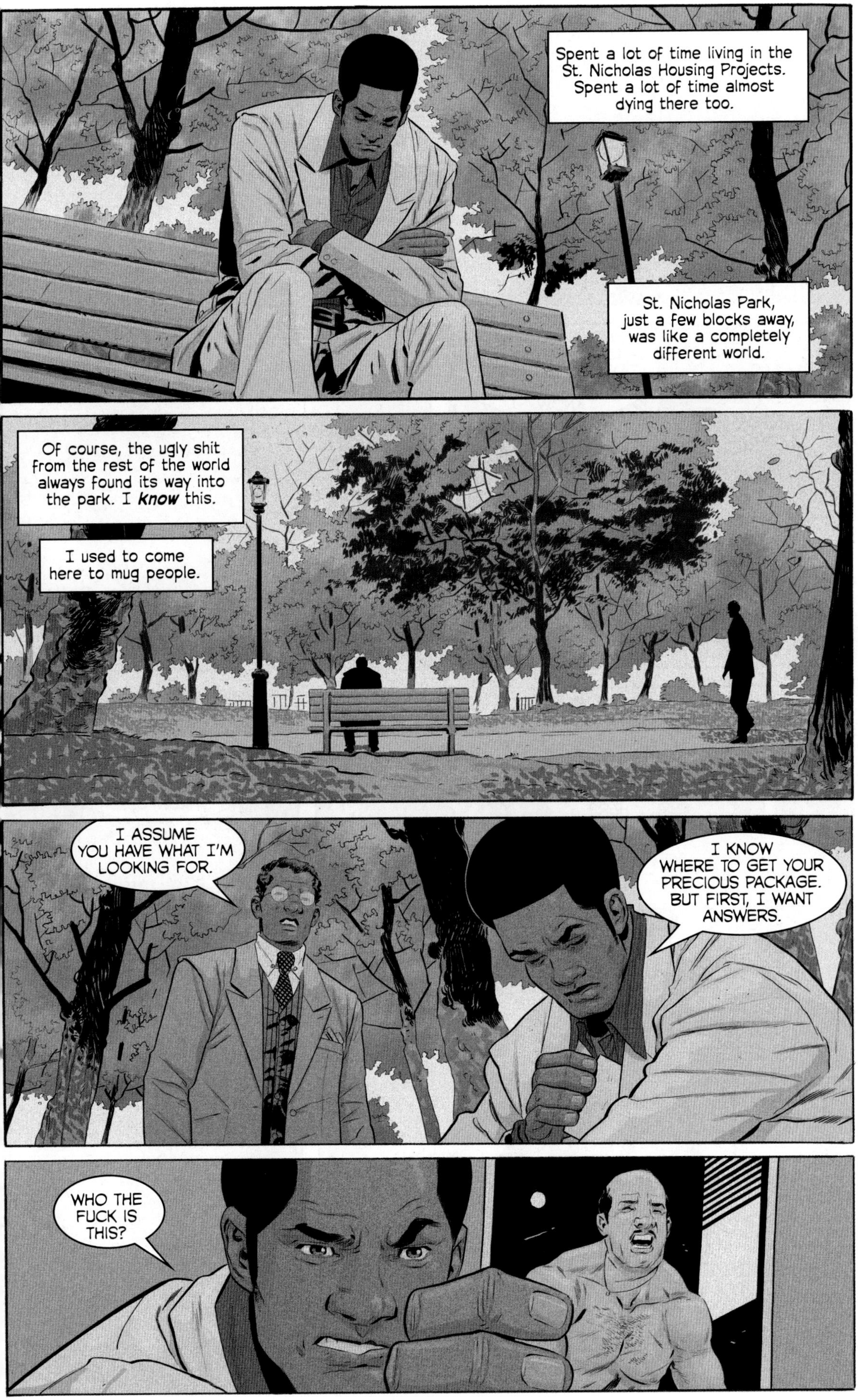
Spent a lot of time living in the St. Nicholas Housing Projects. Spent a lot of time almost dying there too.
St. Nicholas Park, just a few blocks away, was like a completely different world.
Of course, the ugly shit from the rest of the world always found its way into the park. I *know* this.
I used to come here to mug people.
I ASSUME YOU HAVE WHAT I'M LOOKING FOR.
I KNOW WHERE TO GET YOUR PRECIOUS PACKAGE. BUT FIRST, I WANT ANSWERS.
WHO THE FUCK IS THIS?

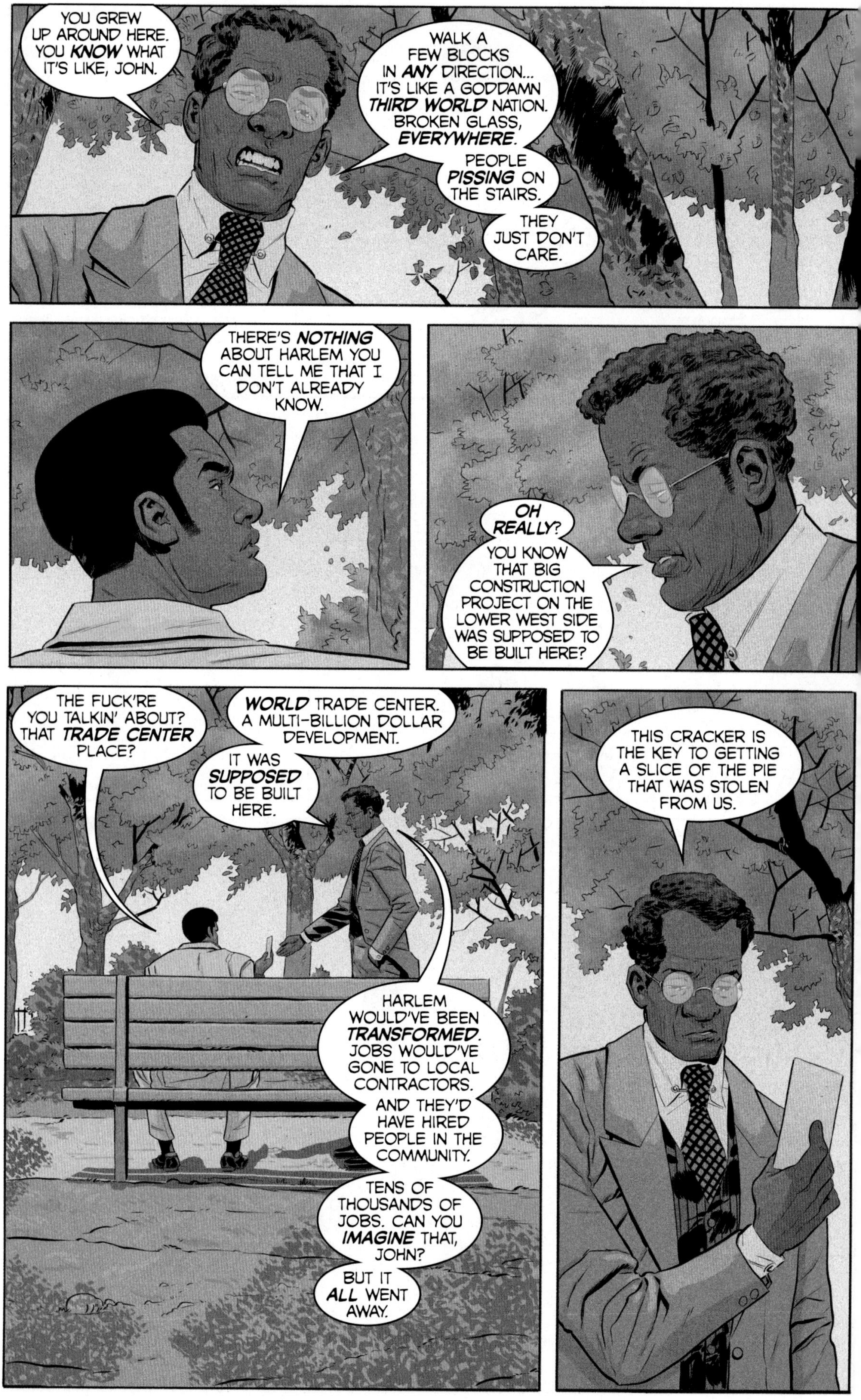
YOU GREW UP AROUND HERE. YOU KNOW WHAT IT'S LIKE, JOHN.
WALK A FEW BLOCKS IN ANY DIRECTION... IT'S LIKE A GODDAMN THIRD WORLD NATION. BROKEN GLASS, EVERYWHERE.
PEOPLE PISSING ON THE STAIRS.
THEY JUST DON'T CARE.
THERE'S NOTHING ABOUT HARLEM YOU CAN TELL ME THAT I DON'T ALREADY KNOW.
OH REALLY?
YOU KNOW THAT BIG CONSTRUCTION PROJECT ON THE LOWER WEST SIDE WAS SUPPOSED TO BE BUILT HERE?
THE FUCK'RE YOU TALKIN' ABOUT? THAT TRADE CENTER PLACE?
WORLD TRADE CENTER. A MULTI-BILLION DOLLAR DEVELOPMENT.
IT WAS SUPPOSED TO BE BUILT HERE.
HARLEM WOULD'VE BEEN TRANSFORMED. JOBS WOULD'VE GONE TO LOCAL CONTRACTORS.
AND THEY'D HAVE HIRED PEOPLE IN THE COMMUNITY.
TENS OF THOUSANDS OF JOBS. CAN YOU IMAGINE THAT, JOHN?
BUT IT ALL WENT AWAY.
THIS CRACKER IS THE KEY TO GETTING A SLICE OF THE PIE THAT WAS STOLEN FROM US.

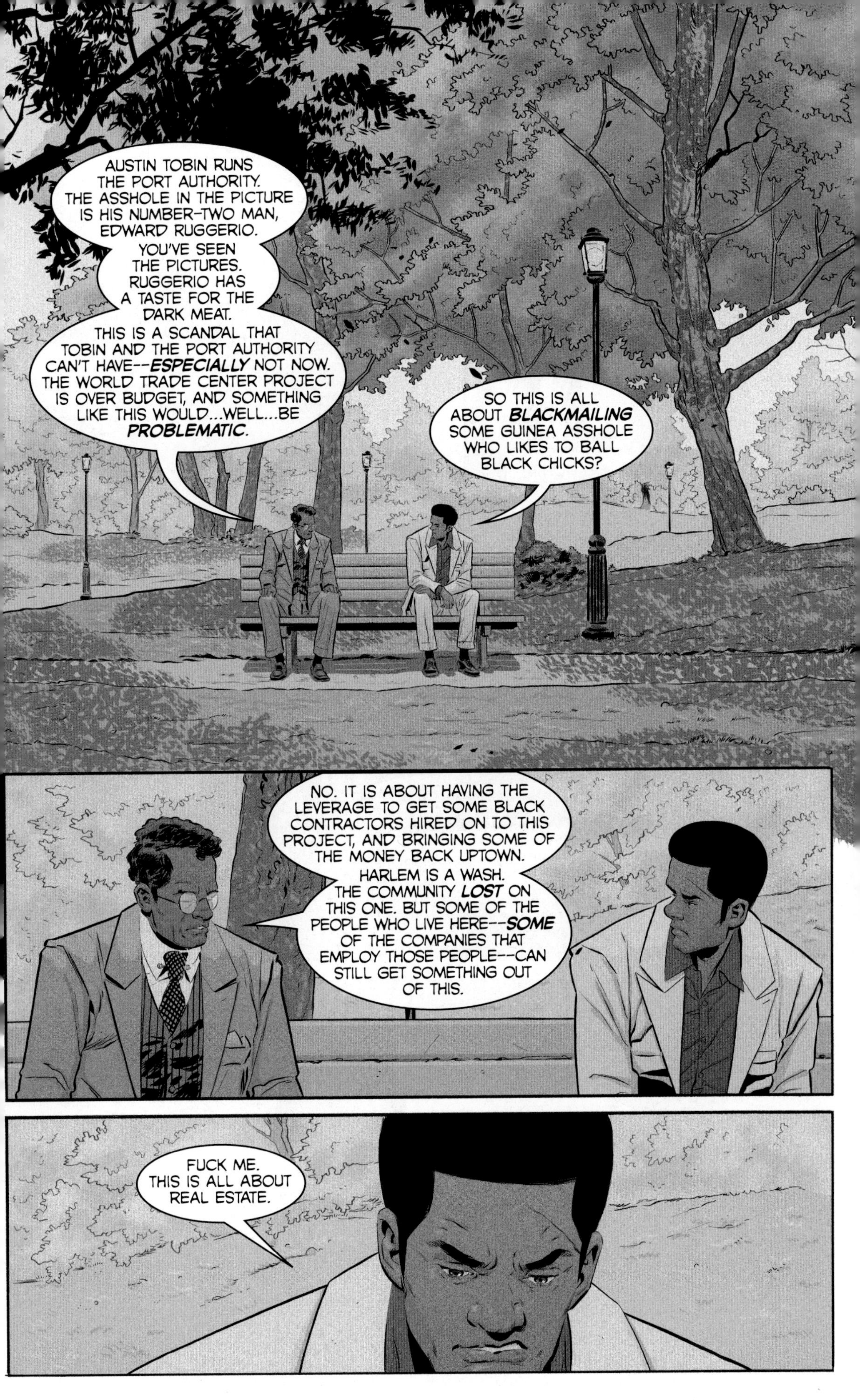
AUSTIN TOBIN RUNS THE PORT AUTHORITY. THE ASSHOLE IN THE PICTURE IS HIS NUMBER-TWO MAN, EDWARD RUGGERIO.
YOU'VE SEEN THE PICTURES. RUGGERIO HAS A TASTE FOR THE DARK MEAT.
THIS IS A SCANDAL THAT TOBIN AND THE PORT AUTHORITY CAN'T HAVE--ESPECIALLY NOT NOW. THE WORLD TRADE CENTER PROJECT IS OVER BUDGET, AND SOMETHING LIKE THIS WOULD...WELL...BE PROBLEMATIC.
SO THIS IS ALL ABOUT BLACKMAILING SOME GUINEA ASSHOLE WHO LIKES TO BALL BLACK CHICKS?
NO. IT IS ABOUT HAVING THE LEVERAGE TO GET SOME BLACK CONTRACTORS HIRED ON TO THIS PROJECT, AND BRINGING SOME OF THE MONEY BACK UPTOWN.
HARLEM IS A WASH. THE COMMUNITY LOST ON THIS ONE. BUT SOME OF THE PEOPLE WHO LIVE HERE--SOME OF THE COMPANIES THAT EMPLOY THOSE PEOPLE--CAN STILL GET SOMETHING OUT OF THIS.
FUCK ME. THIS IS ALL ABOUT REAL ESTATE.

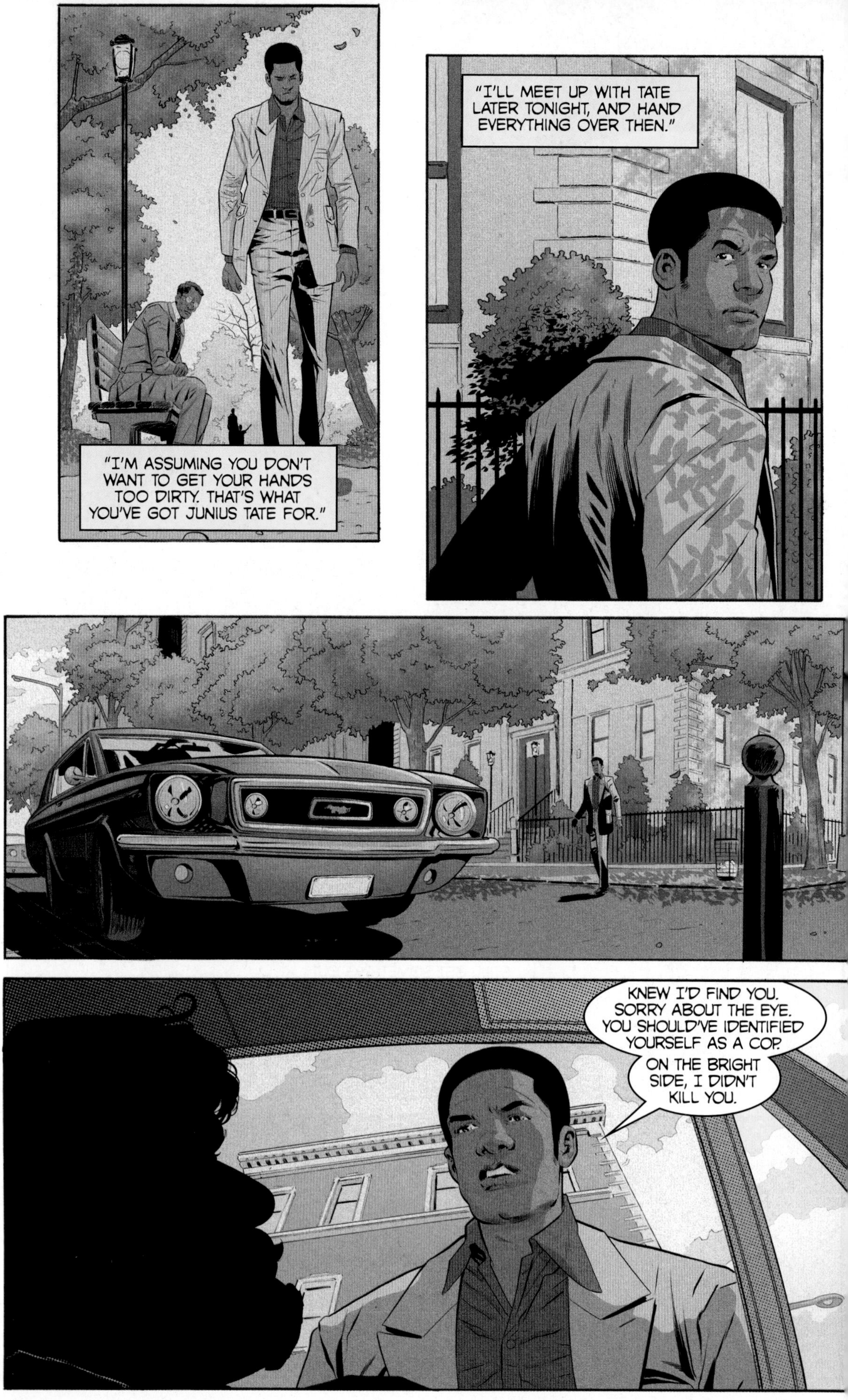
"I'M ASSUMING YOU DON'T WANT TO GET YOUR HANDS TOO DIRTY. THAT'S WHAT YOU'VE GOT JUNIUS TATE FOR."
"I'LL MEET UP WITH TATE LATER TONIGHT, AND HAND EVERYTHING OVER THEN."
KNEW I'D FIND YOU. SORRY ABOUT THE EYE. YOU SHOULD'VE IDENTIFIED YOURSELF AS A COP.
ON THE BRIGHT SIDE, I DIDN'T KILL YOU.

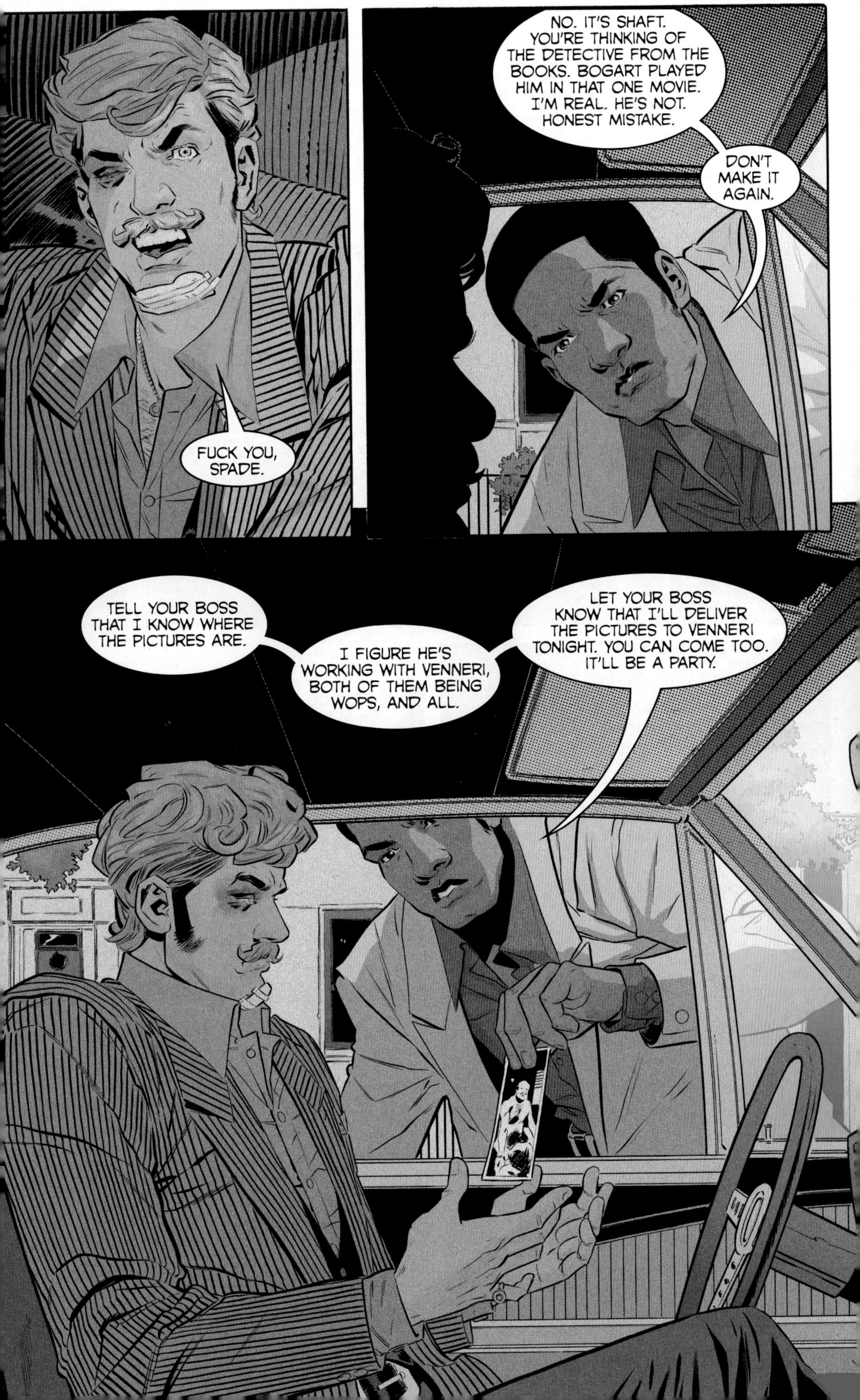
FUCK YOU, SPADE.
NO. IT'S SHAFT. YOU'RE THINKING OF THE DETECTIVE FROM THE BOOKS. BOGART PLAYED HIM IN THAT ONE MOVIE. I'M REAL. HE'S NOT. HONEST MISTAKE.
DON'T MAKE IT AGAIN.
TELL YOUR BOSS THAT I KNOW WHERE THE PICTURES ARE.
I FIGURE HE'S WORKING WITH VENNERI, BOTH OF THEM BEING WOPS, AND ALL.
LET YOUR BOSS KNOW THAT I'LL DELIVER THE PICTURES TO VENNERI TONIGHT. YOU CAN COME TOO. IT'LL BE A PARTY.

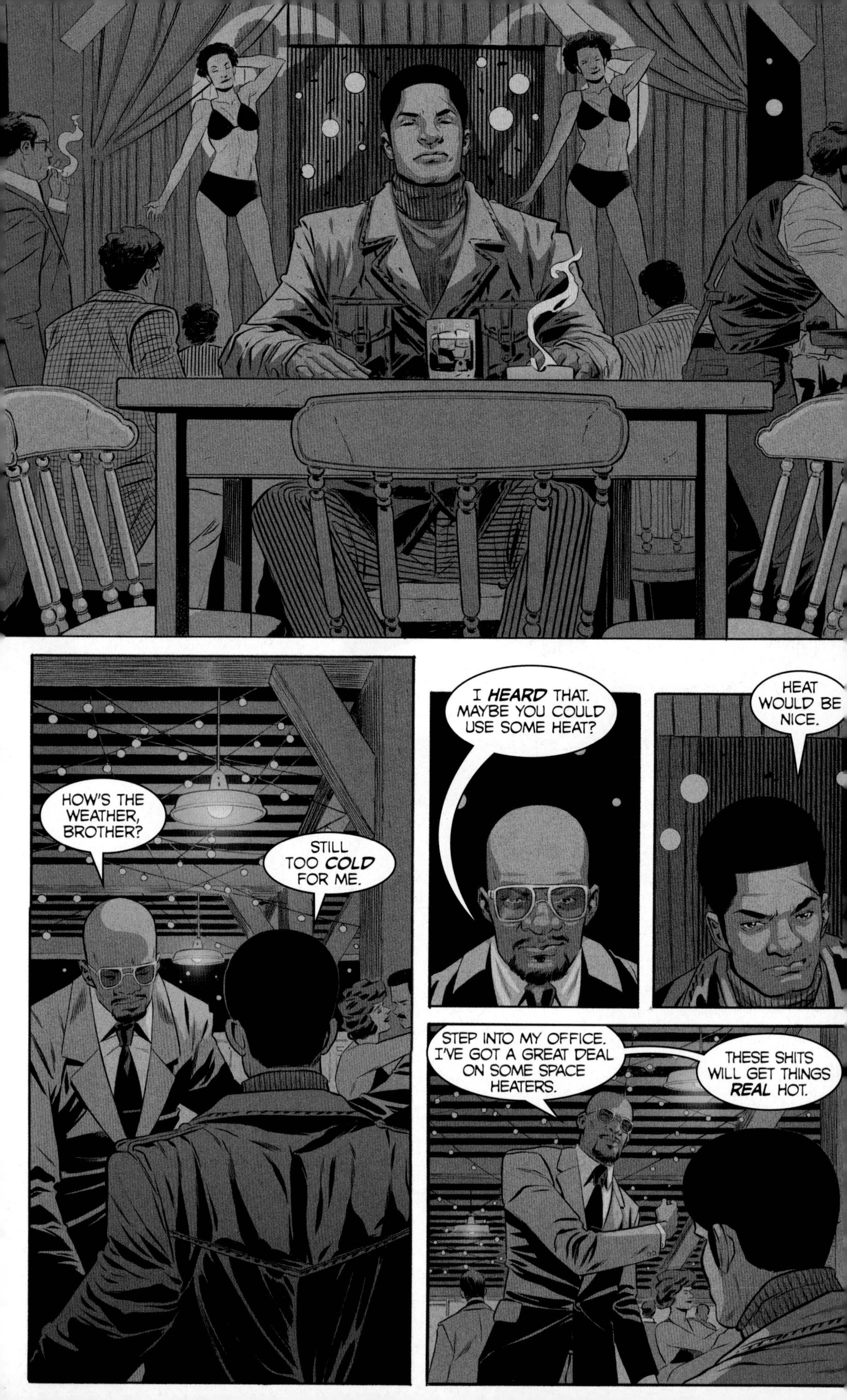
HOW'S THE WEATHER, BROTHER?
STILL TOO COLD FOR ME.
I HEARD THAT. MAYBE YOU COULD USE SOME HEAT?
HEAT WOULD BE NICE.
STEP INTO MY OFFICE. I'VE GOT A GREAT DEAL ON SOME SPACE HEATERS.
THESE SHITS WILL GET THINGS REAL HOT.

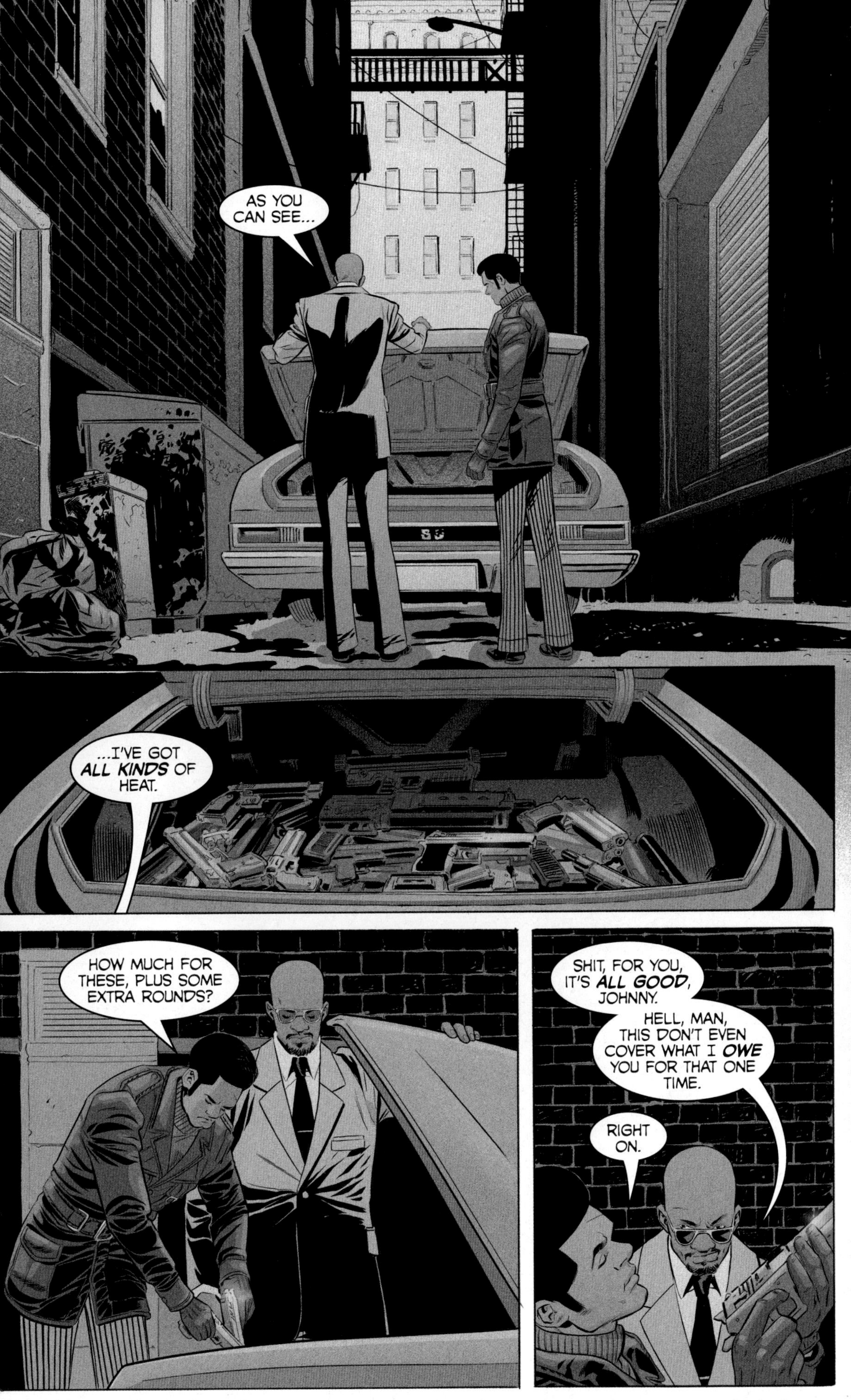
AS YOU CAN SEE...
...I'VE GOT ALL KINDS OF HEAT.
HOW MUCH FOR THESE, PLUS SOME EXTRA ROUNDS?
SHIT, FOR YOU, IT'S ALL GOOD, JOHNNY.
HELL, MAN, THIS DON'T EVEN COVER WHAT I OWE YOU FOR THAT ONE TIME.
RIGHT ON.

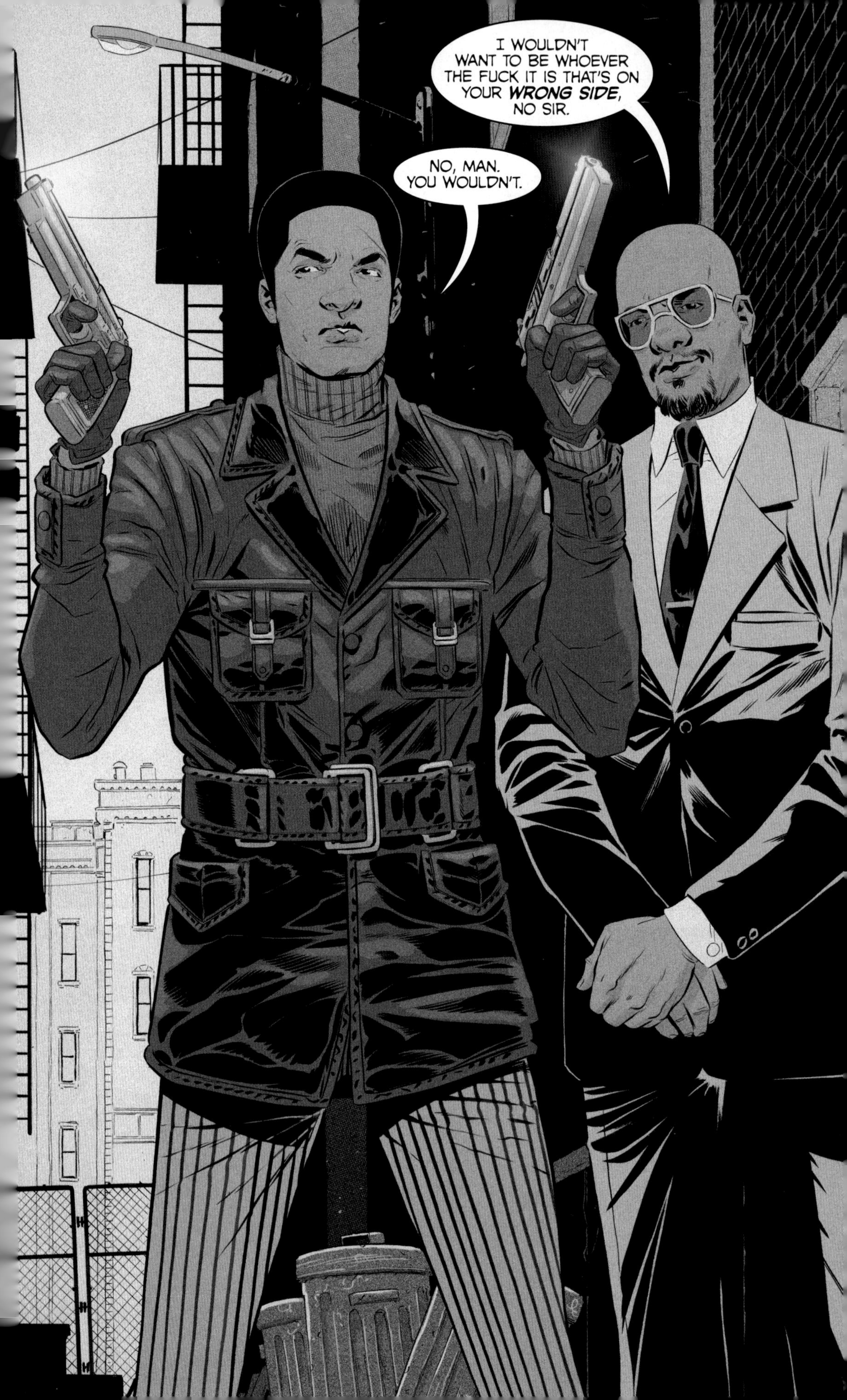
I WOULDN'T WANT TO BE WHOEVER THE FUCK IT IS THAT'S ON YOUR ***WRONG SIDE***, NO SIR.
NO, MAN. YOU WOULDN'T.

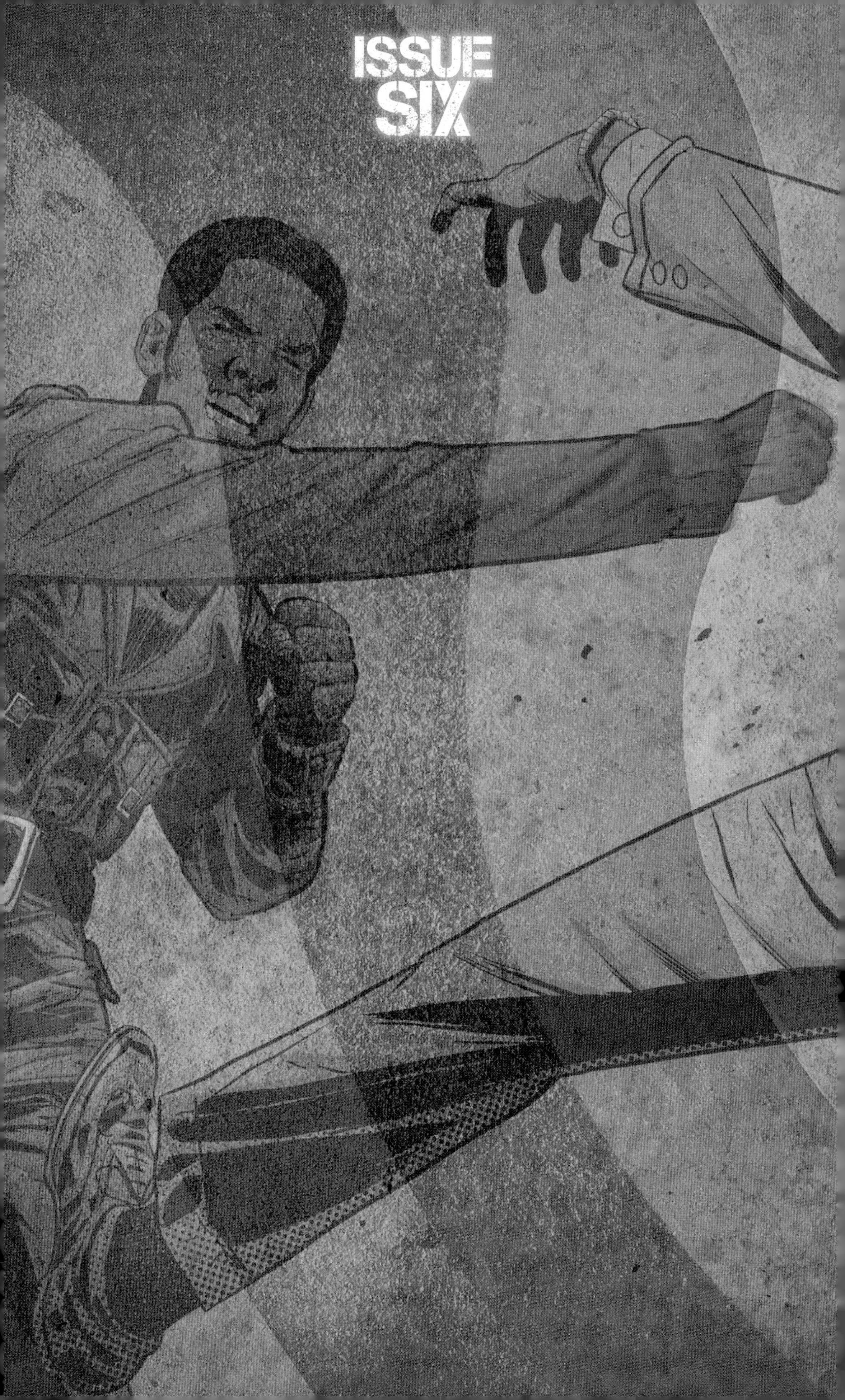
ISSUE
SIX

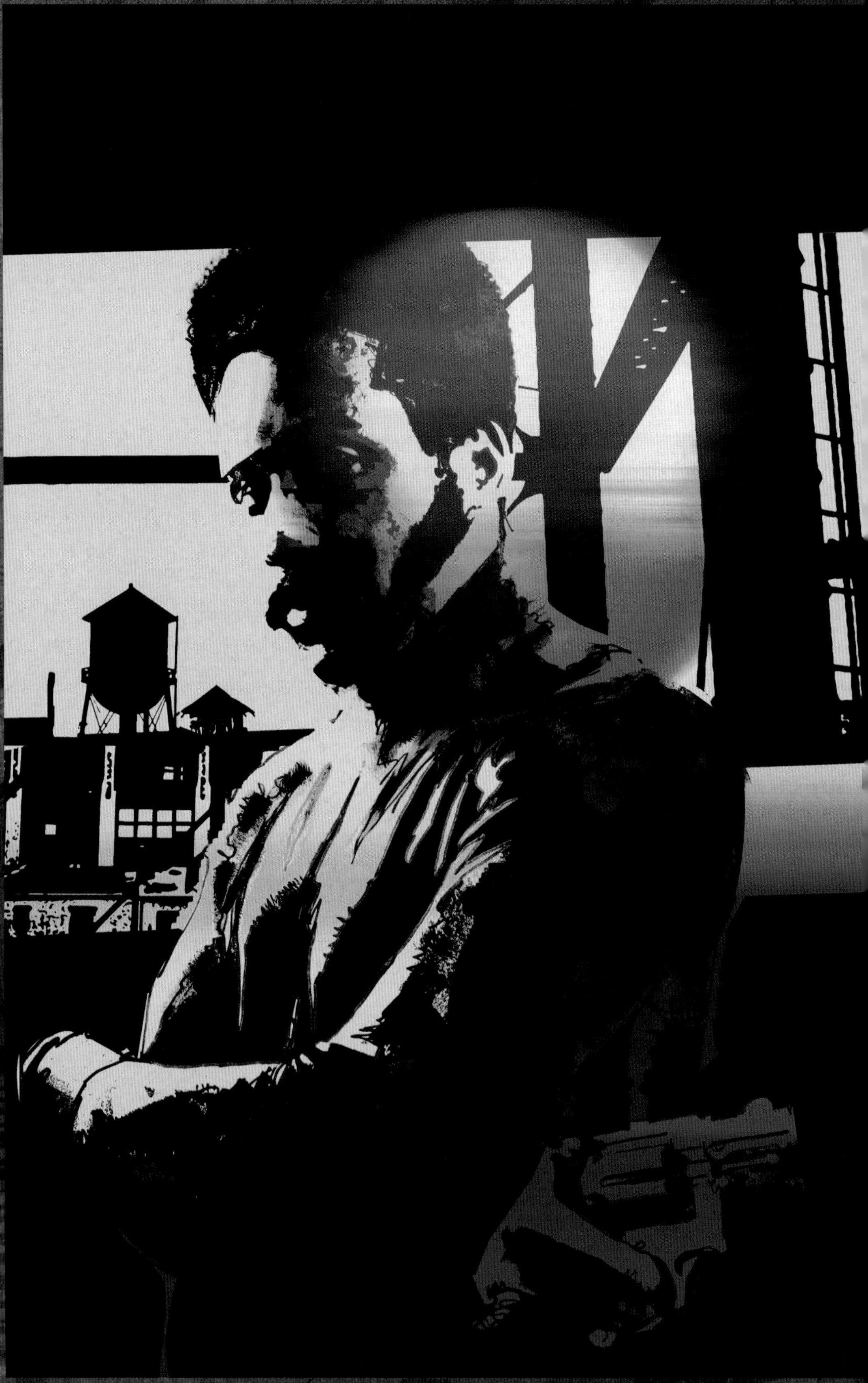

ISSUE SIX MAIN COVER BY
BILL SIENKIEWICZ

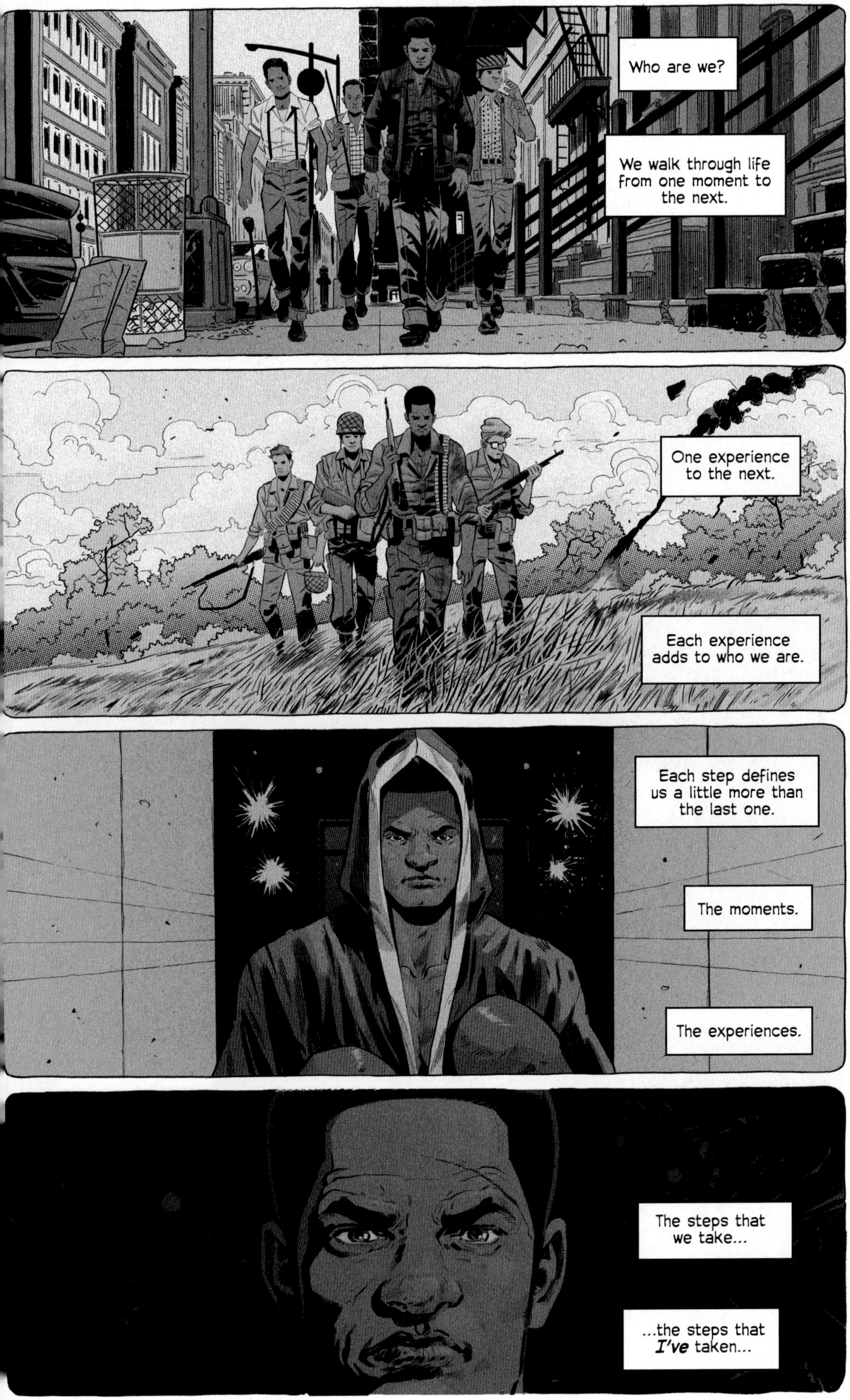
Who are we?
We walk through life from one moment to the next.
One experience to the next.
Each experience adds to who we are.
Each step defines us a little more than the last one.
The moments.
The experiences.
The steps that we take...
...the steps that *I've* taken...

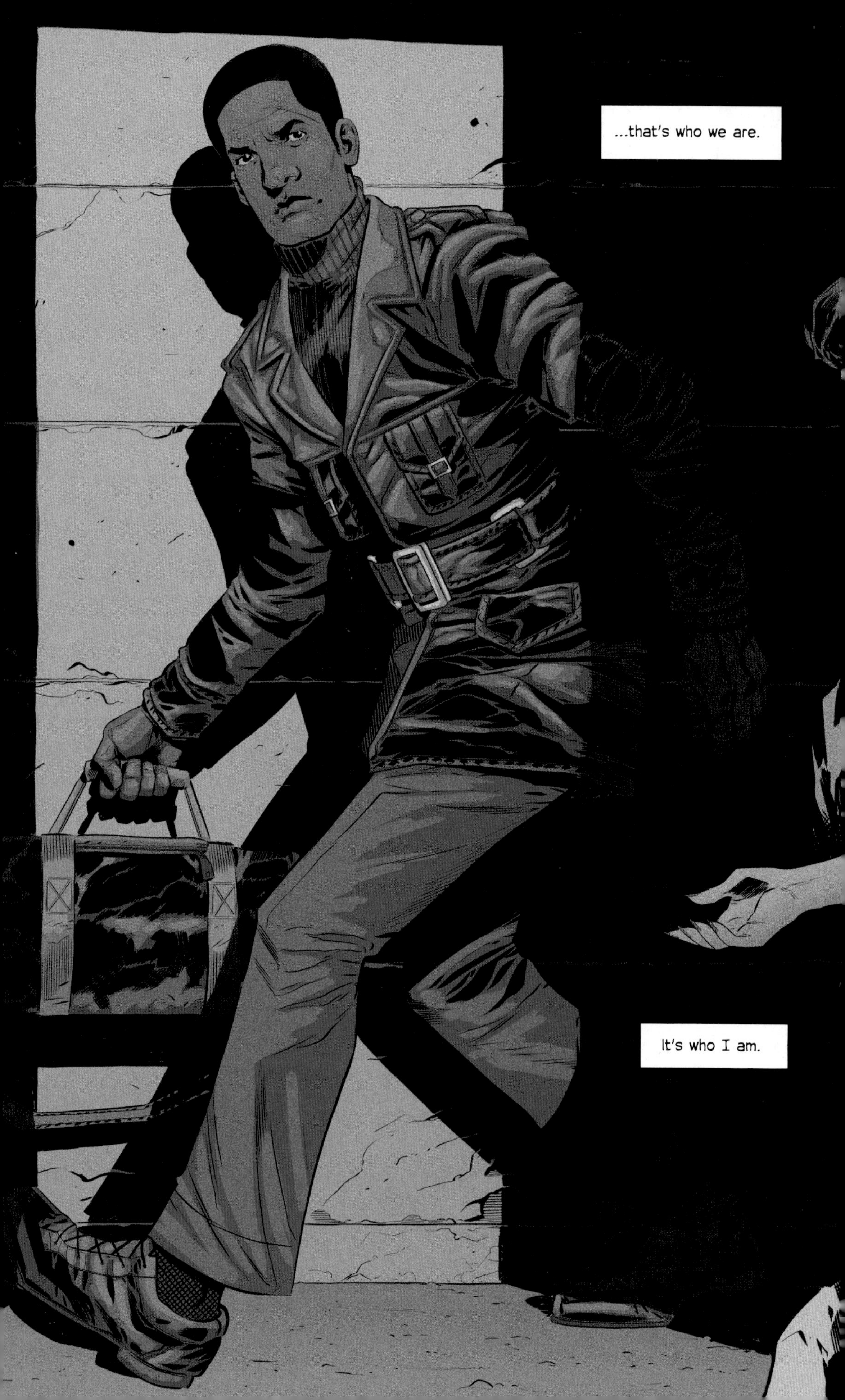
...that's who we are.
It's who I am.

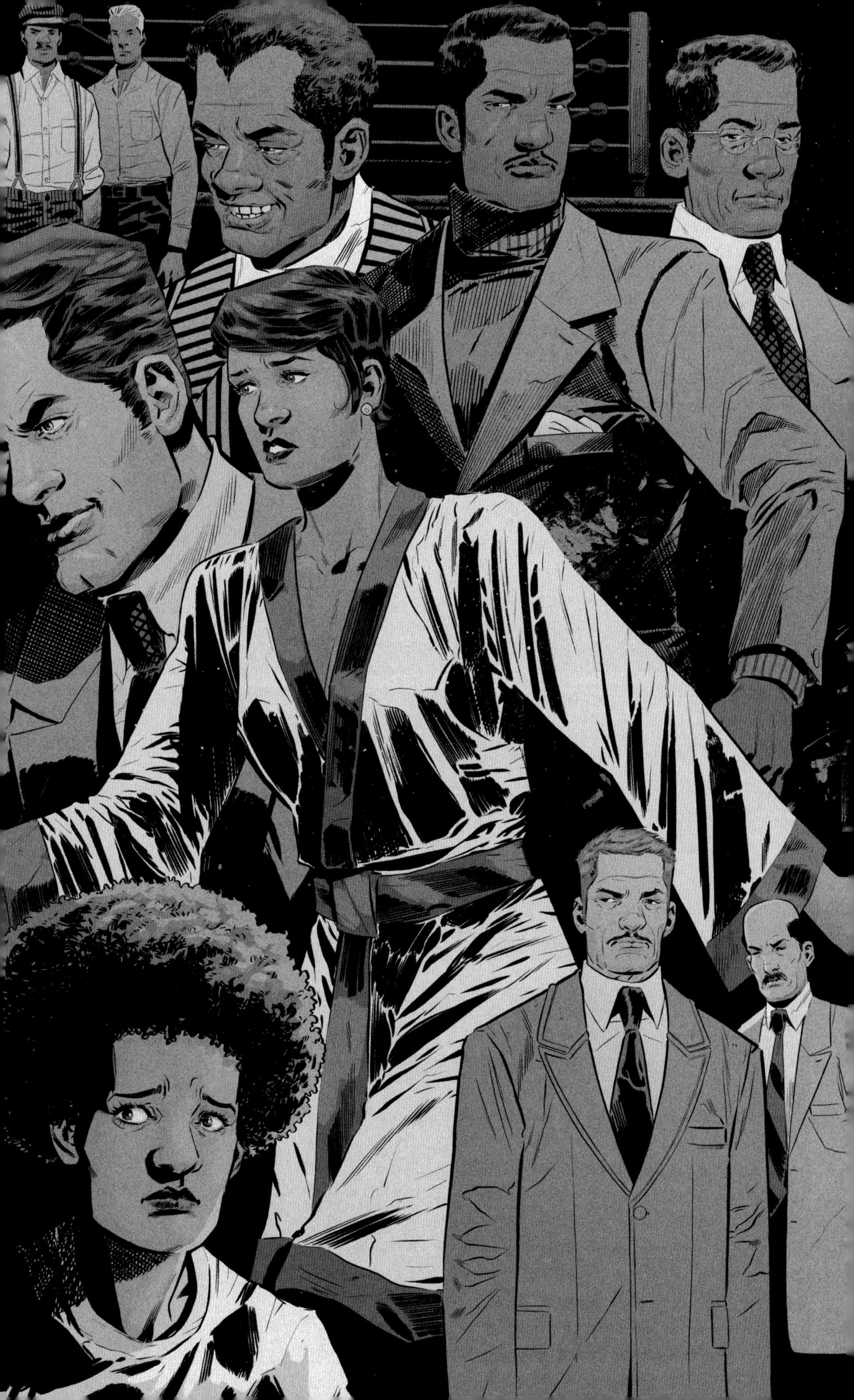

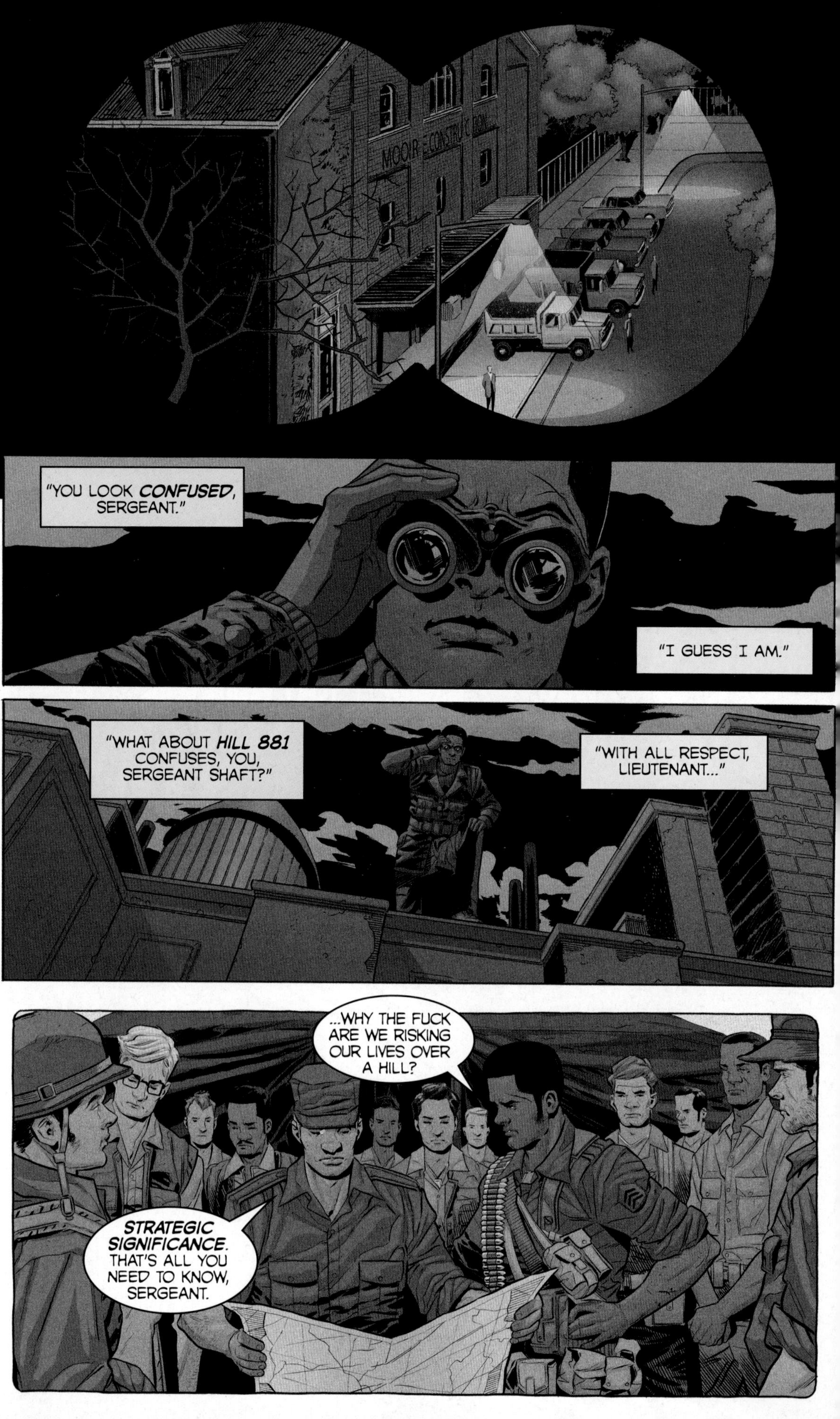
MOORE CONSTRUCTION
"YOU LOOK *CONFUSED*, SERGEANT."
"I GUESS I AM."
"WHAT ABOUT *HILL 881* CONFUSES, YOU, SERGEANT SHAFT?"
"WITH ALL RESPECT, LIEUTENANT..."
...WHY THE FUCK ARE WE RISKING OUR LIVES OVER A HILL?
STRATEGIC SIGNIFICANCE. THAT'S ALL YOU NEED TO KNOW, SERGEANT.

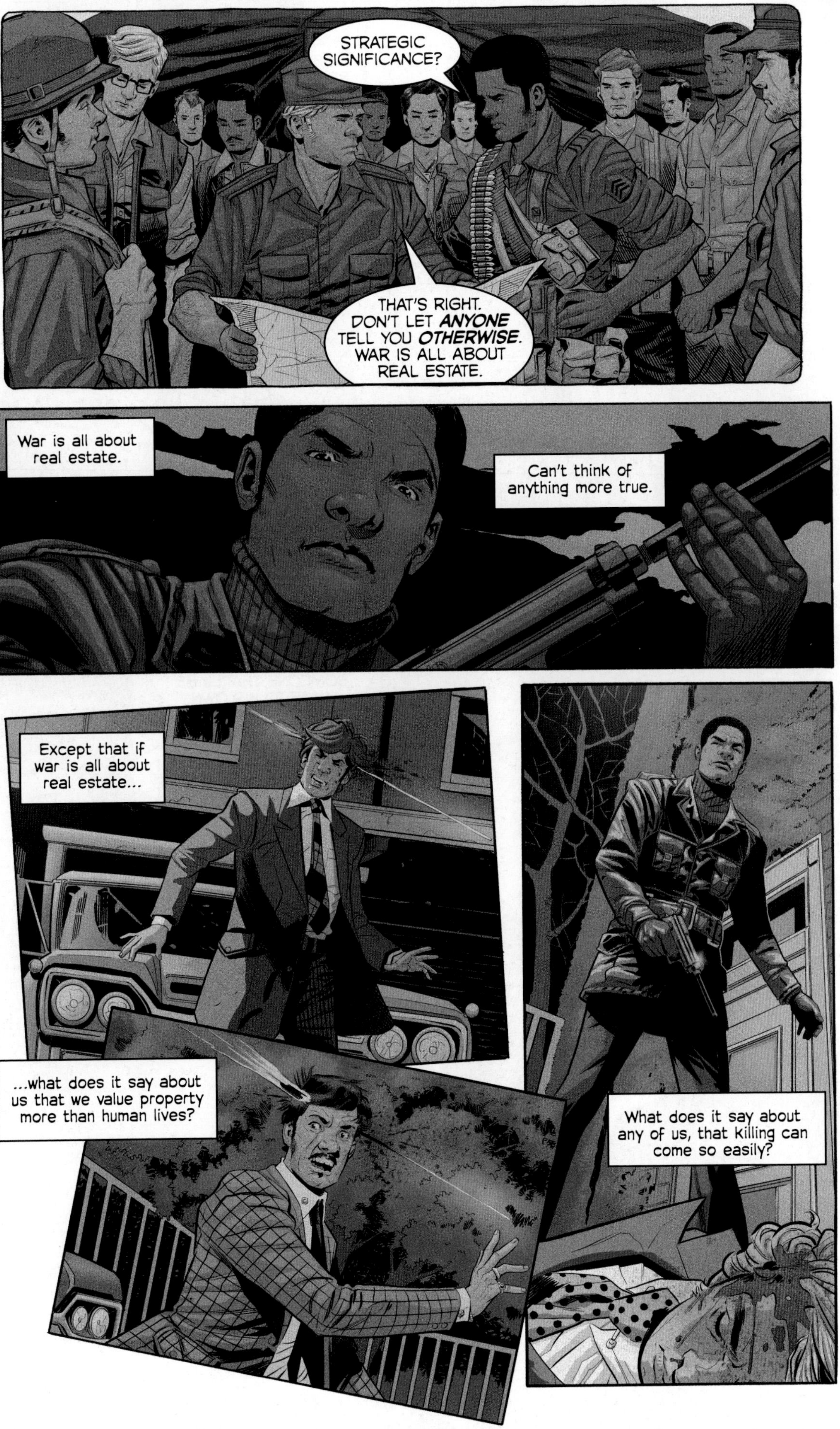
STRATEGIC SIGNIFICANCE?
THAT'S RIGHT. DON'T LET ANYONE TELL YOU OTHERWISE. WAR IS ALL ABOUT REAL ESTATE.
War is all about real estate.
Can't think of anything more true.
Except that if war is all about real estate...
...what does it say about us that we value property more than human lives?
What does it say about any of us, that killing can come so easily?

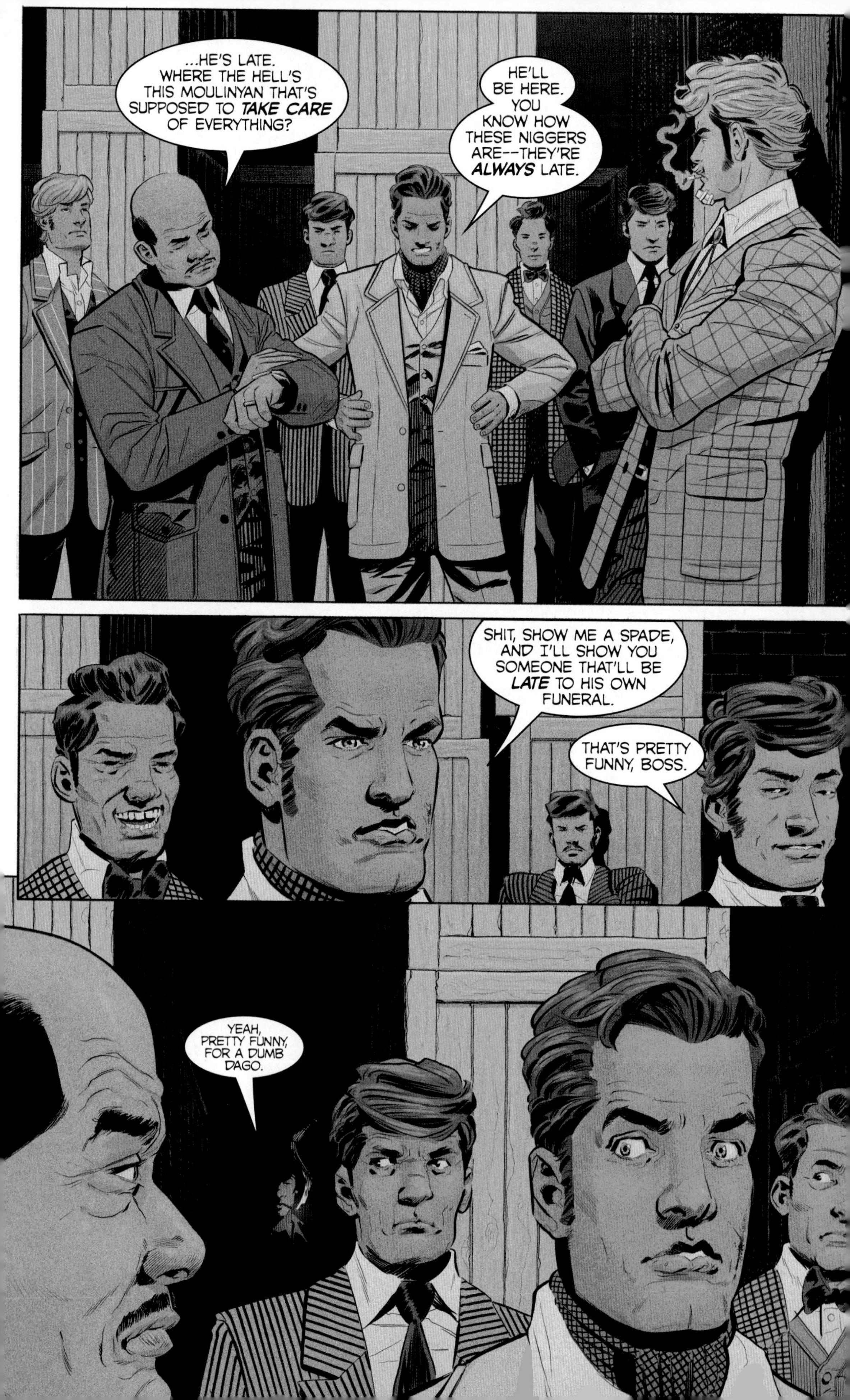
...HE'S LATE. WHERE THE HELL'S THIS MOULINYAN THAT'S SUPPOSED TO TAKE CARE OF EVERYTHING?
HE'LL BE HERE. YOU KNOW HOW THESE NIGGERS ARE--THEY'RE ALWAYS LATE.
SHIT, SHOW ME A SPADE, AND I'LL SHOW YOU SOMEONE THAT'LL BE LATE TO HIS OWN FUNERAL.
THAT'S PRETTY FUNNY, BOSS.
YEAH, PRETTY FUNNY, FOR A DUMB DAGO.

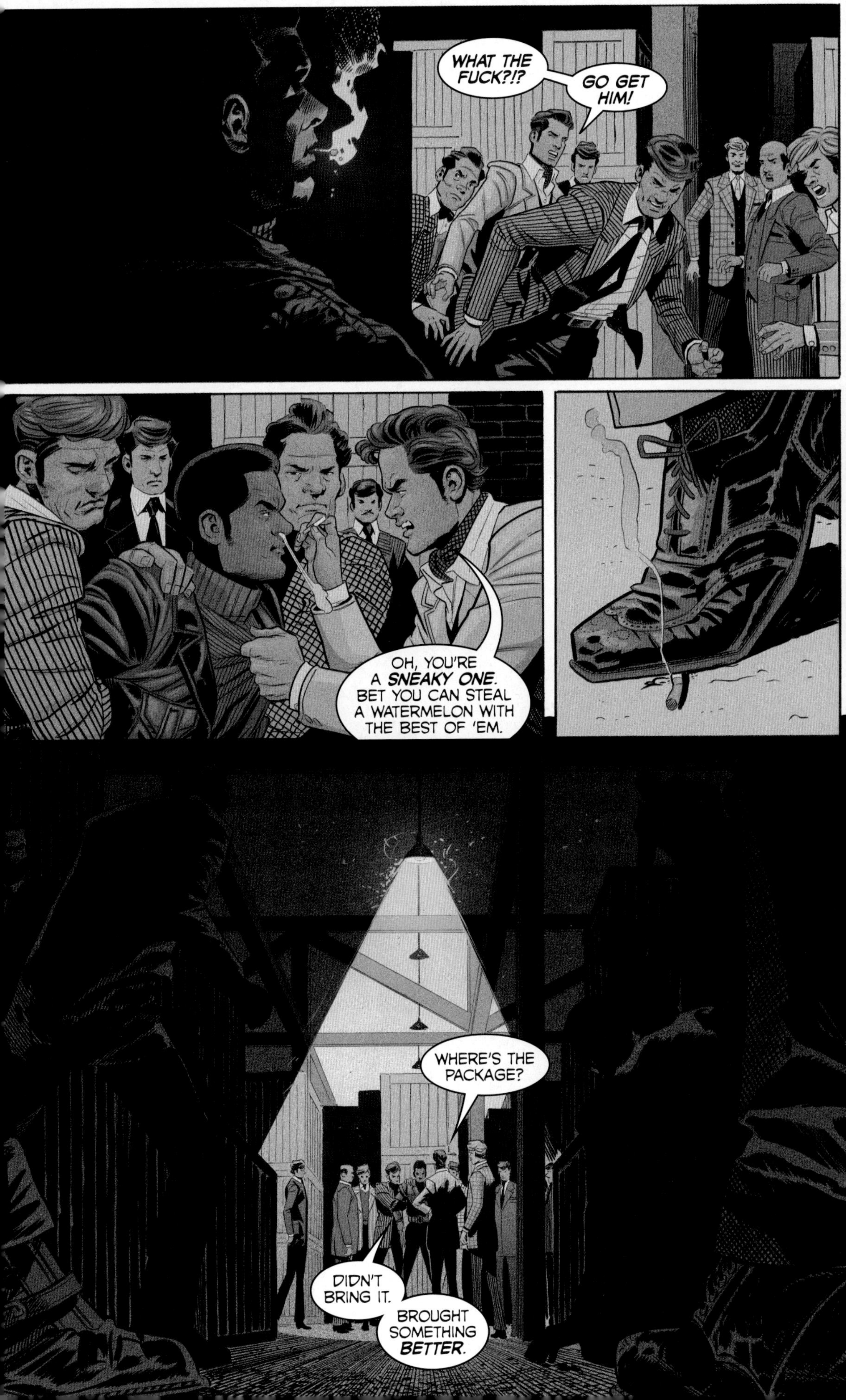
WHAT THE FUCK?!?
GO GET HIM!
OH, YOU'RE A SNEAKY ONE. BET YOU CAN STEAL A WATERMELON WITH THE BEST OF 'EM.
WHERE'S THE PACKAGE?
DIDN'T BRING IT.
BROUGHT SOMETHING BETTER.

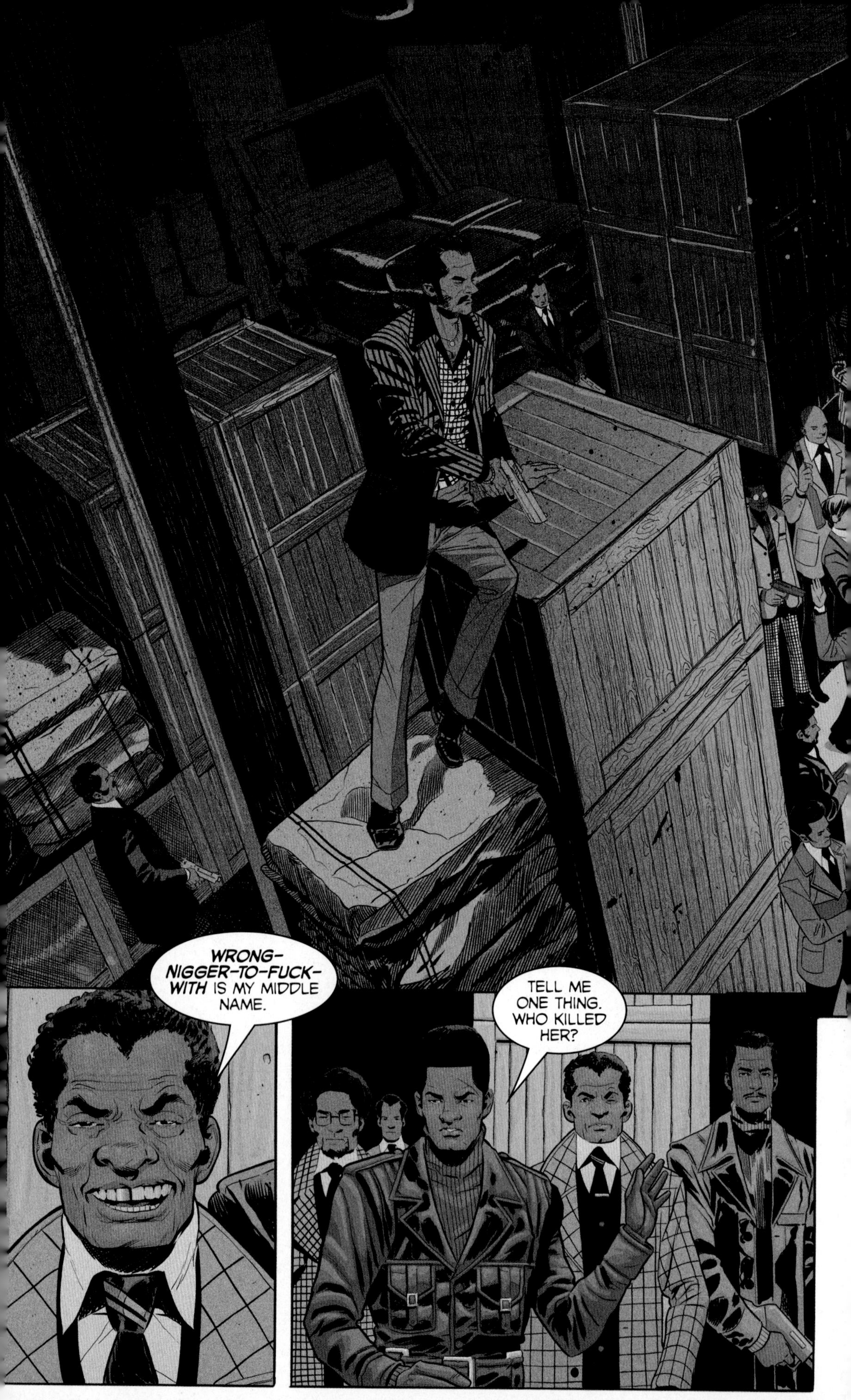
WRONG-NIGGER-TO-FUCK-WITH IS MY MIDDLE NAME.
TELL ME ONE THING. WHO KILLED HER?

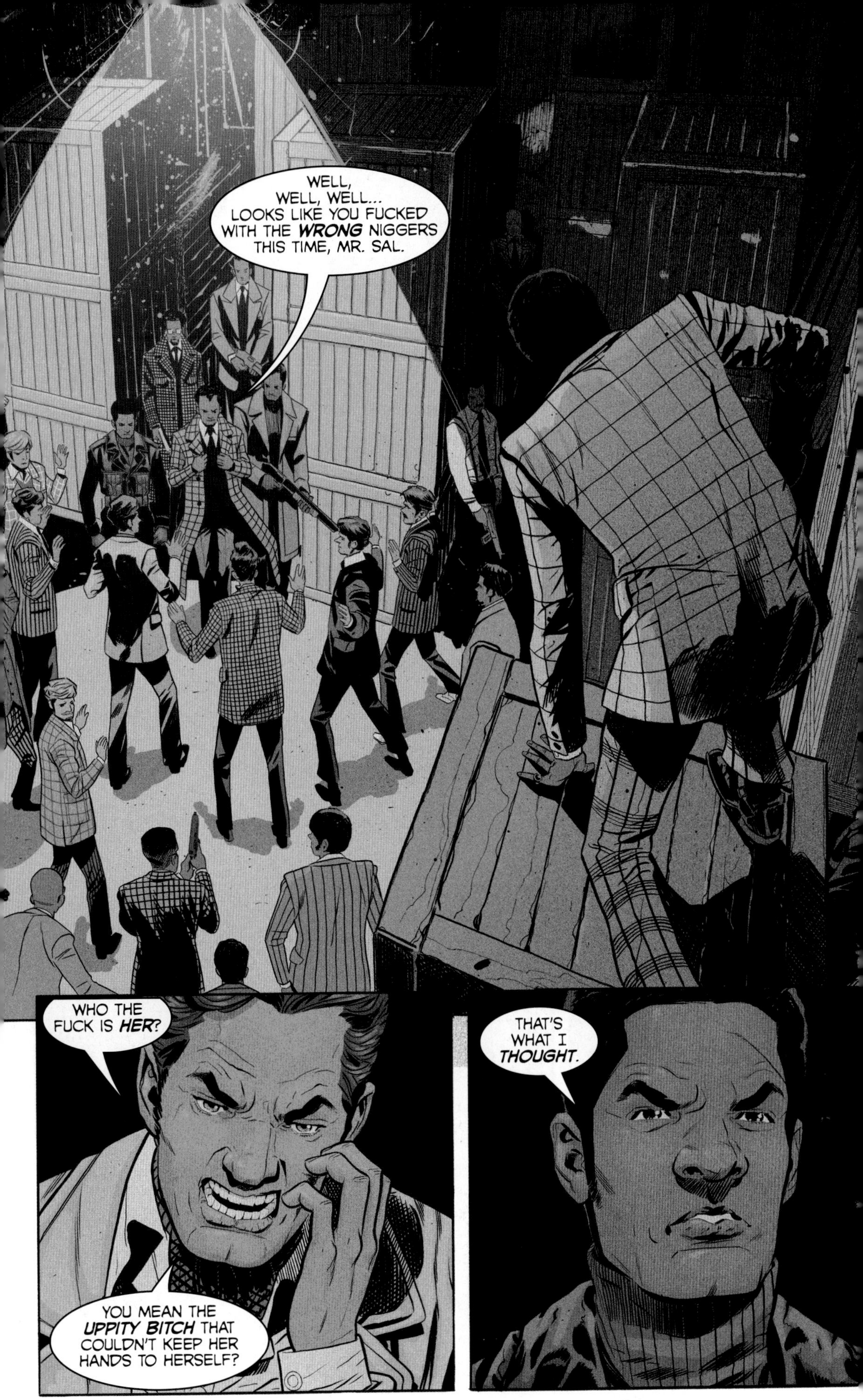
WELL, WELL, WELL... LOOKS LIKE YOU FUCKED WITH THE *WRONG* NIGGERS THIS TIME, MR. SAL.
WHO THE FUCK IS *HER*?
YOU MEAN THE *UPPITY BITCH* THAT COULDN'T KEEP HER HANDS TO HERSELF?
THAT'S WHAT I *THOUGHT*.

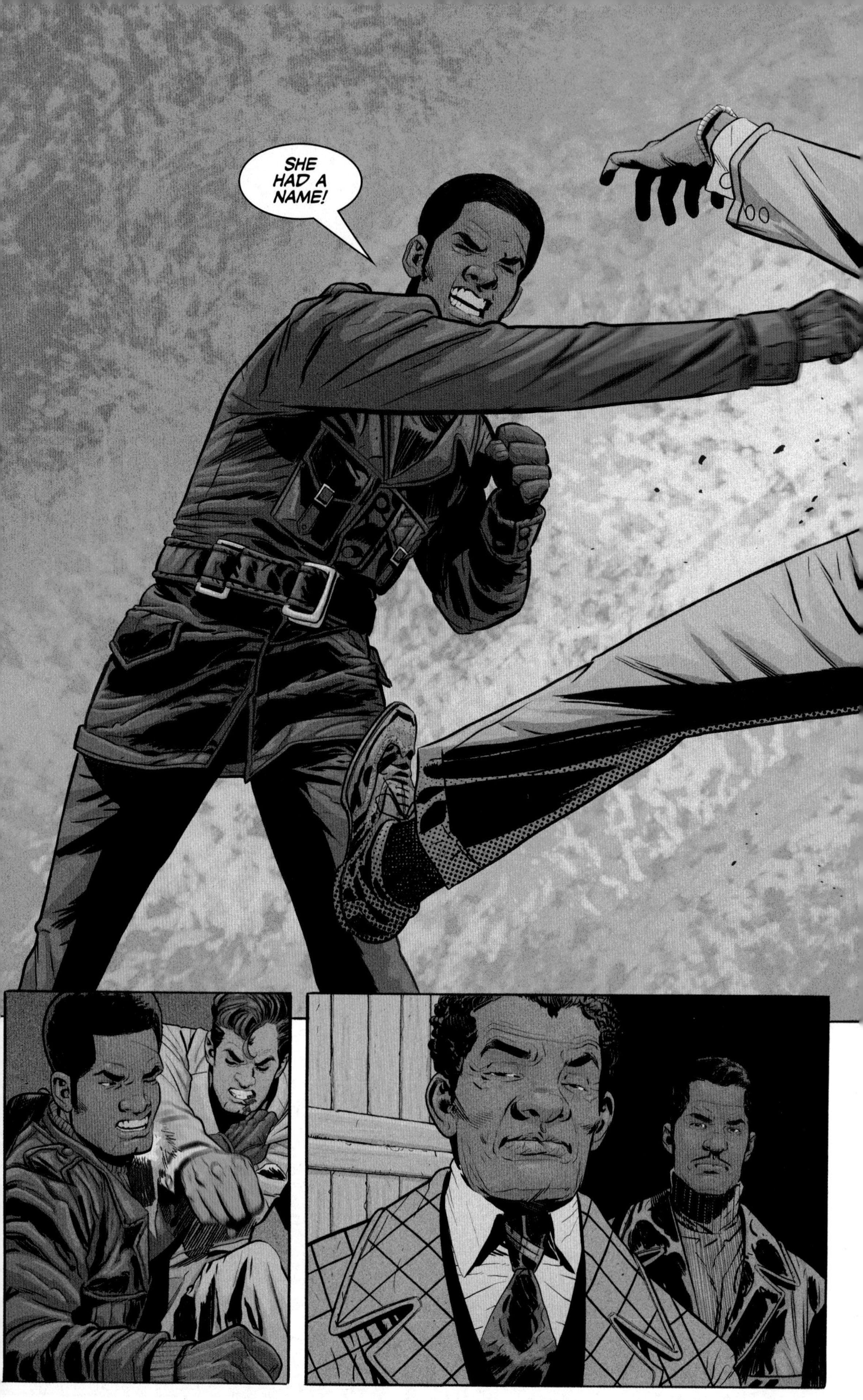
SHE HAD A NAME!

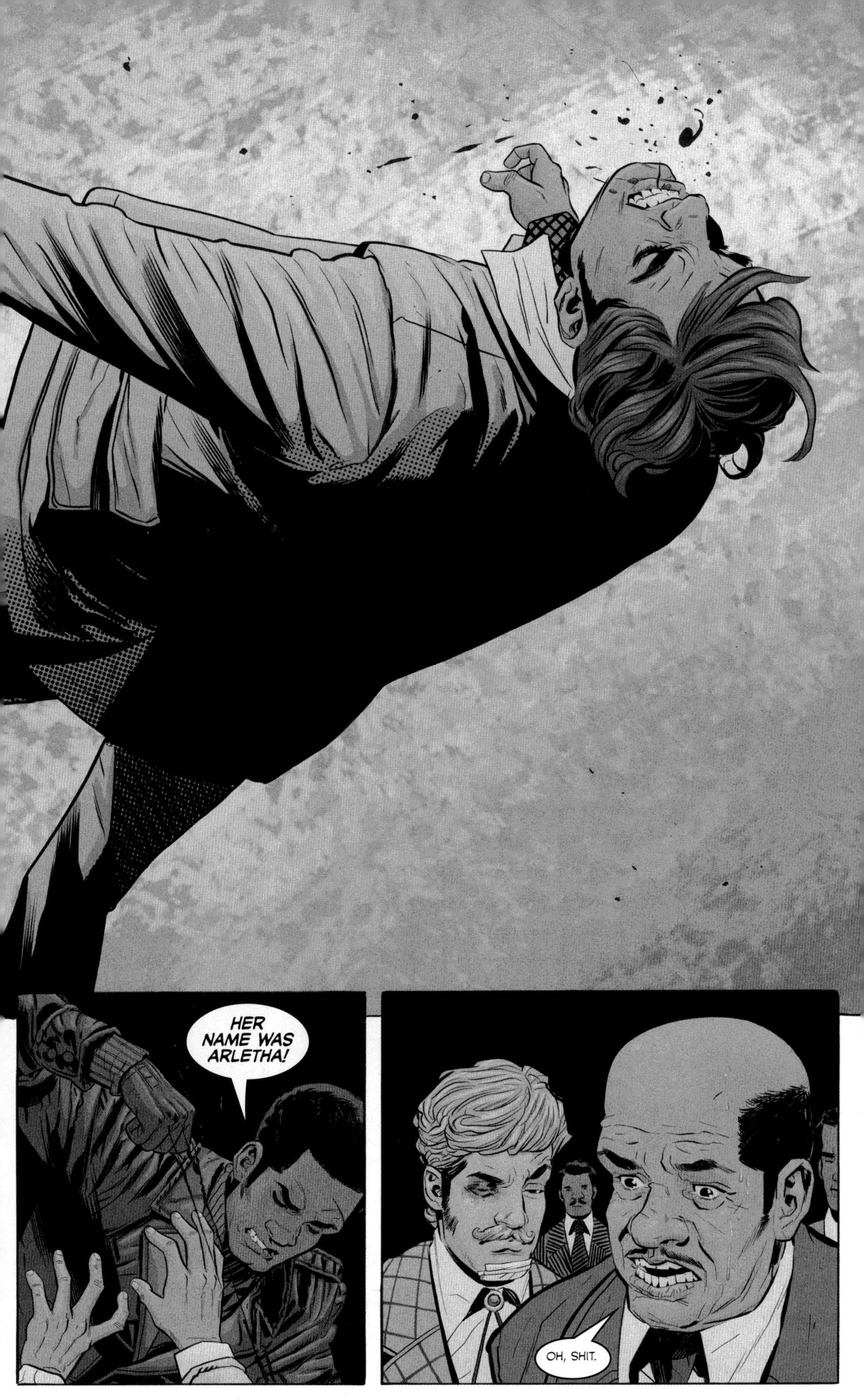
HER NAME WAS ARLETHA!
OH, SHIT.

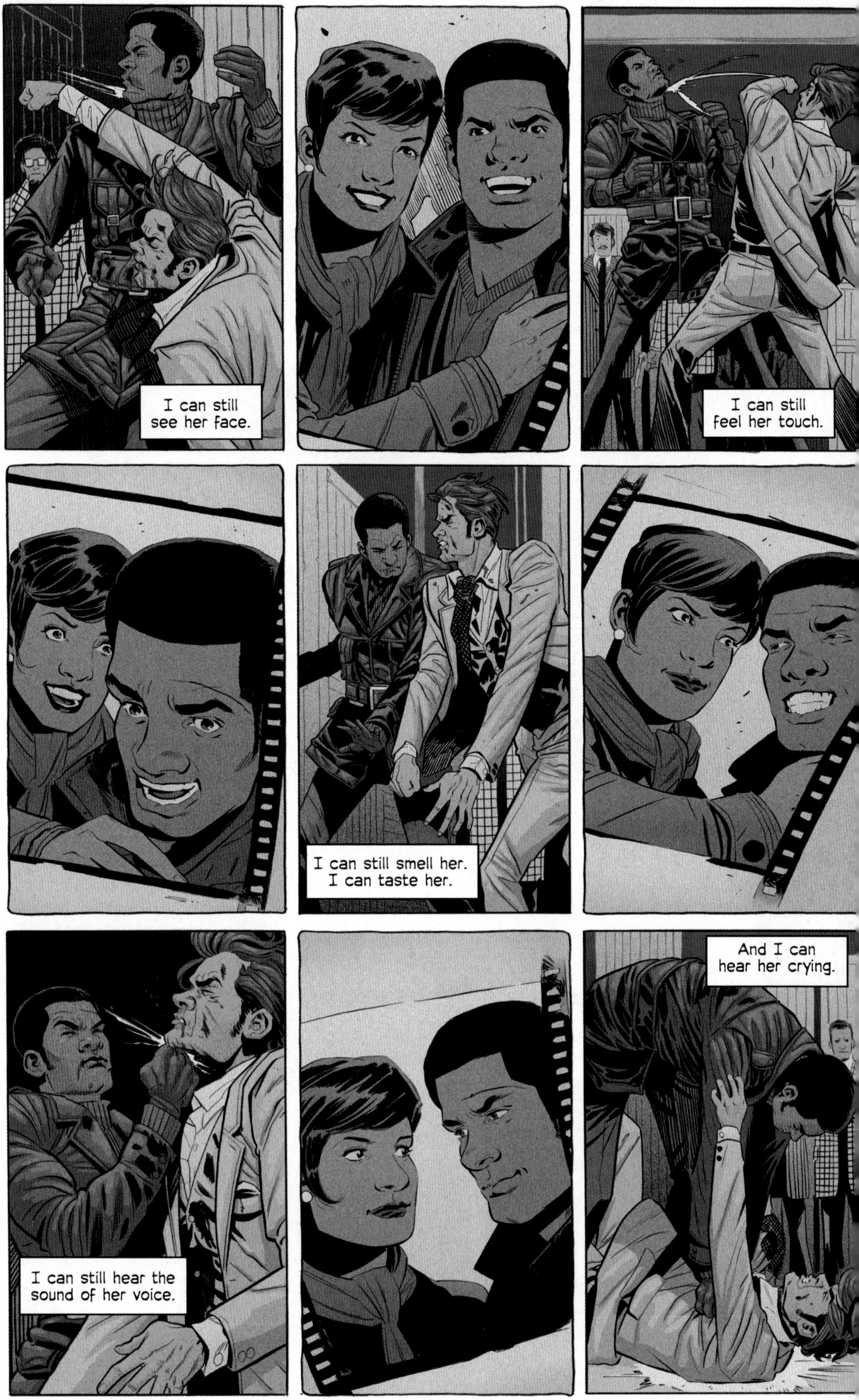
I can still see her face.
I can still feel her touch.
I can still smell her. I can taste her.
I can still hear the sound of her voice.
And I can hear her crying.

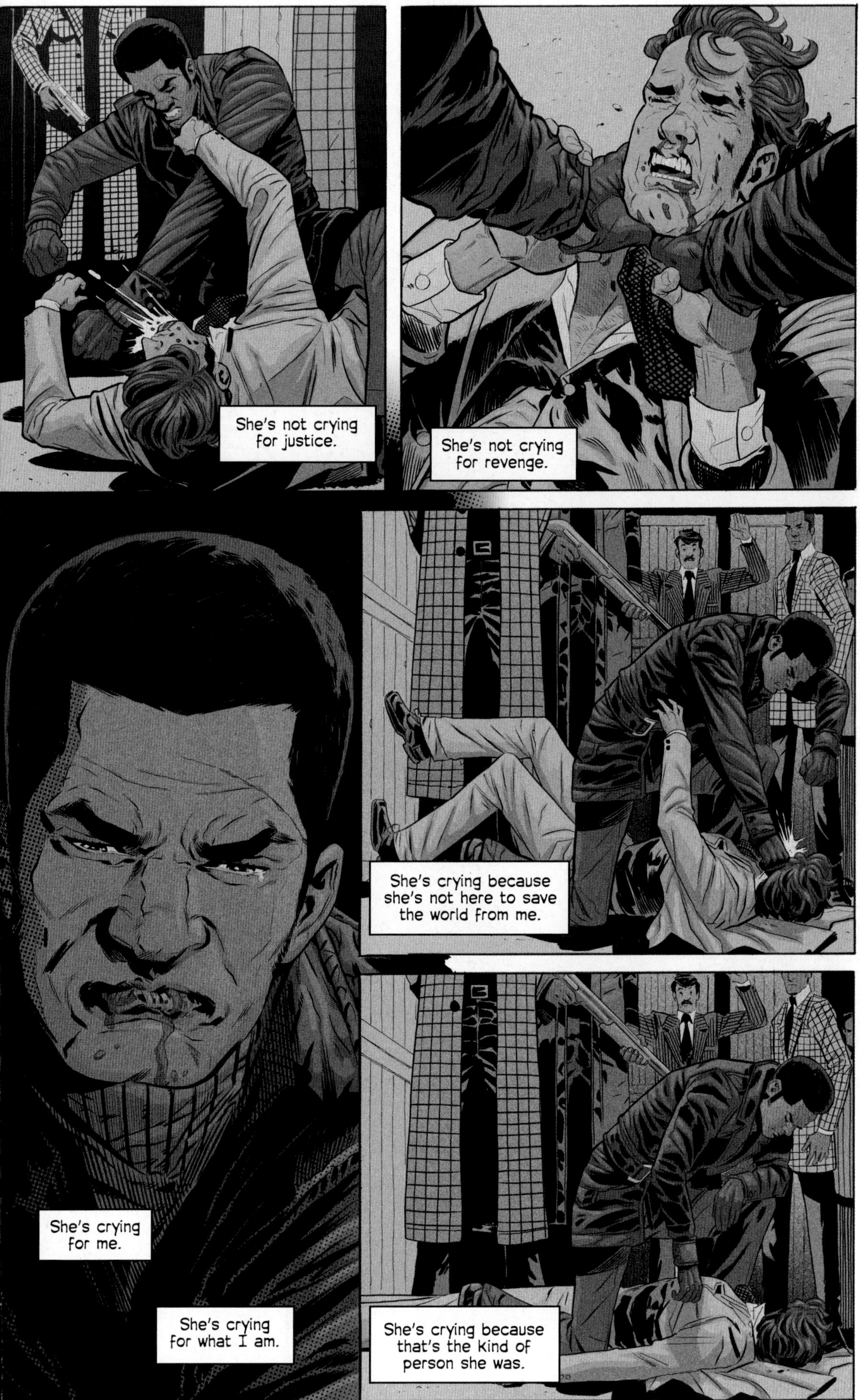
She's not crying for justice.
She's not crying for revenge.
She's crying for me.
She's crying for what I am.
She's crying because she's not here to save the world from me.
She's crying because that's the kind of person she was.

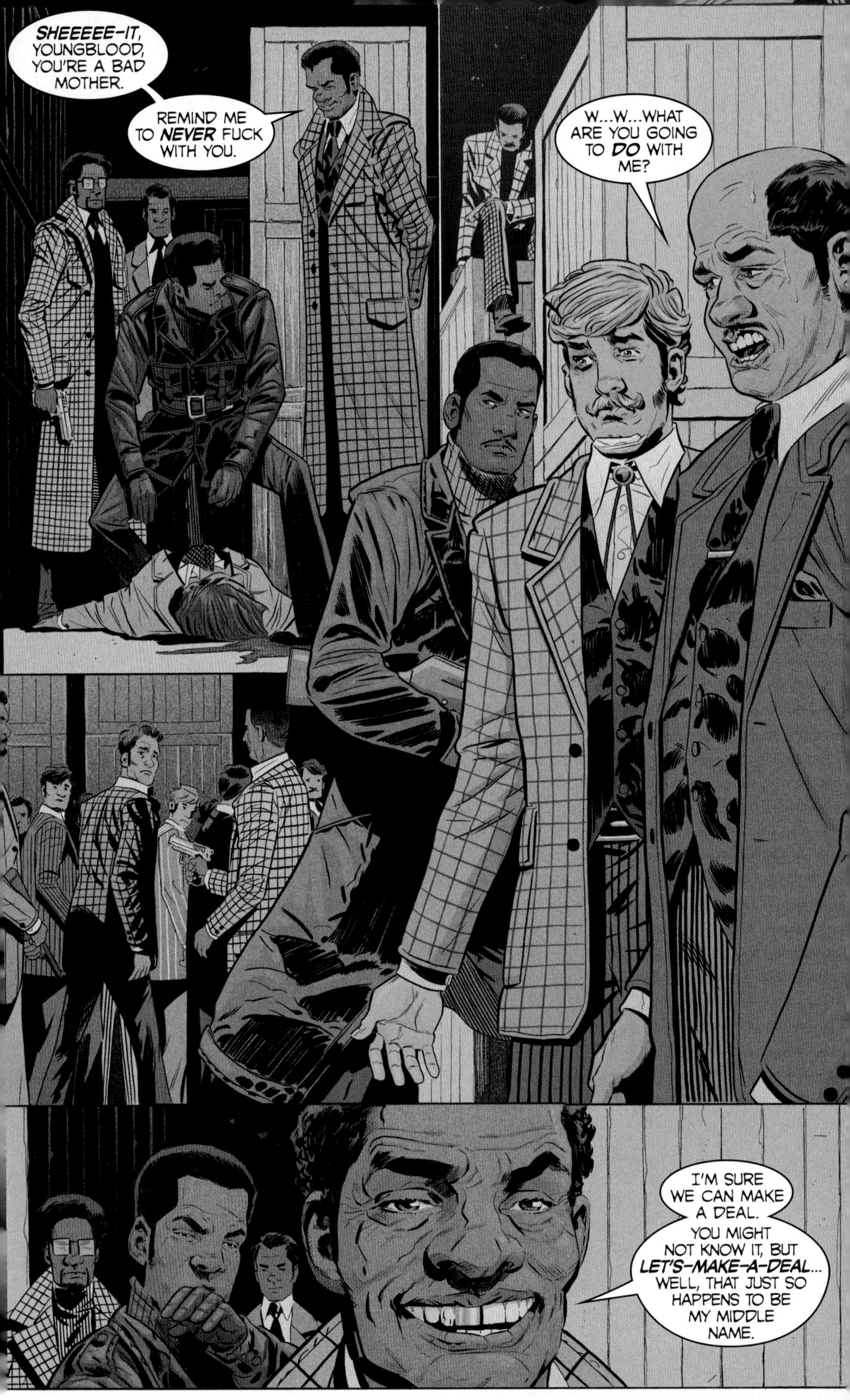
SHEEEEE-IT, YOUNGBLOOD, YOU'RE A BAD MOTHER.
REMIND ME TO NEVER FUCK WITH YOU.
W...W...WHAT ARE YOU GOING TO DO WITH ME?
I'M SURE WE CAN MAKE A DEAL.
YOU MIGHT NOT KNOW IT, BUT LET'S-MAKE-A-DEAL... WELL, THAT JUST SO HAPPENS TO BE MY MIDDLE NAME.

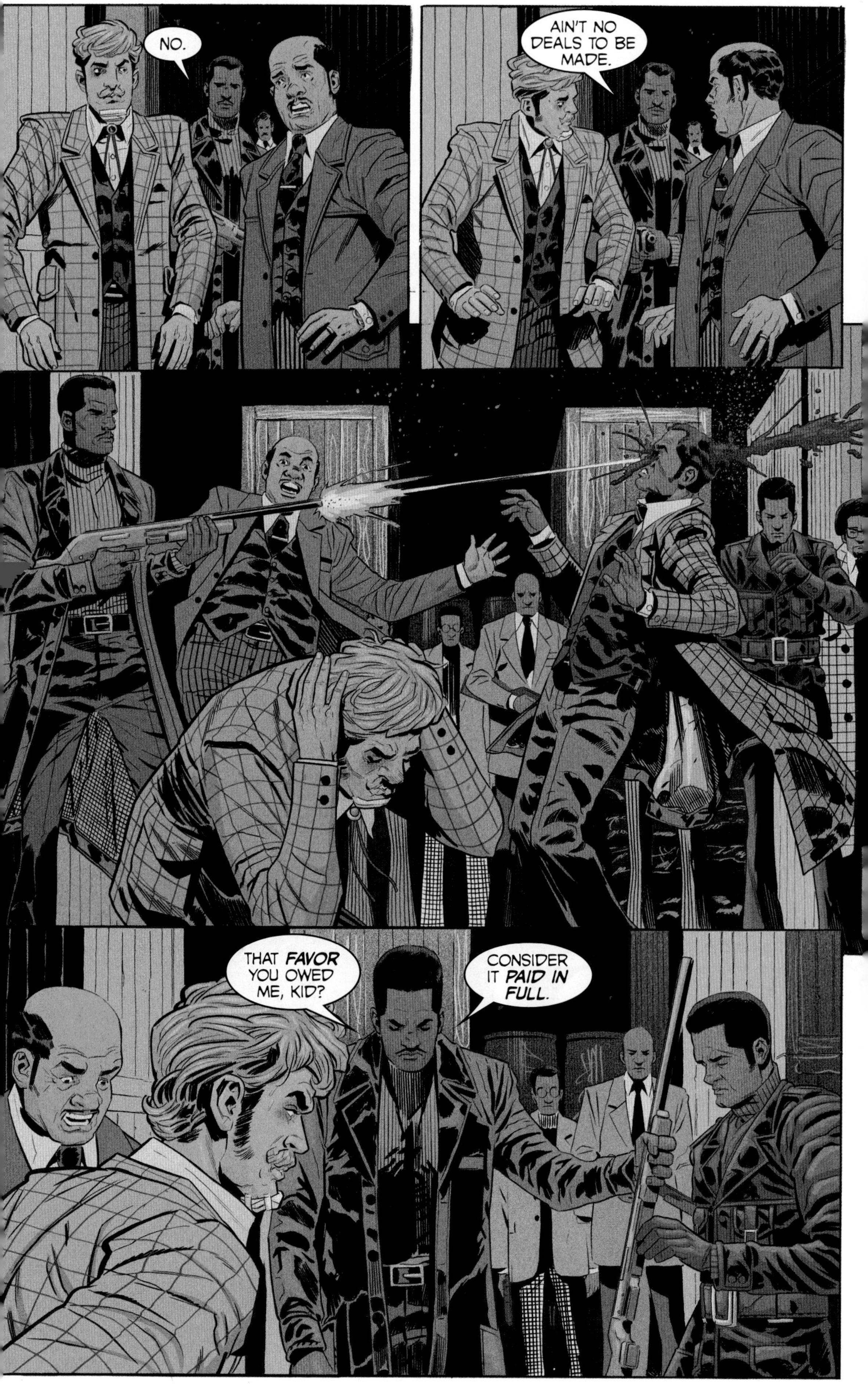
NO.
AIN'T NO DEALS TO BE MADE.
THAT FAVOR YOU OWED ME, KID?
CONSIDER IT PAID IN FULL.

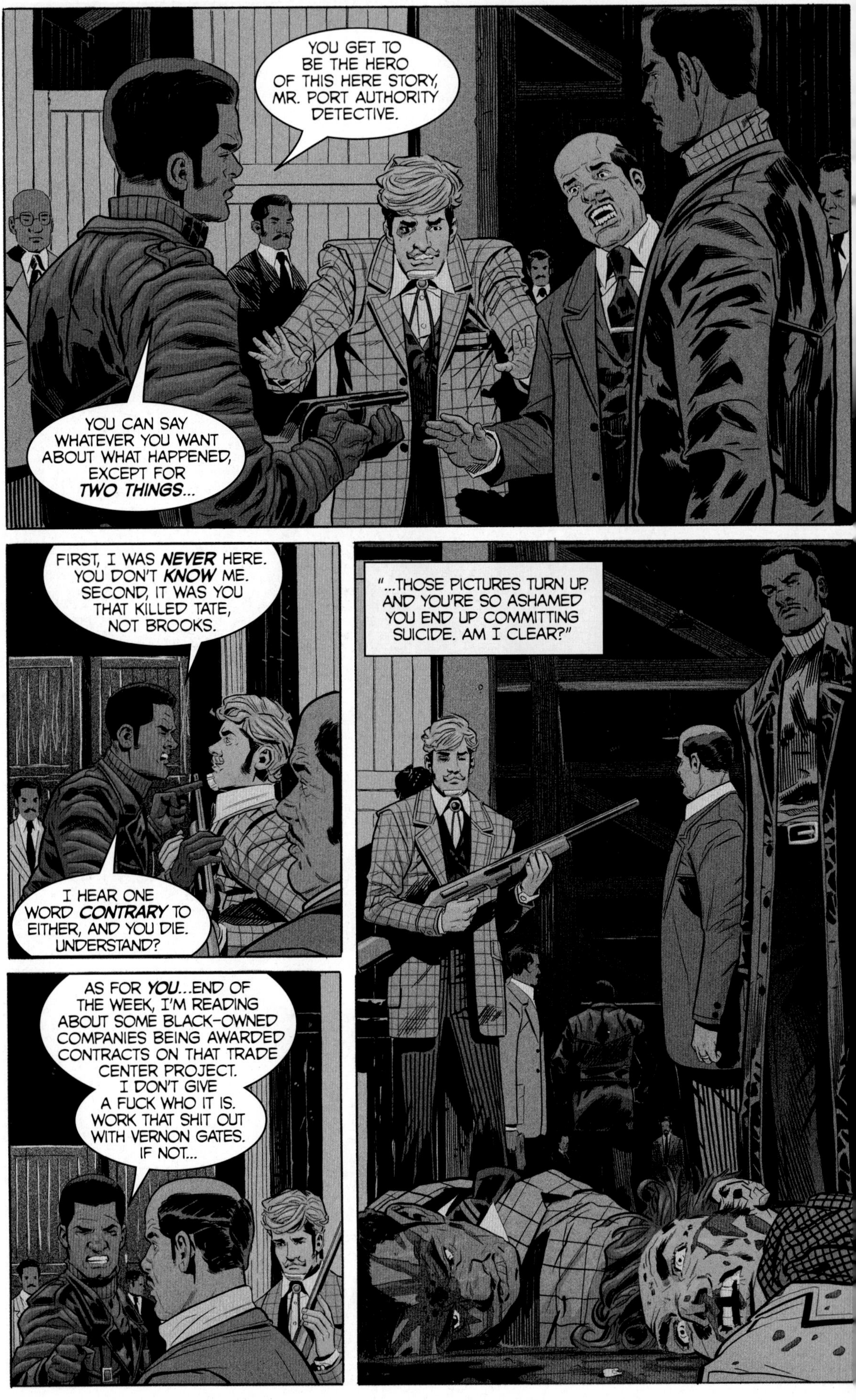
YOU GET TO BE THE HERO OF THIS HERE STORY, MR. PORT AUTHORITY DETECTIVE.
YOU CAN SAY WHATEVER YOU WANT ABOUT WHAT HAPPENED, EXCEPT FOR *TWO THINGS*...
FIRST, I WAS *NEVER* HERE. YOU DON'T *KNOW* ME. SECOND, IT WAS YOU THAT KILLED TATE, NOT BROOKS.
I HEAR ONE WORD *CONTRARY* TO EITHER, AND YOU DIE. UNDERSTAND?
AS FOR *YOU*...END OF THE WEEK, I'M READING ABOUT SOME BLACK-OWNED COMPANIES BEING AWARDED CONTRACTS ON THAT TRADE CENTER PROJECT. I DON'T GIVE A FUCK WHO IT IS. WORK THAT SHIT OUT WITH VERNON GATES. IF NOT...
"...THOSE PICTURES TURN UP. AND YOU'RE SO ASHAMED YOU END UP COMMITTING SUICIDE. AM I CLEAR?"

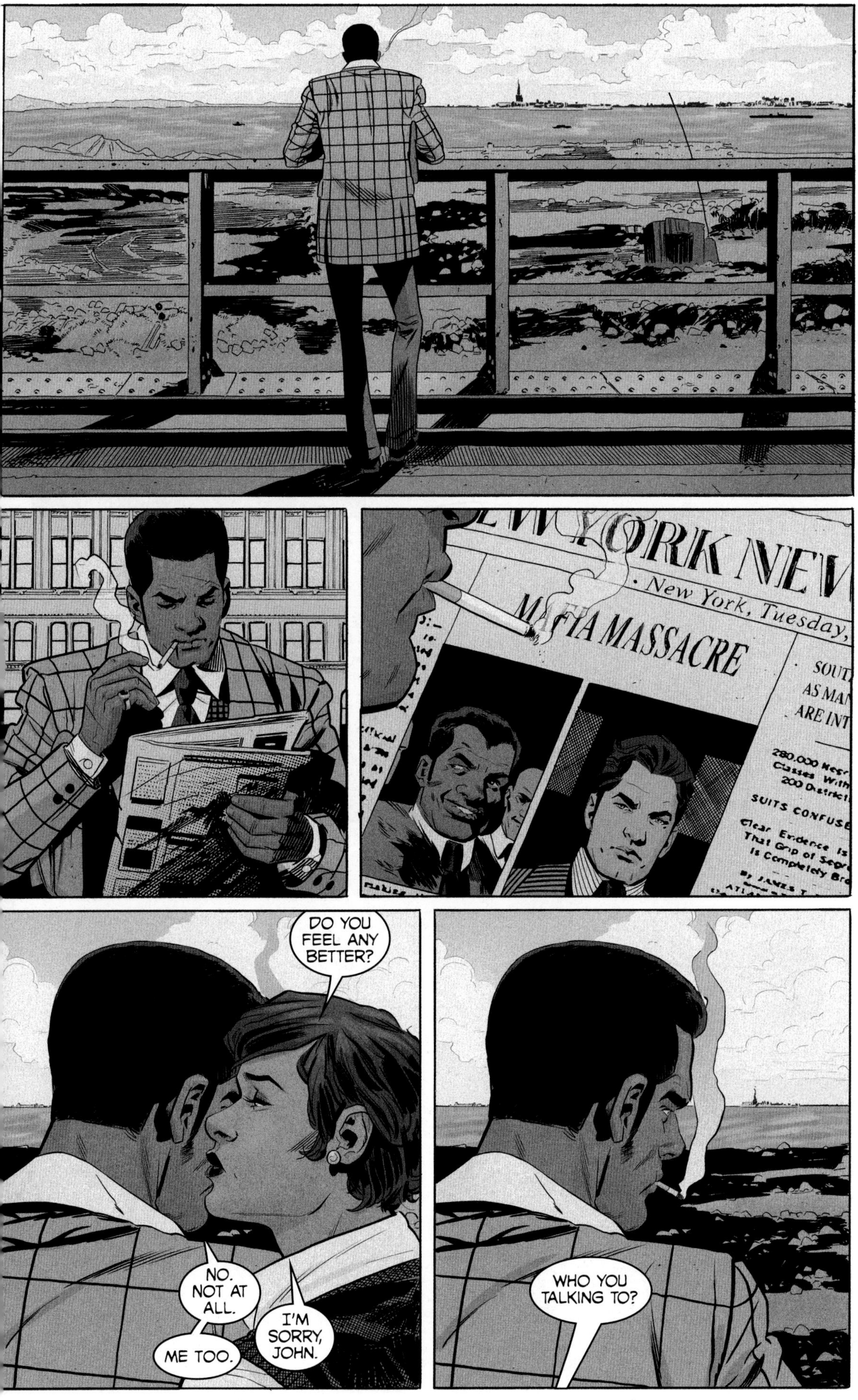
New York, Tuesday,
DO YOU FEEL ANY BETTER?
NO. NOT AT ALL.
I'M SORRY, JOHN.
ME TOO.
WHO YOU TALKING TO?

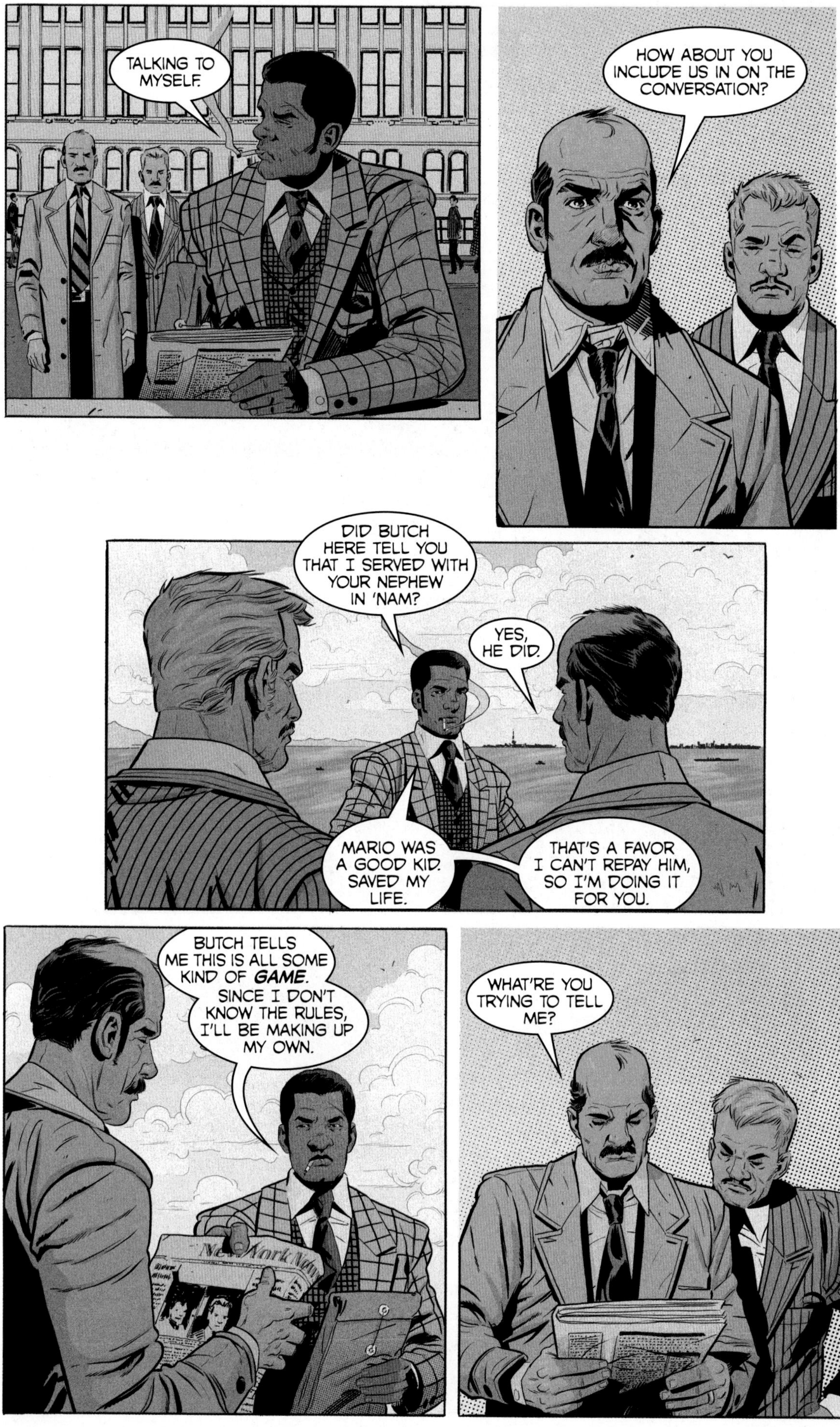
TALKING TO MYSELF.
HOW ABOUT YOU INCLUDE US IN ON THE CONVERSATION?
DID BUTCH HERE TELL YOU THAT I SERVED WITH YOUR NEPHEW IN 'NAM?
YES, HE DID.
MARIO WAS A GOOD KID. SAVED MY LIFE.
THAT'S A FAVOR I CAN'T REPAY HIM, SO I'M DOING IT FOR YOU.
BUTCH TELLS ME THIS IS ALL SOME KIND OF **GAME**.
SINCE I DON'T KNOW THE RULES, I'LL BE MAKING UP MY OWN.
WHAT'RE YOU TRYING TO TELL ME?

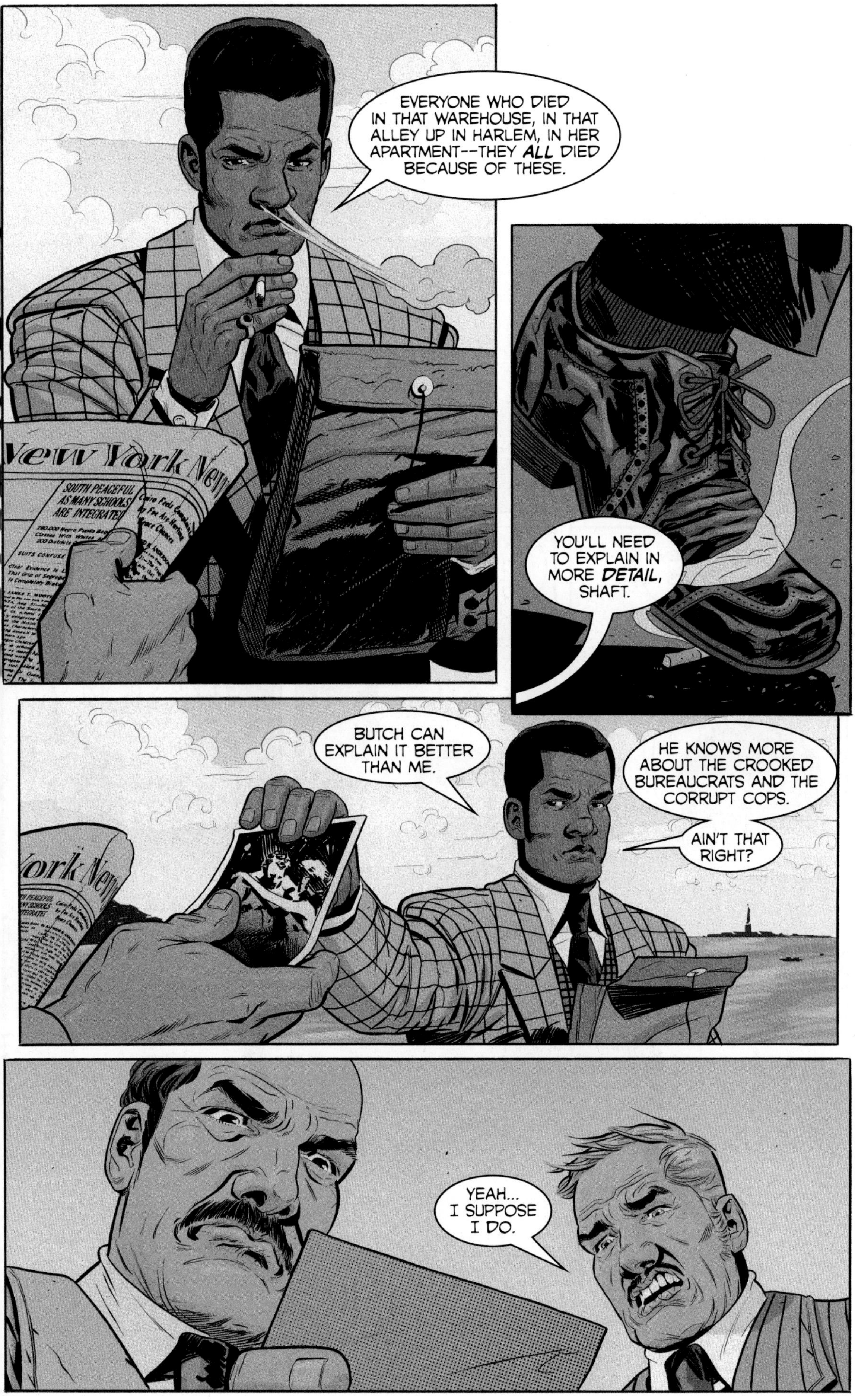
EVERYONE WHO DIED IN THAT WAREHOUSE, IN THAT ALLEY UP IN HARLEM, IN HER APARTMENT--THEY ALL DIED BECAUSE OF THESE.
New York New
SOUTH PEACEFUL AS MANY SCHOOLS ARE INTEGRATED
YOU'LL NEED TO EXPLAIN IN MORE DETAIL, SHAFT.
BUTCH CAN EXPLAIN IT BETTER THAN ME.
HE KNOWS MORE ABOUT THE CROOKED BUREAUCRATS AND THE CORRUPT COPS.
AIN'T THAT RIGHT?
YEAH... I SUPPOSE I DO.

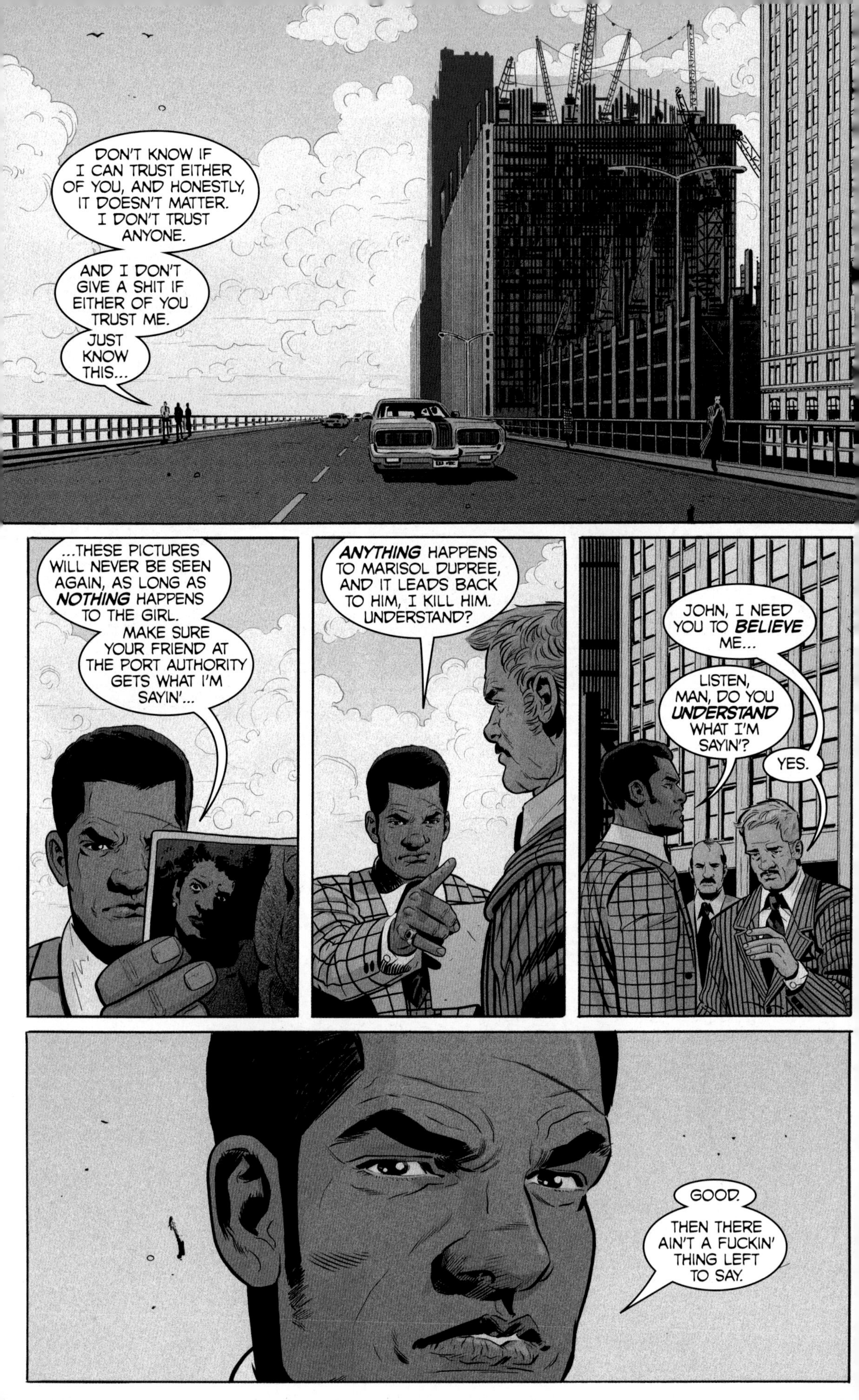
DON'T KNOW IF I CAN TRUST EITHER OF YOU, AND HONESTLY, IT DOESN'T MATTER. I DON'T TRUST ANYONE.
AND I DON'T GIVE A SHIT IF EITHER OF YOU TRUST ME.
JUST KNOW THIS...
...THESE PICTURES WILL NEVER BE SEEN AGAIN, AS LONG AS NOTHING HAPPENS TO THE GIRL.
MAKE SURE YOUR FRIEND AT THE PORT AUTHORITY GETS WHAT I'M SAYIN'...
ANYTHING HAPPENS TO MARISOL DUPREE, AND IT LEADS BACK TO HIM, I KILL HIM. UNDERSTAND?
JOHN, I NEED YOU TO BELIEVE ME...
LISTEN, MAN, DO YOU UNDERSTAND WHAT I'M SAYIN'?
YES.
GOOD.
THEN THERE AIN'T A FUCKIN' THING LEFT TO SAY.

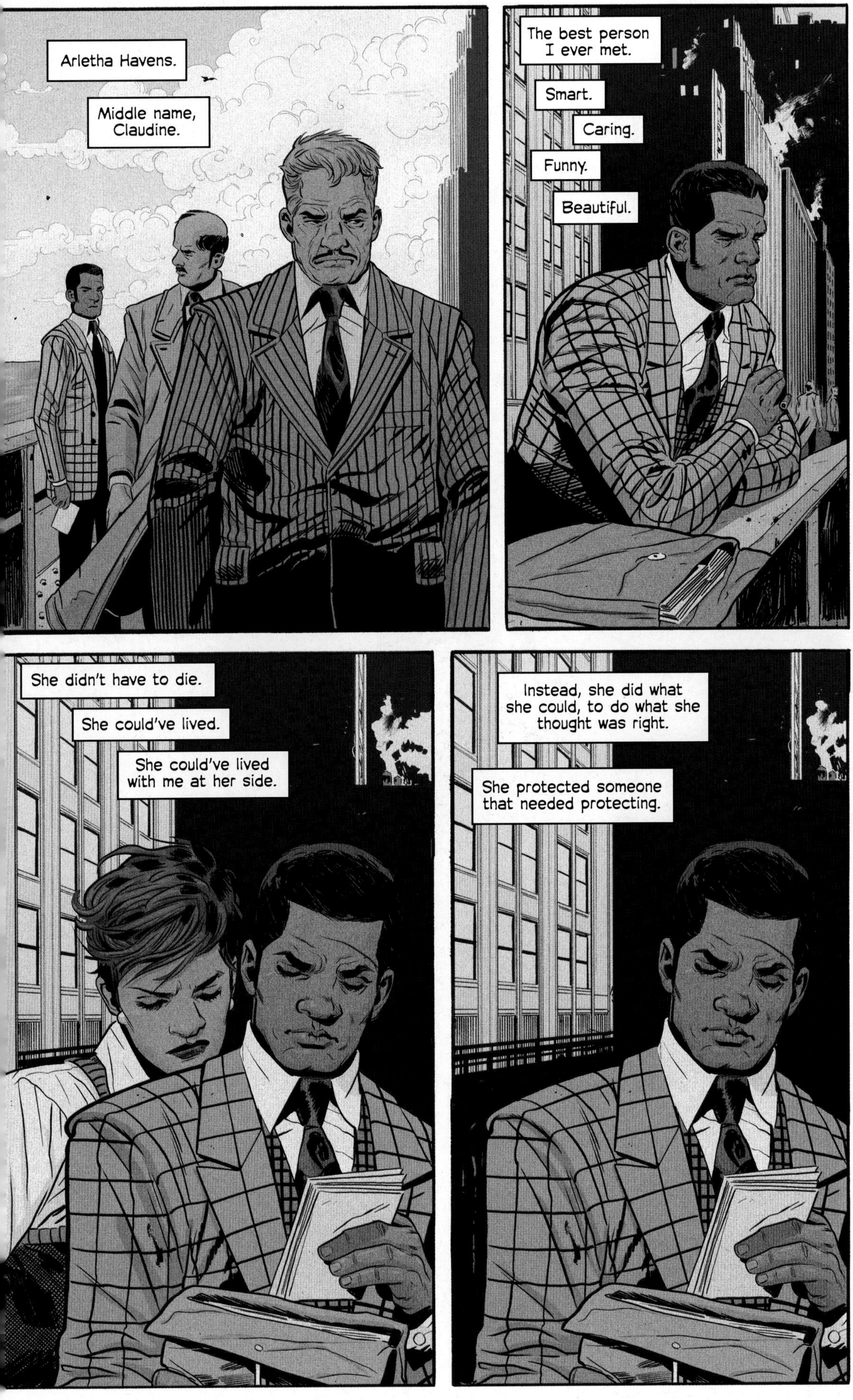

Arletha Havens.
Middle name, Claudine.
The best person I ever met.
Smart.
Caring.
Funny.
Beautiful.
She didn't have to die.
She could've lived.
She could've lived with me at her side.
Instead, she did what she could, to do what she thought was right.
She protected someone that needed protecting.

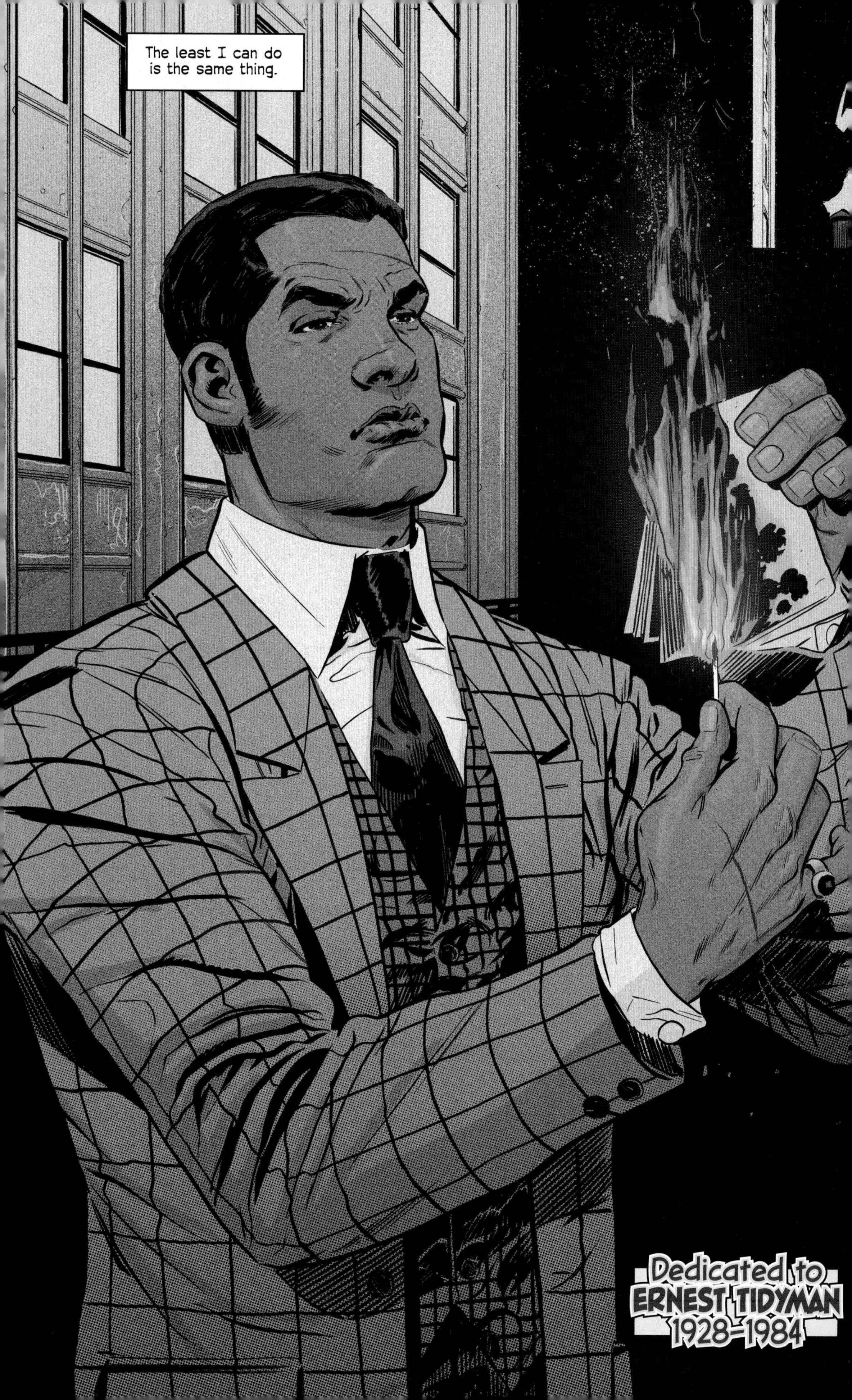
The least I can do is the same thing.
Dedicated to
ERNEST TIDYMAN
1928–1984

BONUS MATERIAL

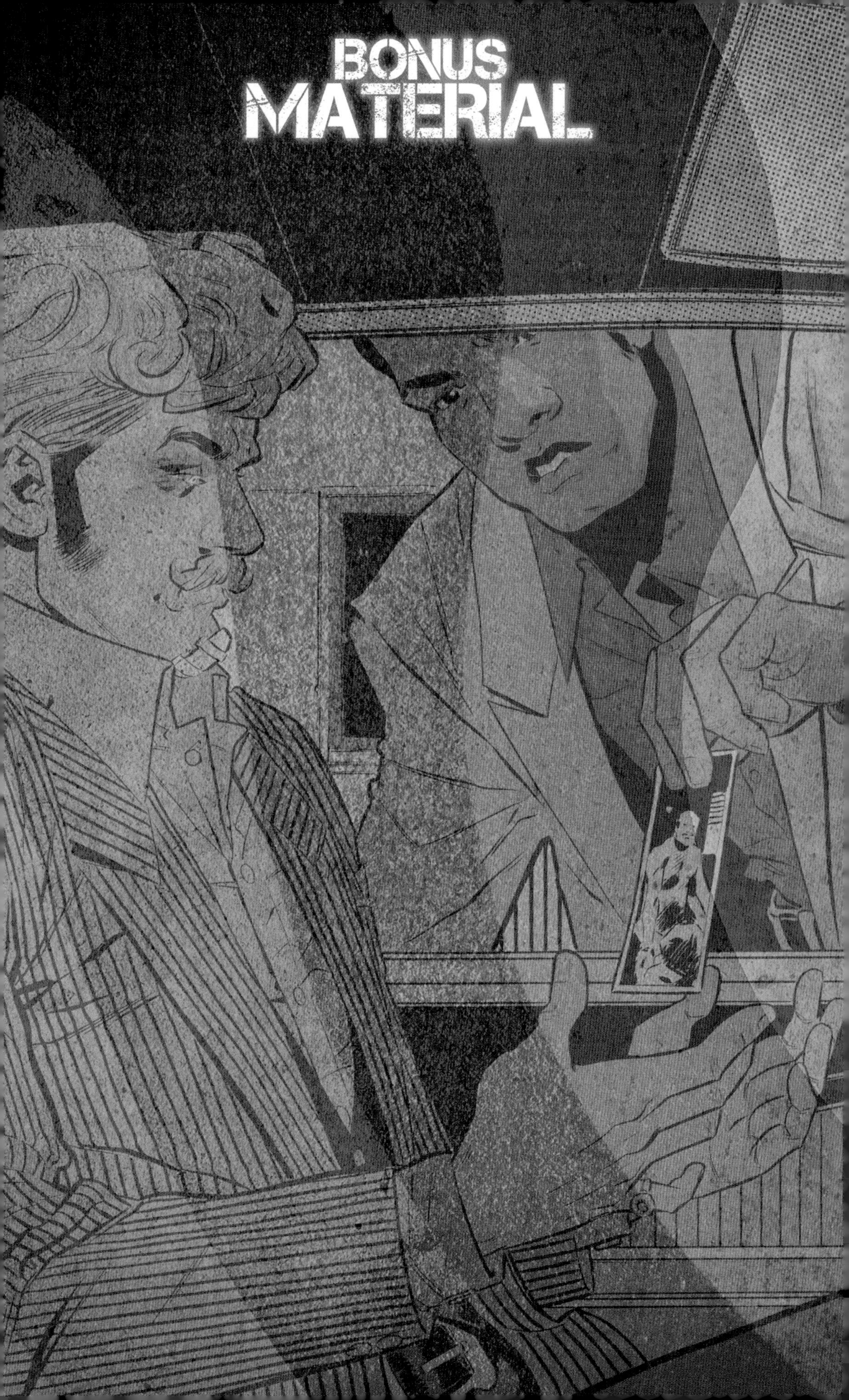

DESIGNING SHAFT

The initial instinct in designing John Shaft for comics would have been to make him look like actor Richard Roundtree. As the star of three Shaft movies and the television series, Roundtree is in many ways the embodiment of Shaft—at least the cinematic version of the character. In reality, Roundtree looked nothing like what Ernest Tidyman described in the Shaft novels. There is a long-running rumor that Tidyman didn't care for Roundtree's looks (he was too pretty), and the author hated the mustache. Since the comic was going to come from the character in the books, I pushed for a design more true to Tidyman's description. I gave Bilquis the photos of several actors that I felt matched the descriptions in the book. Among them were Robert Hooks, Idris Elba, and Tony King, the actor that most looks like the Shaft that I imagine.

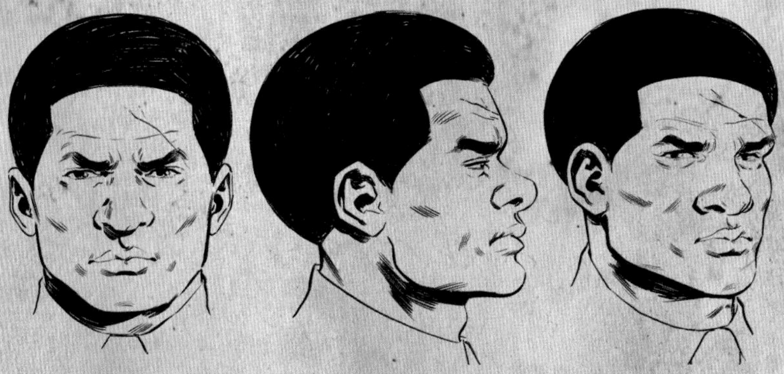

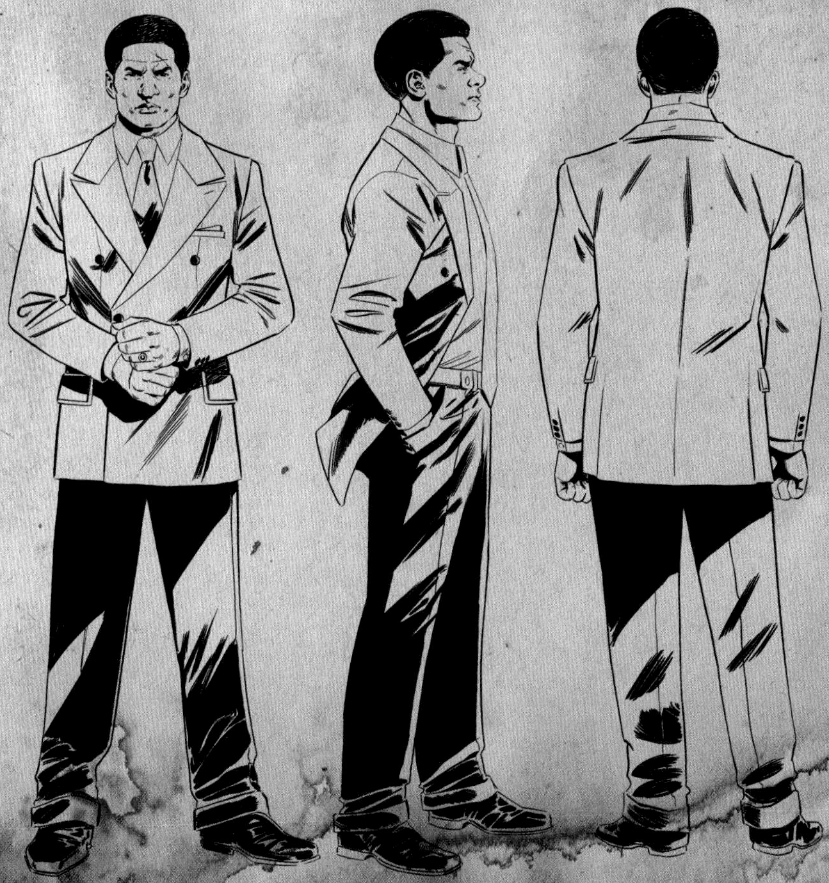

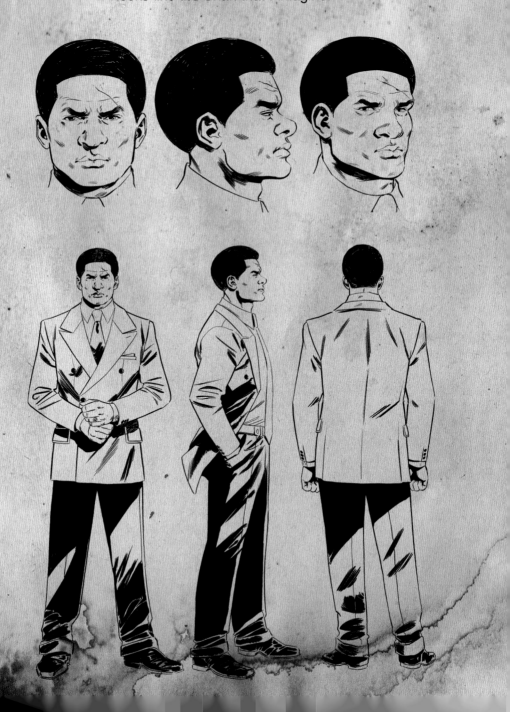

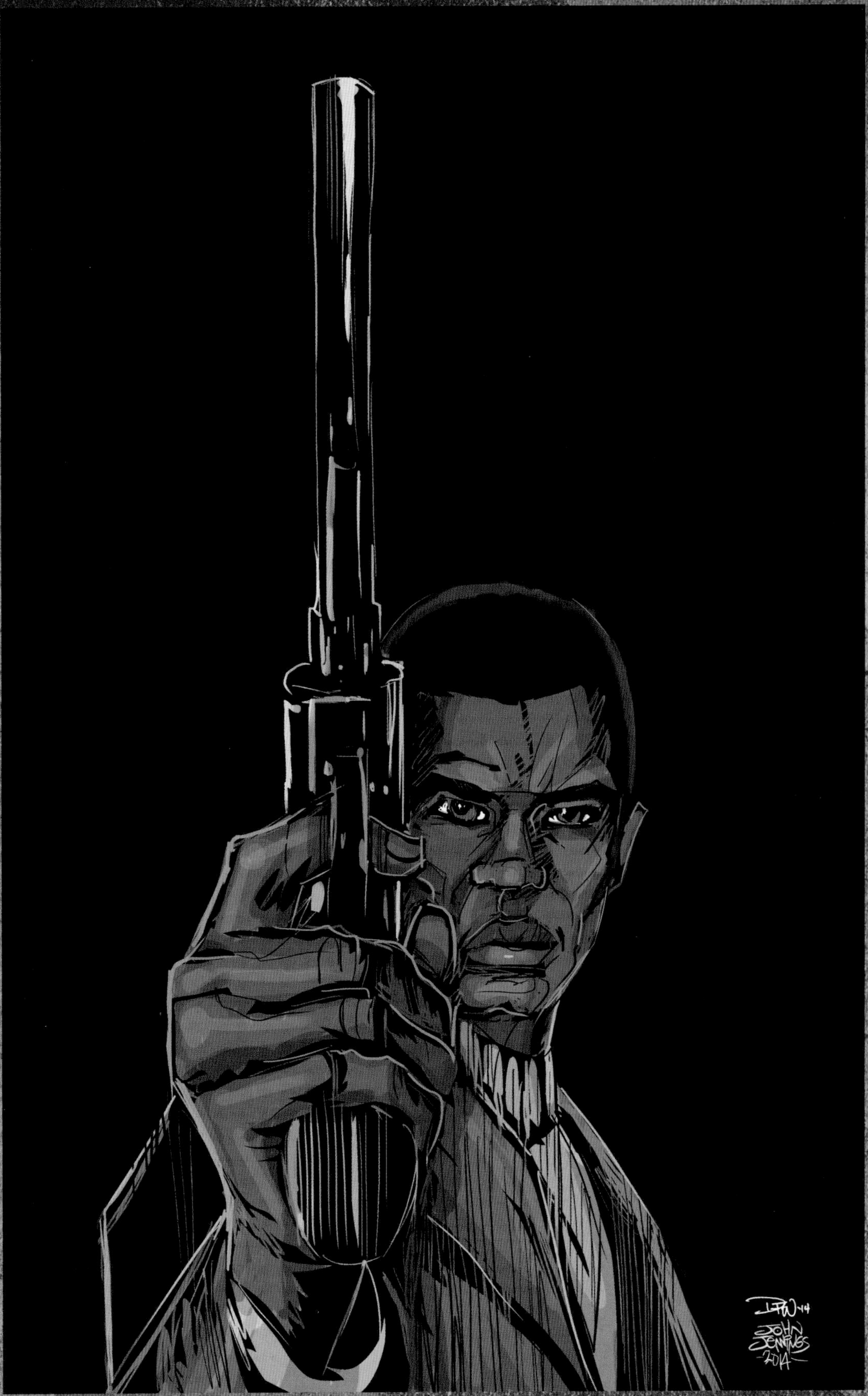

UNUSED ILLUSTRATION BY **DAVID WALKER**
INKS AND COLORS BY **JOHN JENNINGS**

SHAFT SCRIPT PAGES

PAGE 4

Panel 1 - Big panel - Inside the dressing room at the arena. JOHN SHAFT is sitting on a table, dressed in a boxing robe. He is in his early 20s, but can easily pass for older. Shaft's trainer, EDDIE WINSLOW, black, late 40s, is wrapping his hands before the fight. Winslow is working on Shaft's left hand. DOC POWELL is also in the locker room.

CAPTION: Started boxing for real in 1964, when I went into the Marines. Got pretty good. Then I got shipped off to Vietnam in '65.

SHAFT: Where's Eli?

WINSLOW: Don't know. How's that feel?

Panel 2 - Shaft examining his left hand.

CAPTION: Started boxing again after I got home from the war. Needed the money. But more than that, I needed to hit something.

SHAFT: Feels good.

Panel 3 - Close up of Winslow wrapping the right hand. We can see a scar on the back of Shaft's right hand.

Panel 4 - Close in on Shaft. We can see a similar scar on his forehead, just above his left eye.

CAPTION: Thing about me is that I was a fighter long before I became a boxer.

SHAFT: What the fuck're they doin' here?

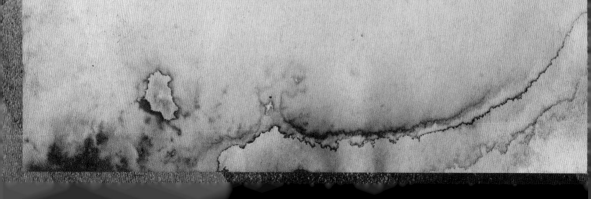

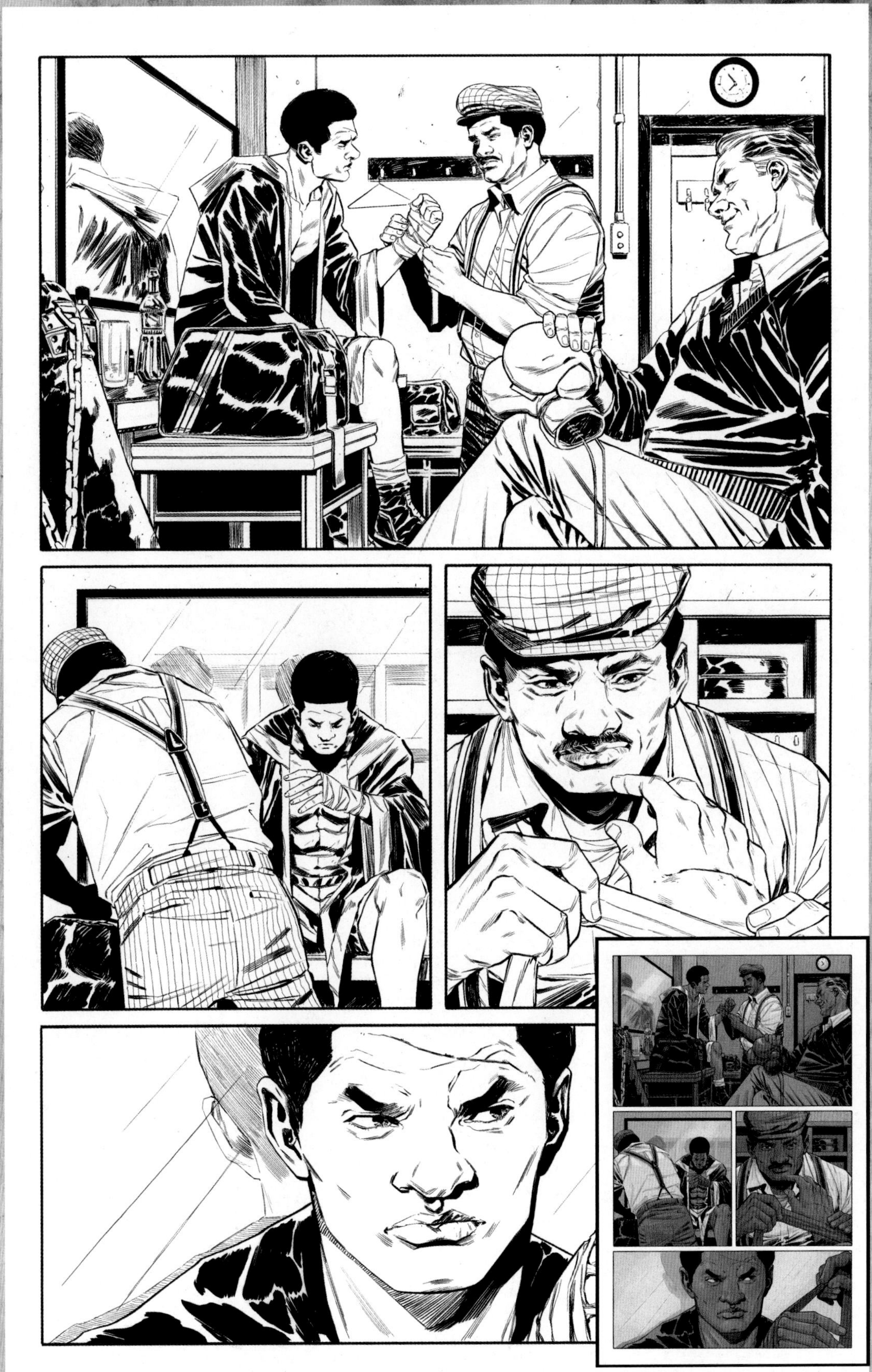

SHAFT #1 PAGE 4

Inks by Bilquis Evely, Colors by Daniel Miwa

PAGE 5

Panel 1 - Big panel - Eli Jackson, Shaft's manager, entering the locker room. Jackson is accompanied by Junius Tate, Bamma Brooks, and perhaps one other goon.

CAPTION: Eli Jackson's my manager. His friends don't need any introductions.

CAPTION: Junius Tate. Gangster. Works for Knocks Persons, who runs Harlem.

CAPTION: Bamma Brooks. When I was a kid, he was the man - the next Joe Louis. That never happened. Took a dive in the fifth, and then became hired muscle for Tate.

JACKSON: Hey, Johnny. You ready for your big night? Got some friends I want you to meet.

TATE: Wha'sup, youngblood? Been hearin' lotta good things 'bout you. Cats 'round Harlem say you the next Cassius Clay.

Panel 2 - Shaft does not look impressed.

SHAFT: Man goes by Muhammad Ali these days.

Panel 3 - Tate still smiling.

TATE: Sheeeeee-it, I don't care what the fuck the motherfucker calls himself. Names don't mean shit to me, youngblood.

Panel 4 - Shaft sitting on the table while Winslow wraps his hands. Shaft isn't even looking at Tate anymore, he's more concerned with what Winslow is doing.

SHAFT: I hear you talkin', but you ain't sayin' anything.

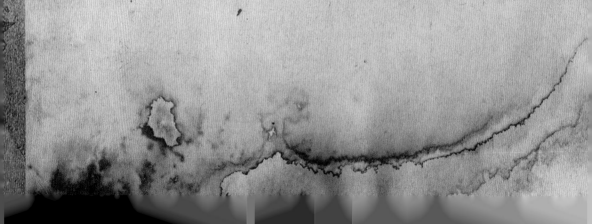

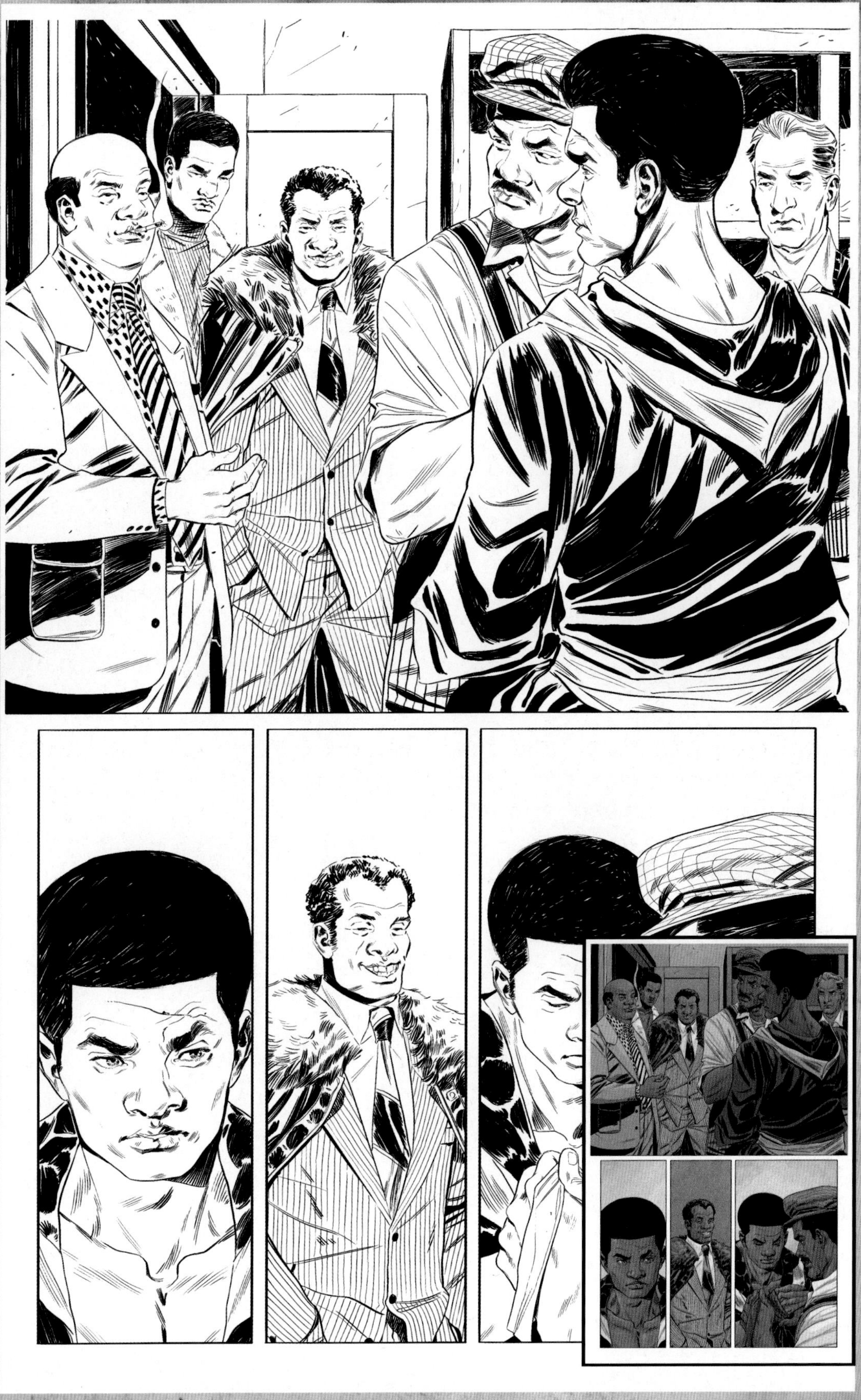

SHAFT #1 PAGE 5

Inks by Bilquis Evely, Colors by Daniel Miwa

Panel 1 - Shaft wearing his robe with the hood up over his head, accompanied by Winslow and Doc Powell, walking out of the locker room, past Tate.

CAPTION: A man like Junius Tate only wants one thing from a boxer like me.

TATE: Give 'em a good show, youngblood.

Panel 2 - Extreme close up of Shaft's face. We can see his eyes, and the scar on his forehead, but that is all.

CAPTION: But like I said, I was a fighter long before becoming a boxer.

Panel 3 - Flashback - Young Shaft, ten years earlier, about 13 or 14 years old. He is in a fight with another teenager, who is armed with a bicycle chain.

CAPTION: You can't ask a fighter to give up.

Panel 4 - Flashback - The other kid whipping Young Shaft in the face with the bicycle chain, as Young Shaft holds up his right hand to protect himself.

CAPTION: Boxing is a sport.

Panel 5 - Flashback - We see the chain tearing into the back of Young Shaft's hand and his forehead - this is where he got the matching scars.

CAPTION: Fighting is life or death.

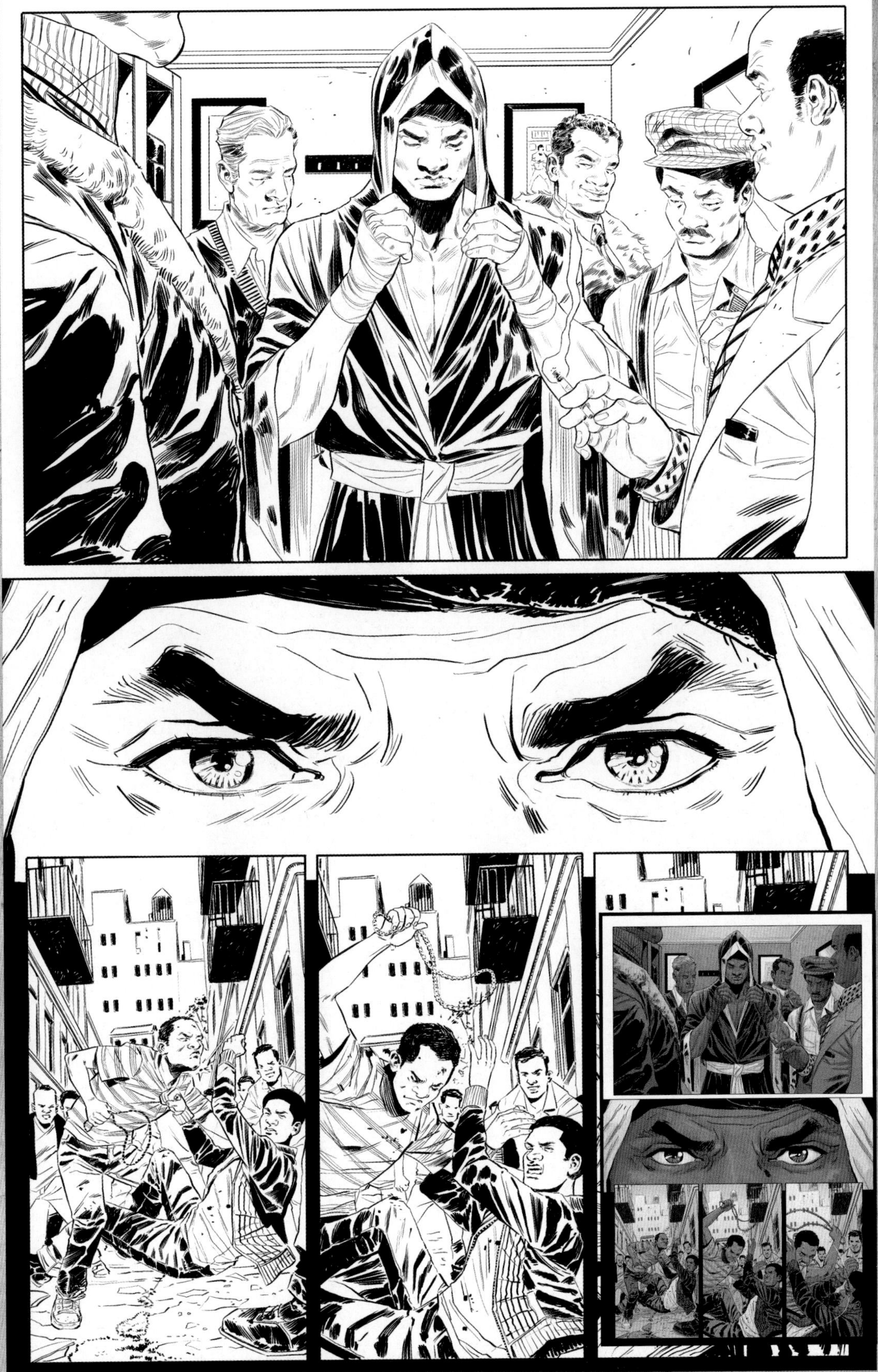

SHAFT #1 PAGE 6

Inks by Bilquis Evely, Colors by Daniel Miwa

PAGE 18

Panel 1 - Tyrone and Shaft are completely in the alley, with their backs against the brick wall. The other gangsters are now in the alley well - four of them in total. Only one has his gun drawn.

CAPTION/SHAFT: Can't really describe what happened, but it was like someone had turned on a light switch.

CAPTION/SHAFT: No, that's not right. It wasn't like someone turned on a light switch. It was like someone unlocked the cage and let the animal out.

Panel 2 - Angle in on the gangsters.

CAPTION/SHAFT: Hadn't felt that way since I was in 'Nam.

Panel 3 - Tyrone, Shaft standing just a step or two behind him. Tyrone looks frightened. Shaft looks intense.

CAPTION/SHAFT: Concrete and skyscrapers had replaced rice paddies and jungles, but the feeling was the same.

Panel 4 - Shaft shoving Tyrone at the gangster with the gun.

CAPTION/SHAFT: Life and death.

CAPTION/SHAFT: Live or die.

Panel 5 - Shaft has grabbed the arm of the gangster with the gun, and has managed to twist the gangster's arm in a way that he is pointing the gun at himself as it goes off.

CAPTION/SHAFT: It'd been two years since I last held a gun.

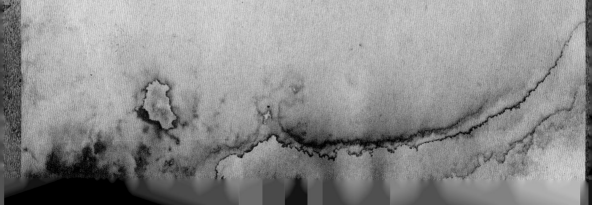

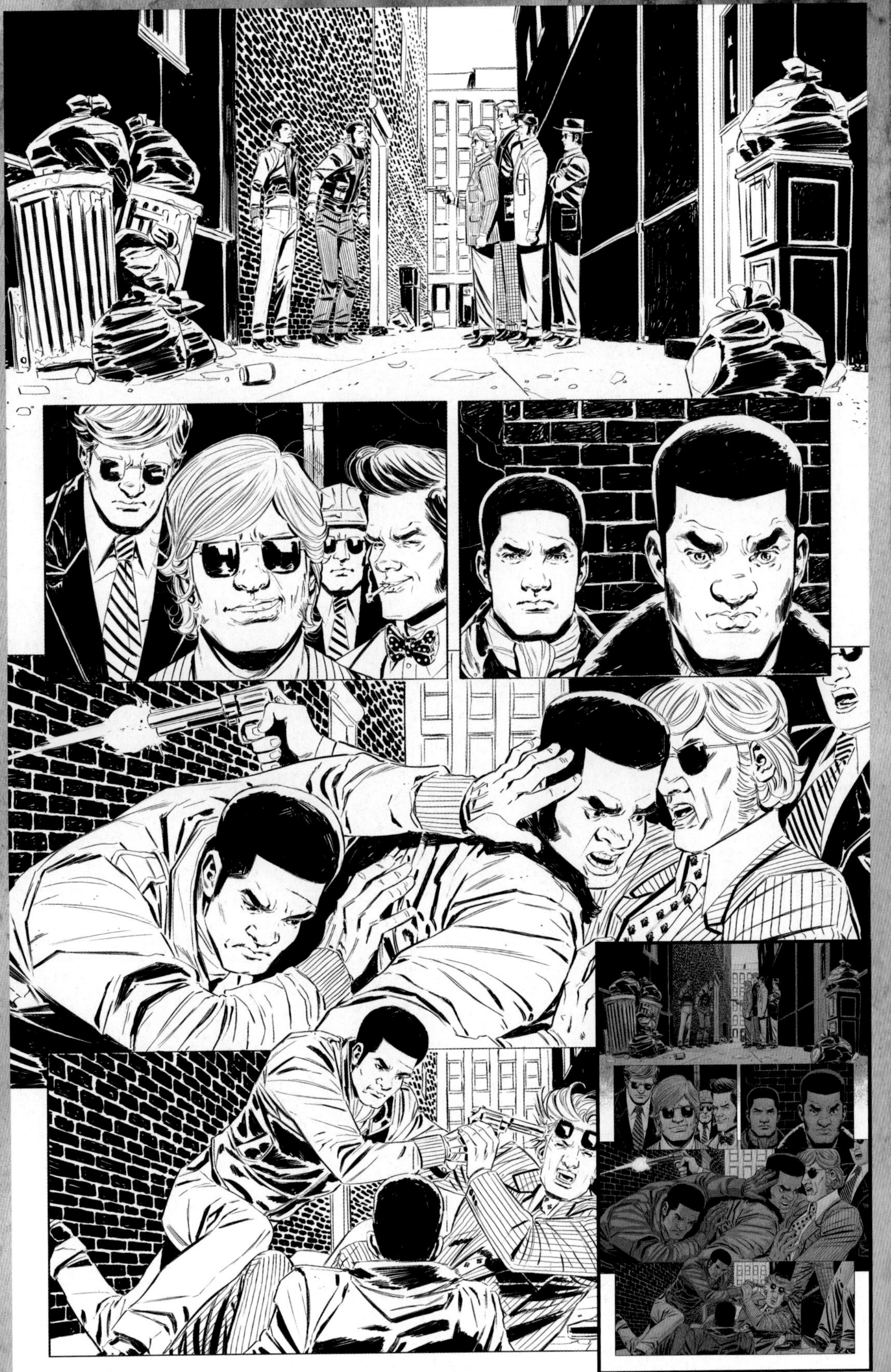

SHAFT #2 PAGE 18

Inks by Bilquis Evely, Colors by Daniel Miwa

COVER GALLERY

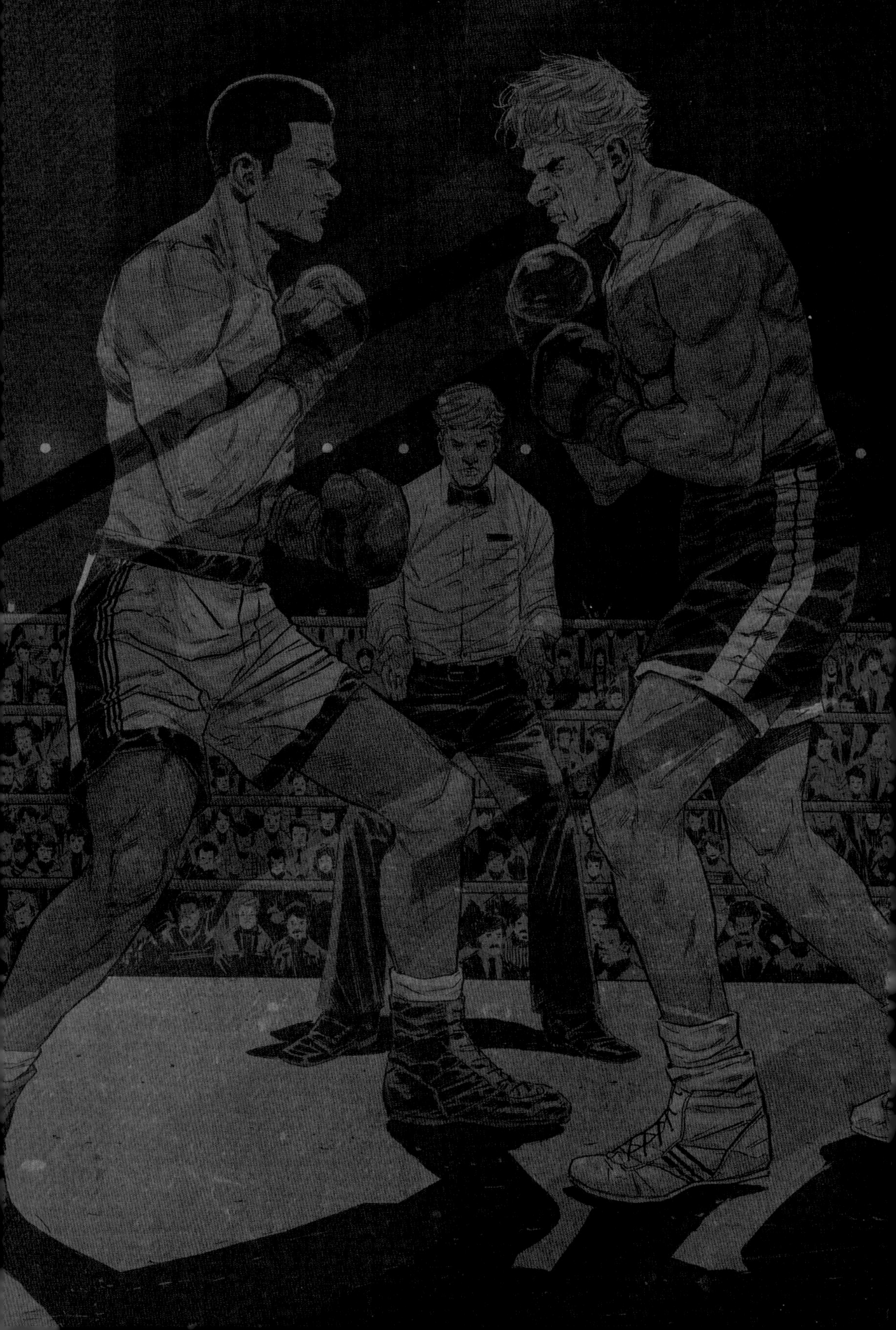

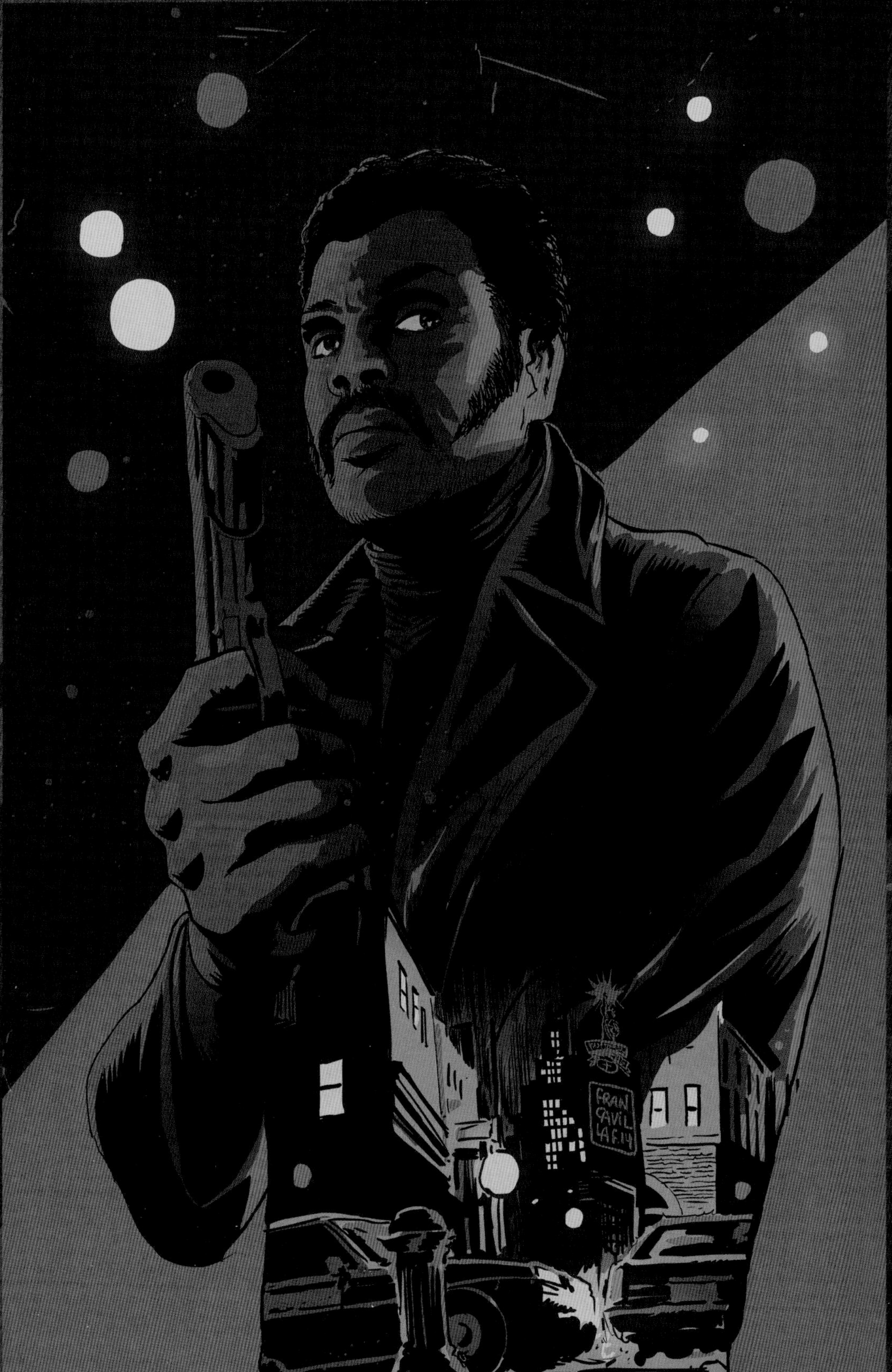
FRAN
CAVIL
LA F.14

ISSUE ONE VARIANT COVER BY
FRANCESCO FRANCAVILLA

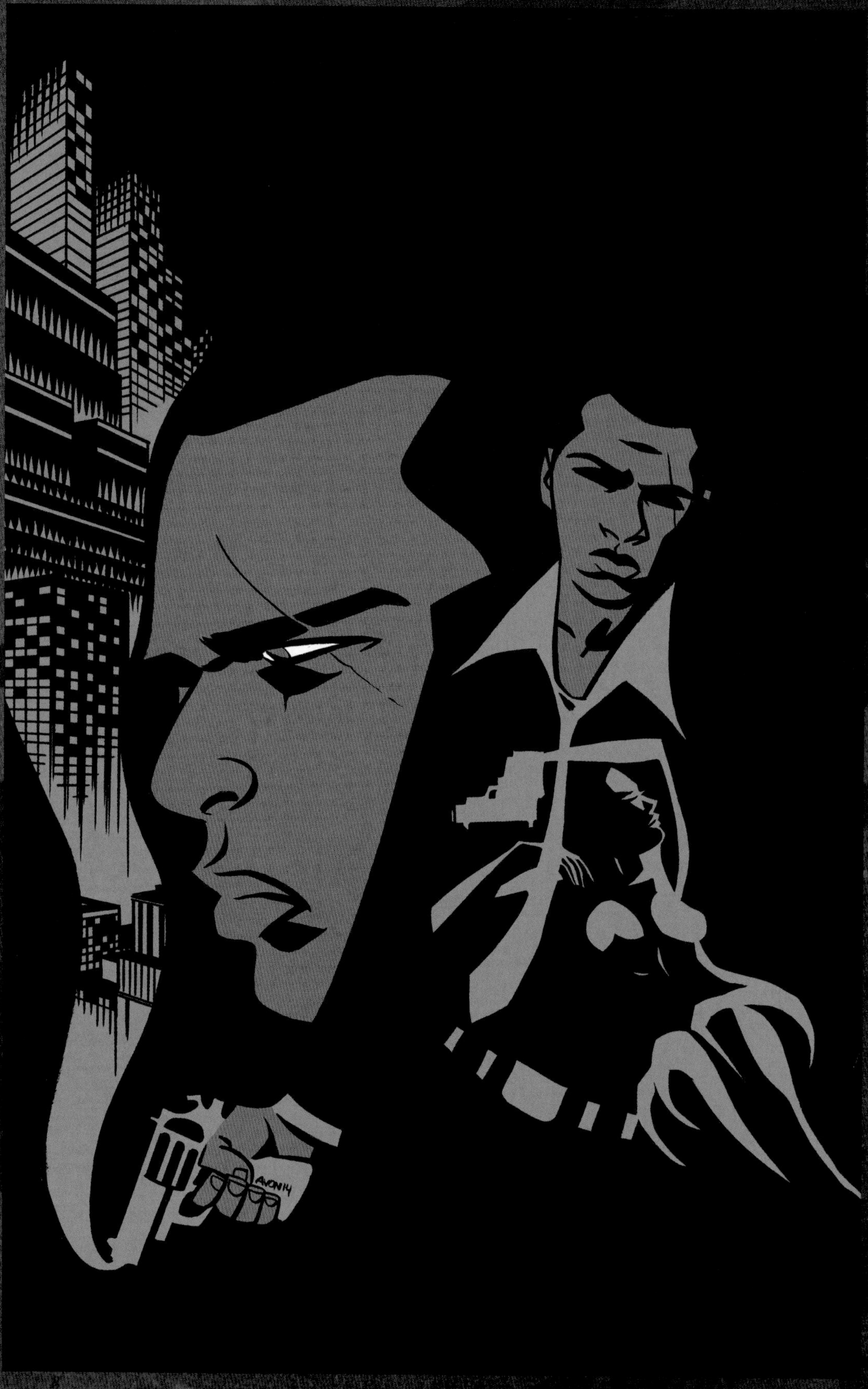
AVON 14

ISSUE ONE VARIANT COVER BY
MICHAEL AVON OEMING

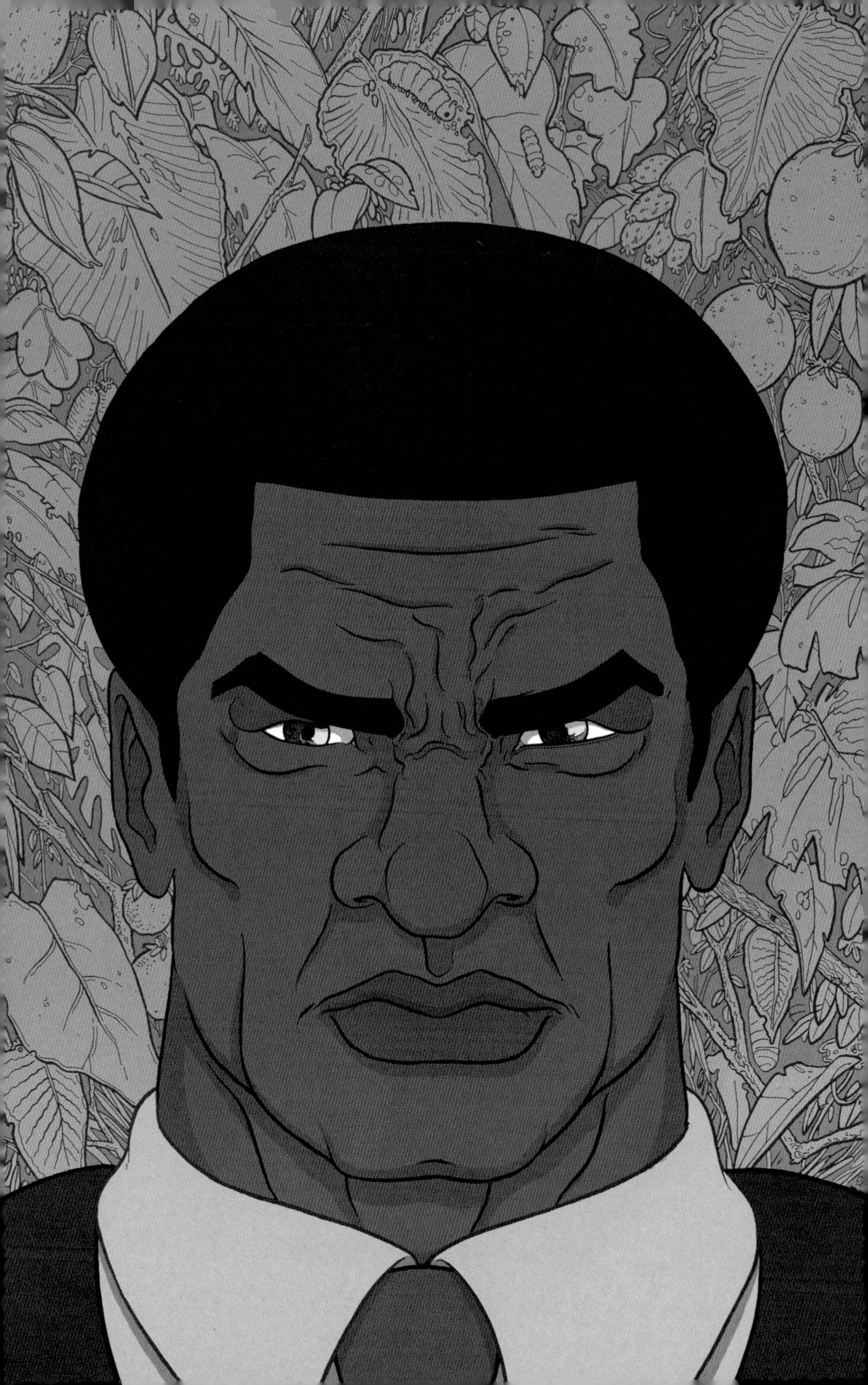

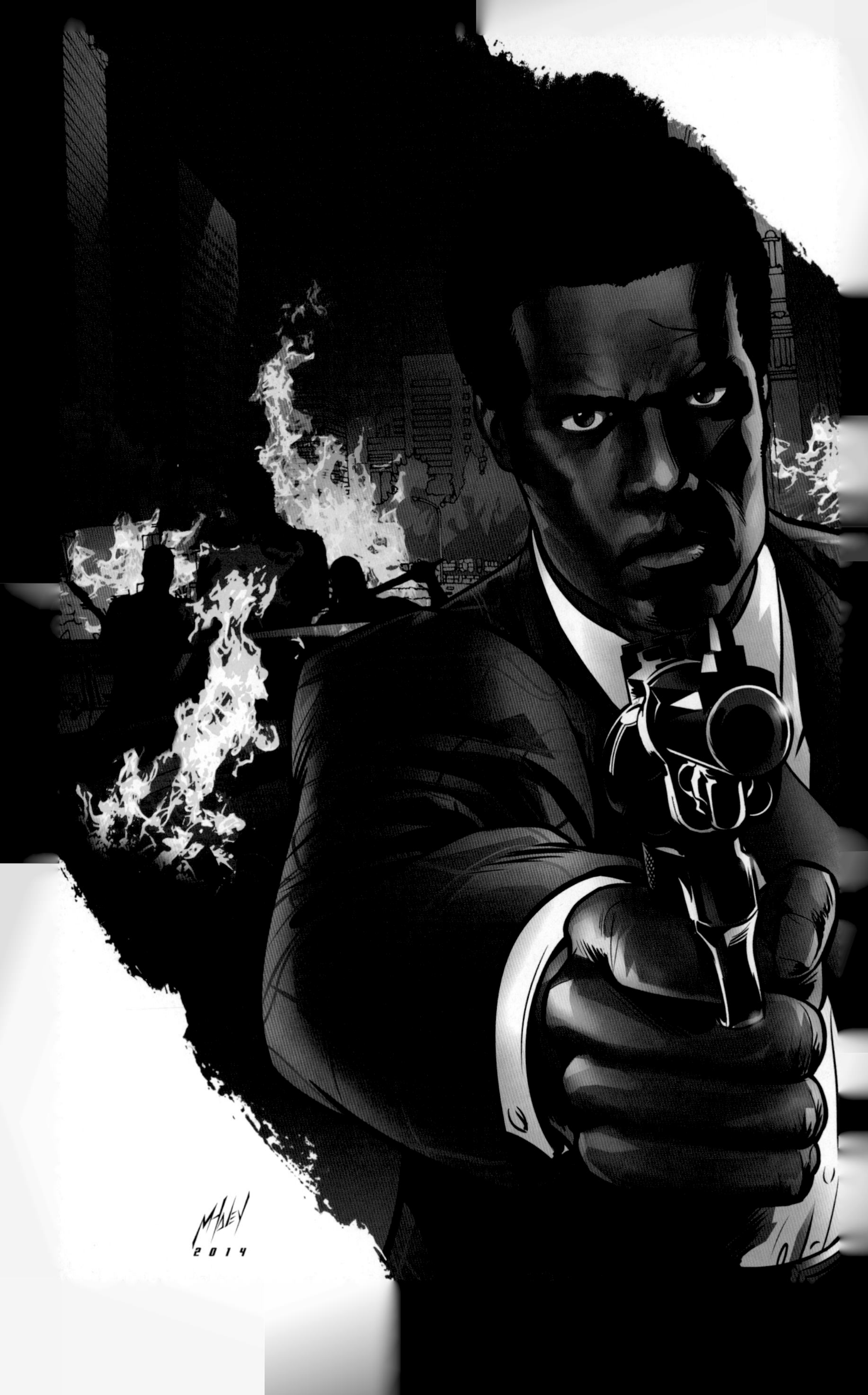
2014

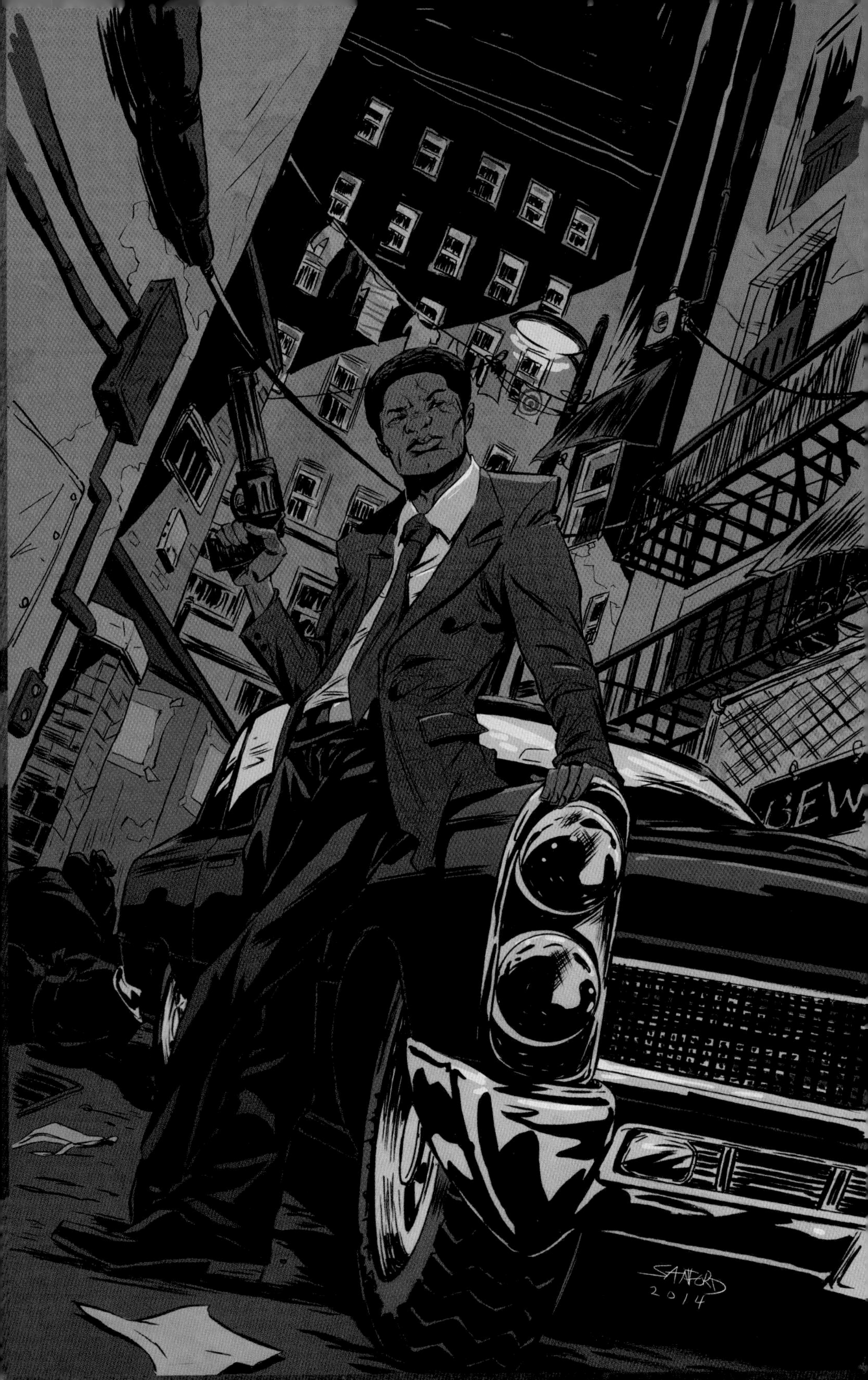
BEW
SANFORD
2014

ISSUE ONE SUBSCRIPTION COVER BY
SANFORD GREENE

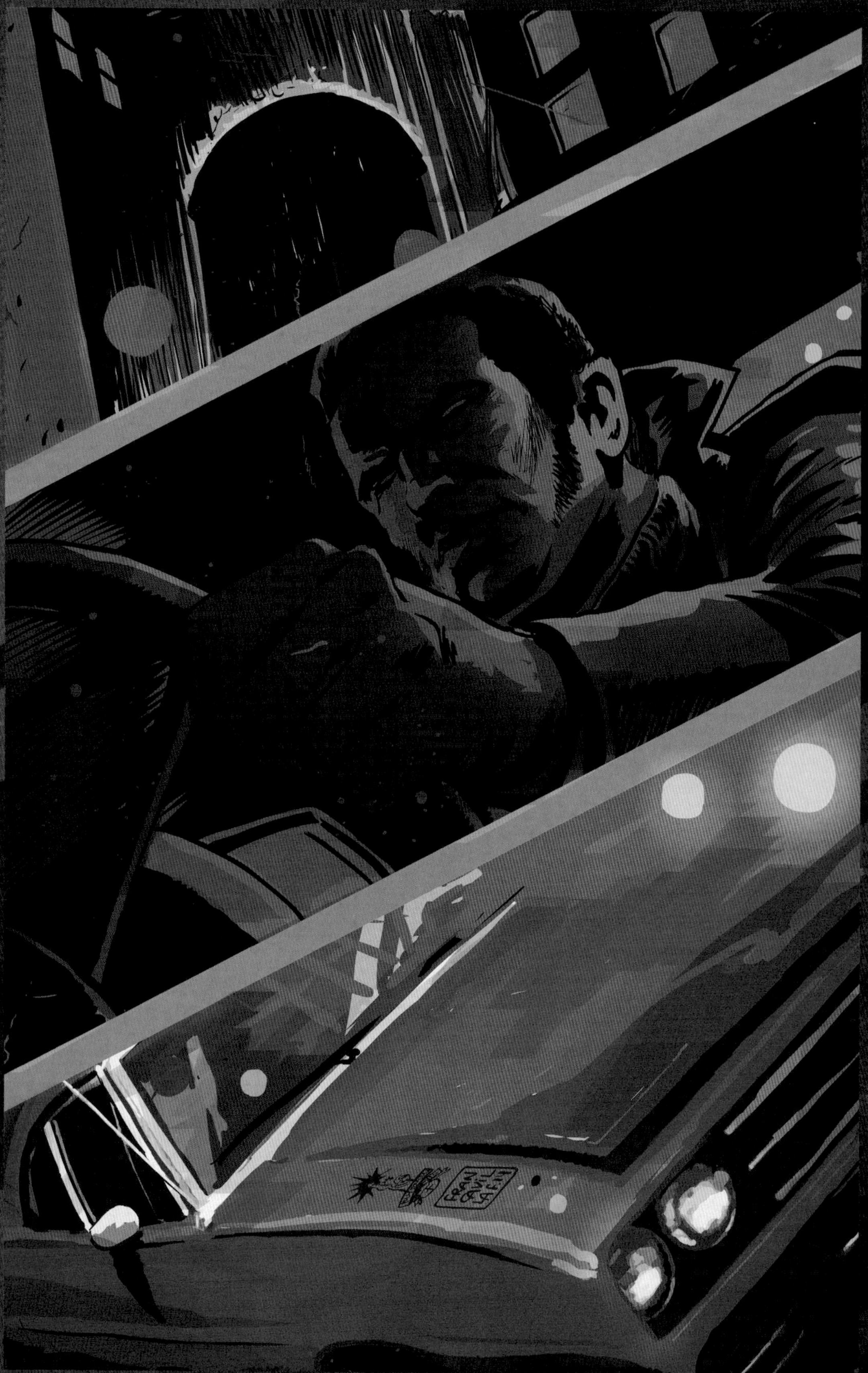

ISSUE TWO VARIANT COVER BY
FRANCESCO FRANCAVILLA

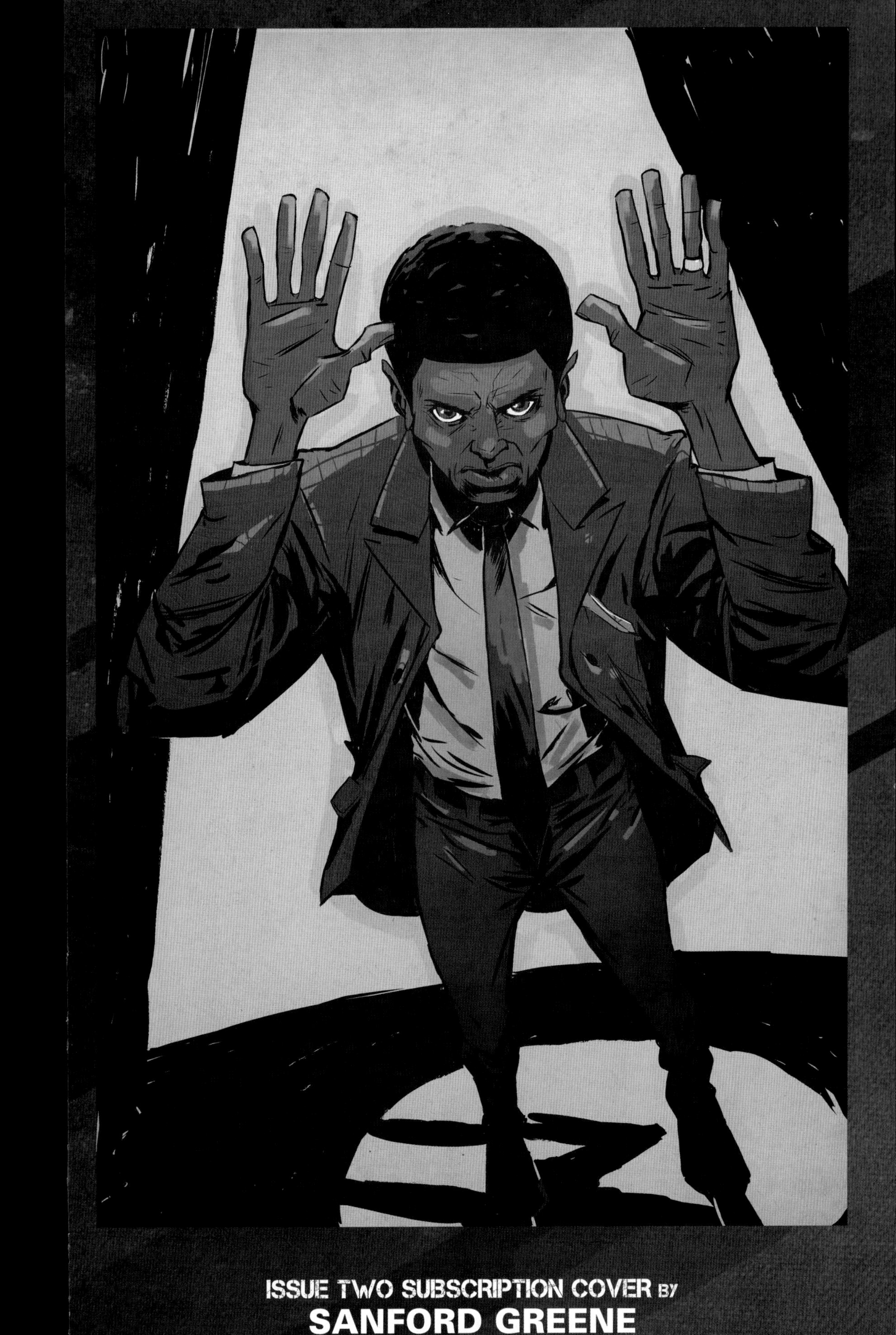

ISSUE TWO SUBSCRIPTION COVER BY
SANFORD GREENE

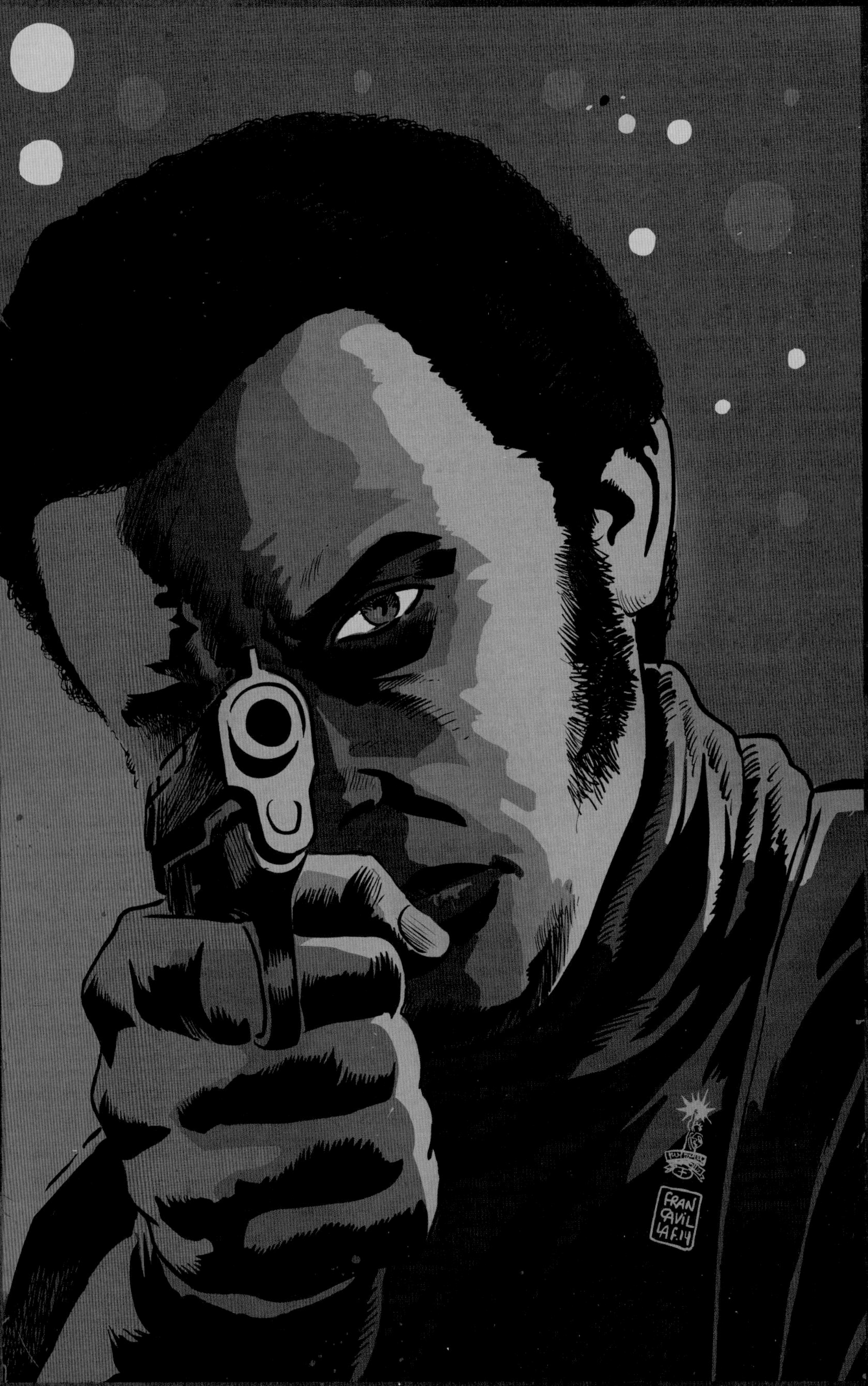
FRAN
CAVIL
LA F.14

ISSUE THREE VARIANT COVER BY
FRANCESCO FRANCAVILLA

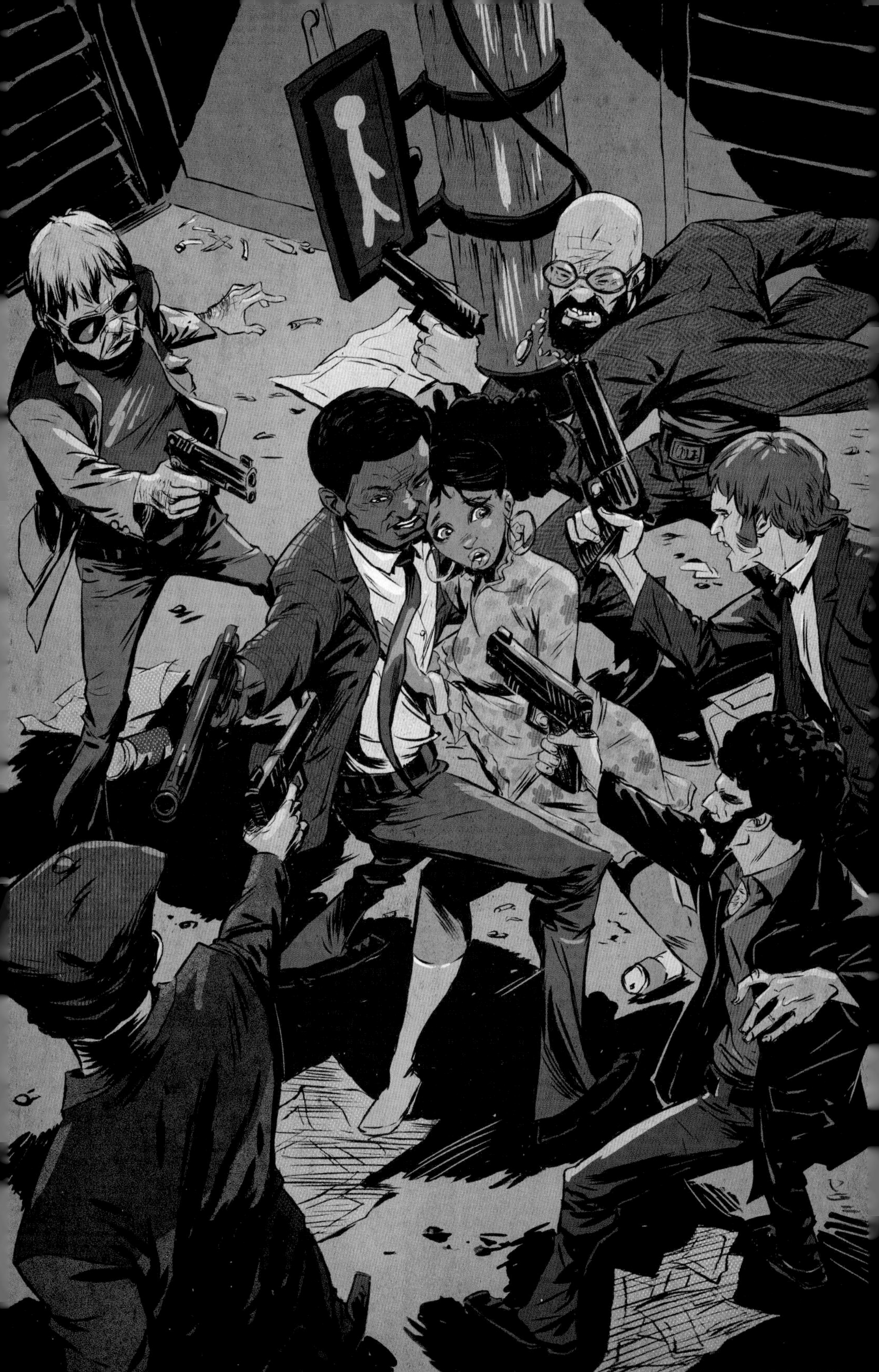

ISSUE THREE SUBSCRIPTION COVER BY
SANFORD GREENE

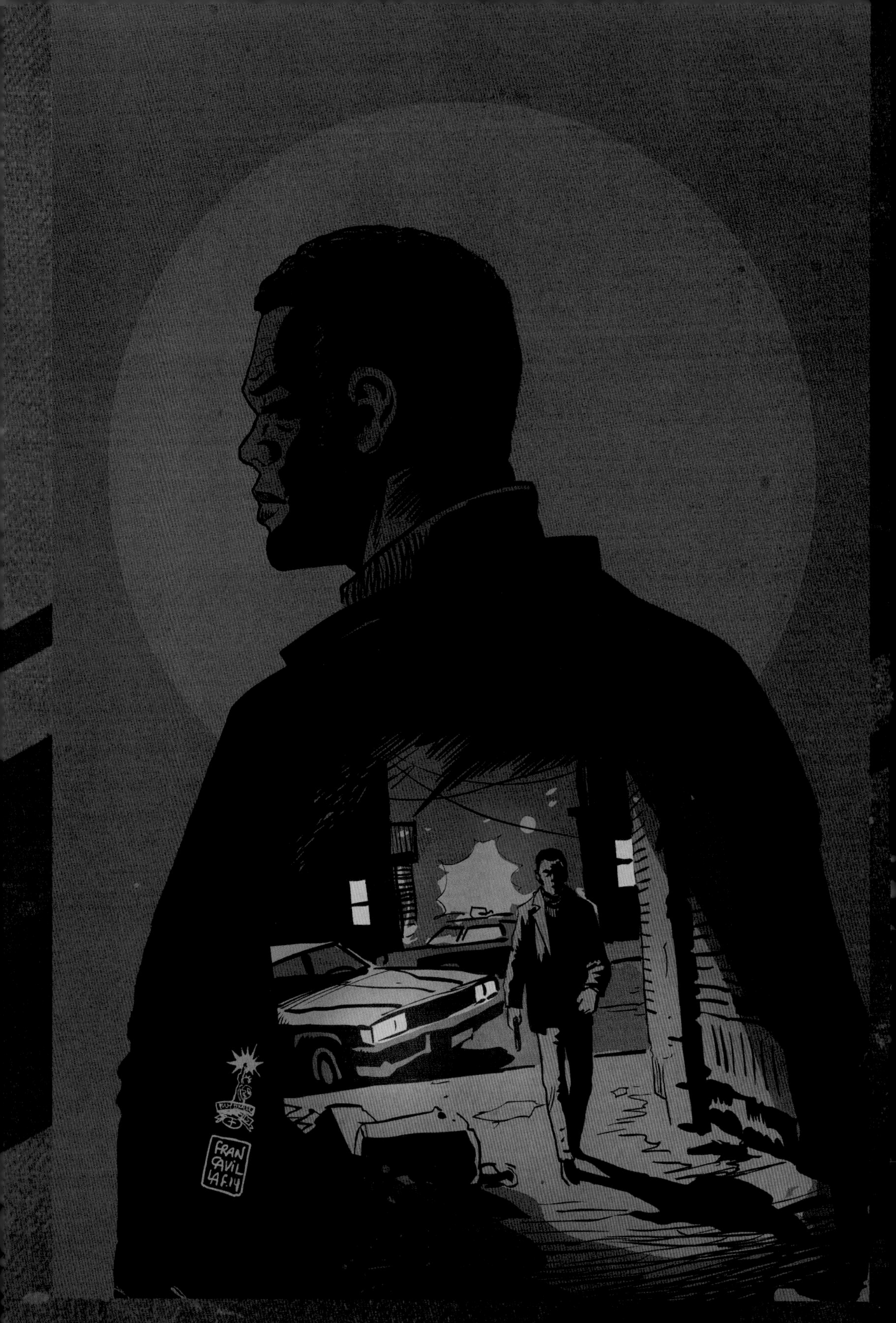

ISSUE FOUR VARIANT COVER BY
FRANCESCO FRANCAVILLA

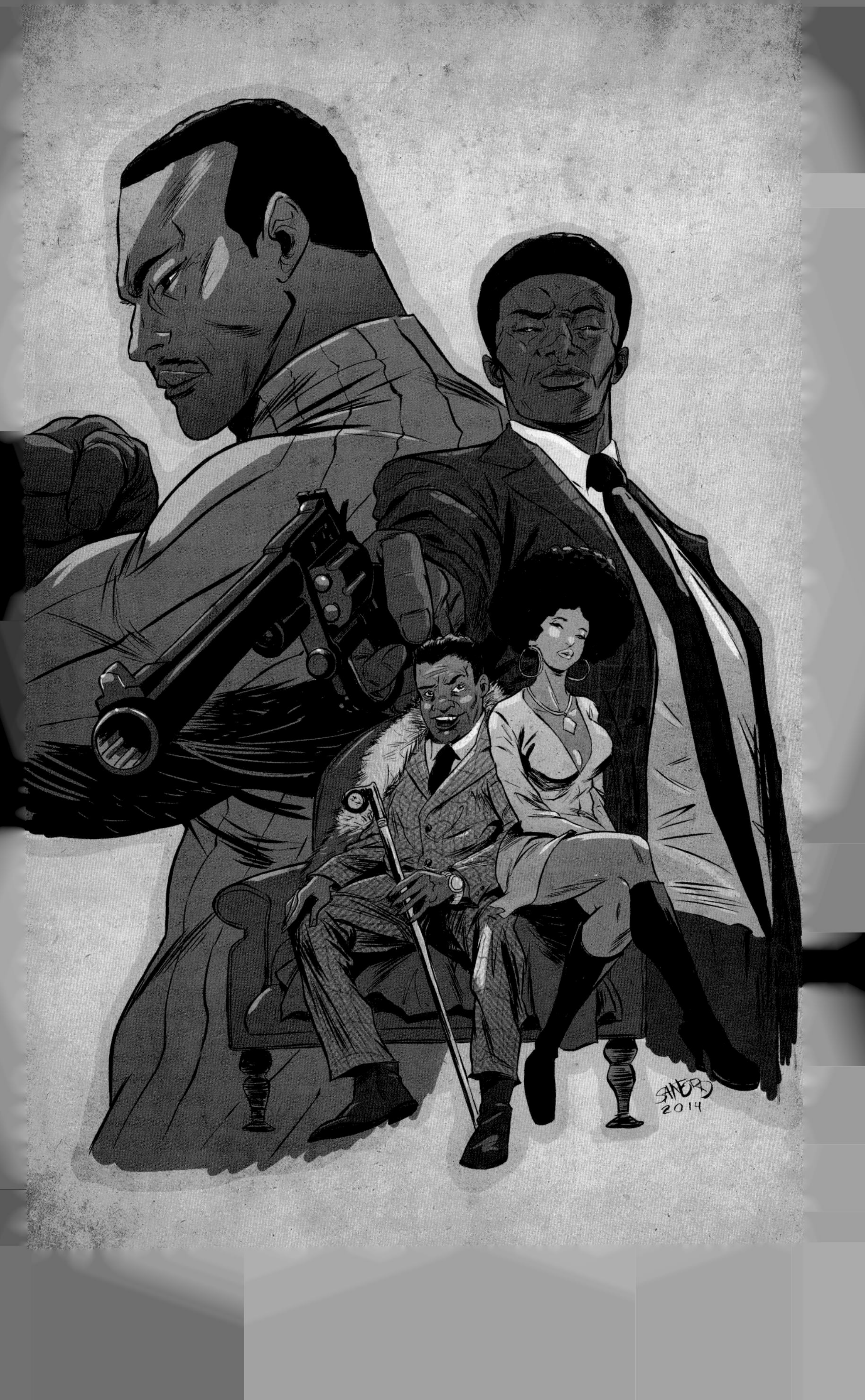
2014

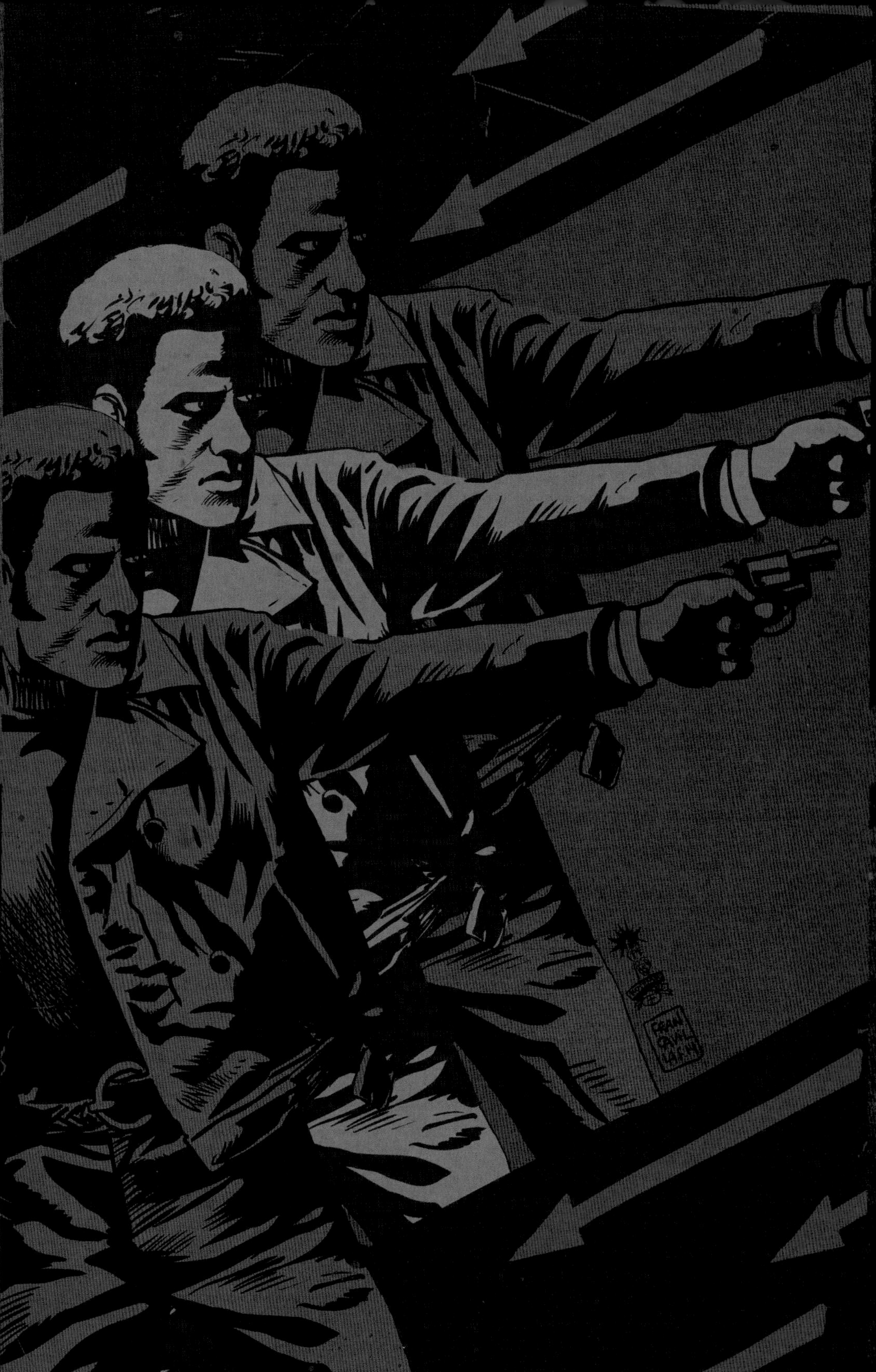

ISSUE FIVE VARIANT COVER BY
FRANCESCO FRANCAVILLA

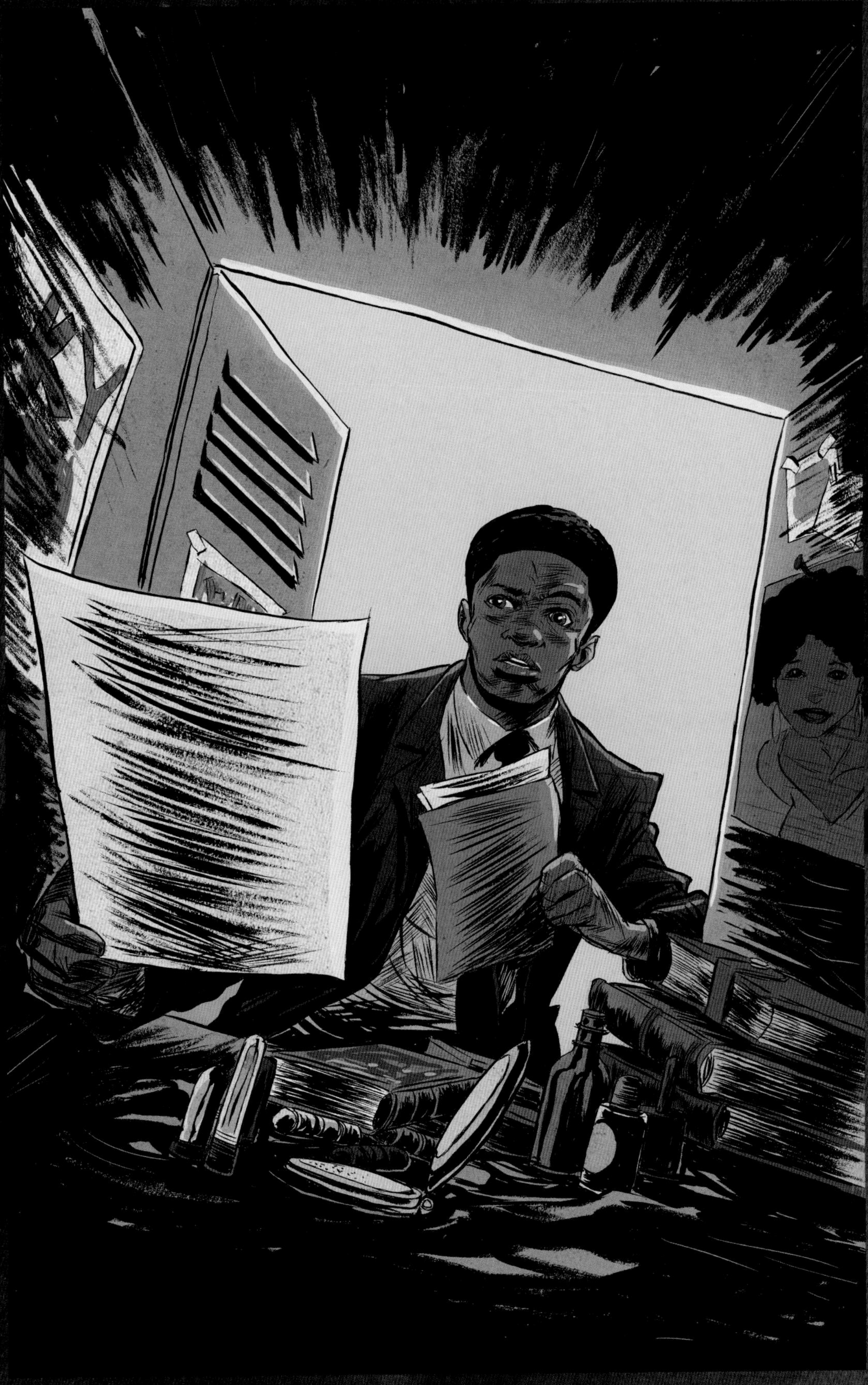

ISSUE FIVE SUBSCRIPTION COVER BY
SANFORD GREENE

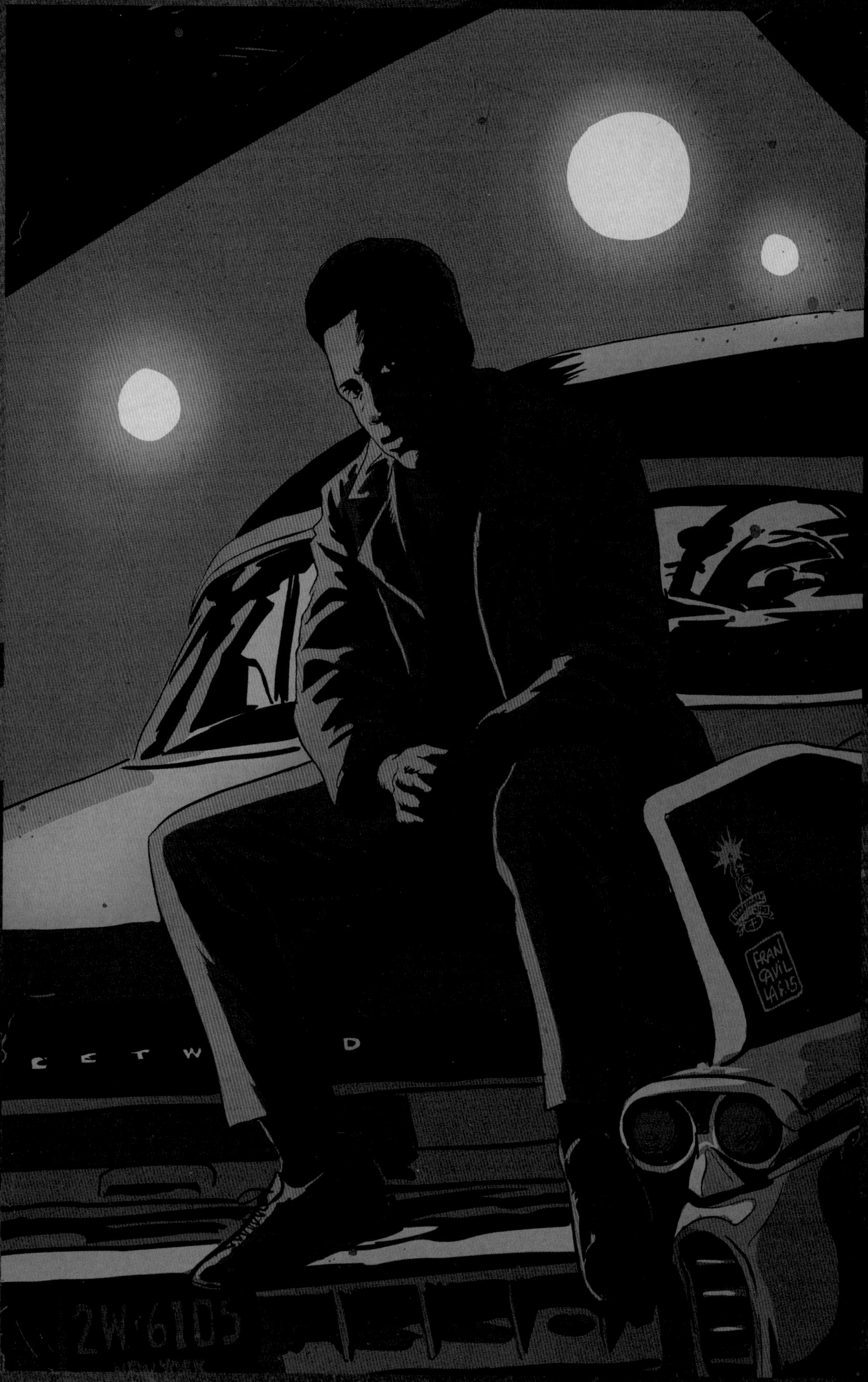

ISSUE SIX VARIANT COVER BY
FRANCESCO FRANCAVILLA

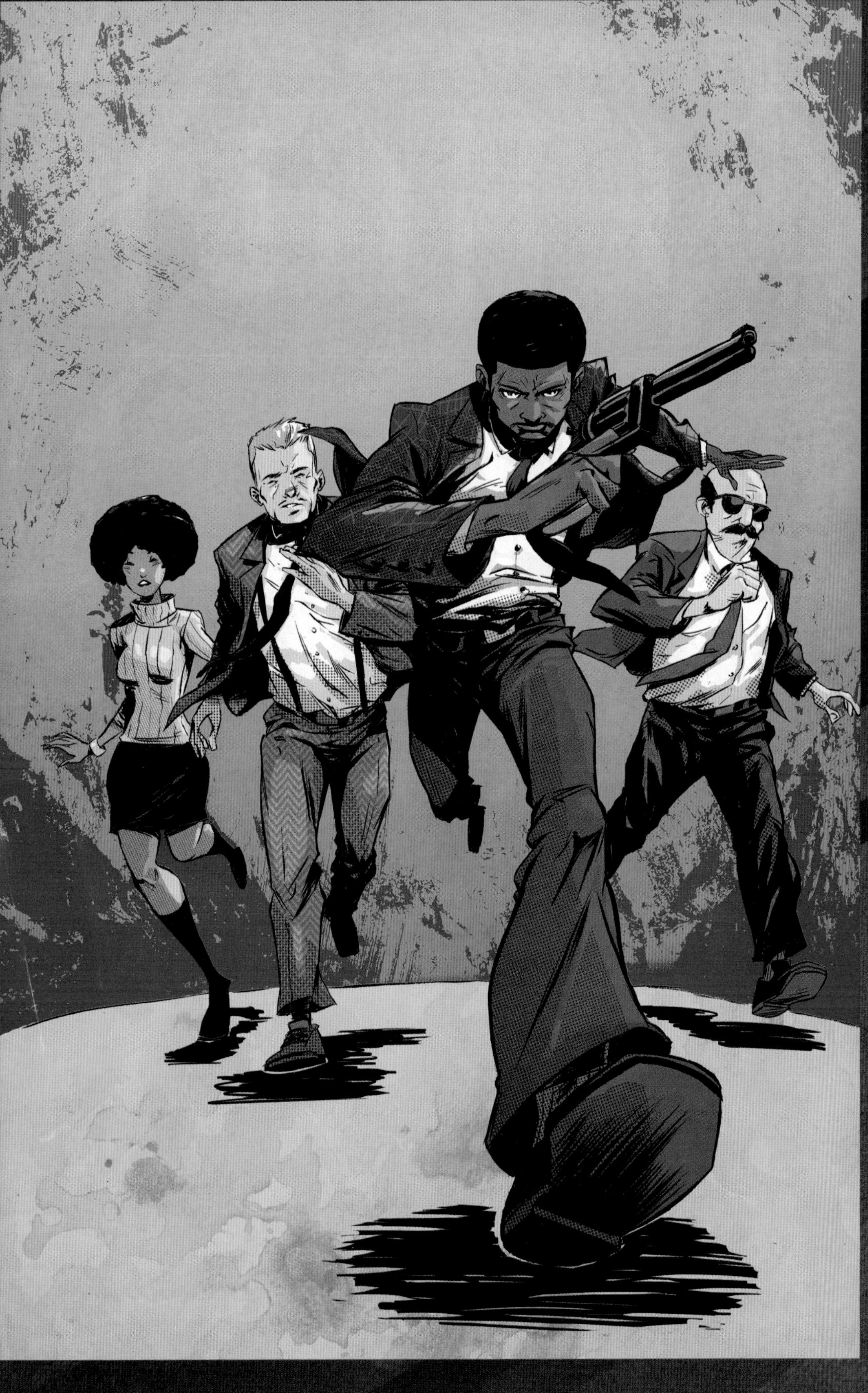

ISSUE SIX SUBSCRIPTION COVER BY
SANFORD GREENE

TATE'S COMICS +TOYS+ MORE

#1 DEC

DYNAMITE COMICS GROUP

RAT M
SUGGESTED FOR MATURE READERS

SHAFT

EXCLUSIVE RETRO-DRESSED COVER
FOR TATE'S COMICS+TOYS+MORE BY
NACHO TENORIO AND **SERGIO MORA**